TO THE BRIGHT EDGE
OF THE WORLD

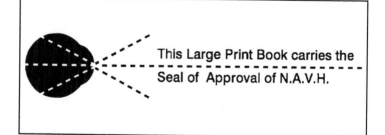

This Large Print Book carries the
Seal of Approval of N.A.V.H.

To the Bright Edge of the World

Eowyn Ivey

LARGE PRINT PRESS
A part of Gale, a Cengage Company

GALE
A Cengage Company

Farmington Hills, Mich • San Francisco • New York • Waterville, Maine
Meriden, Conn • Mason, Ohio • Chicago

Large Print Press, a part of Gale, Cengage Learning.

LIBRARY OF CONGRESS CATALOGING-IN-PUBLICATION DATA

Names: Ivey, Eowyn, author.
Title: To the bright edge of the world / by Eowyn Ivey.
Description: Waterville, Maine : Thorndike Press, 2016. | Series: Thorndike Press large print basic
Identifiers: LCCN 2016026853 | ISBN 9781410492760 (hardcover) | ISBN 1410492761 (hardcover)
Subjects: LCSH: Scientific expeditions—Alaska—Fiction. | Frontier and pioneer life—Alaska—Fiction. | Indians of North America—Alaska—Fiction. | Alaska—History—1867-1959—Fiction. | Adventure fiction. | Large type books.
Classification: LCC PS3609.V54 T6 2016 | DDC 813/.6—dc23
LC record available at https://lccn.loc.gov/2016026853

ISBN 13: 978-1-4328-3998-7 (pbk.)
ISBN 10: 1-4328-3998-5 (pbk.)

Published in 2017 by arrangement with Little, Brown and Company, a division of Hachette Book Group, Inc.

Printed in Mexico
1 2 3 4 5 6 7 21 20 19 18 17

For my husband, Sam,
with love

I looked directly into its eyes and knew that I understood nothing.

— From *Make Prayers to the Raven,*
by Richard K. Nelson,
on seeing an Alaska wolverine

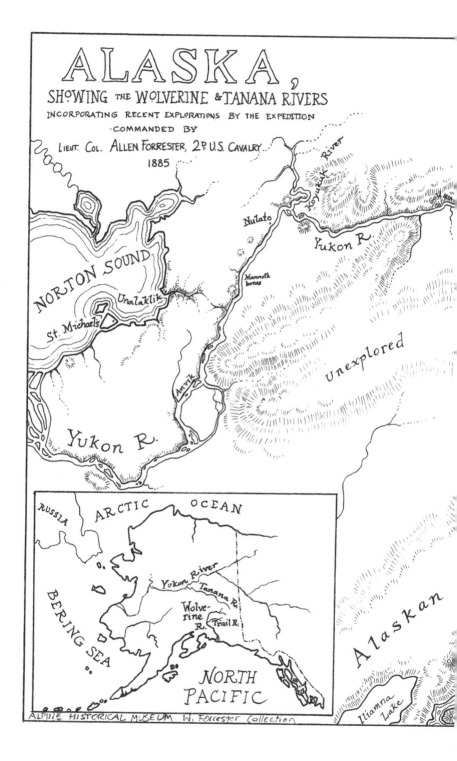

ALASKA,

SHOWING THE WOLVERINE & TANANA RIVERS

INCORPORATING RECENT EXPLORATIONS BY THE EXPEDITION

·COMMANDED BY·

LIEUT. COL. ALLEN FORRESTER, 2ᴰ U.S. CAVALRY

1885

Koyukuk River

Nulato

NORTON SOUND

Yukon R.

Mammoth bones

Unalaklik

St. Michaels

Unexplored

Anvik

Yukon R.

RUSSIA

ARCTIC OCEAN

Yukon River

Tanana R.

Wolverine R.

Trail R.

BERING SEA

NORTH PACIFIC

Alaskan

Iliamna Lake

Attention Mr. Joshua Sloan
Exhibits Curator
Alpine Historical Museum
Alpine, Alaska

Mr. Sloan,

I warned you I am a stubborn old man. These boxes have the papers I told you about, the letters and journals from my great-uncle's 1885 expedition across Alaska. I know you said you weren't able to take them on, but I'm sending them anyways. You'll change your mind once you read through all this. Truth be told, I don't have much choice. I never had children of my own, and all the relatives are dead. When my turn comes, these papers will be thrown out with everything else. For most of my life they have been crammed in trunks and boxes, and they show signs of wear. It would be a shame for them to be lost altogether.

The Colonel's journey was a harrowing one. Maybe it was doomed from the beginning, but I don't see as to how that takes away from its importance. His expedition is surely the Alaskan equivalent of Lewis and Clark's, and these papers are some of the earliest, firsthand descriptions of those northern lands and natives.

Several of his private journal entries are downright fantastical and don't align with his official reports. Some who have read these pages write off the odder occurrences as hallucinations, brought on by starvation and exposure to the elements. Others have accused the Colonel of embellishing his journals in order to gain notoriety. But I tell you, he was neither a hysteric nor a charlatan. He was a West Point graduate who fought in the Indian Wars and negotiated himself out of capture by the Apaches, yet by all accounts he never sought the limelight. I've chosen to consider another possibility — that he described what he saw with his own two eyes. It takes a kind of arrogance to think everything in the world can be measured and weighed with our scientific instruments. The Colonel started out with those sorts of assumptions, and as you will see, it did not serve him well.

Along with the journals and reports, I'm also sending some of my great-aunt Sophie's writing. There are illustrations and photographs, newspaper clippings — odds and ends I've stumbled across over the years. I thought of going through and stripping them all out, but some of it might be of interest to you.

I won't yet mail the artifacts from the expedition. I've held on to everything I can, but most of them are in a fragile state and might not make it to Alaska and back.

I've had them appraised, and you'll find a description of each item and what kind of condition it's in.

Read it all over. If you change your mind and see fit to make room for it at your museum, I will gladly send everything I have.

Sincerely,
Walter Forrester

■ ■ ■ ■

Part One

ARTIFICIAL HORIZON.
MID-19TH CENTURY, UNSIGNED.
ALLEN FORRESTER COLLECTION.

■ ■ ■ ■

Original fitted mahogany case with key. Includes cast-iron reflecting tray and mercury bottle, brass-framed glazed pyramid cover. Designed to aid in celestial navigation when darkness, fog, or land features obscure natural horizon. Mercury is poured onto the reflecting tray, so providing a level reflecting surface, and the image is sighted with a sextant to provide a "double altitude."

Diary of Lieut. Col. Allen Forrester
March 21, 1885
Perkins Island, Alaska

I do not know the time. The depths of night. It may already be tomorrow. I cannot see my own words, but write as I can by moonlight so as to record my first thoughts. In the morning I may deem it outlandish. For now I am slightly shaken.

I rose moments ago & left the tent to relieve myself. With the moon, I did not bother to light a lantern. I slid my feet into boots without tying laces & made my way into the trees. The only sound was of the sea washing at the beach. It is true, I was barely awake, my eyes bleary. As I turned back towards the tent, I heard a rustling overhead. I looked up into moonlight broken by silver shadow & black branches. I expected an animal, perhaps an owl roosted, but it was the old Eyak Indian up in the boughs of the spruce. His face was obscured, but I knew his spare frame, black hat atop his head. Moonlight glinted off the strange decorations at his neck.

He crouched high in the branches, silent. I do not know if he saw me. I made no motion towards him, half fearing he would fall from the branches if startled.

I would find it a chore to climb the tree, but could if needed. An old man with a lame leg — what could propel him upward? Perhaps he fled from a bear. Could he have climbed the tree in a fit of fear? It does not suit his character. The Eyak seems an unflappable sort. He looked as if he sat comfortably in those branches, perhaps even slept.

I am left vaguely uneasy. As if I witnessed a bird flying underwater or a fish swimming across the sky.

March 22

We leave Perkins Island at daybreak, whether we have the men or not. For too long we have postponed on promises from the Eyaks that their men will return from hunting sea otter to join us. We are left with three young Eyaks too young for the hunt & the crippled old man. They say he knows these waters so can pilot us to the mouth of the Wolverine River. I cannot wait another day with the Alaska mainland nearly within our reach. We were weeks delayed by Army affairs in Sitka, only to have fog slow our journey aboard the USS Pinta. All too soon the Wolverine could break free in a torrent of slush, ice slabs, & impassable rapids. If the river runs wide open, we will make it no farther than Haigh's attempt. I fear already for the ice at the canyon.

I write at the tent door. Lieut. Pruitt once again goes through instruments. He polishes the glass pyramid of the artificial horizon & rechecks the movement of the Howard watch. It has become a nervous habit of his that I can understand.

Sgt. Tillman has his own tic. He worries for our food supply. Will we have enough hardtack? he asks three times a day. Says again he is not fond of pea soup, prefers to sledge chocolate up the river. Myself, I pace the shore of this small northern island & look out across the sound. We are men anxious to be about our mission.

The Eyak watches us from where he sits at the base of a great spruce tree, the same one he roosted in last night. The old man is never without his brimmed black hat & gentleman's vest, yet he also dons the hide trousers & shift of his people. His black hair is cropped at the shoulders. At his neck is a bizarre ornament, similar in pattern to the dentalium shells many of the Indians wear, but instead made of small animal bones, teeth, shiny bits of glass & metal. As he watches us, his broad face wears an odd expression. Amusement. Ferocity. I cannot make it out. Even the women & children of the island seem wary of him. The old man glowers, says nothing, only to laugh at inopportune times. This morning Sgt. Tillman slipped on the icy rocks near the row boats, fell hard to his knees. The old man cackled. Tillman got to his feet & went to grab him by his vest collar. The sergeant is no small fellow. Built like a brick s— house, always on the look-out for a fistfight, the general said as way of introduction. I have no doubt he would make quick work of the old Eyak.

— Leave him be, I said, though I sympathized. The old man sets my nerves on end as well. To see him up in that tree in the darkest hours has done nothing to put me at ease. I would take another guide if given choice.

The trapper Samuelson will go with us as far as the mouth of the Wolverine. He would be invaluable traveling farther as he knows rudimentary forms of most of the native languages & has traveled much of the lower river. He expects the Wolverine River Indians, the ones called Midnooskies after the Russian, to bring a message from his trapping partner with plans of meeting him at the mouth before they decide where to spend the season. I continue to try to cajole him into joining our expedition, but he resists. No man's land at the headwaters of the Wolverine, he says. He does not fear the Indians' vicious reputation but instead the inhospitable terrain, the unpredictable river.

As to the character of the upper Wolverine River Indians, the white trader Mr. Jenson does his best to terrorize us with stories. He tells of how they slaughtered the Russians while they slept in their sleds, then cut away the dead men's genitalia to stuff them back in their own mouths.

Mr. Jenson operates the Alaska Commercial Co. trading store here on the island, claims to keep his own Indians in line only through a tough fist. He is one of the more unlikable men I have encountered. He drinks heavily & trades alcohol with the island natives, only to complain of their drunkenness. He brags of his cunning dealings with the natives, how he undercuts them for prime hides. He then advises us to never turn a blind eye to any Indian, as they are liars & thieves.

I avoid the trader as I can, but he seeks me out with stories of murderous plots against him. This island village becomes smaller by the day. We pace, check supplies, watch the skies, ask when the otter hunters will return.

Despite our restless & bored state, we are not untouched by the spectacularity of our surroundings. This land has a vast & cold beauty. Sun everywhere glints off blue sea, ice, snow. The refraction of light is as sharp as the cry of the sea birds overhead. The island is a rough outcropping of gray cliff, evergreen forests, & rocky beaches. Across the sound on clear days, I make out the mountains of mainland Alaska. They are still white with winter.

Last evening at dusk, a brown bear ambled down the beach, shuffled among our row boats. Today we measured a single paw print in the sand to be as wide as a man's two hands outstretched side by side.

My thoughts go to Sophie whenever I am not at work, yet I cannot afford such indulgence. I must keep my mind to the task at hand.

Special Order No. 16
Headquarters Department of the
Columbia
Vancouver Barracks, Washington Terri-
tory
January 7, 1885

By authority of the Lieutenant-General
of the Army conveyed this day by telegram, Lieutenant-Colonel Allen Forrester
is hereby authorized to lead a reconnaissance into Alaska traveling up the Wolverine River. Lieutenant Andrew Pruitt and
Sergeant Bradley Tillman are ordered to
report to Colonel Forrester with the
purpose of accompanying his reconnaissance.

The objective is to map the interior of
the Territory and document information
regarding the native tribes in order to be
prepared for any future serious distur-
bances between the United States government and the natives of the Territory. The
reconnaissance will also attempt to ascer-
tain whether and how a military force
would be sustained in this region if necessary, including information about climate,
severity of winter, and means of communication and types of weapons in possession of the natives. Information should
be gathered and documented thoroughly
along the reconnaissance in the event that

the expedition must be abandoned.

Colonel Forrester is ordered to make full reports to headquarters, including itineraries, maps, and field observations, whenever possible. If needed, as many as five native scouts may be employed. The expedition party should aim to arrive at the mouth of the Wolverine River by the beginning of March so as to travel up the river by ice.

Because of the peculiar, unknown circumstances of such a reconnaissance, Colonel Forrester is left to his discretion regarding travels beyond the Wolverine River. At all times, the men will exercise care and strict economy of their stores. Ample provisions have been provided for the journey.

If the reconnaissance is successful, the party should arrive at the well-mapped Yukon River before winter, where the men might board a steamboat to the coast. Colonel Forrester will then arrange transportation of himself and his men aboard a revenue cutter.

Best wishes for success and safe return,
By command of Major-General Keirn:
Stanley Harter,
Assistant Adjutant-General

USS *Pinta*

Lieut. Col. Allen Forrester
March 23, 1885

We remain tonight on Perkins Island, but at least we are gone from the village & the trader Jenson. We camp on the northern side of the island, directly across the sound from the Wolverine River. The journey so far drags against our will.

Jenson warned we would be unable to launch our boats into the waves. This only spurred our determination. We rose for our departure this morning to a dreary rain & rough seas. The trader was out of his bed earlier than I have ever seen him, only to stand watch over our efforts with much nay-saying. We loaded the row boats in near dark & divided the men. Pruitt, the old man, two Eyaks & I to one boat — Samuelson, Tillman & the third young Eyak to the other. I ordered the three young Indians to give the final heave-ho & jump aboard last.

Too busy fighting the oars against the surf,

I noticed nothing amiss until Tillman's bark.

— Hell! Do we go back for them?

I looked up. Through the gloom I could just make out the Indians at shore. The waves broke at their knees. They gave no expression. One held up a hand. I could not read it. Did they wave farewell, or were they left against their will? Did they intend to stay behind even as they nodded to my terms? Whatever the cause, I would not retrieve them. We had just managed to clear the surf. I cut my hand through the air, out into the sound.

— Onward, I said.

We set into the cold wet gray. Just two strong rowers to a boat. The old Eyak was of no use. We were undermanned from the start.

Daylight improved nothing. Waves chopped at the boat sides. Wind kicked up sea spray, drenched the supplies through canvas tarps. We traveled north along the coast of the island. A cluster of rocks rose before us. I called out to veer to open water. The old man spoke for the first time then, a throaty chortle that was meaningless to me. The trapper understood.

— He says keep close to shore through here.

— What you say?

The boats rose, teetered on the waves, & carried us towards the rocks.

— That's what he says. Keep close in.

I looked to where the old man perched in

the bow. His vest flapped in the wind. His eyes were wild, & he grinned or grimaced, I could not tell.

— It's no good, Tillman hollered into the wind.

I had to agree. The waves would dash the row boats to bits against the rocks. But why bring the old man if not to guide us? He has known these bays & inlets all his long life. The Eyaks said he could get us to mainland.

Our boats threatened to turn sidelong to the swells. Waves broke over the gunwales.

— Do as he says, I called. — Head in.

I had no time to regret my order. The sea took us like driftwood & threw us to the rocks. We scraped our way past the outcroppings only to be swept up by whirlpools at the base of the island cliffs. The boats rotated, heaved, & creaked. Salt spray blinded us. I thought I heard the old Eyak cackle from the bow. Perhaps it was the gulls. What kind of mad man laughs as he drowns?

I cannot say how long we battled the sea & cliff face. Tillman stood at his stern, shoved his oar to the cliff to lever the boat. Even his considerable strength was no match for the sea. Pruitt howled as his hand was smashed between bow & rock. Samuelson let out a string of curses like none I have heard before.

When at last we freed ourselves from the roiling current, we pulled at the oars until our hearts would burst. We kept on until we rode even swells with no rocks in sight.

Tillman navigated his boat closer to ours. I thought he came to set our plan, but instead he threw down his oars, leapt across to our boat. Before I knew his intent, he grabbed the old man by the shirt front to jerk him to his feet.

— What the devil is the matter with you? Tillman yelled into the old Eyak's face. — You'd kill us all!

The old man did not blink. He should have feared for his life. Instead he grinned, his teeth worn nubs. He then spoke with his guttural clucks & hard stops.

— What does he say? Tillman turned to Samuelson.

The trapper hesitated, as if not sure to repeat it.

— He says he's been hungry for many days.

— What?

Samuelson shrugged.

— That's what he says. He's hungry.

Tillman shoved the old man.

— So he'd take us all to hell?

Tillman moved to throw him overboard. The old man squawked a kind of laugh or yelp. I was tempted to let him be sent to the sea, but thought better of it.

— Enough, Tillman. We'll be rid of him soon enough.

The sergeant hesitated. I thought he would disobey. My misgivings about his reputation were roused, but he shoved the old man back down into the boat.

We returned to rowing without talk or pause. Our progress was slow. Not until early afternoon did we round to the north side of Perkins Island.

— The old man says a storm is coming, Samuelson said.

Why should we believe him? None of us trusts the Eyak now.

— I don't know but maybe we should listen to him this time around, Samuelson said. We all followed his eyes towards the horizon where clouds were building.

— He says there is a safe landing just the other side of that point.

This time the old man did not deceive. A cold torrent chased us to shore. We built no fire but quickly raised the tent amongst the trees & climbed in wet, shivering, weary. The old Eyak remains outside, where to none of us knows or much cares. Rain slaps the canvas tent in a noisy pattering. We eat cold beef from tins, all of us crowded shoulder to shoulder.

I asked Samuelson why the young Indians stayed behind.

— Fear.

— Of the Midnooskies?

— No. The trader Jenson. He expects them to help with the otter pelts when the hunters come back.

— It is a notable amount of sway he holds over them, I observed.

— They aren't Jenson's slaves quite yet, but give him time, Samuelson said. — I have seen him yank an Indian child from his mother's hands in trade for furs the father didn't bring in.

— What would a white man want with an Indian child?

— Fear, the trapper said.

We may sail along the border, or be drawn by sledge-dogs over the frozen streams, until we arrive at the coldest, farthest west, separated from the rudest, farthest east by a narrow span of ocean, bridged in winter by thick-ribbed ice. What then can be said of this region — this Ultima Thule of the known world, whose northern point is but three or four degrees south of the highest latitude yet reached by man?

— From *History of Alaska: 1730–1885,*
Hubert Howe Bancroft, 1886

Diary of Sophie Forrester
Vancouver Barracks
January 6, 1885

Oh such amazing news! The General has granted permission so that I will accompany Allen and his men on the steamer north! For days now it has seemed increasingly unlikely, and I am certain it was only Allen's steady, persistent resolve that has won me passage. Of course, I go only as far as Sitka and will return to the barracks the end of February; I will not even set eyes on the northern mainland where their true adventure will begin, but I am thrilled all the same. Allen, too, is pleased. He charged into the sitting room this afternoon and announced, "You'll go, my love! Haywood said you'll go!"

Now there is much for me to do. Until today, I followed Mother's advice and did not "count my chickens before they hatched," but consequently I have made no preparations. We expect to board within the month.

What should I bring? An abundance of warm clothes. Definitely my walking boots, for I am told the deck is often treacherous with ice and sea spray. My field glasses and notebooks of course, with plenty of spare pencils.

There is this, too — a new diary. I resisted when Allen first gave it to me and said my field notebooks suit me fine. His playful reply was that when he returns from Alaska, he would like to hear about more than the habits of nuthatches and chickadees.

I could not then imagine that my days would hold anything of interest: the long train journey to Vermont, the return to my child-hood home. Maybe if I were allowed to walk as far as the quarry pond to watch for the pintails and grebes, or to go to the forest in search of Father's sculptures (how I would love for Allen to see them someday, especially the sea serpent and the old bear), maybe then I would have something to record. Yet I will never be permitted such wanderings. "Shame is the only fruit of idleness." How many times did I hear those words as a little girl? Mother is always at the washboard and rags, the rake and the weeds, and she will expect the same of me. Who would want to hear such a diary read aloud?

But now! Now I will have something to write in these pages, for I am going to Alaska!

I cannot help but be caught up in the excitement. Supplies arrive daily from various parts of the country — tents, sleeping bags, snowshoes, nearly one thousand rations for the men! I do not know how Allen keeps it all in order. This morning, just as he was about to kiss me goodbye at the door, he said, "Yes, Pruitt will be out with the camera, but Tillman can sort the rifles and ammunition. That way I can get to the telegraph office." He must get word to Sitka, by British Columbia and then mail steamer, that he will need several sledges built and ready when we arrive.

And then, during my afternoon walk, I happened across Mr Pruitt with his camera near the stable. Allen says the Lieutenant has only recently learned photography in order to document their expedition, so he is practicing as much as he is able. Today, the blacksmith was his reluctant subject.

They made an amusing scene, Mr Pruitt so studious and fair-skinned, with his red hair trimmed boyishly; the grimed smith, in leather apron and rolled up sleeves, looking particularly unhappy with having to stand for his picture to be taken. Mr Pruitt peered out from the black cloth and quietly asked the blacksmith to turn his shoulder this way and his chin that, to which the smith obeyed with considerable grumbling.

More than anything, I wanted to ask Mr Pruitt how the camera works, how it can be taken afield, and to even see some of his images, but I thought better than to interrupt him.

Such an extraordinary notion, to be able to seal light and shadow to the page in such a way. I often think of the photographs Allen and I saw in a Boston studio — the old woman with her pipe, a little boy riding a giant dog, and a whimsical scene of actors dressed in animal masks. Startlingly vivid, each of them, so that there was a silvery texture to the fabric and skin, and a quality of light that seemed truly magical, as if life glowed from within the paper itself.

I envy Mr Pruitt that he will document the Far North with such a device! (Alas, I will bring on board only my notebooks and poor drawing skills. It seems a curse, that one should love the work of a naturalist yet be so ill-suited for it.)

January 9

I did not expect to be the cause of such a stir. One would think I was to leave on a polar expedition. During tea this afternoon at Mrs Connor's house, the officers' wives reacted with everything from alarm to squealing delight to know that I will go as far as Sitka with Allen and his men.

Where in heaven's name will you sleep? You

must bring extra quilts so you won't freeze in the night! What about the polar bears? They are man-eaters! (I explained to Mrs Bailey that to my knowledge the white bears live much farther north than I will venture, so I will not be in their danger.) The food on board will be dreadful, mark my words. And the seasickness you'll endure! Best pack a tin of good biscuits for yourself.

I should have predicted Miss Evelyn's response. "At least one nice gown. You must have that. You never know when there might be some fine occasion — don't make that face at me Mrs Forrester, you could end up having dinner at the governor's house in Sitka — and it's appalling to be underdressed."

Sarah Whithers was the only one who offered sound advice.

"Do you have a good Mackintosh, to keep off the rain and snow?" And the dear, timid woman said I could have hers, as she had recently been given a new one; I thanked her but told her I had a raincoat, and that I would certainly remember to pack it in my trunk.

And then there was blustery Mrs Connor. "Never mind all this nonsense! Why on earth are you going?"

I apologized but said I did not take her meaning.

"Surely your husband can't make you go," she said.

Not go! I explained that it was my very

37

desire to go, and that if permitted, I would accompany Allen the entire distance across Alaska.

"Absurd. There is no need for a bright young woman such as yourself to join in such idiocy. Leave it to the men to throw themselves off the face of the earth. They are quite adept at it by themselves."

What could I say in my defense?

"But isn't it romantic?" Mrs Whithers interjected. "Imagine a husband so distraught to be separated from you, that he brings you with him!"

It was kind of her to attempt my rescue, especially knowing how painfully shy she is in front of Mrs Connor. Yet nothing could save me from the sense that I had taken several steps back from the other women. I was silent the rest of tea.

If I had found the words, I would have said this: I do not go because my husband orders me. I do not go out of some need to prove or earn anything. And while it will give me joy to remain some time longer at my husband's side, it is not even that alone. Instead, I go because I long to see this wild place for myself.

January 11
Am I truly to believe that Mrs Connor came striding to my front door with only the purest of compassion in her heart?

She would not take tea or cake, but only wanted to warm her hands by the cook stove and insist that I did not grasp the severity of Allen's leaving. I must consider it some sort of holiday to the north! Am I not aware of the danger he will face in Alaska?

I endeavored to remain calm and polite during her visit, allowing myself the occasional, "I see. Yes, I see." Such replies did not satisfy her, and she grew agitated and began to pace about our small kitchen.

"You force me to speak plainly," she said. "My Hugh says that the last white men to venture up that river were the Russians, and they were murdered by the Indians. Every last one of them."

"I see," I said yet again.

"Is that all you have to say? 'I see, I see.' I wonder if you really do see!"

I thanked her for her concern, and led her to the door.

Why would she subject me to such vile talk? Surely I will fret for Allen every day he is gone from me, all the more if what she says is true, yet no amount of worry will bring him back home. Only good fortune and his own skill can do that.

January 12
He has done his best to put my mind at ease. Nearly a hundred years. That's how long it has been since the Indians massacred the

Russians in Alaska. Beyond that, Allen said, there are few details as to what caused the attack. And just as I believed, the American expeditions since have been turned back by the Wolverine River, well before any remote tribes could be met.

"We don't go there looking for a fight, love," he promised. "I'll keep our necks safe."

January 13

At my request, Allen retrieved my travel trunk last night, though he gently suggested it might be too soon to begin to pack. I would not listen to common sense, though, and this morning I set to organizing my belongings. I soon saw the folly in it. It is not as if I have a dozen dresses that I can wear now and another dozen I can pack for later. And so, I have shoved the trunk into a corner and now sit at the bedroom window to write.

It is a winter afternoon like many others in this country — chill, gray, and rainy — yet my view of it has been altered somehow. When we first arrived in Washington Territory, I was enthralled by all the wild country we saw, and even the barracks seemed a far outpost of civilization. With the thought of Alaska in my head now, however, this neat line of officers' houses, the cultivated trees and trimmed hedges and clapboard barracks, the muddy roads — it all seems so tame and ordinary.

Sitka is on the southern-most arm of the Alaska Territory, yet it is well beyond the reaches of common civilization, railroad, or telegraph. We will see mountain glaciers that calve into the sea, breaching whales, and perhaps birds native only to those northern landscapes. And then we will arrive at the end of the map, and Allen will disappear over its edge. It is both exhilarating and terrifying, and I find I can think of nothing else. These next weeks before our departure will be long indeed.

It is good that Mr Tillman has organized a dance, and that Allen and I are obliged to attend. If nothing else, it will provide a distraction.

I will go in search of Miss Evelyn to see if she has a gown I might borrow, since she insists my black wool dress won't do.

Ivashov and his men were sleeping on their sleds when, at a prearranged sign, the Midnooskies crushed each of the men's skull with axes.

— From *Journal of the Russian Geographical Society,* St. Petersburg, 1849 (translated from the Russian)

Lieut. Col. Allen Forrester
March 24, 1885
Point Blake, Alaska

We set foot on the mainland at last, yet the Wolverine River remains out of reach. We crossed in a storm that pushed us two miles to port, made land at Point Blake. The low-tide shore between here & the mouth of the river is mile after mile of slick, blue-yellow mud. Tracks crisscross the tidal flats where Indians slide their dugouts over scant water. Our row boats, weighted with 1,000 pounds of provisions, do not slide so well.

We have made our way into a small cove where we spotted a group of Indians stringing clams. The old Eyak was the first to jump from the boat to the rocky beach. He is agile even with his deformed leg. I thought he meant to flee Tillman, but instead he hopped & ran to the pile of clam shells. He plucked one, then another, slurped at them. An Indian woman smacked him with her hand. Yelled

— Aiii! As if to shoo a pest. The old man was quick on his feet, dodged, then scooped up another clam. Another. The Indian woman chased him about the beach.

— Looks like he was hungry after all, Tillman said. — Crazy old man.

We remain here the afternoon & night, with hopes of catching the rising tide at dawn to row to the river's mouth. Tillman & I raised the tent on the beach. The trapper gathers firewood.

Lieut. Pruitt strives to photograph the Indians. He has a quick mind for scientific devices. When he served under me in Arizona Territory, I was much impressed with his scholarly ways. While most soldiers caroused for leisure, he read books of science & literature. Regularly he would push his wire-rimmed spectacles up his nose, then fire away with his many questions. It irritated some officers, but I found his youthful curiosity a respite.

When I wrote to him of the expedition, I said I would have him collect data for mapping, as I know he is handy with sextant & artificial horizon. Barometer, psychrometer — such weather implements would be his chore as well. In his returning letter, he said he would also like to employ a camera for the journey. Recent advances make it possible for them to be brought easily afield, he said.

— It would be worth its weight, he wrote.

Pruitt has erected the tripod on the beach, attached camera box & now stands with black cloth over his head, so that he appears as a bulbous-headed monster with many legs. The Indians watch from their camp. They point, gawk, whisper. I am not much less mystified. Pruitt attempted to explain the chemistry, the glass plates, silver bromide gelatin, lens, focusing glass. For Sophie's sake, I tried to learn as much as I could.

Pruitt has set his focus on the Eyak, who now stands, cocks his head at an angle, slowly approaches the camera. The old man dips his head, weaves side to side, almost like a fighter, or a wily animal with an injured leg. He is now just a few yards from Pruitt's gaze. Closer. Closer. Pruitt has stuck out an arm, is waving at the old man.

— Back! You're too close. Go back & stay still!

The old man presses his face right up to the camera, reaches up, pulls the black cloth over his head as well. It looks as if he will disappear into the maw of a great monster.

I doubt Pruitt will have much luck with this venture.

We heard an unusual tale this evening. As we prepared our meal on the beach, a young Indian woman walked from the willow brush carrying two dead hares, knelt at sea's edge to skin them out with a sure quickness. She wears a beaded shift of animal hide & a fur mantle across her shoulders. She gave one rabbit to the Indian camp, her family I presume. Much to our surprise she then walked down the beach to our campfire. She slid the other rabbit into a pot of water we had boiling on the campfire. We heated only tins of beans in the flames for our meal so did not hesitate to accept her gift. We expressed our gratitude, but she did not seem to know our words.

— Doesn't she have a man to hunt for her? Tillman asked.

He winked at her, but the girl gave no response.

Samuelson asked her a series of questions in her own tongue, which she answered in a near whisper. They spoke a long time. Never once did she bring up her eyes, as if she feared our gaze would turn her to stone. She then walked down the beach towards her own camp, but before she had gone a few steps, she spoke one last time to Samuelson. He nodded.

— Well? What did she say? Tillman asked.

— She had a husband once.

— Pretty young thing like that. Doubt any man would give that up. So, what happened to the fellow?

— She killed him, Samuelson said. — Slit his throat as he slept.

It was a surprising answer, but no more so than the rest of the story the trapper told us.

The woman said that two winters ago a stranger came down out of the Wolverine Valley. No one had seen him before, but he was a good hunter & quick on his feet. When he asked her to go back to his home with him, she went along. The two of them traveled up the valley, beyond where she had ever been before, until they came to a creek that ran down out of the mountains. He took her to a den in the rocks. It was cold & damp & stunk of fish. For days on end he left her there with nothing but raw fish to eat. He warned her to never leave the den. She was lonely, so one day she tracked him through the snow. After a short time, his prints turned to otter tracks. She kept on them until she came to a bank den. That's when she saw her husband in his true form — a river otter, being welcomed by his otter wife.

Tillman was disbelieving. I had heard similar stories among Indians, but not such a firsthand claim.

— They believe it is a thin line separates animal & man, Samuelson said. — They hold that some can walk back & forth over that line, here a man, there a beast.

Tillman sat forward. He reminded me of a small boy listening to a tall tale.

— So what happened?

— She went back to their own den to wait

for him. When he fell asleep beside her, she cut his throat. In the morning light, she skinned him out. That otter pelt on her shoulders, that there is the skin of her husband.

— Jesus, Tillman said.

— But you don't believe a word of it, do you? Pruitt said.

Samuelson shrugged.

— What did she say at the last, when she was walking away? Tillman asked.

— She says the Wolverine River is no place for men like us.

The trapper leaned towards the campfire & tucked the spindly rabbit legs into the pot.

To Lieutenant-Colonel Allen Forrester:

I am pleased you have come to your senses and will take on this venture. Your initial reticence was unexpected — it has always been my understanding that you were hopeful of an assignment such as this. From your letter, I now better understand your misgivings. I agree that in ways this task might be better suited to a younger man's energy and robust health, but I have no doubt that the depth of your frontier experience, as well as your level-headed approach to leadership, outweighs any of that. In fact, I very much believe it was the brashness and laziness of our young lieutenants that has kept us from launching a successful expedition up the Wolverine until now. Frankly it is an embarrassment, even if some of our politicians fail to recognize it — nearly 20 years the territory has been in our possession and yet we know almost nothing of its interior.

This all said, I have had grave reservations about your plan to keep the travel party so small. You would be better served with a group of a dozen men or more, including a surgeon and a cartographer. Yet you will have it as you wish, not because I am conceding, but because we have been granted only enough funding for you and two other men.

With such, I must insist on one appointment. Normally I would trust your judgment and allow you your own selection of men. However, I am convinced Sergeant Bradley Tillman will prove invaluable. Do not pay much mind to his records of court-martial — he is rough and tumble, but I can think of no other man I would want covering my back if I were setting out as you are. If it weren't for his poor education, quick temper, and taste for liquor, I have no doubt he would be a Colonel already. I insist on his appointment, but you will be left to choose the other member of your party.

I cannot impress upon you too strongly my desire that all of your party's communications with the natives of this land be friendly. You have shown yourself to be even-tempered and fair in your dealings with the tribes, and I believe it could be crucial to the success of this endeavor. I am not sure how much credence to give to the Russian reports. However, if at any point you cannot proceed without provoking hostility, then you must turn back. As much as I am anxious for this expedition to be successful, we do not need another Indian War on our hands.

You know the conflicting dispatches which have been received in regard to this reconnaissance, and the difficulties the adjutant-general of the department has encountered. Despite that, the paymaster has been instructed to transfer to you $2,000 as an advance to pay yourself and the members of your detachment. I trust that you will now be with ample provisions to ensure safety, comfort, and success.

I understand from General Haywood that you are recently married. Congratulations, Colonel. I surmise that may be the root of some of your reticence in leaving on such an expedition, but you can happily retire to domestic married life upon your return.

With sincere wishes for your safe return,
JAMES KEIRN
Major-General, U.S. Army

Sophie Forrester
Vancouver Barracks
January 14, 1885

I am still not recovered from last night's celebration. Allen is entirely correct — enlisted men do put on the most entertaining affairs that, in comparison, make officers' balls seem stuffy and contrived. Fiddle, banjo, accordion. And never would I have dreamed that my staid husband could dance the polka! All the laughter and merriment. There is something truly wondrous about such a gala, with its lights and music spilling out into the dark forest.

Many toasts were made in honor of the expedition, more often than not led by the boisterous Mr Tillman, and all the night people clamored to ask Allen and his men about their plans. When it was discovered that I will go as far north as Sitka, I, too, became a subject of interest. It is a position to which I am unaccustomed, and I do not enjoy.

Thank heavens for the few times Allen swept me away to dance. Too often, though, he was drawn into conversations, and I was left to fend my way through the many people.

Miss Evelyn was unusually dull, as she was distracted by all the handsomely dressed men in attendance and not particularly interested in conversing with me except to ask the name and marital status of this or that gentleman. I was of little assistance, and she quickly abandoned me. Mr Tillman proceeded to spend the rest of the evening trying to woo her, and while I am certain she has her sights set far higher than an Army sergeant, she seemed dangerously enamored. I doubt General Haywood would approve of such a match for his niece.

Perhaps the most perplexing, and troubling, part of the evening, however, was my exchange with Mr Pruitt. He is quite different than I expected — severe and brooding, and he managed to offend me in several instances.

Since that day at the stable, I have been eager to ask him about his camera, so when I found myself near him in the crowd, I mentioned to him my interest in photography. What could he tell me of the process?

"It is much too complicated for idle chit-chat," he said.

Everything in his tone was dismissive and unfriendly, and I would have excused myself, but the jostling crowd would not allow an easy escape. He and I stood for some time before the silence between us became unbearably awkward.

"I understand you have known my husband for many years," I ventured.

"I met him at Fort Bowie, ma'am. Nearly nine years ago."

"Yes, he has told me something of his time there. He very much enjoyed becoming acquainted with you."

Mr Pruitt looked at me sharply, as if I said something deceitful or quarrelsome. After a long pause, he turned his eyes away and said with grave conviction, "It has been my greatest honor to serve with him."

Perhaps I had found an agreeable subject for Mr Pruitt. I told him I would be most interested to hear what it is like to have Allen as commander.

With some encouragement on my part, he described how Allen arrived at Fort Bowie and set to asking so many questions, about the terrain and water sources, the nearby tribes, everything down to the types of grasses that grew there, that the men began to joke that he would next ask about the traits of the dust on the bottom of their boots. All this time he gave no inkling as to what he intended to do with the information.

I laughed, and said that Allen is true to form — he keeps his thoughts to himself, and it is only once he has quietly determined his course that he reveals his plans to those around him, soldier or wife. Yet it filled me with pride to see how much this young man admires him. He said Allen always expects the best of his men and never sets them to a task he would not do himself.

"I've seen him more than once help to dig a well," Mr Pruitt said.

"But my husband must have some flaw?" I inquired.

"I have seen his temper, ma'am," he said.

This was unexpected, for Allen has never displayed to me any fury or undue impatience. When I asked Mr Pruitt to explain, he recalled an incident when Allen received an unwelcomed telegram from a general in Washington, D.C., and he marched into the adobe telegraph office at the fort, seized the machine from the desk, and threw it out the door and into the dusty yard. Mr Pruitt said he and the machine's operator were dumbfounded.

"Your Colonel smoothed down the front of his uniform, apologized for the disruption, and left, stepping over the machine on his way." Fortunately, Mr Pruitt said, it was repairable, for during the next days Allen sent many telegrams of his own, but it seemed his commander was unmoved in his decision.

I believe Mr Pruitt thought this story would amuse me, and I smiled and shook my head at Allen's bad humor, but I was left to speculate about what could anger him so. And how is it that he never told me of it? It did not, however, seem appropriate to discuss such matters with one of his men, and I endeavored to change the subject yet again.

"Allen tells me that you have seen the condor. Is it true?"

He gave me that same look of surprise and doubt, as if I could not truly be interested in such matters. Yes, he said — it was a giant, with a wingspan of nearly ten feet and a bald head of many colors.

How I would love to see such an amazing creature! I described some of the less exotic birds I have observed near the barracks and asked him what species we might hope to see during our journey to Alaska. Just as Mr Pruitt seemed to show some sign of enthusiasm for our conversation, however, we were interrupted by one of Mr Tillman's passionate but brief toasts: "To Alaska!" to which the crowd cheered, "To Alaska!"

As the roar settled, Mr Pruitt leaned closer to me, his eyes on Mr Tillman, and said, "Do you know, Mrs Forrester, that your husband is the only military man I have ever known who is always sober, dutiful, and faithful."

How could I respond to such a pronouncement?

"Yes, well, it is a lovely evening!" I offered. "So many beautiful gowns, and the music! Allen told me I would enjoy this dance more than most, and he was absolutely correct."

Any bit of interest or liveliness on his part seemed to wane and he only stared blankly over the crowd. I was preparing to excuse myself, when he said something unexpected.

"You are fortunate, Mrs Forrester."

What on earth could he mean?

"You still believe everything is golden, all dances and fine stitches and silk," he said, and here he looked over my gown, which made me quite self-conscious. "But this is all just an illusion, a dream," he went on. "You have been spared truth. Your Colonel and I, we know. Once seen, it cannot be unseen."

And then Mr Pruitt urged me to leave him, to dance and enjoy myself rather than have my evening darkened by his mood, and I was all too happy to oblige.

I know Allen says he is an intelligent and hardworking officer and that he is glad to have him on the expedition, but Mr Pruitt seems to me to be an unhappy young man.

All in all, the evening quite wore me out with the noise and discourse. It must account for this ill feeling that plagues me today.

January 15

What a dreadful morning! I never imagined it would cause a row between us, and I hate that Allen went off for the day without our making amends. I meant no cruelty or provocation — I only wanted to know how he could be so angry at a commanding officer as to throw about a telegraph machine.

I have long suspected that Allen shields me. When he reads to me from his desert journals, I notice that he skips entire pages. He will begin to tell of a courageous lieutenant he once knew in the war or of an encounter with the wild Apache, and he will pause thoughtfully and then turn the conversation with grace, like he spins me on the dance floor, and when I realize what has happened, it will be too late and I will be talking of some poem I read or piece of art we admired in San Francisco. And these past weeks, all that he has told me of his coming expedition, yet never did he mention the Indians' massacre of the Russians.

It is true we have been married only months, but I would know him more fully, and not just the buttoned, ironed, and mannerly husband who takes me dancing and presents me with gifts. What of the man who has lived for weeks, months even, without bath or civilized meal, who has seen the deaths of enemy and friend alike? What of that medal that sits upon his bureau? I can see for myself that it is a commendation of great significance, but he will only say that he was a young lieutenant and it was a long time ago.

It is something more, too. I feel a bit as if I've been put in my place. Just because I appeared before Mr Pruitt as a well-married woman in a fine gown (borrowed at that), who is he to assume that I have therefore led a charmed and unmarred life, that I am ignorant of suffering?

Worst yet, is it possible that Allen in some way shares this opinion? If he conceals a part of himself out of a misguided desire to protect me, it would sadden me terribly, for it would mean that neither of us knows the other as intimately as marriage would presume. And here is my most callow admission — it wounds my pride to think Allen's men know him better than I might ever hope to.

Ah, and this is the trouble with a diary. We are allowed to stand too long before its mirror and gaze at ourselves, where we unavoidably find vanity and fault.

I should keep to the field sparrow in flight. The cedar waxwings in the ash tree. Make note of their plumage and bills. Observe the habitats they frequent, the seeds that they pluck. Keep my pencil to wing shape and migration patterns, for these are the more sublime and worthy observations.

Sophie Ada Swanson

Medal of Honor
Forrester, Allen W.

Rank and organization: Second Lieutenant, 8th U.S. Cavalry

★

Place and date: At San Carlos, Arizona, 30 May 1868

★

Date of issue: 4 August 1868

★

Citation: While leading a detachment to persuade an Apache band to surrender, Lieutenant Forrester and 12 men were surrounded by hostiles. The Lieutenant's horse was shot out from under him, so that he engaged in savage hand-to-hand fighting. Under a most galling fire, he assisted three of his wounded soldiers to safety before returning to the fight. He and his eight remaining soldiers were able to hold the 50 Indians at bay until reinforcements arrived.

Lieut. Col. Allen Forrester
March 27, 1885

We have struck ice so will abandon the row boats.

Aided by the tide, at dawn we rowed to one of the mouths of the Wolverine River. Gone from Vancouver Barracks since the 1st of February, we are nearly a month behind schedule. Yet I am glad to see this rugged scene at last — the west bank stacked with heaps of ice, some blocks as thick as four feet. We rowed upriver through a dreary sleet for most of the day along a clear main channel, but at times were forced to halt our progress as slabs of ice floated past. As one large berg scraped against our boat, I felt the deep chill it casts off.

When we fatigued from rowing into the current, we attempted to walk the boats upriver by cordelle — one man pulling the boat along the shore by rope tied to the bow, another keeping the stern into the current with the aid of an oar. It was impractical. The ice along shore required us to climb uneven ground. At times we were forced to wade streams. Pruitt stepped from a bank ledge only to sink to his chin in icy water, but still he managed to hold to his bow line. In other circumstances, it would have been amusing, but we know too well the deathly threat of it. All of us are left cold & wet.

Where we ran aground of ice, we climbed ashore to start a fire. Conditions were not favorable, our hands numb & useless. While our matches were kept dry in canisters, they fizzled in the wet wind. Samuelson managed with a bit of bark & clump of winterkilled grass to light the flames.

Once we have dried our boots, we will unload the boats. Samuelson says there is a nearby village where we can employ Indians to assist in carrying supplies upriver. All food, ammunition, equipment will have to be hauled by sled or pack. We will require at least four strong men.

We are out of the weather. For that I should be glad. Instead I want for fresh air, room to stretch my legs. More than two dozen Indians, three dogs, and the four of us, packed into a hovel the size of a small woodshed. In the center, a greasy fire sends more smoke into our faces than out the hole above. I envy Samuelson, who snores beside me. I too would like to sleep off this day.

Earlier we cached the supplies in a stand of willows near the row boats. As we carried crates ashore, Lieut. Pruitt spotted the old Eyak coming across the snow towards us. He moved slowly, elbows & knees askew, clothes flapping in sleety wind. At his pace, the journey was sure to take him hours, yet too quickly he was beside us.

When I had Samuelson ask him if he knows where we can find this village, the old man shook his head & poked about in the crates.

— He's lying, Pruitt said.

I concurred. I advised we would give him some tea if he would tell us how to find our way there.

Still the Eyak offered nothing. Samuelson said he wasn't sure of the exact location but that we should be able to follow a nearby dry creek bed to find it. He suspected that some of the Indians we met near Point Blake were already making their way to the village over land to warn them of our coming.

As we prepared to leave, the old man sat beside the supplies. I ordered that he was to have no tea, since he offered no guidance.

— We can't leave him here. He'll rob us blind, Pruitt said.

— He says he is old & slow so he'll make his own way, Samuelson said.

I would waste no more time on the matter, so we left him. For two hours we walked, crawled, beat our way through the willows. Pruitt took a branch to the face that narrowly missed his eye.

The dry creek bed petered out to leave us in a thicket. A graying dusk made passage more difficult. At times we considered we had made no progress at all, but at last we broke out of the willows & stumbled into the village, which is nothing more than a few hovels made of sticks & hides.

There, waiting for us, rested as if he had arrived hours before, was the old man. He crouched with a sly grin beside a heap of firewood.

— The devil! Tillman said.

Tillman seemed more amused than angry, but Pruitt wanted to search him for any of our supplies. The old man dodged his efforts.

Now, inside this overcrowded, poorly ventilated shelter, the troublemaker continues his pestering. We don't need Samuelson to translate. The old man stands in the middle of the shelter, hops around the campfire & talks in his sing-song chortles. He waves his arms, gestures towards us, takes exaggerated steps like a clumsy hunter stalking his prey, then he spins in circles like a dizzy child. The Indians all look at us & laugh.

— Glad we could provide the evening entertainment, Tillman grumbled.

I continue to try to write here in my journal. When the old man forces my attention, I do not smile but nod politely.

Just now the old man knelt in front of me, reached into a pouch at his neck to pull out his prize.

— Chocolate! He has stolen chocolate from us! Tillman shouted & jumped to his feet, as much as he was able in this squat shelter. — I'll be eating pea soup, while this scoundrel feasts on chocolate.

Even Tillman proved too worn out for a fight, however. He has returned to his bed, rolled on his side to face the wall.

Despite the rowdy laughter of the Indians, I will try to sleep now as well.

March 28

I had hoped for five strong men. Instead I'm given three reluctant Indians, the young woman who claims to have skinned out her husband, & a dog.

The Indians resisted being employed, except the woman. She is not much more than a girl, yet despite her youth & small frame, I am wary of her. At best she is slightly mad, at worst capable of slitting a man's throat as he sleeps. It did not increase my trust to know that she was amongst those who went ahead of us to warn these Indians of our approach.

Samuelson, however, argued for employing her.

— I'd wager she'll be more help than the

rest of them put together. Their women are hardworking. When a village moves, the women carry all the heavy loads. They fetch the wood, water, pack up the hides. To top it off, this one can hunt. She'll earn her way.

I am doubtful, but I conceded to Samuelson's greater knowledge of these people. Still we were in need of several men. Contrary to my conscience, I again followed Samuelson's advice.

— They love a game of chance. If they think joining our party is a lucky win, they'll want in.

We announced they could draw sticks. Only those who won would be permitted to join us. To my surprise, a dozen Indians volunteered. However, the five selected lost much enthusiasm when they were told we would be leaving this morning, that they would be towing sleds full of supplies as far up the river as we could manage. Two flat out refused to be conscripted, so we are left with three.

When the old man indicated his desire to travel along with us as well, I said that we have no more need for his services. Samuelson translated my message, to which the old man gave a sly look & tipped his black hat as if to bid us adieu.

The dog, a burly husky-wolf much larger than most of the Indians' dogs, seems to have been offered in trade for tobacco & sugar already acquired from our stores without our knowledge. I suspect that, like the Indian woman, the skittish animal will be more trouble than it is worth.

Sophie Forrester
Vancouver Barracks
January 17, 1885

Such an unwieldy title. "The ABC of Modern Photography . . . Comprising Practical Instructions in Working Gelatine Dry Plates." That alone should have deterred me.

Allen brought the book home to me last night, sent by Mr Pruitt along with an offer to further explain the camera's mechanism during our ship ride north. He must have reconsidered his earlier brusqueness, and I am grateful, particularly because I will need every bit of help if I am to understand any of this. An entire chapter devoted to chemicals! Neutral oxalate of potash. Sulphate of iron. Hypo-sulphite of soda. Methylated spirit. Bichloride of mercury. My brain spins.

From a distance, it seemed such a simple and nearly magical art. A black cloth. A mahogany box. Glass plates. Darkness and light. Yet in truth it is both more material and more complex than I could have imagined.

Books have always been my most reliable teacher, but Allen is correct that some skills are better understood in practice, by hands and eyes. He says we should purchase a camera if it interests me so. I have no idea of the expense, and certainly there is not enough time to seek one before our journey north, but if I can learn a bit from Mr Pruitt aboard the steamer and continue to study the manuals over the next months, is it possible that I could learn to make my own photographs?

Well of course, Allen said, and he wouldn't spend too much time fretting over those cursed hand books, either. "You just have to do it and figure it out for yourself," he said, "and I have no doubt that you will."

It is something I love very much about him. He goes not in search of obstacles, only the paths around them. Anything seems possible.

Yet for all my keenness, I see now that I have a great deal to learn.

January 21

It is well after midnight, yet I cannot sleep a wink! Today it was confirmed that we will board the mail steamer "Idaho" on its February 3rd stopover in Portland. Though it is still some time away, being in possession of a firm date and the precise name of our ship has beset me with worries and excitement. Are the women right that I will suffer seasickness? Mrs Connor mentioned a bromide remedy. I will have to ask at a pharmacy. Oh, I do hope I am so fortunate as to see the puffin bird. Are the illustrations I have seen accurate? Does it possess such a sweet and comical expression? As for the Wolverine River tribes and their frightening reputation, I should not let myself fret. . . . and on and on trail my thoughts.

I have given up on sleep altogether and have come to the kitchen table with my diary so that my candlelight might not disturb Allen as he sleeps. I have put on a kettle for chamomile tea and wrapped myself in a blanket in hopes of settling my nerves.

To be awake at such an odd hour, the windows dark and the house quiet, with a daring voyage on the horizon, causes me to miss Father more than I have in some time. If he were still alive, I would be writing to him just now. He would have been so glad for me, for he was always one to favor adventure and the promise of something extraordinary.

I remember that when I was quite young, I overheard him talking of flying mice, how he had seen them swoop and dive across the night sky. If he was in a fervor with a new sculpture, once the form began to come alive in the marble, he would bring lanterns to the forest and work long into the night, and it was then that he had seen them. He said they flew silently, like furry shadows.

For days I could think of nothing but these winged mice. I gleaned every small detail I could find in Mother's schoolhouse book about the animals of North America, and at any opportunity, I pleaded with Father to take me with him at night.

"They are only bats, nothing more," Mother said.

Father whispered to me alone, "These are no ordinary bats. These are mice who swim with the stars."

Loud enough for Mother to hear, though, he added that they appear only when the sun goes down, when children are to be tucked into bed. (It was not like him to be concerned about arbitrary rules such as bedtimes, but I eventually discovered that it was the subject of his statue that made him wary. He was working on his Mary Magdalene, with her unbound curls falling around her naked torso. Needless to say, Mother would not have approved, so he kept the sculpture hidden far into the forest.)

Finally, despite her objections, he allowed me to join him one evening after supper. As we walked into the trees, I was made to promise not to tell Mother of the sculpture.

That first night I lay bundled in Father's big coat and stared up into the darkening sky, but eventually I fell asleep to the sound of his chisel. I awoke to him putting me to bed — I had slept even as he carried me home.

"Did I miss them?" I asked.

"Yes," he said. "But they'll come again."

He allowed me to go with him again the next night and the night after, and I forbade myself from giving in to sleep. I pinched my arms and hopped up and down while Father worked at his sculpture, but the bats did not appear. And then at last it happened — just after sunset on the third night, a dark spot flitted through the trees, so quick and small that I doubted my eyes, but then it came again, and dozens more with it.

Thinking on it now, I am surprised I was not somewhat disappointed, for there was little to observe. In the dusk, especially to my inexperienced eyes, the bats could have been barn swallows or oversized moths. Yet for all that, it was marvelous — the nights of anticipation and then, in the sky above me, the fleeting silhouettes of their wings.

That is the excitement. We catch only glimpses, a burst of movement, a flap of wings, yet it is life itself beating at shadow's edge. It is the unfolding of potential; all of what we might experience and see and learn awaits us.

January 22

Too little sleep is not good for my constitution, and I think I may be coming down with a cold or some other illness, I feel so poorly. I could not bear the thought of lying in bed all day, so although it was blustery, I went for a walk on the wagon road behind the officers' homes. I tired more quickly than I would have liked, however, and have returned after only an hour or so.

January 23

Still I cope with this queasiness and general malaise. I had hoped that exercise and fresh air would chase it away, but again it comes upon me unexpectedly. These past days I have not cared to draw attention to it. Allen, however, insists I visit the barracks hospital tomorrow to see Dr Randall. He says it will not do for me to board the ship if I am coming down with some sickness.

I am loath to go — I've always had the irrational thought that if one consults a physician, it only confirms an illness that might otherwise be ignored away — but I will go nonetheless.

A WEDDING PARTY FOR SON OF GEN. FORRESTER

Lieut.-Col. Allen Walton Forrester, son of Gen. James Forrester, and Miss Sophie Ada Swanson, daughter of Mrs. Helen Swanson, were married at 12 o'clock yesterday at the Grace Presbyterian Church in a quiet ceremony. The bride and groom were attended at the altar by Miss Swanson's mother and Mr. George Forrester, brother to the groom. The ceremony was officiated by the Rev. Dr. Daniel Rodgers. The bride wore a dress of heavy white satin and a tulle veil, and carried a bouquet of pale pink Bennett roses.

The newlywed couple was then escorted to the nearby Forrester estate by the elderly Gen. and Mrs. James Forrester. Despite the small size of the wedding party, the reception was an impressive affair, with numerous gifts and distinguished guests. In light of Gen. Forrester's stature in the Boston community, it does not come as a surprise that his son's wedding would attract such attention. The event was attended by the likes of Gen. Joseph Lovell, Lieut.-Col. Robert Jones, Sen. Henry Dawes, and Augustus Flagg.

The newly wedded couple leaves next week for Vancouver Barracks in the remote

Washington Territory where the Colonel is to be stationed.

Dear Mr. Forrester,

I was surprised when the boxes of documents came to my office last week. As I said during our telephone conversation, we probably aren't the best institution to receive this collection. I think you misunderstood me. I'm sure they are historically important. Unfortunately, we just don't have enough staffing or resources to properly archive them. Our funding was cut this past year, and we are now relying almost entirely on volunteers. I am sure the university or one of the larger museums in Anchorage would be happy to take this donation.

Having said all that, I did read through some of the Colonel's diaries. It isn't easy to translate his shorthand, even with the key of abbreviations you've included, and some of the pages are so water-damaged and faded, it's hard to make out the writing, but they are really incredible. My interest isn't just as a museum curator. I am a member of the Wolverine River tribe through my mother's side. I know many of the places the Colonel describes. Our family still keeps a fish wheel on the river to catch sockeye salmon each summer.

I am curious about the black leather journal that you included. It's not identified in any way, but I can tell it's not your great-uncle's handwriting. It is mostly filled with mapping and weather data, but there are also more personal entries — sketches and poetry. Do you know who this belonged to?

I'd like to talk with you more about the documents and the artifacts you describe. Maybe I can do some research and help you find a home for the collection. Do you have an email address?

I'll drop this letter in the mail and wait for your reply.

Best wishes,
Josh Sloan
Alpine Historical Museum
Alpine, Alaska

60°26' N
145°11' W
33°F, exposed bulb
27°F, wet bulb
Barometer: 29.15
Sleet in morning. Wind ESE, steady & cold.
  Clear by nightfall,
allowing for navigational readings.

We calculate unseen horizon by mercury
pool, pace off distances between our point
and theirs, measure the wind and the speed
by which the river flows, count the very
droplets in the atmosphere. If we can measure, we are sure we can grasp and claim as
our own. What then of the six-winged Seraph
and Cherubim with sleepless eye? No such
celestials dwell here. The Midnooskies have
not met our God. Their own fearsome beasts
fly through these skies. Will we find them with
our civilized eyes? Will they flap out of glacier
crevasse and over black river valley, while we
crawl, scrabble up their mountains?

Otter Tracks

The hymns do have their siren call. I hear them as I row. "Feeble, trembling, fainting, dying, Lord! I cast myself on thee; Tarry with me through the darkness." O we tremble — man and child alike. None of us so different from the clear-fleshed jellyfish that wash up on salty rocks. Cnidaria. Scyphozoa. We name. Dry. Pickle. Exhibit with pins and tabs and stoppered vials. Yet there is no how or why in that taxonomy. Just the Latin tongue. Incantation of cold science. Between Science's measuring and my God's condemning, I find no room for the Soul. No room for my feathered lungs to expand. I would gasp and gasp, only wanting the cold fingers to release their hold.

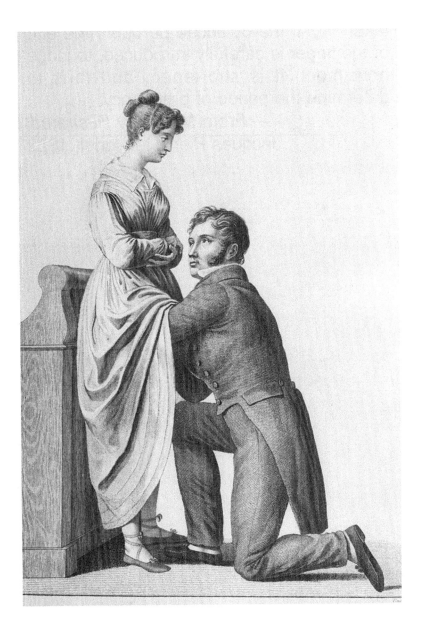

Of touching, — the female standing. This mode is advantageous in every respect. The parts of the female are in their natural position, and the physician cannot be mistaken . . . if the os tincae be open, the end of the finger is carefully introduced, to judge how much it is shortened, and thus to determine the period of pregnancy.

— From *Midwifery Illustrated,*
Jacques Pierre Maygrier, 1822

Sophie Forrester
Vancouver Barracks
January 24, 1885

Can it be so, after these months of failure? We had thought to wait until Allen's return from Alaska to seek out a physician who might advise us, yet it seems that our wish has been granted sooner than we dared to hope. A child!

I feel like a fool that I did not make it out myself, yet the post surgeon seems nearly certain. Such unexpected good tidings! Dear Allen is beside himself with joy. He was ready to announce it to all who would listen from the barracks to Boston, but I suggested that would be neither proper nor wise. It is still much too early, and until the surgeon detects a heartbeat or I feel the quickening, it cannot be certain.

I then had to tell him my one great disappointment. I will not go to Alaska. Dr Randall has forbidden it. I was incredulous at first —

have women throughout history not traveled and lived their normal lives with no ill effect to their unborn children? What could be so particularly dangerous about riding on a steamer ship for a few weeks?

It vexed me the way Dr Randall ignored my questions but instead stood for some time at his shelf with his back to me. He thumbed through his books, mumbled to himself, all as if I were not in the room. At one point he even shushed me. That was too much! I am not a simpleton to be treated with such disregard. (I fear I am sometimes too quick with my words.) When I regained my composure, I proposed that on the ship I would have regular food and rest, and could even sit in a deck chair to watch the glaciers calve, if need be.

That is when he stated it plainly. Under no circumstances am I to go aboard the steamer, and I will need to take great care throughout the pregnancy. When I asked why, if there was something in his examination that gave him concern, he said I am not to worry myself with it, and unceremoniously sent me away.

In Dr Randall's defense, Allen says he is an old battlefield surgeon, more comfortable sawing off limbs and digging out lead balls. Female patients must put him ill at ease.

Be that as it may, how could his discomfort compare to mine? To be poked and prodded in such a way! To be coldly questioned about the most intimate concerns! He presumed I understood nothing of reproduction because I hadn't recognized my state sooner. I had to explain the irregularity of my cycle, that I have often gone months with its absence, so thought nothing of it when it occurred this time. He only sighed as if this were yet another inconvenience and went back to his books, with no word of reassurance or gesture toward kindness.

It is agreed, though — we must obey the surgeon's orders. It would not do to risk our child only so that I might have a bit of adventure. It seems impossible to hope, but maybe someday I will be afforded another opportunity to go to Alaska.

January 26
Everything has turned topsy-turvy, and at times I cannot remember which dream greets me when I wake. For a moment I nearly forget, but then it returns with a jolt — I will not go to Alaska, yet a child comes to life within me! Even when I give it no thought at all, its tiny heart beats. It can be no bigger than a finger. What does it have for eyes and limbs and sense? (Oh that I could read something on the subject!)

Only a few times in my life have I had such intensity of emotion as to feel as if the moment were not entirely real, and I was overcome in such a way just this morning. It rained throughout the night, but with dawn, the clouds lifted and the sun made a rare appearance. I went to the porch in hopes that the fresh air would dispel my queasiness, and standing there it occurred to me that my entire self is being altered, steadily and dramatically, and that something tremendous has begun. As I thought on it, the morning seemed to break into a million shards of light and color, and I saw and felt and heard everything at once — the water droplets that dotted the porch rail in a perfect glittering line, the chill river air that entered me and left with my breath, the sunlit fog that rose from the river valley. I heard the far off whinny of a horse, and when I looked down the hill toward the stables, I saw that the rain drops gathered and glistened on every surface, every bare tree branch and stone and blade of grass, and the sharp brilliance of it all nearly brought me to tears.

How is it that my maternity, such an ordinary, everyday occurrence of humankind, can feel utterly singular and overwhelming to me?

Allen, too, is affected in ways I did not expect. Though I show no outward signs of maternity, he falls over himself to help me to my feet when I leave a chair, and even while he is working at the desk, his eyes are often upon me, as if he is in awe of something I have done.

"Are you really sure?" he said last evening as he watched me in such a way. I was undressing in our bedroom and preparing to put on my nightgown. "The doctor is absolutely certain?"

Isn't he happy for the news?

"God yes!" he said. "It just doesn't seem real somehow. That it should happen to us, that we will have a baby together, and just as I'm leaving you. Everything at once. And here I thought I'd die an old bachelor."

Allen reached out as if to touch me, but then he hesitated, as if he feared he could hurt me in some way. I took his hand with my own and held it firmly against my bare belly, and we were both still and quiet, standing together beside our bed, as if we might either of us see or feel some sign.

"I don't like to leave you this way," he said, with his hand still rested there.

Of course he will go, and I will manage best I can. I am still the same woman he married, I remind him — no more or less competent. Yet there is something quite tender, even vulnerable, about this new side of Allen.

January 27
It occurred to me last night as I drifted to sleep — am I also forbidden to travel by train East? These past days, we assumed I would go home to Mother while Allen is gone, but then I recalled the surgeon's warnings.

When I went to the hospital this afternoon, Dr Randall was mending the broken foot of a young soldier (run over by an ammunition wagon, I have since learned) and even with all the man's cursing and howling, it was clear the surgeon preferred that patient over me. "Take her to my office to wait," he told his assistant, granting not a word or look in my direction.

When at last he came to see me, I apologized for bothering him but said I must clarify his orders.

And it is so. I will not go to Vermont, but instead must remain here until the baby is born. I do not know what to make of this. I never imagined I would stay in Vancouver alone without Allen.

Also during my visit, I made the mistake of asking the doctor if I could please borrow one of his books on midwifery or obstetrics, as I wish to learn more about the physiology. What does the fetus look like? What anatomical features has it developed? He has several books on his shelves that I am sure could satisfy some of my curiosity.

I might as well have thrown a dishpan of dirty water over his head. For a moment he was speechless, and then at last sputtered that it was not "suitable reading."

I told him I only wish to know more about the process, that I possess a rudimentary knowledge of the sciences and have even assisted in birthing. (I saw no need to mention that such midwifery on my part involved a barn cat when I was a young girl.)

Dr Randall could not be swayed. He said his books are completely inappropriate for women and laymen, and that the reading would bewilder me.

If he were to refuse me one of his books because it was precious or necessary to him, that I could forgive easily enough, but to do so out of some paternal censorship or doubt of my intellect — it is entirely displeasing!

I cannot say I am used to such restrictions (and I know my fortune in that). We might not have been able to afford many books in our house, or even in Mother's schoolroom, yet all were open to me, and it was much the same at normal school. What I wouldn't do to have the Sommerton library here with me now!

January 28

Allen has written letters to everyone near and far, sharing our news, but I wish us to wait just a while longer before sending them. Especially to Mother. She will fill my head with worries and dangers. Even before we were married, she warned that my irregular cycles predicted a difficulty in carrying a child. I will allow this maternity to settle upon me more firmly before I engage with her pessimism.

I am ashamed to admit it, but as lonely as it might be here in Vancouver without Allen, I am glad to not be returning to stay with Mother. There is a great deal I admire in her, and I am grateful for everything she has taught me, yet there is so little pleasure in her presence. All is devoted to labor before God, and always she is casting her eye for any aberrance or wasteful delight. I often wonder how much of it is Father's influence — she strained to counterweight his reckless nature by imposing order and frugality in our household, and now that he's gone, she is set in those rigid ways.

I can recall the exact day when I chose a different life for myself. It was at Sommerton Normal School, and I was walking to the dormitory on a bright autumn afternoon and fairly skipping through the fallen leaves. It occurred to me that if I wanted to miss my supper and spend the entire night reading page after page of poetry, there was no one to tell me that I was ruining my eyes and any chances at a good marriage. If I chose to ignore my studies and sneak tea cakes back into my room and nibble on them beneath the covers, once again I answered to no one but the monitor if I did not sweep up my crumbs.

I experienced such complete gladness, and I told myself I would never take it for granted — the freedom to choose my own dress, to plan my days, to walk where I desired and see what I would.

There is, of course, some irony to my circumstances: here I set out on my own path, only to discover that it has brought me to confinement and restriction after all, this time by orders of a doctor rather than Mother.

January 29

Why is it that our disappointments are so often magnified by the reaction of others?

So you won't go to Alaska after all! Did you lose your nerve? Good heavens, it is all for the best. Wouldn't you have had a miserable time? Did the General forbid you? They probably thought you'd be a nuisance or suffer horribly from seasickness.

All in all, afternoon tea was even more unbearable than normal. Since I do not yet feel free to share the true reason for my staying behind, I endured their remarks without retort. Sarah Whithers, bless her, seemed genuinely disappointed, as if she too were being denied the journey, but Mrs Connor gloated, as if she had known all along it wasn't to be.

Ordinary causes of abortions are such as weakness or corruption of the womb, or by outward force such as falls, blows, wrath, madness, fear, running, leaping, cutting of wood, and immoderate exercise.

By way of caution: avoid the presence of ravens and other carrion eaters, for they are Death's envoys, tasked to deliver souls from this world unto the next. If such bad omen visits upon you and signs of abortion appear, the usual way is to lay toast sopt in Muskadel to your navel. This is good medicine.

But to take the womb of a hare beaten to powder, half a dram, in Malmsey each morning is far better.

— From *Midwifery: A Pocket-Companion for Women in Their Conception,* Benjamin Fielding, student in physic and astrology, London, 1743

Lieut. Col. Allen Forrester
March 30, 1885

Rain has softened the snow in the river valley to such a degree that we wallow in our snowshoes, the sleds are useless. We set out each day as soon as there is light enough in order to travel quickly while the snow is still crusted from night's cold. Before long, though, the morning warms to rain. We attempt to tow four sleds, including two made from sawing an Indian canoe in half. The loads, several hundred pounds each, cause us to flounder no matter how many of us throw our shoulders into the work.

The Indians resist leaving the campfire each morning. This morning if Pruitt had not knocked down their lean-tos & forcibly dragged them to their feet, we'd be there still. The woman refuses to assist in pulling, but instead straps a large load of supplies to her back, a small pannier to the dog, & the two head upriver each morning without a glance in our direction.

— She doesn't follow orders, Pruitt complained.

For myself, I did not count on her assistance, so it is of no matter to me where she goes each day.

This stretch of land is dreary, flat, gray, without the beauty of the island coast. We are near enough the sea that precipitation never halts, only changes from rain to snow then back again. Water runs atop the river ice so that we are soaked from ground & sky as we wade through knee-deep slush. More than once we plunged to our necks as we tried to ford open water. Evening campfires do not dry our clothes. However, the sleeping bags of linen sailcloth, waterproofed with linseed oil & beeswax, are proving most valuable.

Tonight I miss my Sophie dearly.

April 2

We have abandoned the tents & half our ammunition, food, clothing, etc., all cached in tall cottonwood trees. If our travel improves, we will send Indians to retrieve as much as possible.

Our stores are reduced to 100 pounds each flour & beans, 40 of rice, but now the sleds can reasonably be towed through slush. Lieut. Pruitt carries little food to make room for scientific equipment, including camera & dry plates. We have kept also some bacon,

extract of beef, tea, deviled ham, what chocolate the old man did not pocket. Luxuries,
but they earn their weight in morale.

We now travel more quickly & with God-
speed we will make it to the canyon before
the river ice gives way. The decision did not
come easily, particularly to have Pruitt's load
contain so little food. Tillman argued against
it.

— We'll go hungry, for pretty pictures!

Pruitt insisted the photographs are invaluable, began to berate Tillman for his ignorance. Here I cut them off to avoid a scuffle.
I reminded Tillman that we expected to
subsist off the wilds during the journey. In
truth I had hoped to make it farther upriver
with more supplies, but I did not say this.

Tillman filled his own sled with such a
heavy load of food that I had to give a push
from behind to get the sled moving. The
sergeant is a strapping fellow but will not be
able to pull that load for long.

The supplies we carry will not last us but a
month. We will supplement with game & ed-
ible plants. The Indians express doubt. The
tall one, called Skilly, said until the salmon
return in summer, the Wolverine River is the
'place where men starve.'

— What of these river tribes, said to be so
fierce? They must eat something, even in the
winter months, I asserted.

Several of the Indians responded, but the

trapper seemed reluctant to translate, only did so after I prodded.

— They claim the Midnooskies above the canyon survive only by relying on human flesh.

As for the woman, she is silent, but clearly has thoughts of her own.

April 3

This morning at breakfast, Sgt. Tillman sat beside me with his tin cup of coffee, inquired about my family in Boston. He knows of my father & his respectable career in the Army. We talked some of our childhoods. Tillman is the son of a coal miner, from a rough life I suspect.

Eventually he asked me about Sophie.

— You've been married for some time? he asked.

I answered that it had been not yet a year.

— You must have had another wife before this. Did she die?

The question surprised me. — No, I said, — I have never been married before.

— You seem like the marrying type. No spring chicken, either. What took you so long?

I have grown accustomed to Tillman's blunt ways, so took no offense. I explained that until Sophie, I had never met a woman who held my interest.

— You & I must not run in the same circles. I find girls aplenty.

Yes, I am sure he does. Yet I speculated that many of them are silly, or if they are quick-witted, they are worldly & cynical.

In reply, Tillman gave a devious grin.

— Ah! But that's how I love them best. Both at once. Silly & worldly!

It made me uneasy. I have no desire to bring Sophie into such low talk. How could I tell of her intelligence, her humor, her gentleness, to a man like this? She is too good for his ears.

I said nothing more on the subject but instead asked Pruitt if he has a sweetheart. The lieutenant shook his head without looking up from his diary.

Sophie is right that Pruitt is different than I remember him. When we went up against Apache in the desert, even after long days of riding, he was rarely silent. — Did you know, Colonel . . . he would always begin, then rattle off one interesting fact or another. A species of plant with gastric juices & a giant flower for eating insects. A cave in North Carolina that breathes like an animal, blowing out air in the summer, sucking in air in the winter. Lantern-like creatures in the depths of the ocean; the speed of a comet through the heavens. Other times he would recite bits of poetry that to this day stay with me: 'Soldier rest! Thy warfare o'er, sleep the sleep that knows not breaking; dream of battled fields no more.'

We fought Indians in savage country. He proved himself to be both tough & astute, as young as he was. I was certain those traits could serve us well on this journey. Now I find him quiet, somber, on edge. He is prone to sitting alone, sketching in his notebook. Does my memory fail me, or have these short years changed him?

April 5

Some good to report — the trapper Samuelson will continue with us, although not of his choice. He expected by now to have word from his business partner, who in the autumn traveled up the Wolverine River to scout trapping & mining prospects. Samuelson heard rumors from Indians earlier in the winter that Boyd had built a cabin some 40 miles from here. Since then there has been no sign of him.

— I'd like to find him whole & alive, Samuelson said. — We had plans.

— Not an overly sentimental fellow, Tillman said in an aside to me.

Sentimental or no, the trapper is great help. Steadfast. Capable. I did not look forward to being without his expertise. I suspect he knows far more than he lets on, not that he is secretive, but instead simply a man of few words.

At mid-day we rested on a cottonwood log to eat cold biscuits. I asked Samuelson about the old Eyak we had left behind. He remains something of an irritation to me. Would he go back to Perkins Island?

— Eyak? Samuelson said. — He's no Eyak.

I asked who the old fellow's people are then.

Samuelson said no one claims him. — He's just always about, sometimes wanted, sometimes not.

— What language does he speak?

— He likes to toy with me, he does. He'll start out in Eyak, then as soon as I catch my rhythm, he'll go to Midnoosky, then he'll change again. All along, he knows our English well enough, I reckon.

It seems that each in their own tongue, the natives call him the Man Who Flies on Black Wings.

— He is something of an odd bird, isn't he? I said with amusement.

— Not just an odd bird.

Samuelson says the natives believe the Old Man can change the weather, make people sick or cure them, as suits his mood. Years ago, they say, he stole an Eyak's wife & the husband shot him. The Old Man just coughed up the bullet, spat it on the ground, & went on unharmed.

Most of all, he says, the Old Man is unpredictable. Today he'll rob you blind, but tomorrow he might give you a warm blanket when you need it most.

— He's a devil & angel in one, he said. —

Nothing to depend on, except that he's always looking for something to eat, & he's always looking for mischief.

It seems impossible that the Indians should truly believe he can fly or spit out bullets that have struck him. I asked the trapper what he made of such nonsense. All humor left him.

— Doesn't matter a God d —— d what I think. Or you for that matter. Have no doubt, Colonel, we are traveling through their world, not our own. Whatever the Russians & politicians say.

I asked no more. The trapper may be right on one count. Despite government treatise, this frozen Wolverine River Valley yet belongs to the Indians, as they are the only ones who claim it. That will change if white men find use for it.

As for the Old Man, I give no credence to the idea he is anything but a thieving rascal with tricks up his sleeve. I will admit this, though — the memory of him crouched in the top of that tree in the black of night stays with me.

April 6

The weather has turned more disagreeable. A storm pounds us with heavy snow, blown into our faces so that we barely make our way along the river ice. Travel is slow at best. The dog is the only member of the party that remains undaunted. It disappeared early in

100

the day so that I suspected it had slunk away to join a pack of wolves, pannier still strapped to its back, but upriver we found it curled in a drift of snow. As we neared, it hopped to its feet, shook off the snow, vanished ahead into the storm. This happened through the day. Even the Indian girl cannot keep up with the animal's pace, so has fallen back to travel with the others. How the dog predicts our route, I do not know, except that we follow the river.

We camp the nights damp & cold with none of us sleeping soundly. Without tents, we rely all the more on our sailcloth bags as our only shelter. Once inside, I pull my poncho overhead to make a small tent beneath which I can eat, read, write somewhat protected from the storm.

Lieut. Pruitt's efforts to take celestial observations are frustrated by the weather.

Sophie Forrester
Vancouver Barracks
January 31, 1885

Allen is gone. I must accept it. Last night I could make do with the thought that he was just at the wharf in Portland, sleeping aboard the docked steamer, and that by some chance I might see him one last time. Tonight is different. The sun has set, the barracks fallen quiet, and I am alone in this house. The ship was to depart this morning at daybreak, bound for Puget Sound. By this late hour, could they near British Columbia? Will it truly be months, even a year before I hear word of him again?

I am feeling sorry for myself, and it is senseless. Of course this day would come.

I wonder, if I had stood on the river shore this morning and waved goodbye as the ship left for the coast, if we had a grand farewell and watched the distance between us grow, if I had witnessed his leaving, would I then be more settled with it? Would his absence be more real to me? Instead, my thoughts play tricks. Maybe the ship was delayed for some reason, or at the last minute Allen decided he could not leave me behind, and I will soon hear him in the hall, bumping his loud boots against the bench, and then, "Sophie love, I'm home."

Everything became a mad rush in the end, with word that the steamer was in the harbor days earlier than expected and set to leave immediately. There were crates to be sealed, lists to check, messages to send.

When I suggested I go to Portland to see him off, he said there was no sense to it. They would board the ship at night and leave at daybreak. There would be no time to visit or say farewell. I suspect he also worried for my health, even traveling those few hours by carriage and ferry.

At least I sent him with my letter. I had little time to compose it, but may my words remind him of my love and allow him to feel the touch of home.

And we did have yesterday morning. Oh, but that it could have lasted forever. The joy of waking to the scent of warm, fresh popovers. (How did he ever convince the barracks cook to bake them? And with blackberry jam and butter! By chance, Allen discovered the antidote to my queasiness.) As the first rays of morning came through our little kitchen window, it was as if we had all the time in the world, and when he laughed and held my hands, I felt as if the sunlight poured through me.

The silver comb is beautiful. It is his birthday present to me, as he will not be with me in April. I wear it in my hair now as I write. The engravings of the fern fronds are so delicate, so lifelike. It is evidence that Allen knows my preferences well. He must have planned this for some time. Did he purchase it in San Francisco on our travel to the barracks, and then keep it hidden away these past months? Surely he couldn't have found such a fine piece in Vancouver.

Oh, Allen, still you are a surprise to me. Soldier, fearless adventurer — yet your heart is gentle. I will wear the comb in my hair every day, so as to feel as if you are always near.

February 2

I am expecting a young woman named Charlotte this afternoon — she is to move into the small bedroom and tend to chores here each afternoon. It seems the Connors have enough help that they are willing to part with her a few hours each day, if we take on the girl's room and board. I have not yet met her, but I'm told her father is an enlisted man and her mother a washerwoman at the barracks.

Allen made the arrangements before he left.

I resisted when we first came to Vancouver and he wanted to hire help — it is one thing to send out the laundry, but I am perfectly capable of cooking meals and keeping a house. (What would Mother think, to know that even with no husband or children to care for, I am being afforded a housemaid!) But now that my tasks are restricted, and I no longer have Allen's assistance, I suppose it is unavoidable.

Allen would have preferred that I move into one of the newer homes down the lane. A room with, say, the Whithers or the Connors would be more economical, and even more luxurious; their houses are equipped with piped-water baths and beautiful parlors. This old staff cabin was never meant for an officer or his family, he said, and in fact, the General intends to raze it next year to make room for a new officer house. It was to be only our temporary quarters until Allen left on his expedition and I returned to the East.

Yet I abhor the thought of taking a room and living under someone else's thumb, and so we came to our compromise — I will keep my own house, but with assistance, and I am glad for it. This log cabin is tucked in among the fir trees so that it feels more of the forest than of the barracks. It is drafty and sagging, it is true, but it is humble and private and suits me well.

The girl is younger than I had imagined, perhaps only ten or eleven, and when Mrs Connor described her family, I somehow pictured a strapping, boisterous girl. This one is instead quiet and waifish. I have hardly been able to pry two words from her, but I am hopeful we will grow accustomed to one another.

Evelyn came to visit yesterday and was baffled to catch me trying to sweep and straighten before Charlotte's daily arrival. "You are an odd card, Sophie Forrester. Dusting when you have a hired girl coming to do it."

My efforts did not deter her company, however. She reclined on the sofa in a beautiful new gown and told me all about the monsieur who designed it. (Her talk of Europe's salons causes me to feel shabby and provincial in one minute and shocked and amused the next.)

It is, however, one of the benefits of her friendship, if I am prepared to call it that — it requires very little of me. All I must do is nod now and then, and she will continue on like a well-cranked musical box.

I learned that her ailing father has sent her West, and to her aunt and uncle's stern oversight, in hopes of removing her from the temptations of the cities and finding her a suitable mate among the officers. They want her married and settled down. From everything I observe of her nature, this seems highly unlikely.

At one point as she sipped her tea and fiddled with the beads on her gown and chattered on, she appeared an exact mimic of the cedar waxwings that come to the ash tree — splendid in painted feathers, hopping from branch to branch among the red berries, beautiful and flighty. I found myself smiling against my will, then trying to hide it in a cough that turned into an unfortunate snort.

"Are you quite all right?" she asked. She was, however, too enthralled with her own conversation to take notice for long.

Later it seemed she had guessed my secret. I had sat down in a chair, and without thought, rested a hand on my abdomen. I should have been listening, yet I daydreamed — what would the quickening feel like? Would I recognize it when it happened?

Evelyn ceased talking and stared at me.

"Will you have children someday, Sophie?" she asked archly.

"Perhaps . . ."

However, this subject did not hold her attention either. She asked if I had gone to tea with the other wives last week, if I had enjoyed it, and then went on without pause.

"Boring old biddies, aren't they? And they don't know what to think of you, Mrs Forrester. Mrs Connor says it is unseemly the way you wander about the woods by your-self."

When I protested, she cut me off again, this time to praise me with backhanded compliments, calling me "diverting" and going on for some time about my queer nature, staring at little birds for hours on end. "With field glasses, and those clothes! You look positively the vagrant in that floppy hat. Where on earth do you traipse off to? Even in the rain and wind! And now to catch you sweeping before the help comes. At least you aren't like the others. So dreadfully predictable! It is what they want of us, though, isn't it? A good woman is predictable, and seeks out a predictable life. They would have us kept safe and quiet and insipid."

This last bit was a pleasant surprise — a glint of an independent, thinking spirit! I decided I would be candid. I told her of the surgeon's refusing to lend me a book.

Instantly, and for the first time that I can recall, I had her complete attention. Not lend a book! The pompous old so-and-so. She would complain to her aunt and uncle on my behalf . . . but no, they would likely side with the doctor. There's a book shop in Portland — they have very little on their shelves, but perhaps they might order it from San Francisco. It could take weeks, months even!

"What is the topic of the book?" she thought to ask, then without a breath, "But

108

no, it doesn't matter, does it? Would he deny the same to a man? I should think not!"

And here she stood up dramatically and raised a finger in the air. "We should take it!"

Steal from the barracks hospital?

"Oh, steal! I only mean for you to borrow it for a few days. That old clod — he'll never notice one missing book."

It's madness clearly. I suspect Evelyn is not solely motivated by the injustice, but also entertained at the thought of goading me into mischief.

However, I think she is right that no one would notice a book's absence right away. Even just an afternoon alone with it.

February 13
Evelyn Haywood, you are a devilish friend!

Just now a boy came to the house with a message — Miss Evelyn says you should know the post surgeon is seeing to the General at two o'clock and will likely stay for some time, so if you were wanting to see Dr Randall, you won't find him at the hospital then.

And so it seems this afternoon is my chance.

We could not stop laughing, so that still my cheeks hurt. Evelyn ran into the house just as I was pulling the book out from beneath my coat, and I held it up over my head like a prized trophy, and we began to laugh until we couldn't speak. It took me some time to tell her of my adventure.

I had waited until a little after two, and then walked the short distance to the hospital. Just as Evelyn said, his assistant informed me that the surgeon was out and not expected to return before the end of the day. Unless it was dire, he said, I should come back tomorrow. I said I was fine, but could I please sit in his office for a moment to rest?

When the assistant left me to return to the main hospital room, I quickly studied the various titles on the shelf. On Deafness and Noises in the Ear. Disorders of Digestion. Treatise on Gunshot Wounds and Other Injuries of the Chest. I was sure that on my earlier visits I had seen at least two or three books on maternity. And then at last, "A Manual of Obstetrics." I heard footsteps approaching the door, so sat quickly down in a chair with as much nonchalance as I could muster. The assistant passed by without looking in on me. I quickly grabbed the book off the shelf and shoved it beneath my coat.

It was only as I neared the outside hospital door that I thought to look again. "A Practical Treatise on the Most Obvious Diseases Peculiar to Horses"! I had taken the wrong book.

As I turned back into the hospital, I ran nearly headlong into the assistant.

"Are you well, Mrs Forrester?" he asked

with genuine concern. He noticed the way I clutched my abdomen as I tried to hide the book beneath my coat.

"Yes, yes, just a bit tired. Might I sit down one last time? You don't need to trouble yourself — I can find my way back to Dr Randall's office."

In such a way, I was able to borrow the correct book and depart again without notice.

"Well, let me see what all the trouble is about," Evelyn said when I had finished my story. "Oh, Sophie. Are you?" So I told her my news and begged her confidence.

As I write this, however, I am anxious about it all. I do hope I remembered to rearrange the books on the shelf as I should have, or the empty space is sure to be noticed.

February 15
From "A Manual of Obstetrics," Philadelphia, 1884

Third Month. — Foetus grows to length of 2, 2 1/2, and by the end of month to 3 or even 3 1/2 inches. Fingers and toes formed, but are webbed. Head large compared with body. Eyes prominent, lids joined together.

Fourth month — Sex distinguishable. Nails begin to appear.

Fifth month — Weight increases to 6 or 10 ounces. Head one-third the length of whole foetus. Hair and nails visible.

Fingers and toes webbed like a waterfowl — how extraordinary! Dr Randall estimates that I am at least four months into my maternity. Any day now, according to this book, I should feel the quickening.

I tried this afternoon to lie flat on our bed perfectly still for a long time, in hopes of feeling some flutter or twinge. Instead, I fell asleep without ever sensing any movement. I do begin to feel a new weight in my belly, however, as if I have swallowed a small sack of grain.

OREGON POST
NEWS FROM ALASKA

April 10, 1885 — The following news from Alaska has been received via Port Townsend: Commander Daley of the USS Pinta reports an Indian uprising on Perkins Island off the southern coast of Alaska.

On the night of April 2, the Indians of the village, under the influence of a new batch of "hoochenoo," attacked the Alaska Commercial Co. trading store operated by Mr. Wesley Jenson. When Mr. Jenson attempted to beat back the attack, an Indian bludgeoned him with a club. In defense, the trader shot down the Indian. During the rest of the night, the hostile Indians rampaged through the village.

A visit from the fourth-rate man-of-war Pinta, even with her small armament, had a quieting effect upon the malcontents, said Lieut.-Commander Daley. The recent shelling of a nearby village by the US Revenue Cutter Thomas Corwin certainly served as deterrent to the Perkins Island Indians. By all accounts, these Indians respect force, and, when ruled with a firm but just hand, behave well.

According to the trader Mr. Jenson: "They are learning to respect our authority, and as long as false sentimentality is not allowed to rule, their respect will increase."

When the surgeon from the Pinta went

ashore to care for the wounded, he found black measles and scarlet fever raging fearfully among the half-breed children on the island. The surgeon has since been kept steadily occupied.

Attention Mr. Josh Sloan
Alpine Historical Museum
Alpine, Alaska

Mr. Sloan,

I don't have an email. Or a computer for that matter. I'm not too fond of chatting on the telephone either. I'm afraid we will have to rely on the United States Postal Service.

I am glad to know it all arrived safe and sound. Those pages have meant a great deal to me. I used to hide away in the attic when I was a boy and read through the letters and journals. It took me some time to make out the Colonel's writing, what with his shorthand, but I felt like I was breaking a secret code and it only added to my fun.

You'll see I took care in how I packed them all inside grocery bags, then wrapped them in newspaper, taped them all up, and packed them in the boxes with old magazines. I wanted to be sure that they'd arrive up there in one piece, and I sure wasn't going to give my right arm so the shippers could do their ridiculous work. Nothing I hate worse than those foam peanuts. I had 70 years of National Geographics and Billings Gazettes around the house here. Seems they finally proved useful.

Now to your first point — I thought about getting hold of a university or the history museum there in Anchorage. It seems to me, though, that the closest these papers have to a home, outside of the Forrester family, is the Wolverine River. I did my research. The woman down at the library looked it up on her computer for me. She said your museum and your town of Alpine are located on the banks of the Wolverine and that you curate collections about everything from Native people to mining history in that area. Now that I know you have your own deep roots in the place, I'm all the more sure about my decision.

Now to the other matter. Pansy politicians. They have no trouble filling up their jet planes or writing checks for their own salaries, do they? But they can't see fit to care for our very history. It's a shame.

All that said, it can't cost much to find a place to store these boxes. Put them on your lists or whatever you've got there, so people know you have them. Keep them safe. I can't tell you how many times I read over these papers, first as a small boy stirred up by the adventure, then as a man trying to understand a man's concerns. Of course I never did meet the Colonel and Sophie, but I feel like I know them all the same.

I always thought I'd come up your way and see Alaska for myself. A lot of shoulda, woulda, couldas. When a man gets to be 70-some years old, there is no time left for sniveling. But I do have a favor to ask of you. Do you think you could send me a photograph or two, just stick a camera out your window there at the museum, so I can have a look at the river? Maybe a few words, so I can picture it all.

Much appreciated,
Walt

Lieut. Col. Allen Forrester
April 7, 1885

Like a salve to me, her letter. I waited as long as I might, but after this hard day of travel, I needed the comfort of her words.

For two long months, I have carried this letter unopened in my breast pocket, yet I swear the pages are still touched by her fragrance. To read those words, written in her hand. 'Our child.'

I have aimed not to think on it. A commander will make poor decisions when hampered by thoughts of home. Yet now, with it fresh in mind, I think of nothing else. If I had been alone, I would have danced around camp like a fool & celebrated anew. Instead I fold the letter, unfold it, read the words again & again.

— What is it? Tillman asked.

He had put a hand to my shoulder. Perhaps he thought the news was bad.

I saw no harm in telling him. She is far into

her maternity now. Likely the child will be born, half-grown even, before we return home.

— My wife will have a baby, I announced.

Tillman whooped, boxed me in the ribs, nearly sent me sprawling into the flames.

— A papa! Our Colonel is to be a papa! We need a toast.

He took a flask from his coat pocket. The men had been told to leave the liquor at home, especially in light of the sergeant's reputation for violent intemperance, but I was not surprised to see it. We each swigged. Tillman cuffed me in the shoulder. He called out for Pruitt, but he had gone for firewood. This didn't stop Tillman, for he again raised the flask, drank on his behalf.

When Pruitt returned with his armload of driftwood, Tillman told him my news. He gave a polite nod, but not as joyous as Tillman. They are two very different men. The sergeant boisterous, strong tempered. Pruitt brooding, thoughtful, quick to retire to his solitude. The Indians went to their lean-tos, paired up as they do. Just Tillman & I remained by the fire.

— This'll be your first, then? he asked.

I nodded. I asked if he has any children.

— Probably left a few here & there, but none that've owned up to me yet. Probably for the best. My bent doesn't fit much with a family. It'd put a damper on my spirit, knowing others needed me, even time to time.

I cannot fathom such sentiments. The thought of Sophie bearing our child overpowers me with joy.

It would have been better if she could have returned to Vermont. The Washington Territory is yet too wild a place for a woman alone. I am all the more pressed to return within the year. I have no desire to spend the winter with Indians. We must make it up the river before the ice breaks, but our pace so far is lacking. I had thought to be through the canyon already.

My dearest Allen,

I wonder where you are now as you read this letter? Have you encountered the Wolverine tribes yet, and are they peaceable, or are you alone with your men in some icy wilderness? Are the mountains as grand as I imagine, and the land as wild? Are you warm and safe? Oh how I wish I could be there with you, to see what your eyes see.

Just now as I write this letter to send with you, the steamship is in the harbor, and you briskly pace the house and check off lists. Your shirt sleeves are rolled to the forearms, an intent furrow to your brow, and you speak quietly to yourself. It causes me a spark of mischievousness, this stalwart manner of yours, so all the more I want to kiss you on the ear and wrap my arms around your chest, to distract you from your work and tempt you into our bed.

How is it that your leaving is suddenly upon us? So much has occurred these past days — you go off to Alaska without me, I will not see those northern shores, but instead I begin a different adventure. I am dizzy with it all. Can you imagine, Allen? When you return, I will greet you with our child in my arms.

I dread these coming months of separation. Filling pages with such unhappy thoughts will bring relief to neither of us, however, so I must search out words that might cheer you when you are far away.

Let me write this instead: do you know the precise moment when I fell in love with you? You would probably think it was the evening of the military ball, when you first escorted me in your dress uniform. You looked striking that night, and I was smitten, I assure you. I had never attended such a grand affair on the arm of such a man. I was dazzled by it, the officers and ladies swirling around me, your sure steps, the splendor of it all.

Yet what of love? That is another, more solid thing; it is not tricked by fine lights or spirits. It is more of earth and time, like a river-turned stone.

It began with a walk. Do you remember? New England seems so very far away, yet that day with you I can still recall like a clear sky. You came to the schoolhouse at the end of the afternoon and asked me to follow you to the pond. I hesitated, not knowing your intentions, but the sunshine and breeze beckoned, and I yearned to be free of the musty, shaded room where I had been sorting books. I closed up the school and followed you along the path. You said you had a gift for me. I asked why you could not have given it to me in the schoolroom, but you kept your secret.

When we came to a poplar sapling at the water's edge, you stopped and went to one knee. I will confess to you now — I thought you meant to propose to me, and I am ashamed to say that my mind spun like a top and I did not know how I would answer. You see, I wasn't yet sure of my feelings for you. I enjoyed your attention, and I admired your strong bearing, but long ago had I passed the girlish age when that alone could charm me.

You surprised me and slapped at your knee, as if you wanted me to sit down upon it. I must have frowned in confusion, because you explained that I should step up, and you pointed into the branches of the tree.

"There is something you must see," you said.

I worried I would injure your leg or embarrass myself by toppling to the ground, but you held out a hand, and I trusted you. I knew it suddenly and surely. I took your hand and stepped upon your knee.

"What am I to look for?" I asked, and you said, "There. In the crook of that branch."

I took hold of the trunk of the small tree and peered into its lowest branches, where at last I saw it. The smallest, most precious thing — the nest of a ruby-throated humming bird. The nest was not much larger than a child's cupped hand, and cradled in its thistle down and fern were two white eggs the size of peas.

Days before I had mentioned to you how I had once seen a humming bird near the schoolhouse. I had watched it hover among the jewelweed and blue phlox, such a tiny, feathered burst of life. As it turned in the sunlight, it flashed crimson and velvety purple, so much light and movement concentrated in its small form. More than anything, I told you, I wanted to see the nest of this tiny bird.

I could have remained there for hours, studying the fragile curve of egg-shell and the intricate weave of thistle down and spider silk. But I heard a muffled groan, and I knew my weight and the hard heels of my boots were taking their toll after all.

"No, no," you insisted. "I'm perfectly fine. Look as long as you want." I stepped to the forest floor and looked down into your kind eyes.

Never before had I felt such wonder and magnitude — I told you I wanted to see a humming bird nest, and you heard me, not just my words, but my longing.

Was there such a moment for you, when you knew for certain? I cannot imagine it was that same afternoon — as I recall, I advised that we should take a shortcut through the forest, and I managed to walk us into a marsh where I was forced to pick up my skirts and our boots were traipsed through mire and muck. Yet I was too elated to give it any care. I had found your love in a humming bird's nest.

Come home safely to me, my dear Allen.

With all my heart's love,

Sophie

Lieut. Col. Allen Forrester
April 9, 1885

At last some evidence of progress! We stand at the base of Kings Glacier, with Stone Glacier in view upriver. Even through the sleety haze, they are a grand sight. Having many times read Lieut. Haigh's account of

Kings Glacier, April 1885

this section of the river, I recognize the landscape. Near the delta, the Wolverine is a wide plain of braided channels, but here it narrows to a deeper flow, bordered by these glaciers. Haigh reports that in spring the water rises 40 feet, overturns boulders weighing half a ton. In this season we see little sign of this impending force but for thick slabs of ice jammed into piles along shore.

Kings Glacier is a wall of ice with a vertical reach of at least 300 feet. There are rough fractures where, in warmer months, large sections must break away, crash to the river. Some cracks stretch higher than a city building. Such a falling mass would surely sink a row boat, kill a man.

The shades of the ice hypnotize — Tillman & I stood beside each other, stared, speechless for some time. Even from this opposite shore of the river, a man is pulled into the blue of the deepest fissures. Within are the hues of cold itself. The sight chills me, yet I thirst for more. I wish Sophie could see it.

Pruitt measured width of river & height of glacier using sextant. He then quickly assembled camera tripod. He curses the weather. Even in sunlight, I suspect the colorless photograph could never capture this grandeur.

We camp tonight in the lee of giant boulders near Stone Glacier. The boulders number more than a dozen, some taller than three men standing on shoulders. Without our tents, we are grateful for the shelter they provide. The size, scope of these rocks is an oddity set down in the middle of this vast riverbed. Tillman conjectured they rolled a long ways from the mountains. Pruitt says it is the work of the glaciers, carrying the rocks down valley thousands of years ago, then dropping them as the ice melted out from beneath. Tillman is skeptical. It is a wondrous truth to be sure.

April 10

We are shut in an ice fog. This morning we left our boulder field, pressed on through Haigh Canyon where waterfalls of ice rupture from the cliffs. We then emerged onto a wide flat section of the river. The fog is settled in the lowlands so that we can see only a man's length in front of our own feet. More than once I bumped into the sled in front of me. I believe had I closed my eyes, turned thrice, then tried again to find my way, I would not have known upriver from downriver, left from right. Only a white nothingness in all directions. Pruitt keeps compass in hand.

Difficult enough to find our course, but added is the problem of Boyd. Based on Indian reports, Samuelson believes his partner's cabin should be near. But which side of the river? It is doubtful that he would build on the river's plain, as spring flooding would threaten any structure. Hills rise at some distance on either side of the river. None of us would be able to spot a clearing or cabin.

Samuelson advises us to watch for any sign of a trail, as Boyd should be coming down to the river to run traps. We do not speak it, but must consider it the same: if Boyd is dead, there will be no tracks to find.

Such icy stillness. Our breath turns to hoarfrost in our beards, hair. Our eyelashes stick together in clumps of frost. Our lungs ache with cold. The others look to me like creatures with fur of snow; no doubt I to them as well. The harder we work, the more our sweat & breath encase us in ice. The Indians at times lag far behind, so appear like phantoms trailing us up the river. Our voices become lost to the fog; we cannot tell who is speaking or from where. It adds to our disorientation.

Though it is several hours until sunset, I have decided to halt, set camp. Perhaps overnight the fog will dissipate or be blown down the valley.

April 11

My hope was unfounded. We woke this morning to the same conditions, if possible even more chill & impenetrable. Tillman fried flapjacks & bacon. Pruitt has estimated our location as best he can with no ability to track stars, sun, horizon. The men would like to wait out the fog, but I think we had best pack up. The Indians, too, are reluctant. One of them would not leave his fire until I put it out with snow.

We have found Boyd, though not in any good condition. We are at his cabin & for the first night in nearly a month, we will sleep indoors.

We remained at our riverbed camp until near mid-day. The fog was unchanged, so we loaded sleds. Travel was difficult. We stayed near the river's main flow to keep our bearings, but then had to traverse open creeks, decaying ice. Our snowshoes were soon coated in a frozen slush. We stopped to remove them, struck them against each other to break free the ice.

Just then came the blast of a gunshot.

— That'll be him, Samuelson said.

— He's northwest, Pruitt read from compass.

For the next hour, we made our way in the direction.

— Sure wish he'd fire off another round, Samuelson said.

— That would be a help, Tillman said. — Also hoping he'll have supper on when we find him.

But there were no more gunshots. In the fog we could not make out hillsides, but at last we spotted a snowshoe trail that came out of the trees, led to a square cut out of the river ice.

— His water hole, Samuelson said.

The track was deep-set in snow, so had been used often during the winter, but Samuelson was grim as he made note of the fresh snow filling it in.

— He's not been down here in some time.

The trail led away from the river & quickly turned steep. We left the Indians & sleds to retrieve them later. Even without the weight of the sleds pulling at us, at times we had to grab tree branches to keep from slipping down the slope.

Tillman observed that he wouldn't want to haul water up such an incline.

After a strenuous climb, we reached a bench land of large spruce. Samuelson spotted a cabin through the trees.

A ghost of a man stood outside the door. Tall, gaunt, so weak he could hardly stand so he leaned on his rifle like a crutch. Boyd's cheeks & eyes are sunken so that his face appears a skull. As he led us indoors, he showed us the many notches in his belt where he had tightened.

— I suppose it was folly to think you might have supper for us? Tillman said.

Boyd pointed to bare shelves, empty pots.

— I'll go fetch the grub, Tillman said.

Pruitt said he would split kindling so as to build a fire in the woodstove.

Boyd did not seem to know what to do with himself or our company. He grinned, stared. Again & again he clasped Samuelson's arm.

— Jesus on high, I've never been so glad to see you.

— Why the hell didn't you fire another shot? We could have used help in finding you.

Boyd had been reduced to his last round of powder. He saved it, in case help came & he needed to alert someone to his whereabouts.

— Or in case help never did come, he added.

Samuelson asked why he didn't travel downriver before now. Boyd's answer was cryptic.

— She wouldn't leave. She said she'd already come down too far out of the mountains.

When asked of whom he was speaking, Boyd said that he has a wife, that while there was no preacher to do the work, they are married before God all the same.

— I never would leave a wife, he said.

Samuelson became impatient, demanded to know who he was talking about. I advised we should get food in him as his thinking may be clouded by hunger.

The cabin is warming with the heat of the woodstove. We have boots, socks, wool underwear, drying along a beam. Tillman is cooking ham & rice, a kindness to share the last of our meat. Out of doors, the Indians have built a lean-to of boughs against a spruce tree & cooked their own meals beneath.

Once we have eaten, I will be curious to hear how Boyd met this fate.

I will here do my best to capture Boyd's story.

He was hunting ptarmigan up in the hills behind his cabin when he first spied her. He claims she was the most beautiful woman he ever put eyes on.

— There was a mist, hard to make anything out, so I thought I was seeing things. She was moving over the rocks just like an angel. I hollered out to her, but she didn't make that she'd heard me. Before I could catch her, she was gone.

Boyd returned to the mountainside again, again, in hopes of seeing her. He was going to look for her forever if need be. — Head over heels like a wounded bear, he says.

At last, one day he saw her through the fog. He approached her gently, so he wouldn't spook her off.

She didn't speak English, but with hand gestures & his smattering of Midnoosky, they were able to communicate. Over the next weeks, they met each day high on the mountainside. Boyd would bring pemmican to share. They would sit together, watch the mist move across the hills.

— I couldn't get my fill of her, Boyd said.
— She was like a little trickle of cold water

from a mountainside that you just want to drink & drink, but you're only getting a sip. I begged her to come on back home with me. She kept pulling away. I told her straight out — if you don't love me, just say so. I'll leave you be. She said it wasn't that. She said she liked me fine, that's why she shouldn't come. There was no sense to it.

While he talked, Boyd ate three helpings of supper, then smoked a pipe with a bit of Samuelson's tobacco. I suspect it will take several such meals for him to regain his strength.

— Gave her a pair of beaver mittens I'd stitched myself, he went on. — Promised her I'd keep her warm & dry in my cabin. I just wanted to wake up to her face every morning. Finally won her over, I did. One day, she followed me back home.

Boyd stared glassy-eyed at nothing for some time. — The fog was like nothing I'd seen before, he said. — It came that night & hasn't left since.

He was nearly out of provisions, as he had planned to leave before spring. He always could rely on his hunting skills. During the winter he had eaten rabbits, porcupine, a moose now & then. With this fog, though, he couldn't see but six inches in front of his nose to hunt.

— She says, I told you, I told you I shouldn't come. Pretty soon, we got to starving, so that we were scrounging for any bit of something. We stewed straps of moose rawhide, tried chewing on that. We were sleeping too much, couldn't even find the strength to fire up the woodstove. I figured we were going to die in each other's arms.

Boyd spoke his next words with much difficulty.

— Two days ago she left me. God help me, but I was too weak to follow her. Now she's gone. She told me she's going over the mountains somewhere I can't ever find her. What she said is crazy, that she & the fog are one & the same, that there can't be one without the other. She says she leaves me because she loves me, that I'll be better off. I don't see that she can be right.

— For a woman? Christ Almighty! Samuelson said. — You lose your head over a woman so you nearly kill yourself? I'd have thought better of you.

Tillman seems equally disgusted at the display, yet Boyd has my sympathies. He wept like a child at his kitchen table. I was grateful to have this journal to take my eyes away from his suffering.

April 12
We woke this morning to a welcomed sight. As we heated water, prepared breakfast, a camp robber called. The noisy chatter went on as we ate. Tillman threatened to search

out the annoyance & bring it down with a rock. When the squawks did not cease, I stepped out of the cabin to see if I could scare it off.

Instead I found sunlight breaking through the mountains to the east. Blue sky stretched overhead. Upriver, along our intended route, I spied the last of the fog as it crept up the narrow valleys to the northwest. I could not help but think of Boyd's Indian wife traveling over those mountains, taking her mist with her.

The camp robber set to calling again. It flew past, landed in a tree just down from the cabin. My eyes followed it, down to the riverbed — out on the snowy plain, there were dozens of caribou!

Boyd is still too weak, but the rest of us grabbed rifles, sprinted down the hillside.

Without much cover on the open riverbed, it was no easy task to stalk the animals. The Indians scattered upriver from us. Samuelson warned us to stay low, quiet as we approached the herd.

— Once they stir, they'll be gone over those hills before you can blink.

We crouched as we ran, ducked behind willow shrubs. Each time one of us raised a rifle to shoot, Samuelson waved us down, gestured for us to get closer.

The animals twitched their ears. Those that had been bedded down got to their feet.

— I've got that one in my sights, Tillman whispered & put his finger to his trigger.

Samuelson nodded approval.

Tillman shot & the caribou's legs buckled. Shots went off all around us. The animals leapt & ran.

We continued to load & shoot, except Pruitt, whose rifle had misfired.

The caribou were like a flock of birds, suddenly across the river, gone into the trees. In our haste we all missed our targets. We were left with only Tillman's kill.

As we approached the dead caribou, we were pleased to see that the Indians had downed one nearby as well. We had meat!

Samuelson set to disemboweling the animal. He directed Pruitt to hold back a hind hoof so as to expose the pale-gray fur of the belly. As they worked, several camp robbers found their way to our kill. They hopped about in the bloody snow, heads cocked, black eyes watching. The Indians skinned their animal & tossed bits of meat to their open beaks.

Tillman asked why they threw scraps to the birds.

— They're saying their thanks, Samuelson said.

—To a camp robber?

Samuelson looked up from his work, grinned.

— Let me ask you this. How did our Colonel first spot the herd?

I recalled the camp robber that squawked outside the cabin.

— Not the first time, the trapper said. — Not by a long shot.

When the work was done, all of our hands frozen in blood, Pruitt & I each picked up two caribou legs, carried one over each shoulder. Tillman took on the rib cage. Samuelson wrapped heart, liver, kidney in burlap he had thought to bring.

We left the entrails to the camp robbers & a raven that flew in just as we packed up.

Most of the day was gone by the time we returned to the cabin. We cooked pieces of meat on the woodstove. It is good, tough but flavorful, improved I am sure by our intense hunger.

We could use the meat of several more animals. I asked if there was any chance we'd see the herd again.

— Hard to say, Samuelson said. — But I shouldn't count on it.

We will remain at Boyd's cabin in hopes that the caribou return.

60°53' N
144°41' W
25°F, exposed bulb
19°F, wet bulb
Clear. Night cold. Aurora Borealis.
The fog and blood have left us, yet I cannot wipe them from my eyes. They seep from me, the remains of massacres. The shots echo in the valley still. If only I could shed tears as pure and clear as those of this solitary prospector who mourns his lost love, Love for God's sake mourned, at his rough-hewn table. If I could shed tears like those, then perhaps my grief would not sicken me so. Bathed in such tears, I would have the strength to cut out my own half-frozen heart, dripping in the blood of a caribou, & hand it to the Lord, if there was such a Lord and He would have such a heart.

Easter Day, Christ's Ascension, come and gone without notice, faith so frail it is eroded by cold wilds. What if, beyond the echo of

Caribou Tracks

those shots, I could hear the sound of Heaven? The crackle of electric current through colored glass. Thunder vibrating through steel. Would the angels cry out?

I once thought to kill myself so that I would no longer wander through a fog such as this. How could it be any greater crime than that which I have already faced, committed, failed to undo? Yet I am a coward. I have written the truth on this page. Cowardice, sickly yellow thing, I found you like worms writhing beneath an overturned rock — I peeled back my self and beheld you at my core where a shining soul should have been.

I have lost no lover, yet I grieve, the days before: clean blue sky, dry dust of the earth on my skin so that I could recall Man's very Creation, my brain afire with the printed pages of curiosity, I could not have enough of it.

That is my love lost. Curiosity, Purity, my Soul.

Sophie Forrester
Vancouver Barracks
February 21, 1885

A heartbeat!

"There, there it is," Dr Randall said after some time of searching with his stethoscope, and I do believe he almost smiled. After I begged, he even allowed me to try to listen, but I could hear nothing but the gurgling of my own stomach. He said one must have a "trained ear" but he assures me that the heartbeat is strong and regular.

I told him I have been feeling well, eating the healthful foods he recommends, but that I am in desperate need of more fresh air. He was persuaded to permit me longer walks, but only on days of fair weather, and still I should keep mostly indoors. When I asked if I might venture up the hill behind the house, however, his stern irritation resumed.

"What would be the sense in that?"

It is no matter — I am content to roam the

barracks grounds. My field notebooks have been too long ignored, and I look forward to seeing what new wild birds March brings to this place.

(When the surgeon came to the house, I thought to hide away his book, and he made no mention of missing it. Yet I almost wish I had given it back while I had the opportunity.)

February 27

Miss Evelyn has planted an ugly seed in my thoughts. She has suggested that Mrs Connor allows me to employ Charlotte only so that she might wheedle gossip out of the girl. I scoffed at the mention of it. "You're telling me that shy, mousy child is a spy?" I asked.

Evelyn raised an eyebrow and shrugged.

"All I know is that Mrs Connor is no good Samaritan. She is a nosy gabble mouth. You keep too quiet and frustrate her, so she has come up with this scheme."

I confess, as trivial as it all is, I am bothered. I would prefer to keep my own house and, with it, my privacy, yet I am afraid I cannot do without Charlotte's assistance. What would I have done when the water wagon came today? Dr Randall said I must not lift anything heavier than a small sack of sugar. Charlotte, however, put quick work to filling the barrels and jugs. She is much stronger than she appears.

I am embarrassed by how little I can do, and so earlier in the week confessed to Charlotte my condition and apologized for requiring her to do nearly everything. At times I wonder if she isn't a little slow, for she only stared at me and said nothing.

March 3

I should have trusted my intuition and declined the invitation, and would have done so if Evelyn had allowed it. "You absolutely must come, Sophie. I insist. Everyone will be there. They've shipped in pineapples, and the cook is making Peking Duck just for the occasion, and Uncle has invited an Indian chief, so that we might converse with him! Lieutenant Harvey has even promised he will attend."

And so went my entire evening at the General's house: I would be engaged in an awkward and grating conversation, and then politely excuse myself so as to stand in some quiet corner of the parlor, only to be drawn back into the crowd. (And I am afraid I am not so fond of Evelyn's Lieutenant Harvey. He is handsome, but I have always been wary of men so at ease with their own swagger and boast.)

After an hour or so, I quietly told Evelyn that I would leave soon, as I wasn't feeling well. Here she turned to her entourage of young officers and women in gowns and said, "Oh yes, Mrs Forrester is very tired, and we must all know what that means!" and gave her affected giggle. Everyone laughed, though they had no idea why, and I blushed furiously. What could they take from those words!

As much as I dreaded the evening, I did not expect to feel such discomfort with the appearance of the Indian chief. He is a stately, gracious man, and I came to understand that he and several other chiefs are traveling East to convene with the newly elected President Cleveland, yet the women treated him like a performing monkey, clapping and sighing when he properly used his silverware and exchanged pleasantries. Even as the chief rose from the table to give a small speech thanking his hosts, I overheard two men discussing the so-called Dreamer Religion of Columbia River Indians and how they plot to rid the country of all white people.

"I remember the days when Indians were jailed in the guard house, rather than invited to the General's table," one man said with undeniable nostalgia.

The worst part of the evening, however, came when the little Chinese boy was stocking the fireplace in the parlor after dinner. A woman, who I suspect had imbibed more than her share of the General's wine, stepped backward, tripped over her own gown, and nearly fell over the boy. When she saw that she had drawn the attention of many in the room, she accused the boy, and began slapping at him, even booted him.

"I keep telling Uncle to get rid of him," Evelyn whispered to me just then.

I pointed out that she had stepped on him; there was nothing he could have done.

"Oh, I don't care about that. They just make me squeamish, the way they scurry about and never meet your eye. I'd rather have an Irish girl like you have."

Why do I find it impossible to speak my mind in these instances? I am always hopeful that I have misheard or misunderstood, and then I am held by anger and indecision — if I say anything at all, I fear a torrent of emotion will burst forth that will cause embarrassment. I worry too much about offending or rousing conflict.

I suspect, however, that any words would have been wasted. Evelyn would admonish me for being self-righteous. I cannot understand how a woman so bright and engaging can express such ignorance. It makes our friendship a challenge.

Now that I have been brought home by carriage and climbed into my bed, my fury has burned out, and I am left cold and tired. Why do we insist on inflicting more suffering on a world that is already fraught with it? It is here that I must part ways with Father's romantic spirit, for I suspect that it is a curse of nature, some original instinct that we have failed to shed. And I am no better than others, for in the face of it, I would keep quiet and retreat.

March 8

I am disappointed with Charlotte, for it seems that Evelyn was right about her spying. She doesn't utter a word in my company, but as soon as she has Mrs Connor's ear, it seems she must let everything spill.

Newly armed with the knowledge of my maternity, Mrs Connor led the women into my sitting room like an invading force.

You poor dear, facing this all alone. How far along are you? Why, you're hardly showing at all! Is Dr Randall absolutely certain, because sometimes a woman only imagines it? Do you feel that draft? Yes, yes, I feel it too. Hardly suitable lodging for a newborn. My goodness, how old the child will be when your husband returns from Alaska! Are you drinking enough water? You must drink plenty of water every day. I tell you, my sister's children are all brats, and it's because she didn't let them cry when they were babies — you mustn't indulge them when they fuss. Osler's Powder, it is absolutely the best for diaper rash. Oh, I can't abide by Osler's Powder.

They set themselves down in my sitting room and commenced to telling me every dull and horrifying consideration of child bearing and child rearing, as if they did me favor to counter my vast inexperience. Oh, I wish I possessed more gratitude and patience. I know they are well intentioned, but I detest being told that I will surely feel this way or that I must always or never do such-and-such or suffer the consequences. It makes me very contrary, so that I want to say, "Well, I don't think I will use diapers at all. Instead my baby will crawl naked in the yard" or "Water! I never drink water, but only whiskey and coffee."

There was something diminishing about the conversation, too, as if suddenly we had become only, collectively, and forever Mothers, with no room for an entire individual. I would have much rather heard about Mrs Whithers' efforts to learn how to play the flute, or Mrs Burton's recent trip to San Francisco. Did she see the traveling opera production as she had hoped?

When at last they all left and I had my house to myself again, I asked Charlotte to please come into the kitchen and sit down with me. I was certain I had made it perfectly clear to her that my condition was one to be kept to ourselves until I saw fit to share it, that I am by nature a private person, and it is my right. "Yes ma'am," she said. Always "Yes ma'am" but no apology or explanation, and the child would not even meet my eyes. It was only with great effort that I controlled my temper.

March 14

It is not fair that all the women of Vancouver Barracks know, yet poor Mother does not, and so I have written to her at last. She need not worry about traveling all the way here, as I am well cared for, and once the baby is born and Allen has returned, we will go East and pay her a visit. I doubt she would come if I asked it of her. The journey to Boston for the wedding was trying for her, let alone the three thousand miles and week-long train journey across all that wild country. It is better for both of us, as unkind as those words might be.

It occurs to me that there are wives here at the barracks with husbands not unlike Mother. A peculiar observation, but it is true. Some of these poor women are asked to account for every minute of the day and are reprimanded if it is not spent as their husbands see fit. If they turn their time to embroidery and gossip, they are condemned as frivolous. If they attempt to organize a literature club or a discussion of women having the vote, they are mocked for taking themselves too seriously. Mrs Whithers is not even allowed to choose the fabric for her own dresses. She says she is not bothered by it, as her husband has suitable taste. (Oh Allen — what would you pick out for me? I fear it would be duck canvas soaked in linseed oil, so that my dress could serve also as rain coat or tent.)

I make light of it, but in truth it would smother me.

And so that day not long after our wedding, dear Allen, when you returned and asked how I had spent my hours, and I admitted I had done nothing all day except wander Nantasket Beach to seek out the laughing gulls and black-bellied plovers, that your parents had invited me to their club but I declined their company to remain alone at the seaside with my notebook, and you did not scorn or chide me, but rather said we should take off our shoes and let the waves wash over our feet — that day I was filled with more love than I ever could have imagined. And when my hands grew cold, you didn't say we should leave the beach, but instead took them in your own and kissed each of my fingertips, and I was warmed by your breath.

You have been gone from me six weeks. Oh Allen, I miss you more than I can bear.

March 16
More and more I regret my taking the doctor's book on obstetrics, yet I cannot bring myself to return it and confront his disapproval. A guilty conscience has never sat well with me, and it causes me to worry. Does

Dr Randall already know and judge me harshly? Will my mischief cause some embarrassment for Allen?

Yet it is more. I do not like to admit to it, but as Dr Randall predicted, the book upsets me. Even the entries on normal pregnancy and labor are gruesome. The sketches are particularly chilling, the organs flayed and pinned, so that one cannot help but conjure the corpses from which they were taken. Heart, cranium, umbilicus, womb, fetus, all dissected and coldly drawn. I know it is the necessary way of science, this partnership with the macabre, yet it repulses me.

I am always so quick to blame my poor drawing skills, which is true enough, yet even if I had the skill, it seems I lack the constitution for true science. I recall how much I looked forward to visiting the natural history museum while in normal school, and I asked to be shown the ornithology display. Should I have expected anything different? Yet to find myself in a room full of dead birds, staring blankly with their glass eyes, and trays of pinned wings and breasts, and jars of preserved organs. I lost all spirit for the endeavor.

Even Mr Audubon's beautiful paintings that I have long admired — all were done in death. He would shoot the birds down, then re-create their beautiful details. I was foolish to not realize it sooner. Why, in our efforts to understand and observe life, must we so often snuff it out?

Lieut. Col. Allen Forrester
April 13, 1885

We have seen the Aurora Borealis! Tillman woke us in the night. At first we all complained loudly, but when we brought our heads out of our sleeping bags, we understood his excitement. Sheets of eerie green light wavered in the clear dark sky, then shifted, turned, shot through with purplish red. The brightness was enough to put a glow over the white mountaintops. We were struck silent.

Nearby the Indians were also awake. Several whispered, pointed to the northeast where a large wedge-shaped mountain was illuminated by the auroras.

This morning over breakfast we learned more. Skilly says this mountain has its own mysterious power, not unlike that of the Aurora Borealis. For as long as he can recall, the mountain has emitted smoke, fire. Often the earth shakes. Deep rumblings can be heard. They say the mountain spirit is both great & dangerous. Before we leave this morning to travel past the active volcano, the Indians insist on smearing their faces with charcoal, ash, mixed with water into a muddy paste. All but the young woman, who seems defiant.

I asked Samuelson about her.

— She likes to stir up trouble, he said. He pointed to the scrap of bear pelt she sleeps on.

— No good. Bears are strong spirits. Only the men are supposed to look at them, much less lay hand on their hides. See, she's got nothing to lose. She's young, but they say she's barren & that it's her own fault.

I studied the young woman. She is slightly younger than Sophie, perhaps 20 or 25, but there is something older in her thin face — a sharpness to her features that speaks of hardship.

Samuelson said she disobeyed her family to run off with that otter husband of hers. They had already promised her to a chief's younger brother. When she came back home, she took to hunting & wandering alone.

— She comes & goes as if there aren't any rules. No one will have her now.

I asked if he knew her name.

— I don't know what they used to call her, but now it's Nat'aaggi, he said. — Like the geese & cranes that fly through when the seasons change, on their way to someplace else, never stopping for long, always looking for a better place to be.

At last, the weather has allowed Pruitt to take his readings, calculate our location. He estimates we are a day from the canyon.

Samuelson warns me that the Indians will likely refuse to go beyond. With the ice weakening, it is considered dangerous passage. I regret our decision to hold back at Boyd's cabin these past days. We saw no more sign of the caribou despite hunting far across the river in the direction they fled.

Equally frustrating is the lack of reliable information. The Indians who travel with us warn that the river will break up within the week. When we met a small band of Midnooskies traveling downriver to trade with the Eyaks, one said the ice was still strong up to the canyon. Yet another in the very same group disagreed, said there is already open water only a few miles upstream.

Tillman asked what we should do if the river gives way while we're traveling through the canyon.

— Say your prayers, if you're the praying type, Samuelson said. — From what the Midnooskies tell, there won't be any escaping up those cliff walls. Hard, vertical rock. Hundreds of feet up on either side.

Pruitt asked if there is no way to travel around the canyon.

— Through those mountains? You'd be slowing yourselves by weeks, maybe more. Not sure you'd even be able to find a way. This is rough, glacier country. You could run into a gorge or crevasse that would stop you dead in your tracks.

I was impatient with the discussion. Our success depends entirely on traveling through the canyon with the river still frozen. Everyone from Haigh back to the Russians had proven it.

It seemed Boyd could read my expression.

— I suspect your Colonel thought all this through well before now, he said.

I am glad Samuelson & Boyd continue to accompany us up the river. Since Boyd says the 'color didn't pan out' in the creeks near his cabin this past year, Samuelson is keen to explore upriver of the canyon where there is rumored to be gold & copper. Boyd's condition, however, concerns me. He is thin, weak, distracted. I suspect he goes on in hopes of finding his Indian wife.

April 15

We have suffered a considerable loss, delayed our expedition even further. I can blame no one but myself.

As we travel towards the mountains, the Wolverine narrows, deepens, the ice collapses to the center of the river. Samuelson says it is unsafe, so we keep near the shore, where we must traverse the mouths of creeks that flow out of the mountains into the Wolverine.

— I don't like it, the trapper repeated often. — That water would be over our heads, & the ice is weak.

I began to think him overly cautious. At my urging, we passed quickly over the creeks without incident.

We eventually came to a much larger crossing.

— This is not one of your little trickles, Colonel, Samuelson said. — I do believe this is Half Mountain River. Under that ice, it's a powerful current. We don't want to take a swim here.

He advised we travel up Half Mountain River to find a safer crossing. It would push us a mile out of our way, perhaps more, the path slowed by deadfall trees.

Or we could risk this hundred yards, pass over it in minutes. The ice was blown clear of snow but for a few small drifts, & appeared thick, unbroken, rose several feet before dropping down into the Wolverine.

I asked if the crown wasn't strong.

— Maybe. All the same, I'd advise against it.

Downstream of the crown, the ice sloped sharply towards the Wolverine. The ice sunk dark & low.

— But it's just a hop across, Tillman said.

— Why, I'll wager we can make it, if we run quick.

The trapper has never steered me wrong. Yet I begrudged another delay, which might be enough to jeopardize our passage through the canyon. I ordered that we would cross, one by one.

Pruitt volunteered & traversed the mound of ice first, pulling a sled behind him, with no sign of difficulty. Once he was safely across, I followed. Most precarious was the slippery footing, yet the ice stayed solid beneath me.

Tillman came next.

— It's slicker than a greased eel, he said as he neared the crest.

At these words, his sled veered just enough off the crown to begin to slide down towards the Wolverine. As the sled gained momentum, it yanked Tillman's feet out from under him, & he too slipped. As he & the sled fell down onto that dark, thin ice, the sled broke through first, then Tillman, so that he was chest-deep in water.

His sled was heavy, loaded with the last of the caribou meat as well as a large portion of our flour, rice, beans. The current was swift enough to suck it beneath the ice & into the main flow of the Wolverine. Still Tillman held its tether. Even as Pruitt & I ran back across, leaving our sleds behind, I could see Tillman's feet shift beneath him. He leaned forward with all his weight so that his shoulders were submerged. He was losing ground, nearing the point where he would be dragged out into the big river. Once he was pulled beneath the ice, there would be no saving him.

I yelled for him to release the sled.

He growled like an animal as he fought the current.

— Save yourself, for God's sake. Let it go!

I then saw the trouble. The tether was tied about his chest, to make pulling easier, but now it trapped him.

The Indian Skilly was quicker than any of us. He jumped into the water beside Tillman, a knife in hand, & slashed the tether. The sled was lost.

Samuelson handed me a long driftwood pole. I lowered the end to the men, helped each climb out of the water onto the icy shore. Tillman's body quaked, from both the cold & the loss I suspect.

— I've done it, Colonel. D —— d us good, I have.

The blame was all mine. I told him so. I should have followed Samuelson's advice. The trapper, however, was kind enough to not point out my folly. He wrapped his own dry coat around Tillman's shoulders. We stood & watched as the dog ran down the shore of the Wolverine, as if it chased some grind or clunk of the sled beneath the ice that we could not hear.

We camp tonight near the creek that claimed our stores. Our supplies are reduced to meager indeed. Less than a month into Alaska, perhaps a year still ahead of us, our remaining food will last us only weeks. We must be resourceful & also count on the good will of the natives we meet upriver.

Samuelson sets out snares to check at dawn. The snowshoe hares have little meat & no fat, but we will subsist on them as the Indians do.

Tomorrow we follow Samuelson's advice after all & travel up this valley to seek a better crossing. We must then make our way back down the opposite bank to retrieve Pruitt's sled. Two days lost instead of one. I am only thankful Tillman is alive & well.

Sophie Forrester
Vancouver Barracks
March 24, 1885

At last some news of Allen. The general sent word that he and his men have arrived at Perkins Island, but they have so far been unable to cross the sound. I am glad to know he is safe and well. Yet more than a month has passed, and they have not even reached the mainland of Alaska!

These past weeks I studied the map and tried to picture them already traveling up the Wolverine River and into that empty, unmapped territory. I sped them along, my finger skimming the paper through a land of pleasant weather, friendly natives, easy walking. Might they travel even more quickly than they hoped? At this rate, they could be home in another month. I should never have allowed it, but one night I imagined them all the way to the western coast and home in time for Allen to place his hands on my swollen belly.

To learn instead that his journey has not even truly begun, it is a heartbreak indeed. I could brush away my worry when he had only just left, but now, against my will, my brain conjures river ice that cracks into swift water, and Indians who dress in furs and eat their enemies.

March 28

It is past dark now, and I shiver beneath the covers and long for sleep. A gale whips the fir trees around the cabin and sleet pecks at the window; I think the dreary weather must account some for my restlessness. This bed was never so cold and empty when Allen was here. Even with Charlotte tucked in across the hall, I feel wholly alone. The house creaks and groans, and I hear some board or branch outside that knocks in the wind. I do not usually possess a fearful imagination, but I could almost expect a "rapping at my chamber door."

I have given myself a chill to recall Mr Poe's lines. It is absurd, for they are just words of poetry, and this house is no different than when Allen slept here beside me. Yet it is. If only I could hear Allen, his voice in another room and know that he was soon coming to bed. In the warmth and comfort of his arms, sleep would soon be upon me.

Instead my only company are the books at

my bedside. Illustrations of deformed organs and stillborn infants, descriptions of all the ways one might die in childbirth — the stuff of nightmares surely.

The photography book, on the other hand, is numbing, with its "depth of focus" and "width of angle" and chemical formulae, but I will turn to those pages, for at least they might lull me to sleep.

March 30
Such a coincidence. It is as if I conjured Mr Poe's raven. Last night I wrote of a "rapping at my chamber door," and this morning I woke to the noisy calls of a raven outside the bedroom window. It was much too late to be sleeping, well past dawn, yet there I was still bundled beneath the wool blankets. I did not know at first what had wakened me, but then I heard another throaty "caaaaww" and a gurgle, something akin to water being drained from a narrow-necked bottle.

I wrapped myself in my shawl, went to the window and saw the bird hopping about on the grass just in front of the largest fir tree. Its right leg is deformed in some way so that its movements are lurching and strange.

I have spotted many of its smaller cousins, the crows, on my walks down by the mill-pond, but not many of these larger, more impressive specimens. If I were to heed Mother's advice, I should have quickly drawn the curtains. Despite her devotion to reading, teaching, and the Society of Friends, she is astonishingly superstitious about the natural world. The notion that ravens are harbingers of death! I recall once when a local woman bore a stillborn child, Mother told me that she had spied the woman throwing scraps to a raven in her yard just days before.

I suppose these nonsensical ideas arise from the birds' scavenger nature and their midnight color. Myself, I have always found them fascinating. It is said that they are considerably more intelligent than they are given credit for, that they can be trained to speak and perform tricks.

"Birds and Bird-Life" has never been one of my favorite books; it is a bit too fanciful for my liking, but it does include some interesting stories about the various species. For example, Mr Buckland reports that a raven will pluck the eyes out of a sick lamb. I confess it startled me after reading this passage, when I then peeked through the bedroom curtains again to see the bird still on the lawn, black feathers disarrayed, head cocked with an eye toward me. I actually jumped when it opened its great black beak and cawed.

Oh, and now I am doing precisely what I find so frustrating about this book. Mr Buckland would personify this bird as an impudent "busy body," always teasing and playing jokes, and I would turn the bird into a fright. I should like more rational, objective observations. I want to know the facts of this creature. What does it eat? How does it court? Where are its nests to be found?

This, however, is interesting. Mr Buckland states that ravens may live as many as a hundred years! Could it be so? Perhaps this noisy old bird outside my window has seen more than we can ever know.

March 31

So stupid of me! To lose the most precious gift I have ever been given!

Just after breakfast, I decided to take a walk along the lane and down through the barracks. Though it is a trifling distance compared to my previous excursions, it lifts my spirits all the same. Not far beyond the Baileys' home, I noticed a nest high up in the branches. I longed for a closer look, so walked the short distance into the trees. A few twigs and damp leaves had stuck to my hat along the way, so I removed it to shake off the bits.

It was only when I had returned to the lane and walked for a time that I realized the comb had fallen from my hair. Oh why did I wear it out of doors like this!

When I realized it was missing, I returned to the place where I thought I had removed my hat, but search as I might, I could not find the comb. A flushed panic overcame me and I was nearly to tears.

And then I spotted it! It was in the wet grass just across from the Bailey house. I was so glad, and was beginning to walk toward it, when that raven — the one with the deformed leg that has been frequenting the yard — swooped in and landed just a few feet from the comb.

"Go on, shoo!" I shouted.

I don't think I understood before just how large and intimidating these birds can be. It was the size of a house cat, and its black beak looked strong enough to snip off my fingers. It shook its wings at me and hobbled about in its strange way. I trusted that it would take flight. Instead, it stepped closer to the comb, and pecked at it once, twice. I yelled and waved my arms. And then, to my astonishment, it snatched the comb up in its beak! I lost all fear and was overcome with anger. I ran at the bird, but it flapped its wings, hopped, and took to the air. It flew toward a stand of trees, and I thought for a moment it might land on a branch and somehow drop the comb. Instead, the raven kept to the air, flew over the tops of the trees, and continued on his way. Flew away! With my lovely comb!

I am positively sick with guilt. It was a treasure to me, both as a gesture of Allen's affection and for its own beauty. And I am afraid I attached some superstitious quality to it — I hoped to wear it every day until

Allen returned safely.

April 2

I do not know that I have ever been so frightened. I am bleeding. It is slight, almost imperceptible, but oh so brilliantly red and terrifying. If these same drops were from a pinprick at my finger, I would not give it any notice, but this blood I cannot ignore. It was with tremendous dread, but when I discovered it, I asked Charlotte to please fetch Dr Randall.

Hope still lives. The minutes were agonizing as he searched with stethoscope, but at last he found the heartbeat. He conceded that if the bleeding soon stops, I may yet carry the child to term, but he offered little assurance. He has prescribed opium tincture, and has ordered me to remain in bed with my feet elevated day and night. I am to call for him if the bleeding does not stop. He says there is little else to be done, except to rest and wait.

When I asked how long this confinement might last, he said as long as I am so fortunate as to bear a living child.

And then, as he stood to leave, he placed his hand upon my bedside table and looked down to see his book. He exhaled sharply, as if in surprise, then picked it up. For some time, he flipped through its pages, and I saw he lingered on a section. He then set it back down on the table, thumped it with his forefinger several times, shook his head as if I were a fool, and left.

If only I could hear your voice just now, Allen. What would you say to comfort me? But you are half a world away, and I must brave this alone.

April 4

"Does it make you happy, Mrs Forrester, to know all of this?"

Still I cannot answer Dr Randall's question. To know that I am not whole, that my womb is deformed. To know the terrible odds. A flip of the coin, he said, and while it sounds cavalier, I suspect it is the truth — according to the book, half of such pregnancies thrive, the other half abort spontaneously. Often a rupture or infection kills the mother as well. How can I say I am glad to know this?

Yet would it be better to live in ignorance, to be coddled like a feeble-minded child? Isn't knowledge in and of itself always good?

I uncovered the truth when I came across a small piece of paper where, likely during my first visit to his office, he had marked a section in his book: "Malformations of the Uterus."

The symptoms aligned in a chilling way with all that I had experienced, and I could see through the Latin words well enough —

septus, divided; bicornis and unicornis, like some mythical creature with either one or two horns. Such deformities of the womb appear in the illustrations as unsightly hearts, cleaved down the middle or gruesomely lopsided. Which exactly is my affliction? Dr Randall is fairly certain that I suffer a divided and misshapen womb, but its specific nature can only be identified through dissection.

"And does it make you happy, Mrs Forrester, to know all of this? Would it have been better if I told you my suspicions when I first examined you? Not one damned thing either of us can do about it, and now you have the rest of the pregnancy to sit around and agonize. You should have left that to me."

It is true. I agonize. The bleeding has stopped, yet any pang in my side or cramp of my womb causes me to fear the worst.

I cannot imagine how I will endure these next months, kept to this small room with nothing but my own worries.

I have returned the book to Dr Randall.

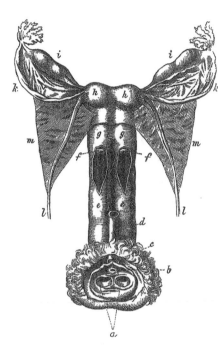

Lieut. Col. Allen Forrester
April 16, 1885

The only good that came of it all is the last of the liquor is gone. I should have seen it coming. The sergeant was in rare form, rowdy, belligerent, no doubt downtrodden by the loss of the sled & provisions.

The Indian woman had killed a porcupine, brought it to us skinned & ready for the cook pot. We boiled it, ate the stringy dark meat with a small portion of flour added. After supper, Tillman pulled out his flask to offer swigs to us, which we refused. Then he took it to the Indians. Over these past weeks, he has become increasingly friendly with them, sits with them after supper to talk & joke. He says their tongue is similar to Apache & he makes progress in learning it.

I advised against giving the Indians any whiskey — I do not wish us to contribute to their ill. In retrospect it would have been better to dilute it among many mouths & have it be done. Instead, Tillman proceeded to drink it all himself.

— He managed to save his flask even if he lost all our food, Pruitt said.

— His flask was in his pocket, that is all, I said. — Tillman would have given his life to save that sled.

Yet I would not have minded if the liquor had washed downstream.

As the evening wore on, Tillman approached the Indian woman, leaned close to her & in slurred speech praised her dark hair & eyes. Samuelson was quick to remind Tillman of her skills with a blade. He was not so drunk as to risk his life, so let her be. Still we were to have no peace. As the rest of us retreated to our sleeping bags, Tillman stepped around the campfire in a ridiculous jig he said he learned from his grandfather. As his gait became more impaired, he tripped over the sleeping dog. It jumped to its feet with a snarl. Pruitt withdrew his carbine from his sleeping bag, preparing to shoot the animal, but I advised him to wait a moment longer.

Tillman growled, crouched, circled, lunged at the dog, then the two were wrestling in the snow like overgrown boys. It seemed all in play, yet the half-wild dog could cause real injury. I moved to break it up, but next came the pinnacle of the evening, perhaps of our entire journey — Tillman on hands & knees, he & the dog with opposite ends of a tether in their mouths, both growling & yanking in a mad game of tug of war.

The Indians watched in humor. Boyd said he wished he had gotten a nip before Tillman downed it all. Pruitt urged me to put a stop to it. I waited to see if the beasts would tire themselves out. At last, with no apparent injury to either, man & dog collapsed in a heap. We fell asleep to Tillman's mumbling — Good fellow. You're a good old boyo, aren't you?

This morning we woke to find the two curled up together by the cold campfire. The Indian woman stood over them. I'm not sure which most disgusted her — Tillman or the disloyal dog.

The sergeant is haggard from his dunk in the creek & long night, but still we set out early this morning with hopes of reaching the canyon today.

Longest day's march yet. Pruitt estimates 11 miles. Our feet are swollen & pain us. All of us, Indians, too, suffer from some inflammation of the eyes, perhaps from exposure to snow, rain, wind, sun. Despite ailments & fatigue, we are within sight of the mouth of the canyon. We stay tonight on the western shore. The bank here is steep & high, but the spruce forest still meets the river & allows us to gather firewood, set a comfortable camp.

Upriver, the Wolverine cuts its way through slate walls several hundred feet high. Once we enter, there will be no more trees or soft ground, only rock & ice.

April 17

We have survived a disturbing night. Not long after supper, we stocked the campfire & went to our sleeping bags. Though it was after 8 o'clock, the northern sun had only dipped behind the mountains & still cast its glow. We sought a long rest in preparation for our journey through the canyon. As I neared sleep, Pruitt's voice stirred me.

— Sir, what is that?

I sat up, followed his point. There at the top of the snowy gully above us was a dark figure. At first I took it for a black bear, standing on its hind legs. I did not think they would emerge from their dens this early.

It was no bear. That would have been preferable.

— I can't make it out, but I think he's wearing a black hat, Pruitt said.

Surely the Old Man could not be here, these many miles up the Wolverine River, when we left him behind in the Indian camp. Yet there could be no doubt.

The Old Man waved his arms, then hopped into the air with what seemed like more height than should be possible for a man of his age. With each jump, he tucked up his feet, so that he appeared airborne.

— What's he doing up there? Tillman asked.

Pruitt left his sleeping bag, took out field glasses. Nearby the Indians were packing up their belongings.

— They're moving away from the hill, Samuelson said. — Believe I will, too. Don't like the looks of him up there.

He rolled up his sleeping bag, jostled Boyd awake.

Tillman wanted to go as well, but I said I would not be moved by a cockeyed trouble-maker.

As Tillman & I tried to sleep, we could hear the Old Man's calls. There were no words that I could discern, only cackles, yowls.

Around dark, Pruitt returned to his sleeping bag.

— He leapt into a treetop, Pruitt whispered.

No matter how we questioned him, he was convinced of what he had seen.

We were all silent in the dark after that. I knew from the way Tillman & Pruitt cleared their throats, turned in their sleeping bags, that none of us was quick to sleep. Yet somehow we must have dozed, for we were startled awake by rumbles in the dark above us.

— Something's coming down the hill! Tillman shouted.

I heard the Old Man's calls, then flaps like that of giant wings. With the noise came another crash of something falling down the gully. We scrambled to our feet, gathered our sleeping bags in our arms, & ran through the dark.

Behind us was a rumble, the cracking of branches, the rush of cold air at our backs.

When we reached the far side of the creek, as far as we could go in such darkness, Pruitt struck a match, lit a candle so that we could see enough to climb back into our sleeping bags.

We remained awake the rest of the night.

At dawn we saw our near fate. The Old Man had triggered an avalanche of snow, ice, earth, & rocks that spilled down the gully, swept through our camp. It was only luck that our sleds, with scant remaining supplies, were just beyond the reach of the slide.

There is no sign of the Old Man this morning. I do not know his motives, but if we see him again, I will not stop Tillman when he takes him by the collar.

&56. THE MECHANISM of these bones is admirable. The shoulder-joint is loose, much like ours, and allows the humerus to swing all about, though chiefly up and down. The elbow-joint is tight, permitting only bending and unbending in a horizontal line. The finger bones have scarcely any motion. But it is in the wrist that the singular mechanism exists.
— From *Key to North American Birds: Living and Fossil Bird,* Elliott Coues, assistant surgeon U.S. Army, 1872

DES OYSEAVX, PAR P. BELON.

La comparaiſon du ſuſdit portraict des os humains monſtre combien ceſtuy cy qui eſt d'vn oyſeau, en eſt prochain.

Portraict des os de l'oyſeau.

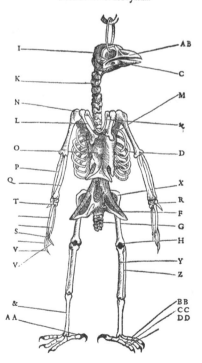

Wolverine River, Alaska Territory
April 18, 1885

Dearest Sophie, my love,

I do not know the chances of this letter
ever reaching you, & certainly it will be a
miracle if it does, but I have to seize this
chance. The Indians we employed on
Alaska's coast are to leave us now. We send
them back down the river with a report to
Vancouver Barracks, letters to loved ones,
& a box of photograph plates Lieut. Pruitt
has taken thus far on the trip. They have
orders to bring everything to Perkins
Island & send via steamer to Vancouver.

Sophie, you do not know how precious
your letter is to me. Your words have filled
me with much joy & love; they keep me
through the toughest days. I travel with
different eyes now, eyes for home & your
arms & your love & our child. It is remarkable, & at times overwhelms me, to think
of how full my life has become. Just a few
short years ago, I had no such ties. Each
night's camp was home enough. It may
be why I had so little fear. What did I have
to lose? Nothing compared to now.

I do hope you are being well cared for
& want for nothing. You must not worry

for me. We are bone tired but safe. Already we've encountered many strange & unexpected adventures, which I do not have time enough to recount here. So often I have wished that you could see this land for yourself. We walk past glaciers that would bring tears to your eyes for their majesty, & the Wolverine River is grand. As is my wont, I have been dedicated to my personal diary. I hope you have been as well. I long for the evenings when we can read them aloud to each other & share our days.

I watch for your birds. So far sighted: camp robbers, magpies, ravens, bald eagles, chickadees, redpolls (Pruitt helped me to identify that flock), grosbeaks. We have also come across a handful of game birds — grouse & ptarmigan — but they quickly went the way of the cook pot when we were lucky enough. When we stop to rest, we hear woodpeckers & owls in the forest, but do not have time to seek them out. The trapper Samuelson who accompanies us says we may also expect migratory birds, waterfowl & raptors, to begin to fill the skies as they travel north. I will keep my eye out. I have no doubt that you would spot & identify dozens of others, & I am sorry for my poor skills as your assistant.

As I write, an Indian by the name of

Skilly sits nearby. He knows some English, but looks as wild an Indian as I have ever seen. A tube-shaped shell, called a dentalium, pierces his nose. His black hair is cropped short as if cut with a dull blade. He wears a parkie made of caribou hide trimmed with wolf fur. Around his neck he carries a beaded scabbard for his knife — these are a source of great pride, & the Indian men do not remove them even to sleep.

Skilly wants to know to whom I write, & when I told him this letter is for you, my wife, he asked if you are pretty & good. Of course, I said.

He says he, too, has a wife at home, though not as pretty as he would like. He says he hopes she is faithful to him while he is gone.

I did not know before now that he left behind a family. He says they have three children, with a fourth born not long before we left. I am sorry to know that we drew him away from these responsibilities. He has proven himself quick on his feet & faithful in his own right. I wish him safe travels back down the river to his family.

Our progress so far has been slower than I expected, but we prepare to enter the canyon I so often told you about. Once we have passed through it, I will be more at ease.

I hold out hope that we will reach St. Michael's, & passage back to Washington Territory, before winter. If for some reason you do not hear from me again for many months, do not be alarmed. I will not be able to send word again until we near the western coast. In the event that we are delayed for any reason, we will spend the winter with the Indians. I beg you, Sophie, do not lose hope.

In your first letter, you asked when I fell in love with you, so I will tell you. It was that very first day, when I rode through the woods near your schoolhouse & passed right beneath you. I nearly fell out of my saddle when I heard the rustle of your skirts overhead. You apologized for startling my horse, but otherwise did you notice me at all? I had never seen a grown woman, skirts & all, in the branches of a tree, but more than that, it was the sound of your voice, gentle, so full of delight. — Didn't I tell you we would find something interesting up here, you said, & you continued. — Yes, you are right! I see that now. You will become an expert before this day is out.

It was only then that I noticed several children sitting on the various branches around you. I asked if it was some insect or bird that you all examined, but you shushed & waved me away. There you were: lovely, brave, & oblivious to me. I think it only served to kindle my affection.

Now you carry our child, Sophie, & you become all the more extraordinary to me. Each passing day as I think on it, I love you more.

I must end this letter. I hope you can read all that I have crowded onto these few pages.

Be sure that the Connors' girl takes good care of you. Sleep late, eat as much butter as you desire, please do not climb any trees, stay well & know that I think of you each & every day.

Your adoring husband,
Allen

PS Know that my love is steadfast. I march back home to you.

Lieut. Col. Allen Forrester
April 18, 1885

The Old Man becomes the bane of this venture. It appears that because of him we have lost most, if not all, of Pruitt's photographs. The fate of our reports & letters is unknown.

Not long after we sent the Indians downriver with the box of photography plates & documents, the one I have called Skilly ran back into our view. We were tying down the loads, preparing to venture into the canyon, when he shouted for our attention. We soon came to understand that the Old Man joined the Indians as they set south downriver. The scoundrel told them that we were trying to steal the very light of dawn, that we had hidden it in the crate to take back to our own land so we could have two suns. He prodded them to open it & release the light. Skilly says he tried to stop them, but they found the glass plates &, perhaps thinking they were contraptions for catching light, stripped them from the protective covers. Skilly demonstrated how they held each up to the sky to inspect them & to shake out any remnants of dawn.

Pruitt was near apoplectic. He is certain all the photographs are ruined.

I worry, too, for my letter to Sophie. The Old Man is fortunate that we will not see him again, as I do not think I could temper my fury.

I thanked the Indian who came to us with the news. In gratitude, I said he should help himself to some of the abandoned food, supplies we cached near his village.

— It was good of him to come back & tell us what happened, I said. — Skilly is his name, am I right?

— That's no name, Samuelson said. — It only means 'little brother.' Would guess he's kin of a chief.

No one in our group seems to know the skilly's real name. It makes me sorry.

As for our papers, there is nothing more to be done. The Indians say the river will soon break. Throughout the morning we heard the grinding of ice on the move. It is here that Lieut. Haigh abandoned his attempt as the water through the canyon became too deep & fast moving to navigate.

If the ice washes out before we enter, we too will fail. If it does so while we are in the canyon, I cannot say we will survive.

Samuelson caught several rabbits in his snares during the night. He & the Indian woman, who apparently continues on with us, are cleaning them so we will have meat.

We leave as soon as they are done.

But with the box containing the sun he was more careful. . . . That was finally given to him, with the strict injunction to not open it. But, turning himself into a raven, he flew away with it, and, on opening the box, light shone on the earth as it does now. But the people, astonished by the unwonted glare, ran off into the mountains, woods, and even into the water, becoming animals or fish.

— From *Alaska and Its Resources,*
William Healey Dall, 1870

Dear Mr. Forrester,

I'm working to organize and read everything in the order of how events would have unfolded. But I keep finding unexpected documents, and I'm so enjoying them. There is this rare sense of immediacy I sometimes encounter with artifacts. I'll be holding one of your great-uncle's small leather diaries in my hands, thinking what a miracle it is that they are still around today, and then I look outside and see the very river the Colonel is describing. I know it probably sounds overdramatic, but it gives me goose bumps. Each time I turn these brittle pages, and imagine the Colonel camped right outside my window, writing by campfire, meeting the first people of this land, it feels like time has collapsed and the past is happening now. This is what made me fall in love with history.

And as I'm going through the boxes, I have so many questions. I'm sure some of them will be answered as I go. Right now, for example, I'm wondering how on earth you could end up with your great-aunt's hair comb as one of the artifacts if it was plucked up by a raven and lost in Vancouver in 1885.

I thought of her when I was at the post office here in Alpine yesterday. A raven had landed in the back of my partner's pickup truck, and it was rummaging through our grocery bags. It was trying to peck its way into a bag of tortilla chips when we noticed it. We both went running and yelling at it, trying to scare it away from our groceries. It flew off, but only as far as a light pole.

There are some great stories about the Raven character in Alaska. In one of my favorites, Raven coaxes his friend Whale into beaching himself in the mud. When Whale is stranded, Raven eats him, the entire whale. The people in the nearby village are angry at Raven because he was so greedy. The hunters begin shooting arrows at him and chasing after him. But Raven is too fat with blubber and can barely flap off the ground. Since he can't fly away, Raven starts turning every arrow into a spruce tree. Even as the arrows fly, the trees grow and grow, and so Raven is able to hide away until the end of time.

On a more practical note, I think it's important that we get these materials into digital form. The journals and letters have been subjected to a lot through the years. I worry about damaging them as I read through them now, but I'm trying to handle them as carefully as I can. Because I'm already doing the work of translating the Colonel's shorthand as I read it, I've started to convert the diaries into a transcript.

I noticed that many of the clippings from newspapers, books, and greeting cards look as if they were once pasted to other backing paper. Do you know where they came from?

And do you know who gathered the medical information — the photocopies in the manila envelope? Some of them have to do with field medicine, others with obstetrics.

The more important question I have to ask, though, is about the official reports. I was able to track them down through the consortium library in Anchorage. I'm reading them at the same time as I read the private journals, comparing them as I go, and it's just as you said — the reports don't reflect his journals. Why do you think he left out so much? In the report he sent back to Vancouver Barracks, the only mention of the man named Boyd is of his cabin, and the Colonel states that they slept there for several days. There's nothing about the man's wife or the fog or the caribou. Never once does he mention the "Old Man" in his reports. Since you are so familiar with these papers, I'm curious to know what you think.

Oh, and I've enclosed a picture for you. That's the Wolverine River, looking down toward the canyon that the Colonel is traveling through. Is? I guess I should say "was." You can see where my mind is — April 1885.

Best wishes,
Josh

■ ■ ■ ■

Part Two

VICTORIAN SILVER HAIR COMB.
ALLEN FORRESTER COLLECTION.
CIRCA 1880.

■ ■ ■ ■

Unmarked silver with decorative hand-chasing, fern fronds. Heavily tarnished, missing two teeth. Measures 4 inches long, 3 inches wide.

Lieut. Col. Allen Forrester
April 20, 1885

Once, as I traveled through desert country years ago, I spurred my horse up a scree slide. The rocks crumbled & fell away behind us as we climbed & I heard the clatter far below. I could not stop to rethink my approach. If I pulled back on the reins, the horse could lose its footing & tumble us backwards. It was a fall neither man nor beast would likely survive. I did not know what I would find at the top of that gorge, if it would be terrain that I could negotiate, but I was certain of this — there would be no going back the way I had come. I was fixed to my path, lock, stock, & barrel.

I don't care to be in that position. Much less when I lead others. Yet it is where I find myself now.

We are passing through a most remarkable, treacherous landscape. It is only through luck & will that our losses have not been greater.

Yet whatever lies ahead of us, we are now wholly committed. Our only way home is north, farther into the mountains.

It was late morning when we left our cliff-side camp two days ago & bade farewell to the one I called Skilly, with the knowledge that our reports & letters had been jeopardized. However, as we set out, the coastal sleet was gone for sun & bright sky. That change in weather alone would have lightened our spirits. Then, too, the Wolverine River at last gave us easy travel. The ice was smooth, snow no deeper than our boots, just enough to give us foothold but not to slow us. Our sleds for the first time worked as intended & glided as if weightless. Tillman dashed ahead, whooped at his own speed. Soon we were all sprinting up the river with the sun on our heads. Even Pruitt gave up his sulk. The dog took to running circles around us, barking sharply, as if to say, 'Now you've finally got it!'

Then, without warning, Pruitt seemed to fall to his knees. As I neared, I saw that in fact he had broken through the ice & had come to a stop only a few feet down. By his expression, he was as stunned as the rest of us. His boots sloshed in a few inches of water.

— But shouldn't he be drowning? Tillman asked. — Thought it was nigh on 20 feet deep.

Samuelson said he had not fallen clean

through, but rather the real ice was still below him.

It was the overflow Samuelson had warned about, when water flows on top of existing ice, freezes, & forms a new, thinner layer of false ice. If the water level drops, a pocket of empty space is left. This overflow ice accounted for our easy travel, but also proved to be thin & unreliable.

— Heart in your throat, eh Pruitt?

Tillman laughed as he helped Pruitt climb from his hole.

From then on, we were wary. We found, however, that if we did not dawdle, the ice held us. It became a kind of race. We ran all the faster. The Indian woman held her own despite the substantial load on her back, & she even outraced Tillman for a short distance. For the first time since she joined us, I saw her smile.

Our exuberant travel came to a halt, though, when we entered the mouth of the canyon. A shadowy cold descended on us & our voices turned eerie against the slate walls.

Gone, too, with the sunshine & cheer was the effortless travel. The canyon binds the Wolverine so that when, over the course of the winter, the ice moves, it is crumpled violently. Great blocks three feet thick & as much as 20 feet high had been torn asunder & turned sideways. It seemed an impassable range of buckles & ridges & upended slabs of ice pressed up against the canyon walls, which are vertical rock the color of lead. They would not allow for any climbing or even a foothold perch if the river ice were to give way.

Tillman asked how far we would travel through the canyon. I estimated three, five, maybe 10 miles.

— If it's three miles, we might make it through in one go, Tillman said. — Much more & we'll be sleeping the night in the canyon.

Samuelson warned us to travel on the crowns & ridges where the ice is the strongest.

He pointed towards a pond-sized dent, where the river ice sunk low & turned a dense shade of blue.

— Avoid that like the plague, he said. — It's too weak to hold you.

Samuelson led. The dog, for once, brought up the rear. Tillman said he did not like the way the animal hesitated to follow, as if it knew more than us.

No one spoke after that.

As much as the canyon invokes fear in us, I think our silence was one of reverence. It is truly a feat of Mother Nature. The slate walls rise hundreds of feet. In places, thick water-falls of ice cascade down the rock. Beyond, to north, east & west, are vast, stony moun-tains & glaciers that stretch miles into the distance. One such glacier reached down into the canyon & to the river's edge, so that we were able to touch the extraordinary blue ice as we passed by.

The Wolverine cuts tightly through the rock, so we can never see more than a few hundred yards ahead or behind to the next turn. We entered one section that was so closely bound, it was like a cavern, with one wall entirely encased in ice to a height of at least 100 feet. Scant daylight entered through the narrow opening to the sky overhead.

There is little sign of flora or fauna in this landscape. Far up on the rocks, small, hardy evergreens cling to nothing but cliff & air. Once, a bald eagle flew down through the canyon & over our heads, its wingspan impressive. Otherwise, we saw no sign of life.

Tillman broke the silence by saying he would prefer to travel along more quickly, to be rid of this God-blasted deathtrap. —We're like mice scurrying into a cat's maw, he said.

Yet I have come to a new respect for Samuelson's plodding approach. We cannot afford to blunder along for it would be all too easy to walk ourselves into a corner, trapped by either giant slabs of ice or one of those perilous low spots. We'd then be forced to attempt the crossing or backtrack to safer ground. We proceeded at a slow, careful pace.

The sleds that had worked so well earlier in the day now became an encumbrance over the rough terrain. Often the sleds overturned;

at other times two of us would have to pick up one, carry it beyond uneven ice, then go back for another. The ice, too, was beginning to show signs of spring thaw; large sections detached & moved beneath our feet. I stepped on what looked like stable ground, only to have the ice block turn beneath me so that I was like a logrolling lumberjack. I just managed to jump to solid ground as the slab bobbed beneath me.

After several hours, below us in the canyon we heard the rumble & grind of ice on the move. No one mentioned it, but no doubt we all heard it.

Tillman began to whistle, perhaps to serve as a distraction. He started with snippets of soldier tunes, but then fell off into the mournful 'Bury Me Not on the Lone Prairie.' Against my will, I found myself humming it, until my brain tripped over the words

. . . Death's shades were slowly gathering
    now,
He thought of home and loved ones nigh.

I called out for him to put a stopper in it.

Tillman was offended, but I was glad to have an end of it.

None of us noticed when the dog first became separated from our group. There was a sudden, sharp bark & we all stopped to look behind. The animal was several hundred yards downriver & against the far canyon wall. We could see its quandary — the animal was separated from us by a large fracture in the ice that began farther downriver than we could see. The dog had been traveling near the cliff & was now cornered. The break looked to be at least 10 yards across, too far to leap. The animal seemed to consider it. It trotted back & forth.

I followed Tillman & the Indian woman downriver to where we could see more clearly. Earlier in the winter the surface must have caved to create an icy pit, with sides more than six feet down. In the depths of the fracture, we could see the flowing water of the Wolverine, so dark surely it was deeper than anything a man or beast could survive.

— If Boyo goes for it & doesn't make it, we won't be able to fetch him out of there, Tillman said.

I agreed. The sides were too steep, the ice too unstable.

At the sound of our voices, the dog became more animated & approached the edge.

With the most expression I have seen the young woman display, she shouted at the animal, waved her arms as if to gesture it away from the pit. Tillman, too, was distraught.

— Go back on down, Boyo. Go back!

For a time the dog paced, then began to whimper.

Tillman volunteered to call the dog, lead him down the river until he could find a safe crossing.

I said nothing. The sergeant understood. We were fortunate to have made it so far without one of us falling into the Wolverine.

We would leave the dog to its own devices. I advised that we should walk away quickly, ignoring the animal so that it would not try to follow us directly. Its best hope, if it has the intelligence, is to retrace its own steps down the river.

As we turned our backs, the dog let out a long howl.

The woman made as if to walk downriver.

— I think she's going to help Boyo, Tillman said.

It is too dangerous, I told her. She should remain with us.

— Boyo, she said, pointed towards the dog.

I stepped forward to take her arm. Her look was quick & alarmed, then angry. But she did as told & walked with us back to join the others.

We explained what had happened, that we had lost the dog, but I had ordered the girl to remain with us.

— Wouldn't have thought she would listen to you, Samuelson said, & I agreed.

The journey through the canyon stretched on through hours. Occasionally the cliffs would offer up a small alcove or a tumble of rocks that met the shore. But for that, the canyon walls were sheer & unbroken.

Tillman asked more times than he ought how far we had come.

Two miles. Three. Not quite four. Pruitt did his best to estimate each time Tillman asked.

— Makes no difference how far we've come, Samuelson finally grumbled. — Only how far we've got to go, & not one of us can tell you that.

Tillman stopped with his question.

It was disquieting when dusk arrived & still there was no sign of an end to the canyon.

The trapper said we would soon lose our light. We had best set camp at the next heap of rocks we found. At least it would get us off the ice for the night.

— & try to sleep in this deathtrap? Tillman asked.

Just as cold night closed in on us, we found a bay in the cliff. When the Wolverine flows, I suspect water eddies in a deep pool here, but now it provided us with large blocks of slate which we could climb upon & set camp. There was no comfort — no campfire, no forgiving ground, no way to sleep but hunched against the rocks. I worried for Boyd, thin & weak. He shivered in the cold. The Indian woman crouched atop one of the higher rocks, as if she watched for something on the river.

Through the night, the black canyon groaned & heaved & gurgled, as if we slept in the belly of a coldblooded beast. I slept little, & when I dozed I dreamt that I drowned or was shoved beneath the ice of a clawing glacier. Even Samuelson, whose sleep is never disturbed, was restless.

— What if we wake to open water, & we're trapped here? Tillman whispered into the dark.

No one answered.

Later, I thought I heard someone mumbling prayers, but it may have only been a dream.

At first gray light, we found that the river was still frozen.

The Indian woman was gone.

— Wondered if she might take off like that, Samuelson said.

— She's gone for Boyo, Tillman said.

I asked why she returned with us at all, if she intended to go for the dog in the end.

— Probably thought it would be easier to leave under cover of night than argue with you.

She had left the supplies from her pack, but taken her personal belongings.

Contrary to every other day before, Tillman was first ready. Boyd was wrapping his feet in animal hide, his boots long since deteriorated to scraps. The rest of us were eating cold bits of rabbit meat.

— Come on! Let's go then, Tillman urged.

— I won't sleep another night in here.

There was no way to have known we were so near, but Tillman will not forgive me for making us sleep in that canyon. Less than a quarter mile ahead, beyond the next turn in the river, we came to the end. It was marked by a slow opening & lightening of the sky. The rock walls eased into steep hills of bluegray spruce trees. The river widened, its ice now laced with channels of open water. The sun was just above the mountains. Pruitt checked his watch. It was not yet 11 in the morning. It had taken us 1 day & 1 hour to pass through the canyon.

I am much relieved. From first contemplating this expedition, I believed this to be our most significant obstacle. The canyon stopped Haigh, & many of the Russians before him, if only because they falsely believed they could navigate its open waters. Only over ice can it be traveled. Even then it is no easy chore.

I have taken a short break to eat the hardtack Tillman has distributed to us & also to rest my hand from writing in this cramped journal. Now I return to my entry, for I fear that if I do not get all of this down, the sharp details will be forgotten.

As we have safely passed through the canyon, I have decided to take a day, possibly two, to rest. We have chosen a stand of aspen not far from shore. Farther up the hillside, we can see bare ground where the snow has melted, but the climb is beyond our diminished strength. We are too worn from our long march & cold sleepless night to do much more than strip off our wet boots & climb into our sleeping bags, though it is yet the middle of the day.

Boyd said he is much relieved to not be sleeping on the ice in the rocky narrows.

— Amen to that, Tillman said. He spoke for us all.

We have slept most of the day, just now woke to warm sunlight & a grinding, steady roar.

— Look, there! Boyd said.

A hundred yards downriver, the Wolverine had come alive; the ice collapsed, churned. We all scrambled from our sleeping bags, pulled on our boots, walked along the shore until we were at the break. Down into the canyon, we watched as slabs of ice buckled & overturned. An impressive sight. From here to Alaska's coast, the Wolverine is a deluge of floating ice blocks, slush, roiling water.

— Nattie!

Tillman ran past us, shouting.

It struck us all then. The woman & the dog were somewhere down in the canyon. A somber quiet descended on us as we returned to camp.

Pruitt set to calculating his survey & meteorological readings. Samuelson fed the fire to dry our wet boots & garments. Boyd was preparing yet another meal of stewed hares with a handful of flour thrown into the broth.

Tillman, however, remained agitated. He paced the river, much as the dog had done when separated from us. He watched as another large slab of ice broke from the edge. His eyes followed it down into the canyon. He marched with determination from camp until he neared the canyon walls. There he cupped his hands to his mouth, shouted. — Boyo! Here, Boyo! Then, — Nattie! Can you hear me? Nattie!

He called until his voice was hoarse & broken.

Boyd suggested that they might have made it through somewhere, or at least found higher ground.

Tillman ran his fingers through his wild hair.

— You think so?

I see little hope that the woman or dog could have survived, but I did not say it.

As for us, for good or ill, our entrance is sealed. Until now, we might have turned back, gone home the same way we came. No longer. We now belong to the Wolverine.

Wolverine River, April 1885

Dear Mr. Sloan,

I can't tell you what a kick I got out of the photograph of the canyon that you sent. I have it up on my refrigerator, and I like to see it every morning when I go to get the orange juice. It's hard for me to imagine what it must be like to step out your door and into that country every day. I do believe it's one of my greatest regrets, that I never made it up there. I should have thought some of that over better when I was laying out my life. But I suppose that's always going to be the case.

Good to hear you're still plugging away at the reading. There are more than a few mysteries in those pages, some that I've worked out over the years, and others that I've just settled with. You best read on and come to your own conclusions. When you're done, we'll compare notes. I will say that I, too, have wondered about the irregularities in the official papers versus my great-uncle's private diaries. I suspect the Colonel was too proud to admit he had witnessed such bizarre occurrences. Or he was wary of how it would be received by his stalwart commanders.

The advertising clippings, greeting cards, and all that must have come from a scrapbook Sophie kept. They were a popular pastime with the ladies back then. Someone in the family saw fit to dismantle it years ago, and I never did find the original book. I don't know if someone was high grading them for profit, though I can't see there would be much money to be made in trade cards and Christmas greetings. More likely a child in the family was using it for art projects. At least some of it remains.

My favorite is the card with the polar bear looking as if it's about to make a meal of a man. It was from the Colonel's brother Harry, the Christmas before the expedition set out. Interesting story about Harry — he and the Colonel were at West Point when the Civil War broke out; my grandfather, the youngest brother, was still just a small child. The cadets were all chomping at the bit to join the fight, so they petitioned the academy and eventually were allowed to graduate early and enter the war as officers. All too quickly Harry landed in a hospital bed with battlefield injuries. He lost both his right arm and right leg. No antibiotics or much for anesthesia back then — they must have knocked him out with chloroform right in the field, sawed off the bloody limbs, and hoped for the best. Tough to imagine how he survived. He was the oldest of the brothers, and from the letters I've read, I think he was the one expected to do great things in the army. Instead that fell to the Colonel.

I'm sure you've also found the few photographs that managed to survive the expedition. The plates must have been left at the bottom of the crate when the Indians were exposing most of them. I wish there were more.

As for the medical references, those are from my sister Ruth's research. She knew I had the Colonel's old papers, and when she was visiting a few years back, she asked me about them. Come to find out, she'd never actually read any of it, so I got the boxes out, and she and I spent the next week or so poring over the letters and diaries. She got so interested, she started looking up information on 19th-century obstetrics and field medicine. Next thing I knew, she was headed out to Portland, Oregon, and visiting Fort Vancouver. The old cabin the Colonel and Sophie lived in is long since gone, but a lot of the other barracks buildings are still there in a historical park. Ruth brought back a bunch of photographs she'd taken. And while she was in Portland, she went through microfiches of old newspaper articles. I'm glad she dug those up — I've always thought Mr. Jenson's fate on Perkins Island was fitting.

With all that happened to the Colonel in Alaska, though, it was our great-aunt

Sophie who really got hold of Ruth's heart. She always said someone should write her biography, and I think she was working the nerve up to do it herself. At one point she marked everything with little yellow sticky notes, about a hundred of them, and had it all laid out in my back guest room, but it seemed to me she was just shuffling everything around and around. It was about that time she came down with the cancer, and she was gone before I knew it. That's how it goes when you get to be my age. Makes me see that there might be some sense to having children after all, just so your entire life and all your family's contributions aren't relegated to Goodwill in the end.

I enjoyed your story about the raven. They do have a comical way about them. They like to harass the dogs, too. I had a golden retriever years ago. The ravens would steal food from his bowl a piece at a time while he was barking and trying to chase off one bird, then another. It drove the dog crazy, and amused me.

One time, though, I watched a raven snatch up a baby rabbit, carry it off into a nearby field, and rip it to shreds. It changed the way I see those birds. They are crueler than you might suppose, or maybe not cruel so much as self-serving.

I didn't mean to end on such a grim

note. But I do hope you'll write again when you have the chance and let me know how the reading is going.

With regards,
Walt

December 22, 1884

Merry Christmas to Allen & Sophie.
   Allen — stay warm and safe in the Far North & don't let the polar bears get a hold of you.

Your brother, Harry

To Allen Forrester, 2nd Class Cadet
West Point Academy, New York

Dear Son,

Your mother has informed me of your intention to study toward joining the Corps of Topographical Engineers. I cannot fathom such a decision. You and I have already thoroughly laid out a strategy for your future, and I wonder that we are discussing it again.

Let me be forthright — I will not allow you to waste your God-given talents as a soldier and leader so you can tramp about the country with a measuring stick. It has been my sincerest hope since you were a young boy that you would continue to carry the torch of honor and service that the Forresters have kept alight for generations. I am confident that between my own connections and the reputation you have already earned at the Academy, I will be able to secure you a worthy commission.

If it is, in fact, adventure you seek rather than service to your country, I suggest you pursue it through some other means than that of your career. And I will tell you this: as an officer and leader, you will soon discover that adventure is a romantic notion, best left behind with childhood, and that you ought to be grateful for the opportunities allotted you.

Your mother might be correct in her assessment. You are a different young man from what I was at your age. Perhaps you are not as ambitious or as desirous of a challenge. Perhaps you will be content to rest on the laurels of our family. I hope this is not so.

I sharply advise you to reconsider your aims, and your duty to family and country, and I trust we will not need to speak of this again.

Your father

Sophie Forrester
Vancouver Barracks
April 6, 1885

I am convinced that all this laudanum and endless hours of sleep do my health no good. Such dreams. The worst woke me before dawn. Allen was there, but he was a stranger, and I was not myself. We ran through an old forest, and it was so dark and overgrown that the roots grabbed at our feet and the branches tore at our faces, and for all our effort, we could not make our way out. I could hear Allen's hoarse breathing and struggle in the near shadows, but because he was a stranger to me, I dared not call out.

April 11

Mrs Connor and Mrs Whithers came for a visit today, but I asked Charlotte to please turn them away, tell them only that I am ill and will try to see them soon.

I am so undone as to not be fit for company.

When Charlotte brings me a basin of warm water to wash, I tremble and cannot stand long enough to see to it. The girl is kind enough to help me wash my face and neck, but I know I must look a fright.

A sickening lethargy affects me. It is the remnants of the sedative, I think, but also all these hours in bed. The sun shines through the curtains, and I lie here like a helpless invalid. It is tedious and fills me with shame, even if Dr Randall has ordered it. I no longer take the opium, as I cannot imagine it is any more wholesome for my child than it is for me, and the surgeon has agreed only because the bleeding has stopped. He takes it as good sign but says the danger is far from passed.

There is some relief in being allowed to sit in a chair at the window for a short while each day. The nuthatches come now and then, and I caught glimpse of a hawk of some sort but could not see it clearly enough to identify. And always the chickadees find their way to our yard.

Ridiculous it may be, but I am glad to not see that raven again.

At last some small entertainment to report. I had moved to the front room to rest on the sofa for a change of scenery, when out in the yard, I spied two chipmunks scampering about. They chased each other, then both would be up on their hind legs, facing each other like boxers, one would hop over the other and they'd run up a fir tree, down again for another tussle on the ground. It was an amusing scene, and I thought Charlotte might enjoy seeing them. I called for her, and when she didn't respond, I called more loudly, and I am afraid I must have sounded the alarm, for when Charlotte appeared, she had some kind of weapon in hand!

"Good heavens, don't shoot," I said, only partly in jest.

"Sorry ma'am," she said. "Thought something was amiss."

I asked about the contraption, a Y-shaped piece of wood with a length of rubber tubing stretched between. She called it a "sling-shot" and with it she can shoot pebbles or small pieces of metal. And why would she possess such a weapon? Charlotte understood it was part of her employment.

"Your Colonel wanted a girl who could cook, clean, and aim straight, just in case there was ever a need."

"But have you shot anything with it before?"

"Nothing out of order," she replied, "just a squirrel or game bird for supper now and then. But my brother Tom says it'll drop a man at forty paces if your aim is good."

I couldn't help but laugh. Nothing out of order indeed. Perhaps this West remains wild yet.

We watched the chipmunks for some time

out the window, but then the men could be heard going through their drills on the parade ground, and the animals were startled back into the woods.

"I cannot tell you how much I long for the out of doors," I said. "To feel fresh air on my face and hear birdsong."

True to her nature, Charlotte said nothing. I told her she had best put up her weapon, as there was no need for it now.

Later in the day, however, she came to knock quietly at my bedroom door. When I called her in, she said in the smallest of voices, "Ma'am, I swear I didn't tell Mrs Connor a thing. I don't say two words to her ever."

It was clear she spoke the truth, and I don't know why it didn't occur to me before — of course it was Evelyn who told the women! It is just the kind of thoughtless thing she would do.

I thanked Charlotte, and apologized profusely for losing my temper over the matter.

"I never seen you lose your temper, ma'am. You don't even holler or throw any pots."

I teased that next time I call for her to come look out the window with me, she need not come shooting, but she remained serious and unsmiling, so I reassured her I was glad to be under her protection.

April 15

I exist in a suspended state between sleep and wakefulness, where nothing at all happens, yet all manner of possibilities exist. I wait to hear word of Allen. I wait to feel the quickening of life within me. I try not to dwell on the future, which seems a vast and unknown territory, but I cannot help but wonder — by this time next year, will I hold a plump, happy baby in my arms, and will dear Allen again be at my side?

April 16

How sharply it returns, even after all these years, that old familiar horror. Heat that roars like a cyclone through the trees, throwing embers up toward the night sky. The hellish glow. And always, always that animal cry from within the flames. In my dream, I shouted to Father, only to wake myself with my own cry.

For a fleeting moment I thought to turn to Allen in our bed and seek his comfort as I had in nights before, but it is the middle of the day, and I am alone.

A lady at this time frequently either feels faint, or actually faints away; she is often either giddy, or sick, or nervous, and in some instances even hysterical. Although, in rare cases, some women do not even know the precise time when they quicken.

The sensation of "quickening" is said by many ladies to resemble the fluttering of a bird; by others it is likened to either a heaving, or a beating, or rearing sensation; accompanied, sometimes, with a frightened feeling; these flutterings, or heavings, or beatings, after the first day of quickening, usually come on half a dozen or a dozen times a day.

> — From *Advice to a Wife on the Management of Herself,*
> Pye Henry Chavasse, 1873

7

Sophie Forrester,
Vancouver Barracks,
April 17, 1885

This afternoon the dreams were so vivid that I could smell burned wood, but it was only Charlotte stoking the cook stove. Hours have since passed, she has long gone to bed and it is dark outside, yet I know I will lie here awake for some time. A body can only sleep so much of its life away.

I wonder what conjures these memories just now. I have tried to put them out of my mind to no avail. I suspect all this lying about and worrying allows the nightmares to grow stronger and more vivid, so that I half expect to see Father outside in the rain.

I wish I could recall him in some other way, kind and laughing, as he was when I was very small, but instead I imagine him in the end, half-naked, his wild gray beard tangled with the mat of gray hair on his chest. Old and

unkempt and mad, but his body still powerful.

I am ashamed to realize it has been nearly
five years since I returned home. Are there
any remains of the barn? Even when I left for
normal school, already the dandelions and
nettles had begun to sprout in the ashes, so it
has likely succumbed to the forest by now.
What of the charred rafters, or the blackened
door frame? I recall that it stood alone, like a
ghostly entrance.

And his sculptures? Father said the marble
would harden with time and shed off the elements, yet I cannot guess how they have
fared. Galloping horses, the women in their
flowing gowns, griffins, angels, tragic beasts.
The way they are littered among the trails
and meadows, as a child I always pictured a
giant letting them fall from his pocket like
pebbles as he walked.

It was not entirely as magical as I should
like to remember. All his wages spent on
marble, even when we owed the grocer.
Father carting the great slabs behind old
Molly the mule as he searched for the perfect
meadow or the precise light through the trees,
so that even I had to fear for his sanity.

Yet they are astonishing creations. Once the
baby is born, we will visit Mother, and Allen
will be able to see them at last. The paths are
surely grown over, but I could find my way
to the bear. He is dearest to me. Full-sized,

taller than a man, so that I remember Father used a footstool as he worked. Such a dramatic pose, standing on his hind legs, roaring at the sky, teeth and claws carved sharply into the marble. I remember those summer days when Father was away at the quarry, and I would sit at the bear's feet and watch the forest chickadees gathered atop his head. A mesmerizing kind of scene, for of course the little birds did not know to be afraid; the bear was frozen harmlessly in rock, but as they fluttered and landed upon him, I could see his ferocious agony.

I am sorry the bear is broken now — I do not know if Father could have mended him if he tried. The sledgehammer had knocked away one of his front paws, and he was riddled with chips and cracks. Still, I should like to see him again.

Even after all these years I can taste the air with its marble dust and green summer leaves. I can hear the echo of mallet and chisel and feel the sunlight that filtered down through the canopy. I was nearly as wild as Father those summer days, my legs bare, my hair untied, and my nose sunburned.

There is a mythical element to our childhood, it seems, that stays with us always. When we are young, we consume the world in great gulps, and it consumes us, and everything is mysterious and alive and fills us with desire and wonder, fear, and guilt. With the passing of the years, however, those memories become distant and malleable, and we shape them into the stories of who we are. We are brave, or we are cowardly. We are loving, or we are cruel.

All my life, I have only considered this through the eyes of the child. Yet now, my view begins to shift. More than anything I want to hold this little baby, to feel his warm weight in my arms and kiss his small fingers. Yet, too, it is such solemn responsibility. To think that these next years, as Allen and I make choices that will seem to us so mundane and ordinary, we will shape our child's vision of the world.

April 18
Father is very much with me just now. It is something of these dreams, but also the time of day. Such a warm and pleasant evening, even observed from the confines of this bedroom. For a few precious minutes as the sun descended, through the doorway I could see that the hall and kitchen was cast in a golden glow, and as Charlotte swept, the dust specks were suspended in the shafts of light. Father would have thought the scene very pretty. The fairy hour, the magical hour, when light moves from gold to silver. A bittersweet nostalgia settles upon me.

Father once told me that every artist leaves behind a self-portrait, whether he intends to or not. In my childish imagination, I pictured a cool, white marble Father, standing silently in the forest. I asked him when he would carve it.

As was common to him, his mood shifted like quicksilver, so that I could not tell if my question amused or angered him, or only made him sad for some reason I could not fathom. There was a dangerous edge to his voice that made me wary.

"Why Sophie — I finished it long ago. Don't you recognize me?"

Why had I not seen it before?

"You have," he said. "You know it well."

It was some sort of riddle, a trick. I tried to guess. Is it the figure with hood and staff? Not the horse with the long mane, or the sea serpent, dipping in and out of the earth?

No. No. His laugh more like a cough, and he grabbed me up in his strong arms.

"There I am," he said, and he pointed to the bear.

I should have known, for it had always been my favorite. I wish I had told him so.

April 19

At last! Oh, it fills me with such joy, and hope, oh dare I write that word "hope," even if good sense cautions me otherwise. Yet how can I feel anything but elation, when I feel you swimming inside of me, little one?

I was lying in this bed, as always, nearly

drowsing, when it came. A flutter in my belly, as if with nerves. Or perhaps an oddly twitching muscle. I lay completely still and nothing more happened. I waited and waited until I had nearly given up, but then you surprised me again, little one. Was it a summersault, or did you wriggle and swim like a tadpole?

It is you. I am certain of it now. My sweet little one, hold fast. I am here waiting for you.

April 21

Nearly three months Allen is gone now. The weather turns fair and warm, and oh great happiness, I am allowed to venture out of doors again. Still I am not permitted to walk far, so Charlotte brings me a chair so I can sit in our yard and watch the birds come and go. My notebook fills with observations and pitiable sketches. Dark-eyed junco, evening grosbeak, golden-crowned sparrow, song sparrow, a large flock of Canada geese in the far distance, and a solitary mallard drake that quacked as he flew overhead, as if he had lost his way.

Now and then the baby turns about, as if to call for my attention. Here I am! It seems more and more like another presence within me, and I find myself speaking out loud to the baby. Do you hear that funny old duck, quacking away? Are you listening, little one? Can you hear the sound of my voice?

I was speaking just like that when Charlotte suddenly appeared at my side with my dose of warm honey water. I started to explain that I wasn't talking to myself but to the baby, and the girl must have seen my embarrassment.

"Don't bother 'bout it, ma'am. Whenever she's expecting, Mam sings to her belly. She says it makes for happier babies."

So I am forgiven this eccentricity. And I am glad, for I do enjoy talking with you, little one. I will tell you all about the wild birds that I see, and I will try to imagine where your father is just now and what adventures he might meet. How I long for the day when he comes home to us.

We came across a grisly scene this afternoon. Tillman & Boyd were stringing snares along the river for rabbits, while Pruitt remained in camp. Samuelson & I set out for a ravine in search of clean drinking water — the river becomes gray & sandy as spring advances.

Within less than half a mile, the narrow creek valley turned rocky, steep enough to halt our progress. There we found the remains of an avalanche not unlike the one the Old Man set down upon us in the canyon. High above, we saw its path. Trees had been torn out by their roots, rocks & dirt churned into the deep snow that was now melting.

At the end of this destruction were the corpses of two white animals so far into decay all that remained were loosened fur & discolored bones. Samuelson said they are what the Indians call tebay, a type of wild sheep that live in these mountains.

A dozen or so ravens & magpies were gathered at the bone piles. They behaved strangely. They did not flap their wings or make to fly off, as one would expect, nor did they utter a sound. They were silent, watchful, & I felt their black eyes upon us as we turned our backs to them.

April 22

Now that we are through the canyon, we are no longer driven by fear that the ice will wash out. Instead hunger is our greatest menace.

This far upriver, the main channel of the Wolverine remains frozen but is too precarious to travel. Much of the valley is now free of snow, so we have abandoned the sleds & rely on packs. Each of us will carry a sleeping bag, blanket, one change of underclothes. Carbines, pistols, ammunition, cooking utensils, account for much of the weight. Lieut. Pruitt continues to carry camera & science equipment. As for provisions, we could easily consume all that we have in three days, but will instead hold them as reserve. We must attempt to live upon the country. Already the men are weakened by hunger — Boyd still recovers from his hard winter, Pruitt seems to waste before our eyes.

It is an uneasy balance, weighing progress in our travel each day with the need to look for food. We heard geese overhead early this morning. Samuelson says we may be fortunate enough to find nesting birds & so be rewarded with both roasted fowl & fried eggs. Such a meal would be very well received.

April 23

All evidence to the contrary, we had a good day's travel. Our only sustenance was a few spoonfuls of beans for each of us in the morning. We then walked 10 miles over granite boulders, rocky shores, with no sign of game. Beset by hunger, the poor condition of our leather boots, & heavy pack loads, our pace was at times a stumbling shuffle.

For all that, we were given blue skies & much sunshine, which carried our spirits. The mountains to the northeast become more visible. They are impressive indeed — their peaks gleam white with snow & ice, break through low-lying clouds.

The riverbed continues to widen to an impressive span, so that it is easily more than a mile across of braided channels of ice. As the days warm, the ice loosens, begins to move. If we were to follow the many bends & twists in the river's paths, we would double the distance we travel. Instead, we leap across the narrower streams, lay driftwood logs over others to build temporary bridges.

April 24

We traveled hard today. It's after midnight, yet we have just set camp & I write by the fire. Earlier Boyd drew our attention to smoke rising out of the spruce trees several miles upriver. It will be a group of the Wolverine Indians we have heard so much about. We approach them with some apprehension, but also with hopes that they will have food enough to trade.

Samuelson saw footprints in the gray mud along the river. Looks as if at least three men, several women & children, travel together. He advises us to salute the Indians with gunshot when we near them. It is a show of greeting & strength. The more rounds we fire, the more respect we earn in their eyes. In turn, the Indians will likely throw a feast in our honor.

I hate to waste the ammunition.

April 25
An unnerving discovery, yet I am not sure how much to draw from it.

This evening as we sought a place to sleep beneath the protection of spruce trees, Tillman came upon a bone. It was broken on one end. Near the break, teeth marks had scraped at the bone, as if the marrow had been sucked. It was weathered, but not so old as to be worn completely clean. Several strands of sinew were still attached. I asked what kind of bone it might be.

— Leg of some sort, Samuelson said.

— What's been chewing on it, that's what

I'd like to know, Tillman said.

— That there was just voles, whittling away at it, Samuelson said. — But these here larger marks, I can't be sure. Porcupine. Fox. Something bigger had to break it open to get at the marrow. Any other sign around?

We followed the sergeant to where he'd found it. Samuelson walked about, crouching now & then to scoop away spruce needles, fallen cones.

— Yes sir, he finally said. — Suspected as much.

In the palm of his hand he held a small plate of bone with strands of long, dark hair attached.

— Looks to be part of a skull, he said. — Judging by the small leg bone, it was a child, I would guess.

At this, Tillman let out a yelp, flung the leg bone to the ground.

Samuelson said Midnooskies most likely cremate their dead or cache them in the branches of trees. We found no other sign. I asked him what he made of it. He only shrugged, eyed the ground & nearby trees.

— Can't really say one way or another.

I think we all would have preferred to camp elsewhere, but we had run out of daylight. We unrolled our sleeping bags beneath the spruce trees, built a fire. We had killed no rabbits that day, found no geese, so we each soaked a small piece of hardtack in water. We face a hungry night.

For a time we were all silent, so I thought the other men were drifting off to sleep. Tillman was the first to speak up. It's always Tillman.

— Those teeth marks, you think they might have been human?

— Could be, Samuelson mumbled as if he had been woken.

Boyd groaned. — Lord, why'd you have to go & ask that?

I offered to take first shift to keep the fire going through the night. As the other men sleep, I write here in my journal, feed branches to the flames. Beyond the firelight, the forest is a wall of darkness. I hear nothing beyond the steady roar of the river & the occasional crackle of the fire.

April 26

We discovered a crude fish camp that likely had not been used since summer, searched for any bit of food left behind, to no avail. We continue to see sign of Midnooskies though the Indians themselves remain out of sight. Smoke rises from campfires upriver, but they are extinguished before we can reach them.

— They're keeping their eyes on us, Samuelson says.

We shot seven rabbits, which we ate before the meat was fully cooked. We become more like the Indians every day. Our hunger, however, is not abated. A drizzling rain turned to snow, yet still we made good time. 14 miles.

April 27
After trailing the Midnooskies up the river, today we at last caught up with them. We fired several rounds, waited for response. We were greeted with silence, which Samuelson saw as bad sign. We spied their hide-covered shelter through the brush & approached with caution, as we did not know how many Indians were concealed within, or their character.

— Do you think they're man-eaters? Tillman whispered too loudly.

Myself, I was not as concerned with the rumors of neighboring tribes, but instead the reports of the fiercely territorial behavior these Indians demonstrated with the Russians.

— Hey, ho there, Samuelson called as we entered the clearing of their camp.

Contrary to our fears, these Midnooskies proved to be a woebegone band. The children peeking from behind the hides were rail thin & vacant eyed; the adults crouched outside, clothed in the most ragged of furs. It was just as the skilly had warned us — a starving land.

Against hope, we asked if we could perhaps trade for some food. The leader, a gaunt man with much scarring to his face, hesitated, then said he would trade us some dried salmon for tea & gun powder. He had a poor muzzle-loading shotgun that he said his grandfather had acquired from the Russians many years ago. He had several copper bullets that he had hammered himself in order to hunt moose. However, he said he has been without powder for some time.

When he ordered one of the children to fetch us the salmon, an old woman began to shout at him & gesture wildly.

He will kill his own children if he takes this food from their mouths, the woman cried. It is all they have, Samuelson translated.

The Indian ignored her pleas, showed the dried salmon to us.

— Good God, I won't touch the stuff! Tillman said.

— When your stomach starts to gnawing at your backbone, you'll eat it & be glad for it, was Samuelson's reply.

The withered flesh was moldy & putrid, looked as if it could make us more ill than not, but I took a small portion of what was offered. In exchange we gave him a sprinkling of tea, explaining that we were nearly without ourselves, & Tillman assisted with the gun-powder.

When we asked if they had seen any geese come through, the Midnooskies were vague. The leader said he, too, had heard them fly overhead recently. Samuelson had trouble translating, but it seemed the Indian was making some kind of threat about the waterfowl.

— Ah, he's just trying to hornswoggle us! Tillman said. — They're as hungry for those geese as we are.

I was interested in gathering information about other Midnooskies in the area. The Indian informed us that a village is located up another river drainage, its confluence about 50 miles north of here.

I asked through Samuelson if the village will greet us in a friendly manner.

The Indian answered that the tyone, the Russian name they use for a kind of chief among their people, is powerful, wary of strangers, but beyond that he was unwilling to provide more insight.

Did he know a passage through the mountains to the north? We plan to follow the Wolverine to its headwaters, but will need Indian guides to find the easiest way beyond.

The man said he has never gone that far.

— His people go to those mountains only after they die, Samuelson said. — They say it is a kind of spirit world. On the other side, you're in the territory of their enemies.

The Indian went on to say that the Trail River tyone is powerful, that he has no fear & that is why he is rich. He has traveled farther than any other Midnoosky.

— Sounds like the tyone knows the way through the mountains, if he'll tell you, Samuelson said.

Boyd then attempted to speak to the Midnooskies in their language. Among his broken speech, I was able to discern the words for woman & fog, so that along with his gestures, I knew he asked after his wife. The Indians had no knowledge of her.

After we left them, Tillman asked how we can know they won't follow us, kill us & eat us all.

— They're awfully hard up for food, he said.

— I think you might be a bit gamey for their taste, Samuelson replied.

Tillman said he didn't find that much amusing.

Samuelson advises me to pay my respects to this Trail River tyone. Though it will require us to travel out of our way in search of the village, I agree. Perhaps we will be able to employ him as a guide through the mountain passes or at least obtain some helpful information about the route.

61°28' N
144°26' W
38°F, exposed bulb
31°F, wet bulb
Barometer: 29.20
Dew point: 17
Relative humidity: 41
Clear.

Oh, fearsome land. I enter the forge of ancient gods: vapors and glaciers and molten rock and time cleaved asunder. Any man would walk this world in awe, yet I am unaffected. I command you — shudder beneath my feet! Rain ice and broken rock down upon my broken head!

And I, tin soldier that I am, will remain cold and unmoved.

Sulphuret of copper and iron, veins of cold water quartz, green hornblende, sandstone and galena and felspathic granite.

With black wing, beat down the subterranean flames, whisk away ash, bare the dead

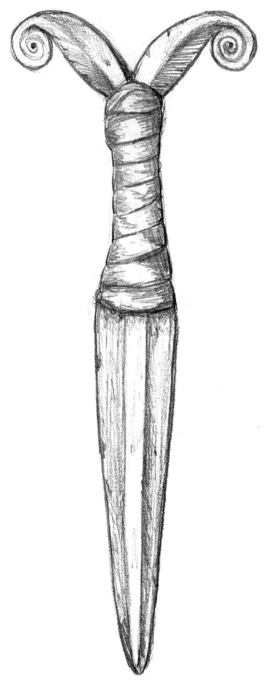

Midnoosky Copper Blade

black in our hearts and the mad glint in our irises: copper knives, flakes of gold, bullets, and brass buttons. Do you not see? Savage white man and Indian alike, our eyes are agleam with it.

The earth shook and trembled. Smoke out of his nostrils, fire out of his mouth devoured. He bowed the heavens; darkness was beneath his feet. He rode upon a cherub, and did fly yea, he did fly upon the wings of the wind.

I would know this place, sudden and pure and without need of conscience or thought, as it was in the beginning, is now, and ever shall be. World without end. I would weep from this longing to know. Instead, I can speak only to the commonest of sins — greed and cowardice, lust and wrath. I speak to them alone because they are written beneath my skin.

Sophie Forrester
Vancouver Barracks
April 23, 1885

I wish Evelyn had told me none of it, for it is an unsettling revelation. I fear it explains something of Mr Pruitt. I try not to let it make me anxious for Allen, as surely he has led all sorts of men and knows Mr Pruitt far better than any barracks gossip can reveal, and more to the point, I am helpless in the face of it.

It had been some time since I had a visit from Evelyn. She was gone to Portland for a shopping excursion for several days. (The town of Vancouver, she says, offers nothing in the way of fashion, and all in the way of dust, saloons, and rowdy men.) When she returned, I was bed-ridden. She came by the house, but when Charlotte told her my condition, Evelyn promised to come another day. I cannot think she was respecting my privacy, but rather that she's squeamish and did not care to sit at my bedside.

Today, however, she found me in the sitting room, fully washed and clothed, and she expressed relief to see me presentable at last. Charlotte brought us tea, and we talked lightly for a while, but at last my irritation overcame my politeness. I asked her outright if she had told Mrs Connor of my pregnancy. "Well of course," she said. She seemed bored by the conversation. "Surely everyone will know eventually. You can't keep a baby hidden in your skirts forever. Why bother with all this secrecy?"

Because I had asked for her confidence, as a friend, and because one should respect other people's privacy. I daresay she puts no stock in these concerns. "Yes, yes, I am all apologies," she said. "You can be so prickly, Sophie. But enough of all of this. I have heard some interesting news I've been dying to share" — and here she gave a dramatic pause and then — "about your Mr Pruitt."

"My" Mr Pruitt? Why would she refer to him in such a way?

"Because he was clearly smitten with you at the dance. You must have noticed how he watched you all the night."

I have no idea what she was talking about, and offered that Mr Pruitt found me tiresome instead. Evelyn waved it off, eager to share her gossip.

"Mr Pruitt was at Elk Creek."

The place name meant nothing to me. Evelyn was disbelieving. How could I not know? She was more than willing to educate me.

It is a terrible, terrible affair. Hundreds of Indians, mostly women and children guarded by a few warriors, slain on a winter's night. Most were killed before they left their teepees.

"The rest were hunted through the snow, like deer," Evelyn said. "Do you know what they do, when the soldiers bear down on them? The squaws rip open their clothes to show their breasts, in hopes that they will be spared, but these men were not so particular."

The commander is a known drunkard, according to Evelyn, who filled the soldiers with whiskey the night before, and rallied them to the unspeakable once the killing was begun.

She insists she has overheard many such stories and does not believe them to be exaggerated. Her uncle was among those who argued for the men to be disciplined, while even at the same time politicians in Washington, D.C., were calling for them to be decorated with medals. In the end, the soldiers were neither punished nor rewarded.

And did Mr Pruitt truly have a hand in this? Evelyn could not say for certain, but she said there is no doubt that he was with the company.

All of this, Evelyn relayed in a breathless, excited manner, and in it, I saw an unfortunate cruelty. If she had been born a man, I wonder if she might have been clever and daring, if not somewhat wild. Instead she is confined to gossip and idleness, and the boredom of it all does her character ill.

As for Mr Pruitt, I hardly know what to think. No matter his part in the battle, it must darken his mind. I can only hope Allen has chosen his men well.

April 24

I spend too much time with this map, as if I could somehow divine your whereabouts if I only studied it diligently. There is so little to go by: the jagged margins of the coast, a thin line marked "Wolverine River," yet I know all too well that its route is only conjecture.

You must be through the icy canyon by now, and into that wild country so little known.

It is all well and good for me to write such things from the warmth of my bed, but I am sure I would rather be at your side at this very moment, suffering whatever cold and hunger you endure, than to sit here with all the comforts of the world, alone and unknowing.

April 25

I was in need of such a day as this! To take in the fresh air, to observe a dozen species of birds, and to have an interesting encounter, all without leaving the back yard.

The weather was pleasant, and Charlotte brought my chair so that I might sit for a while out of doors. I had everything I needed — a lap robe, a stool to rest my feet upon, a cup of warm tea, my field glasses, and notebook.

As I was sitting there, a man came up the lane and then along the side of the house without noticing my presence.

Up close, he cut a somewhat menacing figure. He is near to seventy years old, I would guess, but he is yet broad chested and marked as a soldier — deep scars on his face cause such a downcast to his eye and scowl to his mouth that he looked quite angry, and I hesitated to speak to him at all. However, I screwed up my courage, and called a greeting.

I am afraid I must have startled him. He was on his way to my yard, I am certain, but finding me sitting there, he seemed to consider turning away as if he had not seen or heard me.

"You are welcome," I called to him and waved.

He looked down at his boots, adjusted his sagging cavalry hat, and at last shuffled my way.

"Good afternoon ma'am. Just checking on the fruit trees. I'm the one looks after them."

"Oh, yes, there are several apple trees just over there, but I suppose you know that," I said, and then I realized how strange and rude I must appear, sitting there with my feet propped.

"I am not usually so helpless," I chattered on senselessly, "but you see, I'm . . . I'm expecting . . ."

And here he waited for me to finish my sentence, as if I might say I'm expecting a package, or a visitor.

"A child. I'm with child."

Why on earth did I say all this to the poor man? It must have made him dreadfully uncomfortable.

"Well, then, that's good news I suppose," he said at last.

"Yes, of the best sort!"

The man removed his hat then, out of politeness, and I noticed several fingers missing on his right hand, but I averted my gaze so as not to cause him embarrassment. An awkward silence descended upon us, and I wished Charlotte would come out.

"Oh, please excuse me, I haven't properly introduced myself. I am Sophie Forrester."

"MacGillivray," he said.

"Oh, a grand name!" I exclaimed, for I could not help my enthusiasm. "The MacGillivray's warbler — do you know its call, Mr MacGillivray? I believe it is similar to the mourning warbler."

I did my poor imitation — "churry churry chorry cho."

I feared the man was becoming annoyed with me, for his face contorted in the oddest way, but then he laughed out loud.

"Is that what I sound like then?" he said.

"No, no, not you, just your namesake."

At last, there was some ease between us and I asked him about the work he does.

"General's put me out to pasture, so to speak, which suits me well enough. Always have preferred the company of trees."

Since he knows the landscape so well, I asked if I might have any hope of seeing the elk or grizzly bears for which this wild country is so famous.

"Not likely at all," he said. "This fort's been occupied by hungry men for half a century. They've fairly scoured the land for any bite of meat. Now and then a cougar or black bear might wander down off the mountains, but only two or three times that I can remember."

And what of humming birds?

"Yes ma'am," he said, "they do buzz about in the summer."

I explained that I would very much like to observe their nesting behavior, but I suspected I would have to venture up the hill away from the barracks.

"I'd advise against that," he said. "There are some hellacious brambles up there."

I assured him that I am in possession of both stout boots and a stout heart. To which he said nothing, and we were again at an awkward impasse.

I wondered aloud, then, if the humming birds here are much like those back East. In Vermont, the ruby-throated humming bird often builds its nests near fresh water, I said, in the branch of an oak or maple tree. Certainly there are different species of trees here, but perhaps the Rufous share these same preferences.

He was, I think, taken aback that I should be knowledgeable and curious in such a way.

"Well, that being the case, a body might try following the creek down past there." He pointed toward the northeast and said that if I followed the creek up the hill, it would lead to a marsh where I might "poke about" and find something.

"But you best wait until you are well, and your Colonel returns," he said. "I don't need him chasing me down for neglect."

I told him there is no need for concern — for now, I am very much confined by circumstance.

Even with Sgt. Tillman & Lieut. Pruitt as witnesses, I resist putting this down. How do we account for such an occurrence? We are hungry, it is true, but I have been nearer starvation & not suffered such hallucinations. Is it possible we have encountered a natural intoxicant? I can think of nothing unusual we have ingested. We have not even eaten the salmon we received from the Midnooskies, as we were saving it for more desperate times.

I have no way to account for it, only truth as I have perceived it & which I will try to relay here.

Before dawn, Tillman, Pruitt, & I set out for the marshland to hunt the Canada geese we have seen fly overhead. Boyd & Samuelson were to travel up a nearby valley — they continue to look for precious metals in these mountains.

Our hope was to reach the marsh as the sun was rising, so as to find the geese before they took wing. The morning was clear & cold. We walked up the river valley for a mile or so. As we neared the marsh, through the willows we heard a cacophony.

— Geese? Tillman mouthed silently.

I was not sure. At first, it sounded much like waterfowl — restless honks & the occasional flap of wing & splash. Then my ear would catch something else, a laugh or word.

We crept through the brush, emerged at the edge of the wetland. We faced directly into first light as it broke through the mountains. Frost & brittle ice had formed during the cold night, but a small stream ran open among the hummocks of dead grass. Although not much wider than a stride, the stream was clear & shoulder deep.

Not far off, near a stand of large cottonwood trees, at least two dozen women gathered. Some sat on the grass, others waded & swam. Their hair shone long & black in the sun. They wore hide tunics similar to those favored by Alaska Indians, but these skins were of a paler shade, a near white, & without adornments.

Tillman stumbled out of the brush at this inopportune moment, grabbed at the willows as he tripped. Pruitt put a finger to lips, but it was too late for the commotion had startled the women. Several looked in our direction, shrieked at the sight of us.

Soon all were shouting & fleeing. As they scattered, they splashed through the water and it caught the glare of the rising sun. It was a blinding scene. In that same instant, countless wild geese took flight from the very midst of the women, so that wing & black hair, scream & strangled honk were indistinguishable from one another.

None of us would shoot in the direction of the women, so we were stalled. Then, from perilously near, we heard the sound of arrows in flight. We crouched, raised our rifles, but their aim was not us. The Midnooskies had come with the same intention to hunt geese.

Arrows struck several of the birds before they could gain altitude. The geese fell, flopped in the marsh. The Indians continued to send their arrows.

— They'll hit the women, Tillman said.

Indeed, it was true. Pruitt pointed towards the cottonwoods, where one of the women flailed against a tree.

The Indians lowered their bows. Those geese that had not been killed were now airborne & out of reach. The women had vanished, all but the one who had been struck.

We walked upstream to her, with several Midnooskies trailing us.

At first I thought the arrow pierced her, but

as we neared, I saw that it passed harmlessly through the skin shift at her side & pinned her to the trunk of the tree.

The woman became still at our approach, watched us through strange eyes — so gleaming & black that they appeared to have no center. Her skin was neither white like ours nor brown like the Indians, but instead a translucent gray. Her lips were dull black, as if coated with charcoal, & broad bands of white, like paint, ran down either of her cheeks. Her skin, her hair, her pale tunic, were all speckled with beads of water.

The Midnoosky stood beside the woman, gestured from her to me.

— I don't know, but I think he's asking if you want her, Tillman said.

I reached to pull the arrow from the tree, but the woman seized my wrist. Her grasp was wet & leathery. I then saw that a slick membrane webbed her fingers. Her nails were black, slender & sharp. She turned her head slightly to look at me through one of her peculiar eyes. She blinked — so quickly that surely I am mistaken — but it seemed her eyelid flickered from bottom to top in an uncanny way.

She lowered her head & hissed at me, a frightful sound like a cornered snake.

Overhead, the flock of geese circled, cried.

— Oh, Jesus, Tillman said. — You're not taking her, are you?

With my other hand, I pulled the arrow from the tree. I hoped she would escape, but she was not quick enough. The Indian grabbed her waist, bound her hands with leather thong, led her away. Throughout the marsh, the other Indians gathered the dead geese & stray arrows.

We walked empty-handed back to our camp with little talk except Tillman's occasional mutterings — All my life, never seen anything like it.

I am curious to hear Samuelson's interpretation of these events when he returns to camp.

— No goose for supper, then?

Such was the trapper's response.

I explained how we had come upon the flock & the women at the marsh, the two mingled so that one could not tell them apart. I told him of the strange woman who was pinned by an arrow.

— A real hell-cat, Tillman offered. — I thought the Colonel had lost all sense, when it seemed like he was taking her in.

Samuelson lit his pipe.

— A shame, he said. — Had my mouth set for goose. Bit tired of hare & thin broth.

I asked again if he had ever seen anything like it.

— Nope, he said around his pipe. — I've heard it told, though, that's how they first got their women.

When the world was small & mostly water, he said, women were geese. If a man wanted one, he had to go & catch her before she changed back & flew off.

— Course, then he's got the trouble of bringing her home & trying to tame her.

Samuelson chuckled, as if this was surely the hardest part to believe.

Tillman paced about with some nervousness.

— You're saying that's what we saw, out there in the marsh today?

— I'm just passing along a story I heard told. Make of it what you will.

— It's ridiculous! Pruitt said.

It all amused the trapper.

— So, he said, — a woman from a rib you'll have, but not from a goose?

A small number of Mednovtsy Indians have accepted the Orthodox faith, but their nomadic life and distance from the Konstantin redoubt, as well as their casual attitude toward their new religion, means that they very rarely participate in religious ceremonies, and many have even forgotten that they are Christians.

— From *Captain P. N. Golovin's
Last Report,* 1862
(translated from the Russian)

Lieut. Col. Allen Forrester
April 30, 1885

With the snow rapidly disappearing, we are able to walk easily along the river shore. It is sparse country indeed, though majestic in its span. The mountains to the northeast are wrapped in clouds & what we make for plumes of volcanic steam. The peaks are of such luminous white as to look unearthly.

Pruitt estimates we have gained no more than 15 miles in the past two days. Our travel is slowed by our fatigue & need to search for food. We have seen no more waterfowl. Samuelson caught a few hares last night, but they are not enough.

— I'm sick to death of these d——d rabbits, but I'd swallow a dozen of them if they were on hand, Tillman said.

We are beginning to understand how the natives can be so gluttonous, consuming vast amounts of food in one sitting. It seems the lean meat of this land is not enough to keep up with the physical demands it places on one's body.

We have crossed paths with two other small groups of Midnooskies. Other times we have sensed that the Indians are near but they conceal themselves. So far, they show no sign of the ferocity or cannibalistic nature of which we had heard. They are guarded, watchful, somewhat suspicious of our intentions. The women & children run, hide among the nearby bushes when we approach. We can feel their eyes on us as we talk with their men.

Mostly, though, these people share our hunger. They have no food to trade, say they bide their time until the salmon return. They hunt game in nearby valleys but with little success. Samuelson explained that because of their poor hunting implements the Indians must rely on deep snow to slow their prey.

Their language is related to those of the lower river but has a distinct accented quality. The men's noses & ears are pierced with ornaments made of sinew & hammered copper; the women only their ears. Unlike some of their coastal neighbors, they do not adorn themselves with tattoos, but some of the women & children wear red dye on their faces.

Their belongings are meager — spoons formed of animal horn, vessels made of birch bark & stitched with roots. They hunt primarily with spear, bow, & arrow. There is some sign, however, that they have not gone untouched by the outside world. One woman proudly used a bronze kettle to heat water for us on their fire. She said she had been given it by her mother, who met the Russians on the lower river many years ago. An elderly Midnoosky wore a tarnished silver cross with the ornate design of Russian Orthodoxy, but when asked to explain its significance, he remained silent.

One man treated me with clear disdain when he learned that I was the leader of our party. He did not stand to greet me, looked me up & down. Samuelson explained that it is because I carry a pack as large as those of my men. Among these nomadic Indians, it is a sign of status & wealth to carry nothing. Much of the work falls to the women, who travel with heavy loads on their backs even as they care for children and manage the half-wild dogs they use for packing.

As we visited one of the camps, a Mid-noosky woman appeared from the forest. Her back was bent beneath a pile of firewood, bound together with hide straps. It was only as she neared that I noticed an unexpected detail — atop this heap of sticks was a swaddled infant, strapped in like any other piece of wood, & contentedly asleep.

May 1

This afternoon as we traveled up the river, Samuelson stopped & nodded towards the far side.

— Look there, he said. — I do believe that's our missing company.

Coming down the steep bank was the Indian woman Nat'aaggi & the dog.

When the ice washed out of the Wolverine canyon, I was quite certain we had seen the last of the two of them. If by some unexpected mercy they survived, I thought it likely the woman would return to her own people on the coast.

— I've been watching them since morning, Samuelson said. — They've been making their way down through those alders, off the mountainside.

—You sure it's them? Tillman asked.

— Hard to believe, but it's so. That girl's got pluck, you've got to give her that, Samuelson said.

The woman & dog made their way towards us. They leapt several streams of the river. Soon only the largest channel of the Wolverine would separate them from us & they would be within speaking distance. As we watched, however, the woman & dog turned from our direction, began to travel upriver, parallel to our course.

— Where's she going? Doesn't she see us? Tillman asked.

Samuelson shrugged, said he guessed she wasn't rejoining our party after all.

Tillman shouted & waved at her, but she made no notice.

— What do you care where she has been or where she goes? Pruitt said. — She's not our concern.

While that may be true, I would be curious to learn how she survived her ordeal.

May 2

Nat'aaggi met up with us this morning. She came across the Wolverine in a small skin boat, called a baidarra as in Russian. The dog sat in the bow while she knelt, paddled from the stern. She navigated the swift, gray water expertly, avoided the large slabs of ice that continue to float down the river. Just as she reached us, she swung the bow upriver, sidled the boat alongside the shore. Samuelson stepped into the river to his knees so that he could grab the side of the boat as she neared.

— Well done, woman. Well done, he said.

It is unusual for Samuelson to express this kind of surprise & admiration. I believe it wasn't just her boating skills, but that we were seeing her again at all.

The dog leapt ashore first, nearly knocked Tillman to the ground in happy greeting. The dog then ran about our legs, rubbed its head against us, sniffed at the packs we had set down on the rocks.

Tillman offered his hand to assist Nat'aaggi getting ashore, but she did not notice or chose to ignore it, climbed from the baidarra on her own.

Where had she gotten the boat?

Samuelson said it belongs to a band of Midnooskies who camp on the other side.

— They wouldn't come with her. They're afraid of us. Haven't seen our kind before — 'red hairs on the face.' Seems that's what they call us. Red Beards.

None of us has shaved in many weeks, so we all look bushy. Amongst us, only Pruitt has true red hair, but compared to the near-black shade universal amongst the Indians & the mostly bare faces of their men, our appearances must be unexpected.

We dragged the boat away from the river's edge. Nat'aaggi gathered her belongings. She offered to carry some of our supplies in her own pack, but we explained that our stores are so diminished that we need no help.

As we once again began our day's walk, we asked Nat'aaggi about her journey. How had she survived when the ice washed out of the canyon? Where has she been these many days?

Samuelson translated as she described how she had left us in the night, hid until dawn, then walked downriver until she could reach the dog. She knew the ice would soon break. She continued until she came to a wall of the canyon where she thought there were footholds enough — narrow ledges, spindly spruce trees sprouted from the rocks — where she could perhaps climb out of the canyon. She did not believe the dog would be able to follow, however, so she retraced our entire way back down the canyon.

How did she travel over the weakening ice?

— She says she is lighter & can run faster than we giant Red Beards with clumsy feet, Samuelson said.

Below the canyon, she & the dog were able to climb the hillside where the Old Man had sent down the avalanche upon our camp. As she traveled up the valley, she heard the river ice come washing down in a great roar.

I asked how the travel went in the high country.

— Not easy, Colonel. The toughest land she's ever passed through she says.

According to Samuelson, she & the dog had to cross several fingers of a glacier, jumping over great crevasses. In other places, she had to navigate steep, rocky creeks. When she tried to climb higher into the mountains, she ran into snowstorms & ice fog.

Boyd spoke up then.

— She ever seen any sign of my wife up there? When she was traveling through that mountain fog, did she cross paths with a woman?

Nat'aaggi shook her head.

—Why did she come back up here with us

at all? Why didn't she just go home?

Pruitt's tone was blunt, even insolent, but I shared his interest.

— I do not want home, she said. — I want to see.

It was unexpected. Not just to hear her speak English, haltingly but with clarity all the same, but also the sentiment she expressed.

— If that is all she wants, she could go just as easily on her own, Pruitt said.

— If you believe that, you are a fool, Samuelson said.

An Indian traveling alone through another tribe's territory is likely to be taken as a slave. For a woman, the danger is all the more certain. Her best chance is to remain with us. It likely explains why she waited until she was in our sight before she approached the Midnooskies with the baidarra.

— What then of all her skills & bravery, of which you speak so highly? Pruitt asked Samuelson with some condescension.

— She'd last longer than most, Lieutenant, I'll tell you that.

May 3

We subsist on very little each day. When we are fortunate enough to come across game, we eat every morsel down to bone, so that we are like a plague of locusts on this lean land. Tillman shot a porcupine yesterday, for which we were most grateful.

& salt! Any one of us would trade our boots for a teaspoon of salt. One takes it for granted at the table back home. Now that we have been without it for many days, we thirst for it as if for water.

Boyd's health, remarkably, has improved. He remains thin, but seems to grow stronger from the walking. Lieut. Pruitt, on the other hand, is low in spirits, weak of energy.

I am hopeful to reach the mouth of the Trail River drainage in the next day or two.

With Tillman questioning & Samuelson translating, we learn more of Nat'aaggi's life. Her mother was a Midnoosky from the lower Wolverine River, her father a Russian–Eyak creole. They were both dead before she was old enough to talk, though she did not say if their deaths were related. She was taken in by her uncle's family, who treated her as a servant. Many times she ran away, often surviving for entire seasons on her own along the Wolverine River, though she had never come so far north as the canyon. Each time she was found by someone in the family, she was brought back, beaten, & misused.

— No selnaw, she said. I am no slave.

This explains why she fled with the stranger who came for her. She yet contends that he was an otter man, that it is his fur she wears across her shoulders.

It puzzles me that she can be so self-assured & clever, yet hold to such absurdity.

Sophie Forrester
Vancouver Barracks
April 26, 1885

Oh that I never saw that bird again! Such strange behavior, the way it pecked at my bedroom window.

I was preparing for bed last night and had drawn the curtains when I heard it thump onto the sill. And then came a flapping and beating against the window, an awful, startling noise! I could not imagine what it could be, so that I did not want to look out into the night. Silly nonsense, I told myself. I will not cower in my own house. I pulled back the curtains.

I wonder if its twisted leg contributed to its odd manner; perhaps it had difficulty clinging to the narrow sill, although that still does not explain why it would seek to perch outside my bedroom. When I first opened the curtains, the raven flapped its wings and squawked for some time, its bad leg held out to the side, but then it seemed to settle, only to commence pecking at the glass. I laughed at first, though with a touch of nerves. Such an unexpected, and almost amusing, way for a wild bird to behave. Why are you knocking at my window? I asked aloud. Do not think I am going to let you in.

Yet it continued with its steady and hard rapping, and the sound became more and more horrible. I feared the bird would crack the pane. I tried to shoo it away, sweeping my arms at the window. Could it be somehow trapped on the sill? I took my candle and leaned closer to the window to try to see out into the darkness. The raven stopped its knocking and cocked an eye toward me.

I then noticed something most peculiar. I could not make it out at first, and then thought it only a matter of light and reflection. However, as the bird remained still, its eye turned steadily toward me, there could be no doubt. A bird's eye ought to be flattened in shape, with a dark iris surrounded by a dark-gray sclera, and entirely unmoving in its socket. Yet this eye was round, with white sclera, and it rotated about in the socket. It looked nothing like a bird eye, but rather that of a mammal. More to the point, a human.

It causes me a shudder to think on it this morning. Last night, I shut the curtains and retreated to bed. What else could I do? It would be preposterous to wake Charlotte over such a trivial matter, and certainly I wasn't going to go out into the dark in my nightgown to chase the bird away, although more than anything I wanted it to leave. I pulled the covers up to my chin, the candle still lit at my bedside, and waited with dread to hear that horrid tapping again. Yet all was quiet.

I remained awake far into the night, but never did I hear another sound at the window. I confess it was with some apprehension that I went to open the curtains this morning, and I had to make myself do it in one quick motion. Such relief to see the bird had gone!

If only I were mistaken in my observations, but I cannot imagine how. I saw it clearly, and now even in the light of day I cannot chase it from my brain.

I have slept most of the day, but I have yet to recover from my sleepless night. I intended to sit outside for a while, but have been unable to move from this bed all afternoon. Even the broth and bread Charlotte kindly brought me at noon does not sit well with me. Though I do not complain to anyone, I am quite uncomfortable. My stomach cramps, and there is an acute pain in my left side, but I am not bleeding, and I hold on to that fact. If only I had experienced carrying a child before. Might I then know if a sensation is normal, or that I should be alarmed? Do I fret too much, or not enough?

April 28
This grief is intolerable.

April 30
Such pathetic instruments, this diary, this pen in my hand. What can they do but slice into the wound, flay and pin my sorrow to the page like a dissected organ? I would rather throw it all away, every page, every pitiful hope.

May 2
"You must be strong, Mrs Forrester. You've got to deliver this poor little thing, or it will be your death, too."

Mrs Connor, my unlikely angel of mercy, who came in the night and wiped at me with damp rags, offered small sips of water, while Charlotte cleaned the mess. I did not expect it, but Sarah Whithers blanched and ran from my bedside at the sight of my bloody legs. Not Mrs Connor. Five miscarriages, two stillborns, three live births. She should be decorated with more medals than her husband, she said, her pride matter-of-fact. She survived. She implies that I will do the same.

"You'll have all of the labor, Mrs Forrester, and none of the sweetness. No, it isn't fair. It's a grim business, but it's not up to us, is it? We must never forget it. Our lives are not our own."

Is there nothing we can do? I begged. Please tell me there is something? I'll do anything, but please save my child.

Oh Allen, I have lost our baby.

May 3
There was hope. I did not imagine it, and Dr Randall does not deny it even now. I might have been so fortunate as to bear the child to term.

"But fate came to visit," the doctor said.

Fate. With crooked leg and black feathers. If it had never appeared at my window, would you be with me, little one? Would I even now feel your movements below my ribs? Would I still be dreaming of the day that I would be allowed to hold you and kiss you?

I am a fool to court such thoughts. A hollow coincidence, surely, that the beak struck the glass just as your heart stopped beating.

Your forehead. Your heart. The small flutter of your life. You. You. You are gone, yet still I address you. Still I wait to feel you and know you.

Dr Randall says it is unlikely I will ever give birth to a living baby. If I try, he says, it could be the end of me. My womb, so ill-formed for motherhood, could rupture. I could bleed to death.

May 5

I despise my own propriety. It keeps me to this bed, docile and quiet, hair brushed and pinned, bed clothes smoothed neatly over my lap. I mark the days. I eat. I breathe. I say thank you and please and feign sleep. Yet it is all a lie. In my heart I am something else altogether. I am burning with grief. I should be out in the rain, barefooted and wild. I should roar and claw at the sky. I should rip open my gown and bare my breasts and bare my pain and plead and rage.

It is a selfish daydream. Who am I to claim such boundless sorrow? This heartache, acute and true as it may be, is slight compared to all of this world. Five miscarriages, two stillborns, three live births, and Mrs Connor is one of our fortunate. She is not disemboweled in the snow. Her hands have committed no atrocities. She believes in God.

It is remarkable how we go on. All that we come to know and witness and endure, yet our hearts keep beating, our faith persists.

Lieut. Col. Allen Forrester
May 5, 1885

I do not know whether to count it as bad luck or good that we cross paths again with the Old Man.

Yesterday, we continued to walk upriver even after the sun went behind the mountains. We aimed for a small thicket of spruce we could see upriver. I am certain we must be near the valley of the powerful tyone. Also, Nat'aaggi spotted tebay on a nearby mountain. Samuelson believes the animals are less than a day's hike away. We plan to set snares for rabbits, then search for the village while others go after the tebay. The spruce forest will provide firewood & more shelter than the open riverbed.

As darkness neared, Boyd was the first to spy firelight in the forest. We discussed whether we should avoid the strangers or seek them out with hopes of finding food.

— Nat'aaggi says we should be careful.

When we passed through the canyon, we came into a new land.

Did she refer to a new countryside, or a new tribe of Indians?

— More than that. She says we walk towards the land of the dead. From here on, nothing follows white man's rules. The old stories live. This is where her otter husband came from.

It seems that, out of ignorance, these people attach some superstition to the upper stretches of the Wolverine River. Such fearful beliefs mean little to me. More urgently, we are in need of food, so I decided we would seek out the campfire.

Darkness came on as we entered the forest. There was the scent of cooking meat.

— Now that's something worth sniffing out, Samuelson said.

— It could be goose they're roasting. Or something far worse, Tillman suggested. — These here aren't any blanket Indians. Don't forget about those bones? Why would there be children's bones, gnawed and scattered about like that?

None of us had an answer.

When we reached the camp, we found no sign of tent or hovel, only a large campfire positioned in a clearing surrounded by tall spruce trees.

I called ahead a greeting.

Our eyes adjusted to the light & shadow.

We could see there was a solitary person crouched beside the fire. A slab of meat was speared through by a stick, held close to the red coals.

As we stepped into the clearing, the figure turned up his head, pushed back his hat. The firelight lit up the bronze face, black shadows in the deep lines, so that it looked like a mask carved with a sharp blade.

Tillman cursed. After all his shenanigans, I was no more pleased to see the Old Man. How is it that he, elderly & with a lame leg, could have traveled faster than us up the river valley without our notice?

He beckoned us towards the fire.

— First, ask him what kind of meat he's got cooking there, Tillman said.

— He says we should taste it, tell him what we think it is, Samuelson said. — Seems he cooked it just for us. Been waiting for us to come along.

— No God d——d way I trust that devil! Tillman said.

I had to agree. We remained at the edge of the firelight.

Samuelson, however, did not hesitate. He strode towards the Old Man, unsheathed his knife, knelt at the fire, sliced off a hunk of meat, bit into it.

— Some fine mutton here, gentlemen. Flank meat off a tebay. I wouldn't pass this up if I were you.

It was then I realized Nat'aaggi was no longer with us. I was sure she had followed us into the trees.

Tillman asked how can we trust the Old Man when he has tried to kill us more times than not.

— Not to worry. He says he's not so hungry as he used to be, Samuelson said & roared with laughter.

It was not a comforting answer, yet our hunger was greater than our mistrust.

We joined Samuelson at the fire. He cut away pieces of the meat, handed them to each of us. The meat fell apart in my mouth, smoky, warm, roasted to a crust on the outside, rare & juicy inside. I don't know that anything has ever tasted so good.

The other men were similarly ravenous. We took every portion handed us. When the meat was gone, I apologized to the Old Man for our greed, explained that for many days we had eaten only flour paste & strands of rabbit meat.

The Old Man waved off my words, pointed to a nearby tree. In the darkness I could just make out two shoulders & a rib cage hanging from a branch.

— He says he's got plenty to share.

We consumed most of a side of sheep tonight. We ate until our stomachs were distended. Roasted more meat. Sprawled by the fire in a stupor. The Old Man sat on his heels, watched us.

I asked how he arrived here.

He knew my words because he responded without Samuelson's translation, but he spoke in a native tongue I could not make out.

— He says the same as us. He walked.

How did he outpace us?

— He doesn't carry a pack full of metal & tools. Nightfall doesn't stop him. He follows game trails, because the animals know the easiest way.

It unnerved me to imagine the Old Man creeping past us in the dark of the canyon while we slept.

Why does he follow us this way?

— He says you are wrong. We follow him.

The Old Man nodded towards the forest.

— He wants the girl to come out of hiding so she can eat something.

I called to Nat'aaggi, then whistled for Boyo. The dog ran into the camp first, the woman followed more cautiously.

The Old Man threw a leg bone to the dog, then held up a piece of roasted meat to the woman. She did not move towards it.

— It's all right, Tillman said. — It's just tebay. Tebay.

She knew what kind of meat it was. Something else made her distrustful.

Now we are all well fed, even the dog with its bone by the fire. The men have taken out their sleeping bags, retreated under nearby spruce boughs that will keep off rain & snow.

As grateful as I am for the Old Man's apparent generosity, still I question his intentions. I take first watch. As I write here in this journal, he eyes me from under his black hat.

An oddity, to be sure. Two combs so similar that I cannot deny they are exact replicas of each other. How would the Old Man come in possession of it? Why offer it to me in trade?

The scoundrel crept through the dark, sat cross-legged beside me in the firelight, leaned into me as if we were old comrades. By the firelight, he reached inside his coat for a small sack made of a peculiar, blackish hide. As he opened it, I recognized its form — the sack was sewn from the dried & leathery webbed foot of a large waterfowl, with the toe joints & black nails still intact. He opened the sack, turned away slightly as if shielding a secret. He first pulled out an enamel button, then a few coins, the tooth of some beast, an amber agate, until he came up with what he sought. He closed his hand around it, reached towards the dull glow of the campfire, then, like a conjuror, revealed the prize. A silver hair comb. I took it from him. The same size, shape, the same fern frond engravings. If it weren't for the missing teeth, the tarnish &

gouging as if it had been left out in the weather for many seasons, I could almost swear it is Sophie's.

I gave it back. What use could I have for it?

— He wants to trade you for chocolate, Samuelson said from beneath a tree. I had thought him asleep, his fur cap pulled down over his eyes.

I said there is no chocolate left.

— He says Tillman still has some in his pack.

In its ruined state, what would I want with the comb? Tillman is annoyed to give up his last ration of chocolate — he saved it to share with us in desperate times. Though I think he is most angry that the Old Man had snooped in his pack.

I cannot think why I agreed to the trade. Only that it bothered me, letting the mischief-maker keep the comb in his shaman's pouch.

It's not only chocolate he is after. The Old Man would not leave Nat'aaggi be — he ran his fingers down her hair, whispered in her ear, stroked the otter fur she wears across her shoulders. She did her best to ignore him.

— Why does he pester her so? Tillman asked.

Samuelson says the Old Man is a lecher.

— From what I hear tell, he's got wives scattered thither & yon. Seems he'd like another, at least for tonight.

Tillman moved to box the Old Man. I advised him to let the girl settle her own affairs.

— Nattie doesn't want anything to do with him, he said.

— You're so sure of a woman's heart. Now there's territory I have never been able to navigate, Samuelson said.

May 6

Tillman was correct. During the night, Nat'aaggi remained near the campfire without sleeping — she no more trusts the Old Man than any of us. He whispered at her, poked at her. Though I did not know the words, I could guess their meaning. Eventually, his wooing efforts frustrated, he tried to manhandle her away from the fire & into the darkness. This was too much. I stood to intervene, but Nat'aaggi had already wrestled free. She would not have it. She drew her blade.

That's more than enough, I advised the Old Man.

He laughed, said something. I asked him to repeat himself in English, now that I am certain he knows our language. He refused. I asked again with more force.

— For Christ's sake, can't a man get any shut-eye around here, Samuelson grumbled.

— He says he will never get his fill.

The Old Man gave a last yank at Nat'aaggi's

hair, then retreated before I could respond.

This morning he is gone. He did not kidnap Nat'aaggi in the night, but he did take the last of the tebay meat with him. Tillman, who had the early morning watch, was the only one to notice him slip away before dawn. He says the Old Man left without fanfare, walked from the campfire presumably to relieve himself but did not return. Tillman did not notice the meat gone until daylight.

This late morning we reached what I believe is the Trail River. We split into two parties. Nat'aaggi, Samuelson, & Boyd will remain behind to hunt the nearby peaks for tebay. Amongst us, they have best odds at getting meat. The men & I go east up the Trail River in search of the village & its tyone. Tillman says he has learned enough of the Midnoosky tongue to make do as translator.

I have ordered Pruitt to leave behind camera, tripod, & all but the most necessary of instruments. We have also cached a small amount of tea, lard, & other provisions for when we return. We set out with a few cups of flour & the unappetizing salmon we traded from the Indians. From the Indians' vague direction, we believe the village is about 10 miles upriver, well before the river branches into two forks. The Old Man denied the village exists at all, though I give him no credence.

If their hunt is successful, or if they do not hear from us for more than a week, Samuelson says they will seek us out on the Trail River. If we do not find each other before, we will meet here at the juncture of the two rivers within the month.

Ice is rapidly disappearing. Small patches of green grass emerge along the riverbank.

May 7
No sign of the village yet. Travel difficult, as the valley is snarled with alder, deadfall trees. We are hungry. Soles fall from our rotting boots. We try to mend them with strips of hide, without success.

May 8
All of us quite ill. Out of desperation, ate the salmon yesterday afternoon. Quickly doubled us over with cramps, vomiting. Pruitt so weak, we must at times support him as he walks.

A hardship to travel on, but the village is our best hope.

ALASKA

COFFEE

AT HOME.

It will pay you well to keep a small coffee-mill in your kitchen and grind your coffee just as you use it—one mess at a time. Coffee should not be ground until the coffee-pot is ready to receive it. Coffee will lose more of its strength and aroma in one hour after being ground than in six months before being ground. So long as Ariosa remains in the whole berry, our glazing, composed of choice eggs and pure confectioners' A sugar, closes the pores of the coffee, and thereby all the original strength and aroma are retained. Ariosa Coffee has, during 25 years, set the standard for all other roasted coffees. So true is this, that other manufacturers in recommending their goods, have known no higher praise than to say: "It's just as good as Arbuckles'."

ARBUCKLE BROS.,

NEW YORK CITY.

ALASKA.

THE Russian navigators, Chirikoff and Bering, were the first Europeans to see the Alaskan shore, reaching the lone northland at different points in 1741. These intrepid and ill-fated explorers were followed by the Siberian fur-hunters. In 1799 the Emperor Paul of Russia granted a twenty-year Charter to the Russian-American Company, whose iron-willed manager, Baranoff, conquered the country as far as Sitka, which was founded in 1801, established a colony in California, and opened trade with China, Honolulu and the Spanish colonies. Under the strong influence of Seward and Sumner, the United States bought Alaska in 1867 for $7,200,000 in gold. It has been said that the gold mines of Alaska will produce enough treasure to pay the national debt. These rich deposits were first discovered in 1877 at Silver Bay, near Sitka. In 1880 Joseph Jumeau, a French-Canadian miner, a nephew of the founder of Milwaukee, found free gold in great quantities in the mountain-girt Silver Bow Basin. Over $1,000,000 in dust has since been washed out of these places. The fisheries are of enormous value, and the Government has received from the seal islands a sum equal to that which was paid for the Territory. Four million seals visit the Pribiloff Isles every summer, and up to a recent date the number was not decreasing, owing to the prohibition of killing females. Grave difficulties arose between the United States and Great Britain in 1889 by reason of the American revenue cutters seizing Canadian seal-vessels in these waters.

ILLUSTRATIONS.

Alaskans, Indian Village in Background; Granville Channel, En Route to Alaska; Haunts of the Sea Lion.

■ ■ ■ ■

PART THREE

ALASKA INDIAN INFANT SLING.
ALLEN FORRESTER COLLECTION.
WOLVERINE RIVER INDIANS, CIRCA 1885.

■ ■ ■ ■

Strap of caribou hide, 44 inches long by 6 inches wide, with sinew threading, decorated with a pattern of flattened porcupine quills. Quills dyed with ochre. Used to secure infant to mother's back.

Perkins Island, Alaska
9 November, 1794

Your Grace, Dmitry,

Most Merciful Archbishop and Father.

Blessed be the Father of compassion, God Almighty, who through Divine Providence protects us from our own weaknesses and failings.

I, humble servant, have the honor of reporting that we have conducted 100 baptisms in the past seven days. Since our arrival last autumn, we have welcomed nearly 5,000 natives to the Christian faith. It is still difficult to know how much they understand about their duties before God, but they come in zeal and so we baptize them and instruct them as best we can.

Although their nature is rough, wild, and libidinous, these natives are entirely capable of Redemption. They seem to come naturally to the concept of Christian Charity. Without hesitation they will share whatever food or shelter in their possession, and miserliness is considered greatest amongst sins. They are also as modest in their dress as any good Russian. The women wear simple dresses of bird skins. In cooler weather, they dress in the furs of otter and beaver.

As they come to understand what the

Creator requires of them, we believe they will continue to abandon their shameful dances, polygamy, and worship of shamans.

Yet there are those who do not embrace the truth. Even as the piety of the people increases in the eyes of the Creator, so still is there superstition and partnership with Evil.

There is a sorcerer among them who retains the people's reverence even as they profess faith in God. This aged man mocks civilization by wearing along with his shaman's costume some kind of gentleman's hat that he says he obtained in trade with Shelikhov's men.

This sorcerer is doing much to disrupt our endeavor. He claims to have caused the illness and fever in Father Pavel, and more troublesome, the people believe it is so. He benefits from coincidence. Two weeks ago he claimed that a certain native woman with a black tumor would die before the day ended. Her family begged him to help, but he said he would not. She died at sundown.

Some of the elder natives say that in years past this sorcerer has caused both the sun and moon to disappear, and that his leg is lame because he was shot with an arrow as he flew from tree to tree. They believe he can give and take away the breath of life. He tells them where best they can hunt their animals, and in times of starvation, they say he has called the wild creatures within reach of their spears. They also say he correctly predicted our arrival at Perkins Island.

Before a crowd of devoted Christian natives, I called out this man. I explained that it is only through God that his people may seek Truth and Life after death, that the ways of the Devil can result only in eternal suffering. After listening to my sermon, he repented and firmly promised to halt his practices.

At 5 o'clock that evening, I served Vespers and Matins. At 9 o'clock, we were informed that the sorcerer was atop the log cupola of our modest chapel. A group of native men stood outside and said they had watched the sorcerer fly to his location. It was dark and difficult to see, but I am horrified to report that indeed I saw a black shape atop our blessed chapel.

To please us, the people say they no longer heed this sorcerer. However, we know they continue to look to him for guidance, healing, and Dark Arts.

Eminent Master, I pray that our Creator's benevolence will flow through your heart and bless me with words of comfort, knowledge, and instruction. In your fatherly kindness, inform us as to how best we can continue to bring the Wisdom and the Word of God to this wild land. Forgive me, forgive me, forgive me.

Your humble and devoted servant,
Hierodeacon Joseph

Dear Mr. Forrester,

I had to share this letter with you. I tracked it down in a book about the Orthodox Church's presence in Alaska, and it includes firsthand narratives — diaries and letters translated from Russian — of missionaries who came to Alaska in the 1700s. I read the book several years ago, and thought of it as I was going through your papers. I remembered that there was a reference to Perkins Island.

I have to say, it gave me chills when I read it this time. Nearly a hundred years before the Colonel. Weird.

I'm making good progress on transcribing the diaries, even though I've been able to spare only a few hours here and there. I was out last week. The caribou were just north of Alpine, so I went hunting with our neighbors. But now I'm back, and our freezer is full, so I don't have any plans to be gone for a while. The rest of the winter here at the museum it should be quiet with the tourists gone, so I'll be able to put more time into transcribing. I've resisted bringing it home to work on in the evenings, because Isaac hates it when I spread my papers all over the house. I guess I'm a bit like your sister in that way. And, by the way, I am a big fan of yellow stickies, too.

Since you mentioned your curiosity about Alaska, I'll try to give you a sense of "downtown" Alpine. It's a strip of highway that parallels the Wolverine River. There's a church, a gas station, our museum (which is an old log church that has been renovated), the public library, the junkyard, the post office (which also doubles as a convenience store), and two bars. The main social events are the wakes at one of the bars when one of the old-timers passes away and the flu shot clinics at the library each fall.

There's really not much to it, but somehow I missed it when I was away at college in Seattle. It was just small things — being able to light a campfire in my own backyard and stand around it with friends and neighbors. The cold air off the glacier. Ice skating on the lake in the dark of winter. The northern lights. The mountains. Knowing everyone at the post office. There is the feeling here that civilization is still just a speck, and it makes me feel small in a good way. Seattle made me feel small in a bad way, if that makes any sense.

I've been back home for about five years. It makes my mom happy. She likes to cook dinner for us. We had caribou roast and mashed potatoes last night.

By the way, please call me Josh. Whenever I see "Mr. Sloan," I think I've opened someone else's mail by accident.

All best,
Josh

Dear Josh,

Thanks for taking the time to describe Alpine for me. I've often thought about the boom that came to that area after the Colonel's expedition and the changes it must have brought. I always had it in my mind that Alpine must be a good-sized town. Is there any mining going on around there anymore?

Good on you, getting your meat in for the winter. I'd be curious to taste caribou. I did a fair amount of deer and elk hunting when my knees were still up to it, but it's a disappearing way of life I'm afraid. Most of these namby-pambies down here wouldn't know how to wring a rooster's neck if their lives depended on it. Doesn't matter which side of the fence you look, you can't squeeze a drop of common sense out of the whole bunch. I've canceled my subscriptions to most of the magazines, and I can't stand to watch television anymore. I'm starting to think it's just as well that I won't be around much longer. I don't have much desire to see where these idiots take us.

You'll find a check enclosed, just a small donation to help with the work you're doing there. I wasn't thinking when I sent you everything that in order to preserve it and make use of it, it would require some effort on your end. I only wanted to find a good home for it all. I hope the money helps some, and have no qualms about taking it.

Last of all, let me say, your letters are the most interesting correspondence I've received in some time. It is "weird" indeed that it seems the Colonel's nemesis made an appearance 100 years prior. Maybe it's coincidence — two Alaskan natives in history with similar peculiarities. Or maybe one was mimicking the other. But I suspect it might not be as simple as all that. As I've said, those papers have long caused me to question how I understand the world. Now with you going through the papers, and sharing your own background and knowledge with me, I've got even more to think about.

I won't lie. I've had some lonely years since I retired from the highway department. I used to go down to the cafe some days to catch up with the guys I used to work with, but they mostly want to gripe about how the new hires don't know how to plow the roads, or tell me about their grandkids or their golf scores, which is all fine and good but not of much interest to me.

When I think on the Colonel and my great-aunt, I can't help but wonder what I could have been doing all these years.

My life hasn't amounted to a whole hell of a lot. It's not a very uplifting thought to sit alone with all day.

But then one of your letters comes along, and I've got something interesting to put my mind to. I used to check the mail every week or so, because it was nothing but bills, catalogs, and advertisements. Foolish as it sounds, I go out every day now, and sometimes as soon as I see the mail carrier pull up to the box. Yesterday, darned if she didn't say, "Any more letters from Alaska?"

Sincerely,
Walt

Foetal Pulsation — By far the most important of all the signs of pregnancy, is that which is associated with the name of Mayor, of Geneva, who was the first to discover that the heart of the foetus could be heard beating through the abdominal and uterine walls. . . . These pulsations are much more frequent than those of the mother and are, like them, distinctly double.

— From *A System of Midwifery Including the Diseases of Pregnancy and the Puerperal State,* William Leishman, 1873

Lieut. Col. Allen Forrester
Trail River

The strange baby will not stop its cries. We wander through the forest but find no sign of a village. For many hours we were lost in thick brush, could not find our way back to the river.

It will not leave me. That rooty flesh, that umbilicus string of hideous origins. Clear fluid bubbling up from the ground. Clotted blood & moss one and the same. Can it be true? At times I no longer know — am I awake or dreaming?

Maybe we should leave the infant where it was found, like an orphaned fawn. Yet it would starve, freeze, suffer greatly. This creature has no mother to come for it. — Kill it, Pruitt said. — What difference is it?

He'd seen it himself, he raved. White babies dead by wasting disease. Indian babies slaughtered like calves by white men. He once watched a half-dead Sioux woman give birth in mountain snow, only to be forced by his fellow soldiers to . . . I shouted at him to stop. He has a blackness about him that could sink a man.

Tillman carries the infant. In his coat, swaddled against his chest. He would not leave it, said he'd sooner kill a weasel like Pruitt than an innocent child, weirdly born as this one is.

What could I have done? Ignore the muffled cries? Walk from the forest as if I hadn't heard?

I alone saw them. Four wolves. At a smooth trot along the far side of the river. Silent. Between the trees like shadows. All gray. But the last. It was black. None looked in our direction. Before I could alert the others, they were gone.

The weather is mild, yet does us no good. The illness caused by the rancid salmon is grim. We are all of us weak, at times confused. We need rest, food, but will have neither until we find aid.

We thought we heard voices. Followed the sound, fired our rifles, but heard no more. Our futile stumbling through the woods ended at a cliff face.

Only meal today came when we scraped the last moldy lumps of flour from a sack, mixed into paste with river water.

The child yet lives, though its cries grow weaker. It sucks some of the paste from the flour sack, but will perish soon without food. As will we all.

Godsend! Pruitt shot two rabbits, the first we've seen since we began travel up the Trail River. It revives us greatly. We ate the meat raw, still warm with life. It is gruesome indeed, but we dripped rabbit blood into the baby's mouth, so as to give it some small nourishment. It took to it well, sucked the blood from Tillman's finger. It is, however, a short remedy.

Pruitt argues to turn back, rejoin the others at the Wolverine. Most likely they killed tebay, as we heard gunshots yesterday. But we are too near starvation to make the journey. Our best hope is to find the village. Increasing signs of the Midnooskies — tracks along the river, smell of wood smoke.

May ?

I have much to write, but lack the strength. They feed us. We eat. We sleep. We eat again. Pruitt is most ill, so is fed with a wooden spoon.

I am unsure of the date. The past days are dim. Our health returns, to Tillman most quickly. He is already up & about. I try to regain my legs but remain weak.

I cannot bring myself to write of the found infant.

May 12, 1885
I have done my best to count backwards the days, determine a correct date. I believe I am within a day or two.

Now that we recover, I can at last record how we came to this village.

Though advised to the contrary, we reached the fork of the Trail River without seeing any sign of the village. Tillman, however, said he spied campfire smoke up the south fork of the river, so our direction was chosen.

We staggered along the shore of the river, too feeble to make real progress, too muddle-brained to search the nearby forest. My scope was reduced to the ground directly in front of me as I aimed with much difficulty to step over the boulders. We did not speak, although now & then Tillman uttered a word to the baby in his coat.

Pruitt stopped walking, held up a hand. He had heard something.

Voices to the north. Pruitt & I fired several rounds. Samuelson would have advised more, but I loathed to waste the ammunition that serves as our primary currency. The Midnooskies answered us better; a half dozen shots we heard, although from a great distance away. We decided to stay put in hopes the Indians would seek us out. After some time, we shot two more rounds. An hour or so later, two Midnoosky scouts found us at the river.

Both men were dressed in skin tunics & leggings with very little adornment. One held a small-bore shotgun. Both carried birch bows & quivers of arrows upon their backs. When they spoke, I looked to Tillman for translation.

— I can't understand a word they're saying, he said.

His voice stirred the baby in his coat, which let out a small whimper. The Indians looked to each other in surprise. The shorter one approached, poked an arrow at the bundle.

Tillman forcefully yanked the arrow away. Their response was quick. The taller Midnoosky brought up his shotgun, aimed it at Tillman's head. Pruitt moved for his carbine. I put a hand to his arm. For a tense moment, it seemed we were in for a row. Tillman, however, came to his senses. He slowly handed the arrow back to its owner, fletching first, then leaned forwards to show the top of the infant's head, its small, scrunched face.

Surely it was not what the Indians were expecting to find tucked in the coat of a white soldier. They asked us questions but we could not make out the words.

The one with the shotgun gestured for us to follow them. We could only hope the village was both friendly & near.

The journey was nearly beyond our strength. The Midnooskies led us from river shore to the north, first through shaded woods where the snow has yet to melt, then to the valley wall. The slope that rose before us was so steep as to not allow for anything to grow but shrubs & stunted aspen. Dirt & boulders crumbled down the hillside. It was a climb that in our state would take hours.

— I fear I am too weak for this, Pruitt said.

I ordered him to empty his pack. Tillman & I divided the contents between us. Tillman was disgusted to find several books in the bottom of his pack, including one of poetry.

—You've lugged this up half the country?

Tillman tossed them to the ground. Pruitt objected. I was sorry to do it, but I agreed it made no sense to haul such luxuries. I wrapped the books in a piece of oilcloth and lodged them in a tree branch to protect them from the elements. Pruitt conjectured he might retrieve them at some point, but it seems unlikely.

We tried to assist Pruitt in the climb, but ourselves were too feeble. Tillman fought to keep his balance, pulled backwards by his pack, forwards by the baby at his chest.

While the taller of the Midnooskies was impatient, traveled far ahead, the other was more considerate of our state. He climbed back down to us, slung one of Pruitt's arms over his shoulder, nearly carried him up the hill.

Atop the plateau, the Indians pointed down into the next valley where we could see the huts of their village.

We had chosen the wrong fork of the river.

It took the rest of the afternoon to make it to the village. When we arrived, we were greeted by an Indian, not much more than a boy, who stood in front of the largest of the houses. I introduced myself, then asked if I could meet with the chief.

I gestured towards the skin-covered hut, hoping he would understand.

— Tyone? I asked.

He looked at me in a frowning manner, as if I had mildly amused or annoyed him. He pointed at himself.

I had expected an elderly, hardened man. This one is young, barely a man. His expressions are neutral, but if anything he has a certain mild reserve. There is something in his manner that suggests he is disappointed by our appearance as well. No doubt word of our approach preceded us. Perhaps he imagined something more fierce than the gaunt, unkempt soldiers before him, baby in tow.

We were led into the main hut. Two Indians carried Pruitt, laid him down on one of the benches of spruce poles. In the center of the room, a giant kettle sat in the flames. We collapsed inside, ate all that was brought to us by the Indian women. There was moose meat that came boiled from the kettle, a mush of dried berries fried in animal fat, a wild root akin to parsnip that had been roasted in the flames. They also insisted we eat a broth of rabbit intestines.

Such have been our past two days. We wake only long enough to eat, nurse our battered feet, then sleep again. This is the first moment I have felt well enough to sit up to write for long. A woman cares for Pruitt, propping him up to eat & drink.

May 13

The world comes into sharper focus as my strength returns. All day, all night, all day again I have mostly slept on this bed of hides, but a few times today I have stuck my head out of the skin hut. The sunlight stuns the eyes, has a new heat to it I have not experienced before on this journey.

I cannot imagine how much we have eaten these past days. Tillman is recovered enough to at last notice what they feed us.

— They throw the guts into the pot! he observed.

It is true, the Midnooskies eat every part of an animal — bones, internal organs, skin, & tendons. The varied contents of the cook pot are heated just enough to lend some warmth to the broth, but not enough to leave the meat anything but raw.

I pointed out that we have eaten such meals for several days, suffered no ill from it.

— I can't stomach it any longer, Tillman said.

When next the woman brought him a bowl of the half-raw entrails, he objected.

— I would take it gladly if I were you.

— I'd prefer sirloin, & well done at that.

He has not, however, complained since.

I am not bothered by the undercooked food, yet I feel the lack of salt keenly.

As told by the Indians we had encountered along the river, this is a wealthy village. Though I rarely catch sight of them, the children appear nourished. The adults are clothed in well-sewn skins & furs. They have traded with the coastal Indians for a few white man luxuries — the giant kettle, rifles & powder.

Despite his youth & gentle manner, the ty-one also has an alert vigor to him. It seems he has at least three wives as well as a number of slaves. He is clearly the leader of these people. Even elderly men obey his commands.

I have much to ask him. When will the salmon come? What is our best route through the mountains? Will he guide us? Tillman's translation skills have proven nearly useless. He says they speak a different dialect, so that he can only pick up a few words. We communicate mostly with gestures.

As generous as the tyone has been, I suspect it is in part a show of power. We continue to size each other up, endeavor to understand the other's motivation.

Whether it be for the business man looking for investments, the invalid in search of health, the tourist seeking pleasure or sightseeing, or the sportsman looking for big game, no better opportunity offers than this trip through Southern Alaska.

— From *A Guide for Alaska: Miners, Settlers and Tourists,* 1902

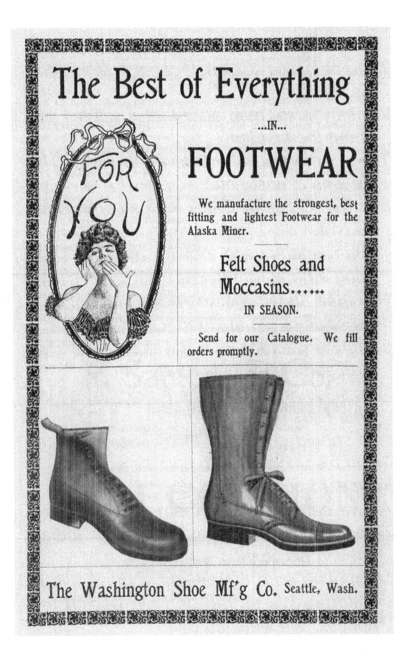

When I First Saw White Men at Trail River

As told to Mary Eaken by her grandmother, transcribed and edited in 1948.

The one called "Colonel" came first. He and
his soldiers.

We saw white men after that. I will tell you
about the first time.

They came from the Wolverine River. The
ice was almost gone.

Man Who Flies on Black Wings came to tell
us first.

"Some soldiers are looking for you. They
bring a baby with them."

He came ahead with the news first.

"The soldiers are at Otters Den Creek."

Ceeth Hwya didn't think it was so. That shaman sometimes puts a hex on us.

"The soldiers will come here next," said Man
Who Flies on Black Wings.

"We should go to see them." So my father
and his uncle went to find the soldiers.

We heard gunshots.

As we came, we saw them. They had red
beards. One of them carried an Indian
baby in his coat.

My mother said they might want to kill us
children. We all ran and hid behind the
houses. We watched them.

They were having a hard time. They were
sick and hungry. They didn't understand

any words.

Ceeth Hwya told his wives to bring them food.

We saw lots of white people later after that. That was the first time.

Lieut. Col. Allen Forrester
May 14, 1885

I have emerged from the hut, sit outside its door on a stump to write. Dawn came some time ago, but just now I watched the sun clear the tall mountaintop to the east. The men of the village have left on a hunt, Tillman with them. Women & children move among the trees at their chores & play. The tyone has assigned one of his men to stand guard. It seems we are not entirely trusted. Pruitt is still abed. His listlessness does not subside.

These Indians have chosen their site well. The village is on a south-facing slope, looking down on the north fork of the Trail River. A fast, clear creek runs out of the mountains, past the camp. To the north rise the tallest mountains I have ever seen, colossal wedges of snow & ice with ribbons of glaciers. At least one of the peaks appears volcanic, sending up a vapor throughout the day.

Here in the valley, much of the snow has

melted except on the north faces & shaded corners. Along the river is a haze of green through the aspen & cottonwoods — leaf buds. Winter leaves us.

I heard the baby somewhere in the camp. Its cry is stronger. How does it fare, I asked Tillman.

— Healthy as an ox.

He says an Indian with a toddler of her own has taken the strange child to breast. With milk in its belly, it grows stronger. For that I am glad. Yet it is a startling thought — a woman nursing the creature.

How do I write of the infant? I have avoided it until now, the memory of its discovery, of crawling beneath the spruce tree, unsheathing my knife.

I had gone in search of firewood. We needed to dry our clothes & warm ourselves but were too weak to chop logs, so I looked for deadfall. It was not yet night. I wish now that it had been. I would have preferred darkness to seeing that unwholesome birth.

I came to a fallen tree with kindle-dry branches that I could break off with ease. As I worked, I heard the men nearby, lighting the fire, gathering other wood.

The cries were muffled so at first I did not distinguish them. It was only when I stopped breaking branches that I took notice. Faint but distinct in the quiet of the river valley, it was the sound of a small creature choked & struggling.

I thought perhaps a rabbit was caught in an Indian snare, or a moose calf injured by wolves.

The sound did not move, but varied in intensity so that at times it was a rhythmic wail, at others a stifled mewl.

I called to the men, asked if they heard the cry — They did not. I said I would investigate.

— Shouldn't I come with you? Tillman asked.

It wasn't far, I believed. I had my pistol so could fire a shot if I required assistance.

The cries led me away from the river, first through sparse cottonwood trees, so that I could still see the river & smoke of our fire, then to the dense band of alders that grows along the bank. I looked for another way around but saw no break, so I entered their shadowy tangle. I had to duck, shoulder my way through, until I emerged at the edge of a murky slough that again offered no easy way around. I thought then of turning back, but the cries continued, smothered, quickened. It was a foolish risk in my weakened condition, but I sloshed through the icy water to my waist.

When I reached the far side, the sound was still muffled, but closer. I walked among the trees, taking a step or two, stopping to listen, then a few more steps.

I was led to the largest of the spruces, a majestic, towering tree, with lower boughs that fanned broadly to the ground. The cries came from the base. I tried to peer through the branches, but could see nothing. In order to enter the low canopy, I had to crawl. The ground was wet & spongy beneath my hands & knees, squelched as if saturated. It struck me as odd, as usually such sheltered ground beneath an evergreen is entirely dry.

It was then that I saw — where the tree trunk met the earth, the largest of the roots seemed to writhe & squirm, like a fat snake that has swallowed a living animal whole. The cry came again, sharper. I crawled closer.

There in the root I spied a small hole, a teardrop rip the size of my hand. I poked a finger into the opening. To my horror, I felt a tiny mouth, opening, closing, crying out. I reached into the root with both hands, tried to rip the opening wider with my fingers, but the skin, the bark, whatever in God's name that it was, was too tough & thick. I took out my knife, then saw the blood on my hands & pants. Blood! It was bubbling up through the moss & needles all around me.

I feared what my knife would release into the world. Yet I also feared cutting the wailing thing. What could I do? I inserted my knife into the opening, sliced upwards sharply.

It was much like the birth of a foal, slick &

bloody & a frightful mess. As I pulled it free of the root, clear fluid gushed from the opening. Trailing from the infant's belly was a long umbilical string, blue tinged, throbbing with life. I held the baby with one hand, tugged the cord with the other. As the umbilicus continued to snake out of the ground, I began to dread what I would find at the other end. Gradually the cord turned rough & coarse & coated in dirt. I had pulled several feet when it stopped fast. Here at the end the umbilicus was no longer malleable & fleshy. It was a tree root!

How did I manage? I cannot say. I was sick with it, the smell of warm blood in the moss, the infant slippery & wailing in my hand. As close to the child's belly as I dared, I slashed the umbilicus with my knife. I cradled the thing in my arms to protect it as I crawled out from under the tree.

Numb with disbelief, I found my way back through slough & alders.

I must have been a sight. Slathered in blood. An infant in my arms. The men were alarmed. — What happened in the woods? Where's the mother?

I tried my best to tell them. They could not comprehend. Perhaps they thought my mind was unsound. I'll take you to the place, I said, so you can see for yourself. Pruitt was too weak, Tillman too revolted by it all.

Yet he was the one, the sergeant, who took

the baby from me, wiped it down with wet leaves, took off his own undershirt to wrap around its trembling little body. He dabbed the afterbirth away from its eyes & nose. The newborn howled.

Its hair is dark, its skin the warm bronze of the Indians. Yet the infant's eyes set it apart. They are not the near-black brown of the Midnooskies, but instead a gold-speckled green.

As naked, warm, vulnerable as it seems, can it be human? Born from the earth like a Greek monster?

We were in precarious condition ourselves. It seemed an impossible task, to care for an infant. Without Tillman, I do not know what would have come of the child. I likely would have left it.

The Midnooskies do not seem bothered by my tale. With few words & gestures, I have tried to tell them of the tree, the root, the blood. Perhaps they do not understand.

One of the men seems to serve as a kind of traveling priest among the Midnooskies. While most of the Indians keep their hair neatly cropped & brushed with bone comb, this man's hair hangs in a three-foot tangle down his back. He is adorned with many necklaces, teeth, & claws, so that he makes a rattling noise as he walks. Equally disconcerting is his lazy eye that rolls upwards so that it is difficult to know where he is looking.

When this shaman overheard my story of the infant, he asked a question, repeated it many times as we tried to comprehend.

— I think he's asking if you are a father, if you have children back home, Tillman said at last.

The question was unexpected.

— Soon, I answered.

Tillman cradled his arms, rocked them as if he held a baby. The shaman nodded.

Sophie Forrester
Vancouver Barracks
May 7, 1885

What is it that causes us to fall in love? We are met with those first, initial glimpses — a kind of curiosity, a longing for that which is both familiar and unknown in the other. And then comes the surprise of discovery; we share certain aspirations, certain appreciations, and that which is different excites us. Before each other, we are moved to bravery and we come to reveal more and more of ourselves, and when we do, those very traits that caused us some embarrassment or shame become beautiful in ways we did not understand before, and the entire world becomes more beautiful for it. There are, too, those intimate and nearly primitive stirrings, the scent at the neck, the delicious tremble of skin and breath. Yet for all their pleasures, they are as tenuous as light and air, and demand no fidelity.

And then there is this: Does not love depend on some belief in the future, some expectation beyond the delight of the moment? We fall in love because we imagine a certain life together. We will marry. We will laugh and dance together. We will have children.

When expectation falls to ruins, what is there left for love?

May 9

My words were so poorly framed, and I am sure now I have done wrong. It would have been better to have deceived. I should have written to Allen of tulips and blossoms in the apple trees, the comforts of this small house, what good company I find in Charlotte and the women of the barracks. Or perhaps it would have been best to have not written at all.

Yet it cannot be undone, as the letter is already sent to the USS Corwin as it patrols Alaska's coast. It seems impossible to imagine, but there is some chance it will find its way into Allen's hands, and I am sorry for it.

"You'd do best to keep your letter uplifting," Mrs Connor said when she came to tell me of the revenue cutter's return to Alaska.

I had all intentions of following her advice, until I set pen to paper.

My dearest Allen . . . with those words, it was as if a brittle dam gave way within me.

How could I not tell you of my broken heart? These weeks I have held myself together, I have not wept in front of Mrs Connor or Evelyn or even Charlotte. But oh Allen. I see now that you are more than husband or lover, for you are my dearest friend. I have a freeness of emotion with you that I have never before experienced. It frightens me to think that the very thing that would ease my pain — your love — might be endangered just when I am most in need of it. What if your affection falters, knowing that I cannot have children and that the life we imagined is no longer to be? Worst yet, what if you blame me? Maybe there was something I could have done to save our little one. I was too eager to be out of bed, too insistent on going for walks. Petty little walks. Is it possible that our child would still be alive within me if I had been more patient? Perhaps you will wonder the same.

And then, in a last great torrent of emotion, I wrote of my worst fear — that you will not return home from this expedition.

Mrs Connor had brought me the recent edition of the Portland newspaper. Did she do so in full knowledge that I would see the article? The bodies of Commander Goodwin and his polar crew have been found on a remote island off the coast of Siberia. They were starved and frozen to death, their ship long lost to the ice, but through all their suffering, the commander kept his log books and papers safe. "His private diaries were found at his side and will be delivered to his wife."

I cannot help but think of this poor woman, who for three years did not know the fate of her husband. Now she will read of his last days in his own handwriting. I wonder — did he leave her some final farewell, and would it offer comfort or only be a new kind of torture?

It is a possibility that I have endeavored to put out of my mind, that one might exist in a state of unknowing for years, only to be delivered the worst news in the end.

Yet, for your sake my Allen, I should have remained resolute.

My thoughts are soaked in guilt; the wretched letter I have sent, the death of our unborn child, the afternoon I stole the book and the moment I read of my deformed womb, the day I wrote to Mother wishing she would not come and the days I did not write to her at all, and all the way back to when I saw Father standing with his lantern, raging at the night, and I pretended not to hear his cries.

Ah, Mr Pruitt, you are not alone with your blame and loathing. I wonder that any life has ever been confined to golden dances and fine stitches and silk, for it seems to me that suffering knows no class or rank, gender or age, and we each of us brave our own darkness.

May 10

Sweet Charlotte. All this time I have tried to shield her from my bleak mood, but today she caught me at my worst. My hands and feet are swollen, my body so waterlogged and wretched from my failed maternity so that I can barely stand and tend to the simplest of chores, but I was determined to do one useful thing. She found me cursing and weeping as I tried to thread a needle to mend a tear in my nightgown. I did not know she was behind me until I felt her small hand on my shoulder.

"It's all right, ma'am. I can sew that all right."

I did not have the strength to conceal my emotions, so I kept my eyes down on the needle and said I would manage, and promised I would compose myself in time. Yet then I did quite the opposite, and began to sob openly. Charlotte's arms were around me and she patted me gently all the time I cried.

"I swear babies aren't all they're cracked up to be, ma'am," she said. "They're always hollering and wetting themselves and spitting up, and they won't give you any blessed peace. Sometimes my mam says she'd like to run off and be a nun but she doesn't think the church'll have her."

For the girl to be so callous to my grief! Utterly oblivious, the girl continued talking, until slowly I began to find some unexpected humor in it.

"It's true," Charlotte went on. "One time when my brothers got to fighting and the littlest was screaming like a banshee and I by accident burnt up my good shoes by the woodstove, Mam threw her apron down and walked right out of the house, left the door wide open, and she got nearly to town before Da picked her up in the wagon. He put her in a room at the hotel for the night, saying she could have it all to herself, with a hot bath and a new dress, if only she would come home the next day. She came back, and I'm glad she did, but I don't think I would have, if I was her. I'm decided — I'm only having dogs and goats, but no babies."

I started to laugh then, and she did, too.

May 12

Only one of Father's sculptures did I not like to see. His Pietà. The word was mysterious to me as a child, and I did not recognize the weeping woman. If only Mother had ever walked down the path into the woods and seen it, I like to imagine that she would have admired it, even with its Catholic effect.

It frightened me, however, even more than his sculptures of pagan gods or the lion hunter that crouched in the densest part of the forest. It was the woman's face, shaped into a melting and howling cry, that horrified me, but also something about the awful weight of the dead man laid out across her lap. He was too heavy for her, he nearly crushed her, and even though I could not understand it fully, it seemed to me an unnatural scene.

"It is her own son, her dead child," Father said.

He would not look away. Everywhere, even in the blackest abyss, he believed one might witness the divine. The shadows and contrast — absence itself — as important as the light and marble, for one cannot exist without the other.

May 13

Mr MacGillivray found me in the yard today, and I am afraid this time it was I who wanted to turn away and pretend I did not see him approaching, but then he called out his friendly greeting.

"How are you today, Mother?" And then, as he neared me, "But where is your chair, Mrs Forrester?"

"I am no longer in need of it, I am afraid."

Such insufficient words. Yet he must have read in my expression the true meaning, for he did not ask anything more of me but only said, "I am sorry to hear that, my dear. Sorry indeed."

He offered his arm to me then, and together we walked back toward the house, fallen plum blossoms at our feet and the evening sun in our eyes.

A miracle, it seems to me, that a man scarred by the cruelest of battlefields could harbor such compassion for my small loss.

May 14

I have been thinking of light, the way it collected in the rain drops that morning I was so full of joy, and the way it shifts and moves in unexpected ways, so that at times this cabin is dark and cool and the next filled with golden warmth.

Father spoke of a light that is older than the stars, a divine light that is fleeting yet always present if only one could recognize it. It pours in and out of the souls of the living and dead, gathers in the quiet places in the forest, and on occasion, might reveal itself in the rarest of true art.

The entirety of his life was devoted to the hope that someday he would create a sculpture so perfectly carved and balanced, set in just the right place among the trees, that it would be capable of reflecting this light. He had seen it in the works of others, yet he believed he had failed in his own.

I wish he could have known the truth. Just weeks after he died, I went to see the bear. It was the end of an autumn day, and as I stepped into the meadow, the light of the setting sun was cooling from oranges and reds to the bluer shades.

He had never looked so alive; shadows dipped and curved along his outstretched claws, his fur and muscles seemed poised for life, and for a moment, the sun just touching the horizon, the marble seemed to be formed of translucent light itself.

I had no doubt of what I was witnessing — this was not simply a flattering cast of sunset; this was the light Father had sought his entire life. The nearest I can describe is when Father took the back off a piano and showed me how a strong, clear note could cause other strings to vibrate without ever setting finger to them. He said the strings were resonating in sympathy to that pure sound. So it was within me.

Shall I allow myself to believe in an immortal soul? If so, then I am certain it was Father's spirit that gathered with the divine light of the world and radiated from that finely carved marble.

He always looked to his angels and gods and his Pietà. He never thought to look so near.

May 16

There is not much time. I could run in five different directions, but today Charlotte and I began by removing all the dried goods from the pantry and then stripping the shelves from one wall, because it was all that I could think to do for now.

"Ma'am are you sure you're feeling well

329

enough? Shouldn't you rest a while? But ma'am, where are we going to put all this?"

I had forgotten all about the crocks and jars and sacks — flour, sugar, rolled oats, coffee — that we had piled on the floor.

"The dining room table," I told her at last. We never use it.

Next we set to taking down the shelves. A chill sweat plagued me from the effort, as I am still weak from my long confinement, but Charlotte is adept with hammer and pry bar. She hesitated at first, as if we did some reprehensible destruction, but I assumed full responsibility and I think she came to relish the task. (In fact, she spoke more words than ever I heard from her, mostly of a rough and colorful nature. "Sorry ma'am," she said each time she cursed. "That's why Mam's always telling me to keep my mouth shut. She blames Da and my brothers, but she swears just as good as any of them.")

Dismantling the pantry took much longer than I expected, and we were dead tired by the end of day. Tomorrow, I told her, we will plug any cracks with rags.

We must get rid of the light. Every last bit of it.

Lieut. Col. Allen Forrester
May 15, 1885

The Indians become accustomed to our presence so even the young ones do not hide from us. Though it remains cold in the shade, with patches of snow in the forest, the children run about nearly naked. They are often joined by one or two of the many half-wild dogs that live with the Midnooskies.

This mid-day I observed a group of boys playing a string game that reminded me much of cat's-cradle. The string was formed from dried animal sinew which they had tied into a large loop. They wove it between their fingers to form different shapes.

When they saw that I watched them, they held up each string picture so I could clearly see. The first was of a mountain. I recognized it even before they pointed to the range to the north.

— Very good, I said.

My tone must have been too stern, for they

frowned, whispered to each other. Once I smiled, nodded, they continued with renewed excitement.

Next they made a star. The horns of a tebay. Then came a complicated interlock of strings that I could not make out. When I shook my head that I did not understand, one small boy pointed to his own ribs. Evidently it was a rib cage. They continued for some time, weaving their pictures.

There was one that was my favorite. I wish Sophie could have seen it. The string & hands formed the shape of a bird. Working together, two of the children were able to make the wings flap.

May 16

Pruitt at last sits up, is aware of his surroundings. The woman who tends him seems to be an outsider among these people. She is well taller than most of the Indians, her skin a paler shade. She carries herself proudly, although I suspect by the way she is treated by the others that she is a slave. She is gentle enough with Pruitt, assists him in sitting up to eat. Yet she expresses no emotion in her dealings with him, neither fear nor affection, but rather complete indifference.

Tillman causes me some anxiety. Already he has scuffled with some who have offended him in one way or another. This morning, he caught an Indian removing the artificial horizon from Pruitt's belongings. Tillman yelled at him, yanked the instruments from his hands, shoved the man to the ground. The Indian jumped to his feet with ax at the ready. It only flamed Tillman's anger. No doubt it would have come to dangerous blows had I not stepped between the two.

Tillman is not cautious enough around these Indians, but dallies with the young women, throws himself headlong into confrontation. The Midnooskies seem peaceable enough, but I remind him to check himself — we remain at their mercy.

MURDER IN ALASKA

May 4, 1885 — News has arrived from Alaska that Indians have murdered the local trading man on Perkins Island.

Mr. Wesley Jenson, operator of the Alaska Commercial Co. trading store at Perkins Island, was shot down inside his own bed in the early morning hours of April 30. This is not the first instance of hostility between Mr. Jenson and the local Indian population. Last month, the USS Pinta, under the leadership of Lieut.-Commander Daley, responded to an uprising on the island in which the trader shot an attacking Indian.

According to reports from Sitka, Alaska, the murder of Mr. Jenson followed several days of mayhem. The Indians had accused Mr. Jenson of causing injury to a young squaw. Three days later, the woman's husband and uncle confronted the trader at his store. It seemed violence was to be averted when Mr. Jenson told the Indians that they were mistaken and that they should go back to their own camp. In the early morning hours, however, the two Indians returned and shot Mr. Jenson as he slept in his bed.

Commander Daley reports that the killers were eventually captured by Lieut. John Lowry. The Indians quickly declared their crimes, claiming the murder was in revenge for Mr. Jenson's mistreatment of a young woman on that island. According to Daley, homebrewed alcohol and the supposed witchcraft of a medicine man on the island also contributed to the violence.

The two Indians are in custody and being transported by steamer to San Francisco, where they will stand trial for the murder.

61°36' N
143°45' W
Barometer: 29.18
54°F, exposed bulb
42°F, wet bulb
Dew point: 20
Relative humidity: 26

I am weary of these days of my own mind. Not the disemboweled, disembodied, charred stumps, not the blackened fields that stretch to the back of my brain. These are mere wounds to flesh and memory that I might endure. I speak to the shadows. Here, and here again, beneath my very skin. They will not leave me be.

I said kill the bawling newborn. What difference will it make? The Colonel would not meet my eyes. He feared the sight of my sick weakness but it is worse, Colonel, oh so much worse. I am worthless weak coward but more appalling I am only this: a true specimen of humanity.

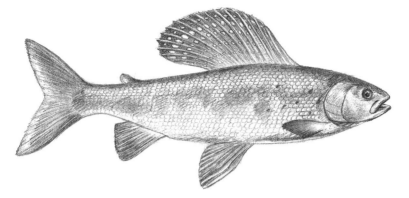

Thymallus signifier, *Arctic Grayling Fish*

Once my heart was full and trusting. I believed. A soldier's shot always true. A soldier's ways steady and forthright. I would wear that code like a mantle. At Elk Creek, I came to a hard truth: the mantle is threadbare, the wind passes through it.

I would believe again if I could. In goodness. In magnificence. In simple benevolence. Yet even in these far and icy valleys, mankind is no different, just more poorly armed. Strip away psychrometer and sextant, carbines and glass plates, skin shifts and quills and painted faces, and we are the same. Quivering maws. Gluttonous. Covetous. Fearful. We say we worship. A word. A man-god. A fiery mountain. But we worship only ourselves. And we are jealous gods.

Dear Walt,

I have just read in the Colonel's journals about the baby he found under the tree. It's incredible! What do you make of it? I'd be tempted to think he was just out of his mind with starvation, but the details are so specific.

The documents continue to strike close to home. I mean, the Trail River — that's where my father and uncle used to go sheep hunting every fall. Now there's a multi-million-dollar fishing lodge there that brings in clients from all around the world. I wish I knew exactly where that spruce tree was.

You're right of course. The Colonel's expedition was the beginning of a lot of changes for this area. At first a few miners did well with gold, but then in 1899, coal was found about 15 miles north of the famous Gertie Lode. Though it wasn't as glamorous as gold, it was coal that brought the railroad, and by the early 1900s, Alpine had become a boom town — saloons, company buildings, hotels, supply stores. There were bunkhouses for the miners, a newspaper, theater, a tennis court and a dress shop. It's hard to imagine now. It's pretty much all gone. Even the train tracks have been overgrown or fallen off into the river. We've managed to salvage a few of the original buildings and have them here on the museum property for visitors to walk through.

All of that came and went just in the relatively short time since your great-uncle traveled through here. In a century, really, it went from Native country to boom town to . . . well, whatever it is now.

It's funny that you ask about the mining. For the past 50 years or so, it's all been shut down. But last year an Australian company came in to scout the area. If they find what they're looking for, they're planning to reopen at least one of the mines. It's a divisive issue here, even within families. My uncle runs the post office, and he believes it's what Alpine needs — an influx of money, jobs, an opportunity for people here to earn an honest living. And then my cousin, his own daughter, is vehemently opposed to it. She's a member of the tribal council, and she is also actively lobbying against reopening the mines. She says the environmental damage will be irreversible and that it would change the whole community. From there, everyone has picked their sides. Up and down the highway you can see spray-painted plywood signs. "Mining Built This Town." "Protect Our Children — Keep Our Water Clean." You get the idea.

Isaac and I keep our heads down. The

librarian likes to joke that she's Switzerland, maintaining a neutral state. We're with her. I have my own thoughts, but I can sympathize with both sides. All the vitriol makes me sad, though.

Thank you very much for the check you sent. It will actually do a lot to help. There's still a part of me that feels like I should encourage you to give the journals and documents to a larger museum, but a greedy side of me doesn't want to give them up. I am in the process of applying for a grant to see if we can get some more money to add to the pot — I'd love to be able to create an exhibit using the artifacts you have. In the meantime, I'm going to continue to transcribe the journals and scan the images. At the very least we can preserve them and make them available online to researchers or anyone else who might be interested.

And Walt, I've enjoyed your letters a great deal too.

With warm regards,
Josh

Lieut. Col. Allen Forrester
May 17, 1885

Our sleeping arrangements are comfortable enough but unlike anything I have experienced before. The dwellings are dug into the earth, their frames of spruce poles covered with bark. Where there are cracks, the Indians have used moss to keep out the cold.

We are given privileged sleeping quarters in the tyone's larger, more sheltered home. The interior is sparse. There is a fire in the center, with a large hole in the roof directly above to allow sunlight in, smoke out. Along the inside of the walls are benches made of spruce poles lashed with rawhide. These are several feet wide, near to four feet high, on which are spread animal furs. We have been allotted space to sleep on top of them. Indian men, sometimes joined by their wives, sleep along the other walls. An astonishing number of women, children, & dogs then sleep beneath these benches, which are small shelters unto themselves with animal skins providing a curtain about them. Throughout the nights I wake to sounds beneath me — a dog growling in its sleep or a mother softly whispering to her child.

Often before we are allowed to retreat to our sleeping benches each night, the Indians gather in the hut to tell stories. Though we understand little, it is evident that the Indians know them well. As one tells a story, the others shout out comments, laugh, contradict. Children at times reenact the scenes, yet they are not allowed to interrupt or become too unruly. Myself, I am grateful for the children's acting, for it allows me to generally follow along. There are battles & hunts, lessons taught. The characters are often both human & animal.

This night I followed enough to understand the first was about a mouse or similarly small creature that shares its food with a starving man. The other was a more gruesome tale from what I could tell, of a woman who betrays her husband by secretly taking a wild beast for a lover. When the husband discovers the treachery, he slays the lover, cooks him in a pot for supper, then sends his bones washing down the Wolverine River.

I wish now that Samuelson had come with us to the village. Communication is hampered. Before supper, the tyone & I tried again with hand gestures, drawing in the dirt, Tillman's few words. In as many ways as I can invent, I ask him if he will guide us over the mountains. He does not seem to understand. He has his own questions, which I cannot grasp. We all are frustrated.

May 18

This afternoon I mend clothes & packs, ordered the men to do likewise. I have also obtained hides to sew Indian moccasins — our leather boots are beyond repair.

I ready us to leave within three days.

Once again I approached the tyone in hopes of communicating with him. We make no headway. It is possible he comprehends my request but is either unable or unwilling to aid us. When I point to the northern mountains, draw a map in the dirt, he studies me with much seriousness. He nods curtly, walks away. I would think him dimwitted if I did not observe him with his own people. He is confident in his dealings with them. Though he does little labor himself, it is evident that he runs all the affairs.

The village seems to be about something, as there is much activity throughout the day. Their tools are of the most basic — beat-copper blades, bone needles. Yet they are skilled in their work. The men gather spruce poles & willow saplings. The women scrape raw moose hides, stitch the large skins together, then soak them in the river.

We, on the other hand, are in danger of settling into doldrums. Pruitt remains mostly abed doing nothing. He insists he is too ill to travel, though I see nothing physically ailing him.

It aggravates me to no end how he fails to take celestial readings or work on refining his maps or repair his clothes. I have found it does no good to lose my temper with him, so I spent some time this morning trying to draw him out. I suspect his illness is partly in spirit.

Poetry did not prove a suitable topic, as he grieves the loss of his books. I mentioned the flora & fauna we have so far observed. My wife would be interested in the birds, I said. She spends every spare minute outdoors with her field glasses.

Pruitt showed some interest in the subject, said he watched a large, pale gray falcon in flight as we made our way up Trail River but was unable to identify it.

My wife is particularly enamored with the humming bird, I said. I went as far as to tell him how I had found her a humming bird nest during our courtship. A tiny thing, yet it won her heart.

— I doubt we will see any humming birds this far north, he said.

Tillman, on the other hand, is wholly content here. He even says he has become fond of their cooking.

— All that bloody meat, it makes a man feel alive!

He has taken up bow & arrow with some of the younger Indians. They place wagers on who can shoot the farthest, with the most accuracy. We are unable to obtain a single bit of helpful information from the tyone, yet the lack of common language has not stopped Tillman from learning several gambling games from the Midnooskies, including one involving a handful of carved bones. I do not understand the game, nor do I care to.

When he does not fraternize with the Indians, Tillman totes the found infant swaddled in rabbit pelts. Tillman makes peculiar noises & expressions at it, seems to enjoy its company. He explains his ease by saying he grew up the oldest of a dozen siblings.

When I informed him we must be on our way so as to reach the coast before winter, the sergeant shrugged it off, as if it made no difference when we return home.

— Why rush off, Colonel? Soon enough the boy will give us some direction. It'll save us time in the long run.

That is what he calls the tyone — 'boy.' It is an underestimation. The tyone may be young, but he has more influence than Tillman gives credit.

The Midnooskies held some sort of celebration last night. After noon, the entire village of more than 30 gathered near the tyone's hut. They lit a large fire, boiled pot after pot of moose, tebay, rabbit their hunters had brought in. The tyone's women carried birch baskets full of different foods — dried berries, tubers, last year's dried fish. It was well after 8 o'clock before everything was prepared. Pruitt would not move from his bed, but Tillman & I sat with the others just as several young men began to sing. They had no drums or other musical instruments, but kept time with the rhythm of the words. Their voices rose & fell in a hypnotizing way.

This near to summer, the sun no longer sets, though it dipped behind the mountains to leave behind a cool, bluish light in the valley. The cooking done, the Indians heaped more wood upon the fire until the flames climbed into the pale night sky.

Next a group of men formed a circle near the fire. They were the most extravagantly dressed of any of the Midnooskies we had so far encountered, adorned with copper jewelry, furs of lynx, marten. One had a particularly large copper nose piercing & ornate necklace of dentalium shells. The tallest, most dignified of the group wore a black wolf hide.

Their steps began slowly, a kind of bowing & stomping to the ground, but soon their pace was feverish. The firelight cast a glow on their faces. They sang with low shouts & a rousing cadence, until against my will my own heartbeat quickened. More Indians joined until the scene was so violent & heated, I believe it would cause some white women to faint.

Tillman was stirred to his feet, made as if to join in. I pulled him back. — It's not our place.

— Looks like good fun to me, he said.

We are outsiders. We can't understand what all this means. I advised him to just sit & watch.

As the night neared the closest it would to darkness, sometime after midnight, the Indians piled more wood into the flames. The women had now gathered in a circle around the men. Their dancing was more contained, the steps smaller, but equally impassioned. Tillman tried to take the hand of one of the young women, danced one of his jigs in front of her, but she quickly pulled away.

At last I implored Tillman to follow me back to the hut. He cannot be trusted to stay out of trouble's way.

May 20
I did not expect to find anyone by the creek this morning. I walked only to stretch my legs. When I came through the bushes, the servant woman who cares for Pruitt was

crouched beside the creek. She gathered water with bags made of animal gut. I must have frightened her for she looked up at me with wide black eyes, then hissed at me.

I maintained my composure. I offered to carry the water. She did not respond. I squatted near her, reached into the creek where she held a bag in the flow of the stream. In evident fear, she withdrew her hand. There, on the inside of her wrist, a patch of gray, downy feathers grew along her pale skin.

It is time for us to leave this place.

It seems we are more captives than guests. An hour ago I left camp to climb the nearby mountainside. My hope was that I would be able to see down into the Wolverine Valley, perhaps determine the location of the trapper & his companions. Without Samuelson's translation skills, our stay here becomes useless.

Part way into the climb, I was overtaken by two Midnooskies, I believe the same two who found us on the other tributary of the Trail River. I attempted to explain to them that I was merely hoping for a better view. They made it clear that I was to return to camp.

I had my carbine, but thought better than to resist them. For now it seems we must wait this out.

45°F, exposed bulb
40°F, wet bulb
Barometer: 28.80
Dew point: 32
Relative humidity: 60
Cold, strong wind.

Have you ever seen the nest of a humming bird? She would march to Kingdom Come in search of one, the Colonel says. He is bemused & clumsy in his affection. He cannot comprehend how she should find so much in that small hold. He is neither blessed nor cursed with a poet's heart.

He does not see. In the palm of the hand, such a nest might become Mr. Blake's wildflower. Infinity, all of Eternity, collapsed like damp foetal feathers inside a thimble egg.

Auguries. Heaven. Or Hell. Joy. Or Woe. Victory. Birth. Death. Defeat. All told in a raven's cry, a vulture's flight. Can I recall those signs of Innocence? The babe that weeps. A skylark wounded in the wing. All

Wolf Tracks Near Trail River

Heaven in a rage . . . the lines escape me.

And what of you, Mrs. Forrester — what do you seek in the break of the shell, the weave of the twigs? Whose future do you divine?

Or, is it possible, that your wonder is truly pure, without expectation or pride? Do you, Mrs. Forrester, still believe? Do you bask in the golden light I once imagined I felt upon the crown of my head? Not simply the light of God, Love, Science, even Truth or Art, but that rarified light of Promise. Thy Kingdom Come.

It is no wonder the Colonel fell in love with you.

Sophie Forrester
Vancouver Barracks
May 17, 1885

The dark room is nearly ready, yet I can do no real work until I have a camera, dry plates, and chemicals.

Since I was a young girl and first caught sight of a mourning warbler and knew it for what it was, or first heard the song of a wood thrush in the forest just as rain clouds lifted, I have sought some form to express myself. Yet I have shown no aptitude or lasting interest in any of them — not watercolor nor pencil, not dissection nor taxidermy.

It occurs to me now, however, that I might work with light itself. It has always captivated me, the way it shifts and alters all that it touches, significant both in presence and in absence.

I am desperate to begin. I have become too mindful of suffering and darkness; they attend to me even when I bid them not to, like scavenger birds perched and waiting for the calf to die. And when I seek a finer grace in the day, some essence of love and life, the light fades beneath my eyes.

I will not abandon the quest before it has truly begun, however. I will let this grief sharpen my gaze, polish and shape it until it becomes a magnifying lens through which I might yet see.

May 18
Evelyn was thrilled when I asked her to accompany me to Portland on Thursday, for hadn't she always wanted to take me shopping in the city, and hadn't she always wanted to get me into something besides my plain dresses? Her eagerness waned when I informed her that we would shop for photography supplies rather than dresses and shoes, and I am sure she would have abandoned me altogether except that I allowed for a quick stop at Mendelson's. (They are expecting their summer shipment, Evelyn informed me. "Fabric comes in choices beyond gray and brown, you are aware of that, aren't you?") I would go without Evelyn except that I need her assistance in navigating the streets and finding the various shops.

I have my list, but only the vaguest notion of where I will find everything. I can be certain of this — it will cost me dearly. As I counted my savings this morning and prepared myself for the knowledge that I might spend it all in one fell swoop, I could not help but hear Mother's voice of reproval: a woman should never depend on marriage alone to keep her safe, as any number of tragedies could befall her, and we must always be prepared for the worst. Hers is the voice of experience, I know all too well, but I will not heed it.

I refuse to assume a long, dreary life. I would prefer to spend every last penny, if need be, and visit every druggist from here to San Francisco; I would place all my faith in something mysterious and joyful and surprising, even if it fails me in the end. And well it might. I have sense enough to know that I might delude myself, that in all likelihood this lies beyond my ability and artistry, perhaps even beyond my faith, but then I think of Allen and know precisely what he would say — nothing is impossible. Take one step, and then another, and see where the path leads. Don't think of the obstacles, only the way around them.

Thursday, then, it is Portland. And tomorrow, I will look for birds.

May 19
It is most difficult for me to express the joy, the complete relief, to at last return to the forest and find that I have the strength and resolve to walk up the hills and down through

the trees, to breathe in fresh air and act upon my own will! After these months of opium tinctures and bed rest and worry and that terrible, ultimate grief, it is as if some precious element of my being has been restored.

I left alone just before noon, and for a time I followed the wagon road behind the officers' homes, but when I heard the laughter and conversation of an approaching walking party, I ventured off the trail. Stepping into that shaded, somber hush is much like entering a cathedral, the fir trees serving as grand pillars, their green limbs arching overhead. Occasionally there came the songs of chickadees, the chattering of dark-eyed juncos, the sweet call of a song sparrow and, far off, the dull thud of a woodpecker. For one thrilling second I thought I would encounter some wilder beast — there was a ruckus through the dried grass and sticks, but it was only a little field mouse or mole, and that, too, made me joyful.

The forest has always had such an effect on my spirits, the moment slows until I can see the intricacies, bright and pure, like removing the back of a pocket watch to see the shining metal gears turning, turning.

I thought I spied a humming bird's nest in a spindly dogwood, and oh that would have been a lovely discovery. Since that day with Allen, they have become all the more precious to me. Yet through my field glasses I recognized it as only a paper wasp nest, tattered from winter's wear.

As I made my way back toward home, it was as if I had sprouted wings on my feet. It was a wondrous sensation, making my way down the hill, a breeze in my face, Mount Hood revealed in all its snowy glory, the Columbia River Valley spread before me in greens and blues, and I felt as if I could bound across the world in weightless leaps. For the first time since I lost our baby, I felt wholly alive.

May 20
Today Charlotte joined me on my excursion to look for nests, and though I did not expect to be so, I was glad for her company.

When we set out, we waved hello to Mr MacGillivray, who is planting a row of maple trees along the lane in front of the General's house.

"See you've got your armed guard," he said when he noticed the sling-shot at Charlotte's side. "Always best to be prepared."

Charlotte's disposition is much changed now, and she chatters along merrily, with little time for a breath. I have learned much about her family — that she has all brothers, several older and several younger, that her family is Irish but her mother named her Charlotte because "it doesn't do anybody any good to be Irish in this country."

The girl is an observant scout and eager to learn. I have done my best to name those plant species I know, and have promised her that we will ask Mr MacGillivray to help us identify others. A few she knows by such muddled common names as bloody hearts, everlastin' pearls, little baby twin flowers, and wolf's mane, and each vivid name induces her to share an equally colorful story. A few short weeks ago I would not have imagined the need, but now and then I must gently ask Charlotte for quiet, so that I might hear the bird calls.

When she is not asking about a type of tree or flower, Charlotte inquires more times than I can count, "But ma'am, what are we looking for?"

A nesting bird to photograph, I say. Why a nest? It will provide a focus for the camera, a place that the bird is sure to return and, hopefully, sit still long enough to be photographed.

All that I tell the girl is true enough, yet there is more: I seek a certain arrangement of light and shadow, a folding of lines and balance of weight so fine as to let me catch sight of something beyond reason. I can only pray that I will recognize it when it is before me.

May 21
Surely a baby's spirit is a slight thing, with little consciousness or will, yet I sometimes

feel its presence. It is not so morbid as it sounds, nothing like a phantom or ghastly haunting, but rather like an unexpected dappling of light.

Perhaps I only conjure it out of lingering grief. Can an unborn child, which has never taken a breath or opened its eyes beyond the womb, be in possession of such a spirit?

And if it is true, what Mother and her Society of Friends believe, that we are each inhabited by some bit of divine light, then upon death, how long before those particles dissipate entirely, becoming unrecognizable except as a part of some greater whole?

I think my little one would like to perch, even for a moment, in that lovely space between light and wing, air and silence. If only I might create such a photograph.

Lieut. Col. Allen Forrester
May 22, 1885

Welcome news! They have found their way to the village.

— Ho hey there! came Samuelson's shout.

There he appeared, along with Boyd & the girl, none the worse for wear, escorted by two Midnooskies up the Trail River. The dog, Boyo, led the charge, to Pruitt's annoyance. We had enticed the lieutenant out of the hut for a dose of sunshine, so he sat cross-legged upon a boulder when the dog lunged into him, barked, lapped his face.

— What's this? Samuelson asked when he saw Tillman with babe in arms. — You work fast, soldier!

— No, no. Not mine. Though that would make a more believable story than the one we'll tell.

We shared our news, though not all the gruesome details of the child's birth. I concede, now the infant is washed & clothed, it is more appealing. It is much altered in this short time, too. It holds up its round head & watches everything keenly.

We told of our stay so far with the tyone & his people, our disappointing attempts at communication.

They, too, had their adventures. When they set up the Trail River in search of us, they followed our same mistaken route. How had they then found their way to us?

— Lucky for us, you left a marker.

Boyd untied his pack, took out the bundle of Pruitt's books.

The revelation brought new life to Pruitt. I thought for a moment he would be brought to tears, but instead he shook Boyd's hand, thanked him repeatedly.

— We were glad to see it in the tree, Boyd said. — From there we spied your tracks up the dirt slope. Once we got up on top of that ridge, we could make out the village.

It seems that not long after we had parted company with them, they shot several tebay in the mountains, but lost one to the cliffs. As they carried the meat down the valley, they camped along a creek where they were happy to find 'color' in a few pans.

— That's not all, Boyd said with much emotion.

— He believes he caught sight of his woman, Samuelson said.

— I did, Colonel. Up high by those peaks,

where we shot them tebay, I seen her wandering in the fog. I ran & called after her till I was hoarse, but she was too far off.

They were reluctant to leave the creek, both for its gold prospects & Boyd's attachment.

— But we were wondering after you, Samuelson said. — It's good to find you well.

Just then, Boyo broke into a scrap with several of the village dogs, so our conversation was interrupted.

Written Record by Lieutenant Andrew Pruitt
Meeting between Tyone Ceeth Hwya and
Lieutenant Colonel Allen Forrester,
Translator William Samuelson
Trail River
May 23, 1885

— Does he know a way through the mountains? We want to travel up the Wolverine River, over into the Tanana drainage.

— *Yes. Yes. You have told him that many times since you first came. He says he is not an old man who can't hear. He knows where you want to go. You haven't told him why.*

— That's the way to our home.

— *It would be better to go back the way you came. He says the way through the mountains is not as good.*

— We are determined to go north. We would like to set out soon, so we will be home before winter.

— *If you want to be home, why did you come here?*

— Tell him the United States of America now owns this land. We bought it from the Russians. We need to know what is here. Now that we know, we can go home.

— *How can this be your home, if you and your family and tyones live someplace else?*

— This isn't our home. We own the land. But it's not our home. Our home is far away. Tell him I have a wife and child waiting for me. I want to see them. To do that, I have to get across these mountains.

— *You must have come for another reason. He says men don't leave home unless they are after something. Is it fur? Slaves?*

— We came to see the country. That is all. Now it is time for us to go home. We need to know the way through the mountains. Will he guide us?

— *He doesn't think so.*

— Why not? Could he at least give us some advice about the best way? He has been there many times, hasn't he?

— *Maybe he has. Maybe not. He wonders why you soldiers are here. He wants to know if an army follows you up the river.*

— Tell him there is no army coming. We want to leave him in peace.

— *He says you'll run into trouble in the mountains. {I don't know the word, Colonel. Think it's something like a ghost or spirit of some kind.} He says you should go back down the Wolverine. It's a lot farther to go over the mountains. You and your men were almost dead when they found you.*

— Tell him we will go, whether he guides us or not. It's just a matter of what he gets out of it. We'll pay him. Guns. Ammunition. Even if he'll just tell us the best way. We think there's a pass, above the north fork of the Wolverine. Is that the best way?

{Here's part of the deal, Colonel. He's the middle man. He's the only one trading goods between the Indians upcountry and whites downriver. He thinks you might be after his trade.}

— Assure him. I have no interest in trading. We are just traveling through. Will he help us?

{He doesn't seem to have any more to say on that, Colonel.}

— Tell him we are very grateful for his hospitality. He and his people have treated us very well. We could not be sure how they would welcome us.

— *If you had been Russian, they would have killed you.*

— Yes. I know there have been battles in the past.

— *It was long ago, before he was born.*

— Does he know about Ivashov and his men?

— *He knows that name.*

— Does he know why they were killed?

— *He has heard the stories of his people.*

— Tell him we have heard the stories only of their enemies. I would like to hear what his people say.

— *The Russians thought they could use his people like dogs. They were made to pull the Russians in sleds up the Wolverine River. The Russians slept while his people were not al-*

363

lowed to rest or eat, only pull the sleds. They also used whips on them. It was no good, so they killed the Russians.

— What about Vasilyev?

— That was later.

— Tell him I have read Vasilyev's account of his time with the Midnooskies. It did not seem like there was any trouble before he was killed.

— They killed that man not because he was a bad man but because he was a Russian.

— Vasilyev wrote that your people treated him well at first.

— Yes. We did not want to kill him. He was respectful. He asked questions about our way of living. He put these things down on his papers. After he was dead, we sent those papers back to his people with his body, so they would see that he had been a good man.

— If he was good, why kill him?

— The Man Who Flies said we must kill him or the Russians would keep coming. It would be the end of the people. The shaman was right. The Russians did not come back after that. We were left alone for many seasons. Most of us have never seen Red Beards before. Until you came.

— The Man Who Flies? What can you tell us about him?

— He is an old man. He wears a black hat. When he flies, he has black wings.

— Tell him we think we have seen this old man, too.

— *He has always been the same, then, now.*

— Is he a friend or enemy?

— *Not one or the other. If a boy is hungry, he sees a rabbit, he kills it. If he isn't hungry, maybe he chases it for fun. Or maybe he just watches it hop along the snow because it makes him happy to see the rabbit hop.*

—Why do you call him the Man Who Flies?

— *Because he flies.*

— Tell him I have never seen such a thing.

— *He has, when he was a small boy. Many winters ago his people were starving. The old people were dying. One day, the shaman with wings came. He said he would bring the people food. The next morning, all the snares had rabbits in them. The people had a feast that night. While everyone was singing, dancing, he says he saw the old man on top of a spruce tree. The shaman jumped into the air, flew to the next treetop, then the next, until he was gone.*

— Tell him we hear other stories, about his people. We hear that when they are starving, or when they kill an enemy, they eat the flesh of humans. Is that true?

— *Is that what your army believes?*

— It's what we fear.

— *He says that's good.*

—What is?

— *That your warriors are afraid.*

365

— But is it true?

{He says he doesn't have any more to say. Best leave that be, Colonel.}

— Please tell him, I meant no offense. I have many other questions. Since we came to the Wolverine River, we have seen women who behave like geese. There is the baby we found in the woods. Can he explain these occurrences?

— *He doesn't understand. You saw them, not him. How can he tell you again what your eyes already told you?*

— We are not accustomed to believing in mountain spirits or men who can fly.

— *He says he hears from the Indians downriver that your people catch light on paper so that you can see something that happened a long time ago or far away. You have boats that shoot fire, wooden boxes that sing.*

—Yes, that is all true.

— *He says he was a small boy when he first went over the mountains. He met the Wolverine People. He was frightened because he had heard many stories. Some of them were true. Some were not. That is always how it is with strangers.*

— Yes, I wanted to ask him about the people on the other side of the mountain. Will we find them friendly?

{Colonel, he thinks I'm not translating right. He says either that or you aren't very smart,

because he answers the question, then you ask it again.}

— Ask him then how long it will take us to reach the Tanana? Should we stay to the east or west side of the river as we travel up?

— *He wants to know why you carry a pack. If you are a tyone like him, why don't your men carry your belongings for you?*

— Because I like to do my own work. Ask him why we aren't permitted to leave when we want to?

— *He wonders why you ask this.*

— The other day I went up the hillside to get a clear view of the valley. His men stopped me. Why?

— *You were going the wrong direction to get to your home.*

— All right then, if we go the way we intend, over the mountains, how long will it take for us to get to the Tanana?

— *He doesn't know because he isn't a Red Beard. You might take longer, or go faster.*

— The servant who cares for Pruitt. Where did she come from?

— *She is not one of our people, but she has lived with us for several seasons. She is getting used to our ways.*

— His knife — it is made of a metal we call copper. We have seen your people with decorations made of gold, too. Does this metal come from these mountains?

367

— *Yes.*

— Where in the mountains?

— *He says he has never met a grown man who asks so many questions.*

— I apologize. There is much I don't know.

— *That is why you ask so many questions?*

— Yes. {Is he getting ready to leave?} Please, just a few more. What about the salmon? They are an important food for your village, aren't they? When are they coming?

{*That's why they're building their skin boats, Colonel. The salmon should be coming into the Wolverine any day now. They're heading out in two, maybe three days.*}

— The entire village goes, then?

{*Every last one of them. The Wolverine is their summer ground. The tyone says you and your men can go along if you want, in their boats down the river to the Wolverine.*}

Lieut. Col. Allen Forrester
May 23, 1885

Many questions are still unanswered, yet I am glad to have at last talked with the tyone. He is an astute leader, with some humor & insight. It is remarkable to think he is probably not yet 20. In return, Samuelson says the tyone finds my character confounding — that I should be so old yet still ask so many questions, do the work of my men.

I would have liked to have been more forthright with him. No army follows me directly up the Wolverine. Yet it will come eventually, in one form or another. I suspect it will be men of Samuelson & Boyd's ilk who will clear the trail. Prospectors have incentive more than most.

All I would offer the Midnooskies, however, is conjecture.

The Mednovtsy invited me to visit their country. I told them, 'I would be glad to come to you, but it is hard to get to your country. I am not a bird and do not have wings. Neither will have I energy and resources to cover on foot such a great distance. It will take two or three months to go through forests, tundras, and swamps and I will have to spend the same time in order to come back home. May those who wish to be baptized come to my place themselves.'

— From Hegumen Nikolai, Travel Journal, July 1860, *Through Orthodox Eyes*

Sophie Forrester
Portland, Oregon
May 22, 1885

It is no chore to find Borax and methylated spirits in a city of this size, but then came hours of futile dashing about the city, sometimes in carriage, often by foot. Evelyn was indispensable in ways I did not predict. She is both bold and charming in her own way, so that while I managed to set against me every clerk I encountered, Evelyn would appear at my elbow with some bit of coquetry, and we would suddenly find ourselves being assisted, although the value of that assistance varied greatly.

When I asked for "negative varnish," one druggist teased that I would better benefit from a "positive varnish," while another suggested I go back to my husband and have him write out the list more clearly so I might be able to make sense of it. A young boy left alone in charge at one shop was too humiliated to admit that he had no idea what I was talking about, so insisted that they were out of stock, of every single item on my list. I began to think that even with its half dozen druggists, Portland would fail me. Fortunately another customer in that shop was kind enough to direct us toward Redington's. "He knows a thing or two about cameras," the man said.

If only we had known to go there from the first! When I entered Redington's, I could scarcely bring myself to ask for negative varnish. Instead of a mocking reply, however, the soft-spoken gentleman said, "Making pictures, are you?"

What glad relief! Not only did he know the items I sought, but he possessed the knowledge and supplies to simplify the process for me. It seems that the book Mr Pruitt lent me, published just two years ago, is already out of date, and that the manufacturers of dry gelatine plates now include their own developing solutions. I had already spent so much money on this piecemeal of chemicals! Even on that account, Mr Redington set my mind at ease, saying that I will need them, as very soon I will prefer to mix my own solutions in order to achieve better results. The prepared developers, he said, are best for beginners.

In less than an hour, I had my Cramer's Extra Rapid Dry Plates, my chemicals, even a ruby lantern for my dark room.

"And do you have your dark room trays? The old books will tell you to use porcelain, but then you must worry about breaking them. We can order rubber pans from back East, but they won't be here for some time."

I could not bring myself to tell him that I had picked out two porcelain platters that nearly emptied my pocketbook, then reconsidered and returned them to the shop where I had purchased them, and instead bought an outlandish amount of paraffin wax and inexpensive fabric with hopes of sealing a container of some sort.

"Whatever you have will be fine, I'm sure. But you know what has worked wonders for me? I cut up an old rain coat and used the India rubber cloth to line several wooden trays. They aren't pleasant to look at, but the solutions don't damage them, and they practically bounce if you drop one by mistake."

He was nothing short of a godsend! Everything about him was gracious, and even his shop was cool and quiet, with the fresh aroma of lilacs in a vase. (While I do not usually concern myself with such superficialities, I admit it was a welcome change from the dust and roughness we had encountered most of the day.) Along with his practical advice, Mr Redington gave me a photography catalogue, from which I can order a vast array of products and tools.

"And might I ask what kind of camera you have?"

A pitiful photographer I must have seemed — I have yet to set eyes on my camera, and could not recall the manufacturer's name. I had purchased it through Bradstreet Mercantile, as it was the only place I could find a camera that could be delivered within the week, and I could not bear the thought of waiting for one to come all the way from San Francisco. All I could say for certain is that it takes four by five plates, and I was regretting the small size. I confessed all this to Mr Redington.

"No, no, you don't strike me as a studio photographer. I suspect a field camera such as that will suit you perfectly. They are lighter to carry and quicker to set up. And the truth is, Mrs Forrester, a camera is nothing more than a shrinking box with a glass lens. All the difference comes from the eye that looks through it."

(I did have to wonder later how Mr Redington could be so sure I preferred the out of doors to the portrait studio. My pondering caused Evelyn to laugh out right. "Good Lord, Sophie, do you ever look at yourself in a mirror?")

My only disappointment is that I have allowed Evelyn to convince me to stay in the city for the night. We are at the Quimby

House, a pleasant enough hotel from what I have seen of it. Evelyn is of course in the dining hall, socializing, while I have already bathed and put on my sleeping gown. My head aches from all the talk with strangers, and I long for solitude.

I would so much rather be at home now. I fear how quickly the season slips away. Many of the fruit trees are dropping their petals. The flower gardens around the city are in full bloom. Time has become suddenly precious and fleeting.

May 24

I save all such notes for my field books, but I must mark this everywhere I can. A male Rufous humming bird! I was granted only the briefest look at it this afternoon, yet I am fairly certain. It passed by the front porch of our house in a quick dart, so close to me that I could hear the furious thrum of its wings. My eyes followed it beyond the honeysuckle, where it paused for a moment at the budding wild rose bush. I ran down the steps then, as I did not want to lose sight of it, but it flew off toward the parade ground and out of my sight so quickly. Yet for an instant, perfection reigned — the way it hovered in the brilliant afternoon sunlight, dark wings a blur, the red feathers of its throat set afire. It positively glowed.

May 25

I do not strive to be mysterious. It is not that I am unwilling to share my purpose, but more that I am ill-equipped to put it to words, and I am afraid the other women read into this an unkind secrecy. Yet how can I describe something so specific yet ethereal? If I could describe it perfectly, there would be no need for the pursuit. Isn't the service of art to bring into focus something that cannot otherwise be defined? So that a sculpture does something words cannot, and, dare I hope, so too a photograph.

Mrs Connor came to the house just as Charlotte and I were unpacking the crates of supplies I had brought back from Portland.

"My dear woman, you do yourself ill gadding about." (As if I spent my hours in dance-halls!) "You must be worried sick for your husband, and your heart broken from the loss of the baby. Shopping in Portland! Rearranging the pantry! You should rest, and make peace with your condition."

I said nothing. What Mrs Connor does not understand, and I am unable and unwilling to explain, is that my love and loss are precisely what I am about.

I am not even sure I will know it when I see it, yet I possess in my mind a scene. The gentle, warm light of early evening. A slender branch. The promise of an unbroken egg-shell; life aquiver in feather and flesh. Yet it is the light that holds my desire.

May 26
It is this time of night, when the house is quiet, that I miss Allen most painfully. During the day, I am wholly diverted by my search for birds, and I work late into the evening to mark my bottles of solutions and organize my dark room, but inevitably I must go to bed, and here is where I find my loneliness.

I've taken to sleeping in one of his nightshirts. Excessively sentimental, I know, but it still smells of him. I wonder if it does more harm than good, to indulge myself in this way, for even as it comforts me, it causes my heart to ache all the more.

I am afraid, Allen. I am afraid my barrenness will become a dead weight that will drag upon our marriage. I'm afraid my condition will mark me as incomplete or, more terrible still, repulsive to you. And deeper in my heart, in a place that is dark and unrecognizable, I am afraid that you will no longer love me.

Lieut. Col. Allen Forrester
May 25, 1885

We wait while the Midnooskies finish packing up their village. I have done as much as I can to repair my clothing & pack. I mostly pace about the camp in boredom.

Samuelson & Tillman have pulled out playing cards, resort to hands of poker to occupy themselves. They have persuaded Nat'aaggi to join them. They have explained the rules to her as simply as they can. Samuelson advised that they switch to betting pebbles, so as to not take advantage of the novice.

Samuelson's raucous laughter just drew my attention. When asked what was so amusing, Tillman grumbled something to the effect that Nat'aaggi has clearly played this game before. In front of her was a sizeable heap of pebbles.

May 26

If this were my troop, we would be well on our way. We were to leave this morning. Yet still the Midnooskies cook meals, gather their children. It is most painful for me to watch the disorder. I am near tempted to march down the shore with my men, leave the boats. For now, I wait.

Tillman says he is in no hurry to go. Most of the morning he has tried without success to provoke Nat'aaggi into another hand of poker. It seems being beaten so soundly yesterday did not sit well with him.

He admits, too, that he fears throwing himself at the mercy of the river.

— Have you cast your eye on those rapids? he asked.

I had. Though not as impressive as the vast, gray sweep of the Wolverine River, the Trail River flows swiftly over boulders so that in places the water churns into a white froth. The Indians' skin boats are but crude structures — odd-shaped moose hides stitched with sinew, stretched taut over a flimsy pole frame. They are impressive in dimension, each of the three boats being more than 25 feet long, five feet wide, two deep. Every part of the frame, from keel to gunwale to ribs, was carved with knife & ax, then assembled with rawhide & willow sprout. These Indians accomplish a great deal with the little they can scrape from this country.

It's as if we prepare to take to the river in giant hollowed animal corpses. I hope they are more watertight than they appear.

I have just come to understand how this village in its entirety will make the journey to the Wolverine River. The baidarras will be filled with the heaviest supplies, & only the men will board! The women will go by foot with loads upon their backs, leading the pack dogs.

I asked Samuelson to relay my disapproval to the tyone. He advised against it.

— It's how they do things, Colonel, Samuelson said. — We're just along for the ride.

A dispute then arose when Nat'aaggi indicated she would join us in the boats.

The tyone spoke sharply to her, but she held firm.

— He says our slave woman must walk with the others, Samuelson translated.

She does not belong to us, I said. She travels with us. If we are to ride, she does too.

The tyone at last agreed. Several village women observed the disagreement with much interest.

At long last. Word that we will launch.

61°30' N
144°23' W
46°F, exposed bulb
39°F, wet bulb
Dew point: 27
Relative humidity: 47
Night cool.

Let me keep to that skin boat. Let me ride the roar and swell. Alive, at the bow, in the face of sun, wind, and freshwater spray. Carry me on and on to the edge of the earth, with children's laughter like a wind-full sail, then carry me beyond. Bent willow boughs and moose hide. Wild ways, bear me well.

Deliver me. I am in your hold. "Make me to know mine end, and the measure of my days; that I may know how frail I am."

Lieut. Col. Allen Forrester
May 27, 1885

An exhilarating ride! Yet no easy chore. During our boat journey yesterday, we were thrown against boulders, doused in icy spray, then suddenly grounded by shallow waters. Often we leapt into the river, waded, towed the boats over rocks, until the river channel abruptly fell off into deep, quick current. There we all scrambled back on board to enjoy the run downriver.

All but Tillman. He cared neither for the wading nor the riding. Amidst the most exciting stretch of river, he was seized by terror, stood with a wild look to his eyes.

— I can't swim a stroke! he bellowed. — I'll drown!

His towering weight nearly capsized the baidarra. I ordered him to sit & stay so. He was a sickly, miserable fellow before the day was out.

The young tyone commanded our craft

with much pride & skill. We men were armed with long poles to aid steering. Our captain would variously shout 'To Kwul-le!' (Shallow water!), 'To Keelan!' (Deep water!), or 'A-to!' (Paddle!) to which we would respond obediently. He evidently knows the river well, so navigated us through narrow turns, turbulent whirlpools that could have easily been the end of us. The light, bendable nature of the boats also showed its worth. I have no doubt that any Army row boat would have been sunk at the first run of boulders.

Most surprising, Pruitt proved an enthusiastic white-water man. At the bow, he paddled with a vigor I did not think his bearing would allow. When we collided with rising waves, Pruitt could even be heard to let out a high-pitched hoot. This caused the two Indian boys in our boat to laugh & cheer.

— I believe that is my preferred method of travel, sir, he said when we had landed.

Tillman did not share his opinion.

— I plan to walk with the women from here on, he said.

Samuelson translated this to the tyone, who laughed for some time after.

With such a swift current, we made good time. Had we left when the sun first breached the mountains, I have no doubt we could have arrived at the Wolverine River within the day. Instead we floated but for an hour or two, then pulled into shore just below the fork. Here we set camp, waited for the rest of the Midnooskies.

Samuelson was correct about the Indian women. They are strong & enduring. Their pack loads rival anything my men & I carried up the river. As small-framed as they are, they trudge along steadily. They arrived at the camp only a few hours after us, in time to prepare the evening meal.

This morning we once again wait for the Midnooskies to ready themselves. Tillman assists the women, secures a large load on his pack that he will carry when he walks with them. This has provoked taunts from the men, but Tillman displays a rare stoicism.

Nat'aaggi has indicated that she will join them on foot.

May 28

Confluence with Wolverine River

The Trail River wrung us out yesterday. More than eight hours at it. Much of that time was lost when we floated down a channel that ran dry. We worked to drag the skin boats back up to the main river, but the current in places was too strong. We were forced to unload all the boats, portage to another part of the river. Pruitt & I considered that Tillman had not chosen badly after all to walk instead with the women. They reached the Wolverine nearly at the same time as the boats & looked in better shape than the rest of us. We did not make camp until midnight.

Sophie Forrester
Vancouver Barracks
May 27, 1885

Oh, it has arrived! And even sooner than I expected!

During these many months since Allen left for Alaska, the infrequent sound of a wagon or horse approaching the house has caused my heart to seize with dread and anticipation — is there some word of him? Can it be that he has returned so early? Please let him be safe and no bad news delivered this day.

It was therefore a most pleasant change these past few afternoons to have my thoughts occupied instead by the small, benign and pleasant hope that my camera might be delivered. And today, the carriage from Bradstreet came with my package!

I suppose Mr Redington is correct — at its most basic level, it is only a box with a glass lens, yet I think I am in love with it. It is not so heavy or cumbersome as I feared, and I am able to handle it with relative ease, but there is an agreeable, substantial weight to its polished mahogany, fine leather bellows, and brass knobs. Indeed, it has the gravity of a well-crafted weapon or tool of cartography, masculine and sophisticated, so it seems something of a wonder that it should belong to me.

(And never again will I be so ignorant as to not know the maker of my own camera: "American Optical Co." is stamped on a brass label, and the name will be so etched in my brain.)

Now that I have removed all the contents of its carrying box, and admired every screw and knob and latch, this afternoon I will set myself the task of understanding its mechanism.

I feel now as if the work can truly begin!

How is it that no one, not Mr Redington nor Mr Pruitt nor the author of this photography manual, ever thought to mention such a peculiar occurrence? Everything is on its head! It is embarrassing to admit, but for some time I had the irrational thought that I must have attached the lens incorrectly, or somehow inverted the camera when I put it on the tripod, but no matter how I turn the camera, the image on the ground glass remains the same — upside down!

It was only after a ridiculous amount of

time that it occurred to me that, of course, it does not matter, for once the exposed plate is developed, one might turn it any way one desires. Yet it is a unique and vexing challenge to try to align the scene before me with that which appears on the ground glass. When I want to include more of the ceiling, for example, I find myself adjusting the camera downward, for that is where the ceiling lies on the image before me!

It is perhaps best that Charlotte is gone these few days (her mother is preparing to have another child), for the quiet and solitude allows me to sort through some of the mysteries of this apparatus. It was great trouble just to determine how to unlatch the tailboard, unfold the camera, attach the lens, also put the tripod upright and secure the camera. I assembled it in the sitting room, pulled the black cloth over my head, and focused the image of our sofa onto the ground glass, and then pretended to take a picture of the sofa, but only by sliding in an empty plate holder.

All this does not seem like much, written on the page, but in fact it took me most of the day. It is unfortunate that all daylight vanished before I could move out of doors and take my first photograph, but there is tomorrow.

May 28
It has been one of the most extraordinary

days of my life!

In the shadowy, red glow of my dark room, a tree revealed itself to me, stark white branches against a black sky, like an other-worldly ghost of a once living tree.

I confess that when I lowered the glass plate into the developing solution, I had no faith that anything would transpire. I gently rocked the tray, the liquid washing around the glass. And then, where there was nothing before, there appeared the poplar tree, and I do not exaggerate when I write that it felt to me a revelation.

I was for a moment transfixed with wonder, but then I recalled all that I must do next. Quickly I rinsed the plate in water (I see now that I will need to haul many pails of water to keep on hand in the dark room) and then I placed the glass in a solution of hypo-sulfite of soda.

I will not lie; the photograph itself is a failure and does no justice to Mother Nature. The tree has been flattened and stripped of its lovely detail. It is blurred, for I must have jostled the camera as I replaced the cover to the lens. Yet as imperfect as it is, I am still in awe of its creation.

May 30
Sunny and quite hot this day. I did not go far afield, but remained near the parade grounds as the men were not at their drills, and still I

was drenched with sweat by the time I carried all of my heavy equipment and assembled it. Many birds were about, but I have yet to see how I will ever capture one in a photograph. The camera requires focus and planning that does not take into account the quick movements of flight.

Also, a letter from Mother today. I am most grateful for her kindness, for she simply wrote that she was saddened that I should suffer such loss and that she hoped I was healing well, with not a hint of her characteristic admonishments. "Be still and cool in thy own mind and spirit." Words I have always found comforting, and I confess I was glad to again be wrapped in Mother's intimate plain speech of thee and thou.

She went on to say that she has volunteered to write a pamphlet in support of equal education, and though she is not comfortable leaving the house much, she hopes she can be an asset to the movement even from afar.

I am reminded that for all her austerity, it was Mother who instilled in me a sense of just treatment of our fellow human beings. Without her, would I be any different than the woman who stepped on the Chinese boy, or those who would see Indian women and children locked in jails?

June 1
Charlotte is returned and says her mother

and new infant sister are faring well. While I wish to be filled only with joy for her family, I cannot deny a certain pang of sadness, even envy.

Mostly, however, I am surprised at how pleased I am to have the girl's company again. As a schoolteacher, I often longed for a single afternoon to myself, and have always enjoyed solitude, but I see now how much I have come to appreciate Charlotte's friendship. I believe she shares my sentiments. "I like your house," she said, "cause it's mostly quiet and we talk about interesting things."

I showed her the camera and handful of plates I have developed so far, and she was wonderfully delighted. She is also eager to learn more about the chemicals, so I shared with her my notebook. I had not noticed until then how much it takes on the appearance of a mad man's ravings — formulae and chemical recipes and mathematical calculations, aperture to focal length to time of exposure. As I ventured an explanation, I at last understood the considerable task undertaken by the author of the "ABC of Photography," and do not judge him so harshly as before.

June 3

Rain! Cursed, damnable rain! I am sorry to write such words, but this country tires me with its weather! One cannot hope to take a photograph with buckets of water poured over one's head, and so we are confined to the house with little to do.

We spent some time cleaning the dark room — I have asked Charlotte never to sweep, as that will only stir up the dust. Instead we must wipe everything down with wet rags. She also filled my water buckets.

As Charlotte now prepares our afternoon meal, I have wrapped myself in a blanket by the front window and am finding unexpected pleasure in the catalogue that Mr Redington provided me. I doubt I would have found it so appealing a month ago, but now every page holds a new delight. Expensive lenses. Drop shutters. Even camel hair brushes for cleaning glass plates. I mentally budget, trying to determine which items I might afford.

June 4

A brief break in the rain this afternoon. Four photographs taken among a flock of pine siskin not far from the house. I can only hope one might appear on my plates.

Miserable weather again this evening.

June 5

I offended the women, but it was not my intention, and I believe they must have some share in the blame.

Mrs Connor and her visiting younger sister, along with Sarah Whithers and Louise Bailey, took it upon themselves to walk through the rain with their umbrellas today and present themselves unannounced at my door. I was at work in the dark room and had just finished ruining a plate by leaving it too long in solution (though the photograph was so poor, it hardly mattered). The appearance of unwanted guests was of no help to my already nettled temper. When Charlotte saw them approaching the house, I joked that perhaps now was the time to fetch her sling-shot. Not that I would want anyone injured, but only chased off my porch.

From the dark room, I heard Charlotte welcome the women into the sitting room, put water on for tea, and say that I would be out in a minute. And then came Mrs Connor's commentary — "Mrs Forrester has been about with her camera a great deal. It cannot leave her much time to tend the household, such as it is."

What desire could I possibly have to venture into this conversation? It was wrong of me, but I began to develop another plate, with hopes that they might leave out of boredom, but then I heard Charlotte.

"Oh no, miss. Leave that be, miss."

And with that, Mrs Connor's insolent younger sister began to pull back the curtain of my dark room. It is not an easy task, for it is made of several layers of heavy wool and quilts, so as to completely block out the light, but the young woman was tugging and fighting her way through the fabric.

"What is back here?"

"Oh miss! She won't be happy at all!"

And with that, a cascade of natural light was let into my dark room, and the image in my hands dissolved away into a smoky blackness.

"What is this place?" Soon, all the women were gathered about to gawk into the red glow.

Mrs Forrester, what have you done to your pantry? I really don't think the General would approve. Why is the lamp red? Oh, but it has the look of hell to it. For this, you have given up all polite society?

The rest of the visit went no better. After Charlotte had ushered them all to the table and I joined them, my eyes eventually adjusted to the daylight, and I began to notice certain things I hadn't before. For one, it had not occurred to me how inconvenient it is to have all of one's dry goods piled on the table, if one happens to have guests. There was little room for the teacups.

Mrs Connor began to sniff and wrinkle her nose, as if struck by an unpleasant odor. Mrs Whithers, who was sitting closest to me, stared wide-eyed at my arms, and then I remembered that my dress sleeves were rolled above the elbow like a laundry woman. As I began to unroll them and try to right myself, I saw that all my fingers were stained and dirty from the solutions, but there was nothing to be done about that. I asked Charlotte if she would please pour the tea so I would not smudge the porcelain.

"You have been missed at croquet and literature club," said Mrs Bailey as she took up her cup of tea.

"Let us be forthright — we have all become concerned about you, Mrs Forrester," said Mrs Connor. "Do you ever sleep? The watchmen say the lamps are lit at your house well after midnight, so that they can see it all the way down at the barracks."

I felt no need to respond to the inquiries and so sat silent, but then Mrs Whithers leaned in close to me and whispered, "Might I ask, what are those devices?"

She referred to several printing frames I had propped on windowsills. I began to explain that I was curious to see how prolonged exposure to indoor light, versus brief and bright direct sunlight, might affect the printing of photographs onto paper. Just then I overheard Mrs Connor's younger sister ask if there weren't any biscuits or cakes.

I apologized and said I was afraid we had not had much time for baking. (In truth I have had to skimp at the grocers in order to purchase the printing frames and paper. As best I can, I aim to keep the ledger balanced in Allen's absence.)

Mrs Connor sniffed again and again, and

then finally, a handkerchief to her face, said, "I apologize, Mrs Forrester, but there is a most disagreeable odor in your house."

"Oh? I'm afraid I have gotten quite used to it. It's the chemicals. I have poor ventilation in the pantry. I nearly fainted for lack of air yesterday, but it won't do you any harm out here."

All conversation seemed to dwindle then, and after a few minutes, when I could see that everyone had finished with their tea, I begged their forgiveness but said I must get back to my work. I meant no unfriendliness as I handed them their umbrellas and hurried them out into the rain; I only wanted my house back to myself. I could see by her long, angry stride, that Mrs Connor was put out, but in truth, I do not believe I behaved any more rudely than they did, appearing at my door without invitation.

Of the pine siskin, not a single fixed image, yet there is one photograph that is of some interest to me. It is only a smudge of wings, so that it requires effort to see that it is several birds in flight, yet there is something appealing about the pale gray ripples.

Dear Mrs. Forrester —

Regarding the fogging, I suspect there may be some light leaking through, whether into your camera box or your dark room. If, instead, a negative appears thin from underexposure, it may yet be saved — try the citrate of soda solution, added just as the negative begins to show detail. It can nicely intensify the image.

As for the stains on your hands, they are a nuisance that cannot be avoided. You might try rinsing them with muriatic acid. I find a solution of 1/4 ounce of acid to 16 ounces of water to work well enough.

I have enclosed a brand of printing paper I have found quite satisfactory, as well as the additional chloride of gold you requested. It does seem a waste indeed that the toning bath cannot be preserved for additional prints.

And let me say, I hope you do not hesitate to write again. It gives me pleasure, perhaps inordinate, to be able to discuss the chemistry of the process, and I am well-pleased to know that you are finding success so far.

Yours respectfully,
Mr. Henry Redington

Lieut. Col. Allen Forrester
May 29, 1885

Smoke rises from Indian camps along the riverbanks. We have observed several Midnooskies fishing with sinew nets on the ends of long poles. One young woman stood on a rocky outcropping, leaned out to lower her net into a churning eddy. The gray water is cold & fast moving. It is a precarious business. Samuelson says every summer the Wolverine swallows several Indians & village dogs.

No salmon have been caught yet. Throughout the day, the Indians dip their nets in the water in hopes of making a catch. They will spend the summer here. They have already set to raising pole racks where they will cure the fish with sun & smoke. They also begin to dismantle two of the baidarra so as to use the poles & moose hides for their summer huts. I obtained the third to assist in our travels upriver.

I have yet to convince Ceeth Hwya to guide us over the mountains. He has agreed, however, to accompany us for a time up the Wolverine.

We wait for the salmon. As restless as I am to be on our way, it would be foolhardy to leave with so little food.

Samuelson informed me today that he & Boyd will remain in the Wolverine Valley.

— We'll try our hand at these creeks. Looks promising. Like to see if we can get a bit more out of the Indians about the copper. Not as good as gold, but there's money in that, too, if a man can get a proper operation going.

Though I anticipated we would part ways eventually, I am sorry he will not continue on with us. I much appreciate his company. I told him so.

I asked if Nat'aaggi would join them. It occurred to me that Samuelson might be interested in taking her as a wife. Such is common practice among frontiersmen.

— Don't believe so. I'd have no objection. But she's got itchy feet. I don't see her settling down with us. Not even with the tyone, rich as he is. I wouldn't be surprised if she tags along with you three.

I asked why she would want to do such a thing.

— You remember what she said. She's got

the world to see.

It was then that he mentioned already having a wife, which came as a surprise to me.

The woman lives in San Francisco. During the course of 10 years, they have only seen each other a half dozen times. They have not been reunited in nearly two years most recently. They are married by law, yet live as if not.

— Gertie's got herself a young dandy to keep her satisfied. Saves me from the opera houses & city life. I love that woman, but I don't much like being shackled down. We came to terms. I tramp about to my heart's desire, take up with a squaw now & then when it suits me. When I hit my luck, I send money Gertie's way. Once in a blue moon, we renew our vows, so to speak.

Samuelson must have read my expression.

— Now then, Colonel. We can't all be as upstanding as yourself.

I declared that if I were to find my wife with another man, I feared what I might do to the both of them.

— It's true that many a man has turned murderous under such circumstances, but seems to me that would put a halt to any good times for those involved, he said.

I cannot comprehend his tolerance.

May 30

A competitive nature has risen between

Tillman & Nat'aaggi. They began the morning attempting to see which of them could skip stones farther across the river. Now they are at some kind of Midnoosky game. Nat'aaggi bends & ties a thin willow branch into a circle, throws it upstream. The two then throw as many rocks as they can into the hoop as it bobs & swirls past. I thought it only idle diversion, but they both sprint after the hoop, picking & tossing rocks with vigor. I take it that Nat'aaggi won the first effort, for Tillman kicked his foot in the sand. He must be in the lead now, for he often whoops. All the commotion has roused Boyo. The dog barks & runs alongside them.

Pruitt mostly reads & sleeps in a patch of sand beside the river. I went with hopes of drawing him into conversation. It was a small book of poetry that he held. I asked him if he enjoyed it, to which he only nodded.

He has been so markedly subdued on this expedition that I worry for his health. I asked if he is well enough, all considered. He said he did not know — an answer plain & candid. Had he sustained injuries over these past years? Long after wounds & fractures have healed they can yet trouble a man.

— Nothing you can put eyes to, he said.

When it seemed he had nothing more to say on the matter, I began to walk back to camp.

— I was at Elk Creek, sir, he called after me.

His words stopped me. He asked if I had heard the stories then.

I was not aware that he served with the regiment at that time, but I admitted I had heard events went poorly there with the Indians.

— That does not even begin to describe it, he said.

Never once did he look me in the eye, but he spoke more than I have heard on this journey. He gave some details of the events. I needed none. I have witnessed depravities in the field. It is a sad fact, but given too much rein, men will often degenerate into animals. It does not require tremendous skill to halt such behavior — a bit of intelligence, a clear sense of morality, a strong hand. Unfortunately, many leaders possess not even one of those traits.

I said I understood Major Townsend was in command. He nodded. I saw then that Pruitt was trembling.

One cannot bear the responsibility of other men's actions, I advised. The blame rests with the commander.

Pruitt was silent for a long while, then he returned to his book. Our conversation was at end.

May 31
A shout just rang up from the river. —

Slukayk-ay! Slukayk-ay!

We joined several of the children as they ran down to the shore. One of the young Indian men had netted an enormous salmon that bowed his pole with its weight. It took all the man's strength to pull it ashore as it flapped against the rocks. A most remarkable fish! It was nearly three feet long & weighed as much as a small child.

Boyd explained that it was a chinook, the largest of all the salmon.

— Not a better fish I've found, for looks or for eating, Samuelson said.

It was indeed an impressive specimen. As one of the first fish of the season, it aroused a great deal of gleeful singing among the Indians.

A delicious meal. The Indian women cut slabs of firm, crimson meat from the fish, then cooked it on sticks over the flames of a campfire. They added green alder to the fire & the smoke flavored the salmon. We all of us ate until we could eat no more.

June 1
The Midnooskies have requested Tillman name the found infant before we part ways. Many suggestions for the child were considered, including the names of people in our party, but none could be agreed upon. I of-

404

fered Bradley, after Tillman since he seems to have a soft spot for the baby, but he said he has never cared much for his own name & would not like to burden a child with it. Other names would draw up some unpleasant association. Michael was the name of Tillman's uncle, who was apparently the 'meanest b —— d' Tillman had ever known. George, a favorite of mine, was tossed out because it called to the trapper's mind some association with "sissy royalty," while Boyd said he had known too many cheating saloon gamblers of the name of Frank.

I suggested we consider a biblical name, in the way of frontier missionaries. As the son of a pastor, Pruitt knew better than the rest of us & made a strong case for 'Moses.' But what of a family name, when this child has no family? Again Pruitt's knowledge proved useful. The scientific name for the spruce tree is Picea.

Moses Picea it is.

Later in the day Samuelson came with the lazy-eyed shaman, as he wanted to tell me something.

— He wants you to know it is good we have given the child one of our names. He says he will need it when it is time to fight the Red Beards.

I said there is no reason to think there will be a battle.

— He says the battle will come. But maybe

this boy will be able to talk over here, talk over there.

June 2

For now, our party upriver consists of myself, Sgt. Tillman, Lieut. Pruitt, Ceeth Hwya, Nat'aaggi, & the dog. Samuelson & Boyd will continue with us for the next week or so to scout prospecting sites.

We retrieved our cached goods, including tea, lard, beans, our last sack with some small portion of flour. I insisted that we leave behind Pruitt's photographic equipment & remaining plates. We arranged for Ceeth Hwya to send these downriver with traders to be delivered to Perkins Island. Pruitt does not believe he will ever see the photograph plates again. I understand his dismay, yet they become unwarranted as our welfare does not depend on them.

We pull our supplies upriver in the skin boat. The current is swift, however, so the work is hard. I consider resorting to packs again, but it would require us to abandon some of the food we have obtained from the Indians. I had hoped to employ several Midnooskies as guides upriver, but the tyone says they cannot be spared from their fishing.

Ceeth Hwya's presence, however, is a considerable asset. It is evident the esteem in which he is held along this river. At each Indian camp, we are greeted with much fanfare, provided with salmon & wild greens. These protracted visits slow our progress, but we are kept well fed.

June 3

I understand that their ways are not like ours, yet is there not some basic level of human morality? In a just world, a man should be given his due. If he works hard, he should be rewarded. If he shirks his duty, he should be punished. One would expect this to be universally accepted, but not so among some of these Indians.

I have made it my habit at each camp to present the local head man with a small token to show our respect. Today we met one tyone who was a particularly lazy, unpleasant fellow. He did nothing for himself, would not even stand in our presence, but shouted orders at his vassals.

A young boy, bright-eyed & cheerful, ran about the camp at the tyone's bidding. The boy fetched water & wooden trays with food for each of us. As the visit wore on, I became decided. I gave the boy a coin. I made no show of it, but neither did I hide it. The tyone was watchful as he perhaps waited to receive his own gift. None was coming.

Samuelson disapproved of my stand.

— You won't change their way of thinking, just rile them.

There was to be no conflict. The tyone

simply called the boy to him, took the coin, merrily thanked me for the gift as if I had intended to give it to him all along. As we turned our back on the camp, he was proudly showing his prize among his men.

I enjoy my conversations with Ceeth Hwya, which become less formal. Though I have no aptitude for it, I learn a few words of his language. Mostly, though, I rely on Samuelson for translation. This afternoon as we traveled upriver, the tyone asked about where I come from, my family, & our ways of living, which I endeavored to answer. He was surprised to learn that a man of my age & status would have only one wife, to which Samuelson offered that perhaps more wives only meant more trouble. This amused Ceeth Hwya.

His next line of questions puzzled us for some time. He approached it in several ways, asking about a certain activity I conducted each day. At last he mimicked the behavior of my writing in my journal.

I explained how one might, through symbols drawn on paper, record experiences & ideas so that they will not be forgotten. I described it as akin to the stories they tell each other in the evenings.

He understood that the Russians had also kept such records. He asked if I would give the books to my tyones, as the Russians had.

I said that while I write reports & a journal for my commander, I also have my private diary.

He asked if he could learn to make these symbols. I assumed so. How could he go about learning such a thing?

— You ask a lot of questions for such a young man, I said.

The tyone nodded seriously, then saw my joke & laughed.

From all I have observed, these people seem to have a quick sense of humor, which is a pleasant trait.

*REPORT TO HEADQUARTERS
DEPARTMENT OF THE COLUMBIA,
VANCOUVER BARRACKS,*
Attention General John Haywood
June 4, 1885

Dear Sir,

Our party is in good health, our expedition so far a success. We are near the confluence with the Trail River at or near 62°14'N, 145°23'W, and prepare to continue our travels north up the Wolverine River. We estimate we have traveled approximately 340 miles from the mouth of the Wolverine River. I am hopeful that you have received my previous reports.

If all continues according to plan, we should pass through the mountains within the month and begin our journey down the river system to the western coast of the territory.

Our encounters with the Midnooskies have so far been amiable and informative. They are a poorly armed people. Mostly they still use bow and arrow, although some small-bore muzzle-loading shotguns are present, out of which they fire pebbles or bullets hammered from copper. Judging by their peaceable, jovial character, I would not deem them warlike.

In the future, good relations with the Trail River tyone Ceeth Hwya will be of upmost importance in securing the trust and cooperation of these tribes.

Strong evidence exists of gold and copper along the Wolverine River Valley. The Indians are adorned with the metals and use them to make a variety of tools. Two trapper/prospectors who accompany us believe there may also be silver deposits nearby. The Indians are not particularly guarded or secretive about these minerals. I believe they will easily reveal their specific locations when pressed.

As to other resources, game is not as plentiful as one might expect. We have seen but a few caribou and moose. Salmon, however, are said to be abundant in the Wolverine River throughout the summer. The tribes migrate to the river in early June for the fishing season. Any military endeavor would be best planned with the annual return of salmon in mind.

The main deterrent to a military presence in this territory is the rough terrain. Even the Indians are stymied in their attempt to navigate the river. The hardiest traders amongst them make journeys to the coast, via skin boat in summer, over the ice in winter, but it is a rare few. This accounts for my scant reports so far this journey.

Due to stretches of boulder-strewn rapids, steamboats will never ascend the Wolverine River. Other than native dogs, pack animals are not suited for this country due to poor footing in the mountains and deadly winter conditions. The only feasible means of bringing a military force into the country would be to march soldiers across the ice in winter. Even with well-packed sledges, however, food stores would be exhausted well before any regiment could reach the headwaters.

In the event of conflict, the Indians would best be controlled by halting the sale of ammunition and arms, then by patrolling the river and restricting their access to salmon during the summer season. A large number of the natives would thus perish from starvation the following winter. It is my firm belief that the destitute nature of these peoples will ensure their quick obedience if threatened with the loss of shelter or food.

This is a demanding country. Any man who ventures here must be strong of body and mind, with great endurance and the ability to live on very little food. He must be warrior, hunter, packer, and diplomat all in one. In my experience, the only class of men to meet such requirements are mineral prospectors and fur trappers.

I anticipate that I will not be able to send another report until we have cleared the mountains and entered the Tanana River drainage.

Very respectfully,
Lieutenant-Colonel Allen Forrester

Dear Walt,

I have just come across the name of the baby the Colonel found under the spruce tree, Moses Picea — I know him! Or I should say, I know of him. He died before I was born, but he is a hugely important figure here in Alaska. He helped organize the first Tanana Chiefs Conference in 1915. Many Natives didn't want the federal government to bring the reservation system to Alaska. Moses Picea served as a translator for those who came to testify before the government officials.

I was transcribing that portion of the diary yesterday and literally jumped out of my chair with excitement when I came across his name. And I'm certain it has to be him — all the details line up.

He died in 1980, three years before I was born. Some people said he was nearly 100 years old when he died. He didn't have a birth certificate, though that wasn't unusual among Alaska Natives back then.

My mom met him several times. She says he was a remarkable man. He reminded her a lot of her own uncles, but she also remembers Moses Picea as being exceptionally tall and broad-shouldered and with unusual hazel eyes. She said when she was a little girl, she was always afraid of him at first because he had such an imposing presence. But then he would crack a joke or wink at her, and then they would be friends for the rest of the visit. He was a favorite among children, she said, because he always shared a bit of "Indian candy," smoked salmon cured with brown sugar.

It's hard to list all that he did. That 1915 meeting was one of the first times Native leaders spoke up in defense of their land rights, and even though it wasn't settled until nearly 60 years later, Moses Picea saw it happen in his lifetime. Instead of reservations in Alaska, Natives were given land and money to set up their own corporations. I'm sending you a copy of a photograph from that initial chiefs conference. I thought you might find it interesting.

I think Moses Picea is most remembered for his writing, though. He was one of the last fluent speakers of the Wolverine dialect of Na-Dene. He helped translate the Bible into the Wolverine River dialect, and he wrote stories and poetry in both languages.

This has always been one of my favorites, and I read it now with new meaning:

SONG FOR MY MOTHER, 1952

You say go to the river, it is time for the
    salmon

And I go to the mountains to hunt for
    nothing.
You say to never let anger chisel me
And I sharpen my words on a
    whetstone.
You say come home at night
but I sleep where I fall.
So what is this Mother's love
but a steady hold against the bore tide
    of a young man?
You say "I did not give birth to you, but
    you belong to my heart."
I say, what is birth but death in reverse
And what is love
but the beat of a mother's heart against
    her son's ear?

My mom saw Moses Picea speak pub-
licly a number of times. She says he was
articulate in both languages and had a
way of bringing really different kinds of
people together. His main message was
always that the government should treat
both the land and its Native people with
care.

It's so eerie to have that all in mind
when I'm reading these diaries.

That isn't the only reason I am writing,
though. It's been a while since I heard
from you, Walt. I don't want to be a pest,
but I've missed your letters and wanted

to make sure you are well.

With warm regards,
Josh

Tanana Chiefs Conference, Library Room at Fairbanks, Alaska, July 5, 1915

We feel that just as soon as you take us from the wild country and put us on reservations that we would soon all die off like rabbits, just as the chief has said. We live like the wild animals, in long times ago our people did not wear cotton clothing and clothes like the white men wear, but we wore skins made from the caribou. We lived on fish, the wild game, moose and caribou, and ate blueberries and roots. That is what we are made to live on, not vegetables, cattle, and things like the white people eat. As soon as we are made to leave our customs and wild life, we will all get sick and soon die. We have moved into cabins.

There is no such thing now as the underground living, and as soon as we have done this the natives begin to catch cold. You used to never hear anything of consumption or tuberculosis. The majority of people say that whiskey brings tuberculosis to the Indians, but this is not true. It is because we have changed our mode of living, and are trying to live like the white men do. I feel that the natives are entitled to their own land, and should not be put on a reservation.

— Paul Williams, front row, right

Hello Josh,

Please excuse my long absence from pen and paper. I'm afraid this decrepit old husk of mine is proving more trouble than it's worth. Of all the damndest things, my plumbing landed me in the hospital for a few days, and I was slow to get back on my feet here at home. I am glad it didn't end me. Not that I'm clinging to life by any means, but it would be an embarrassment to be knocked off by an infection in my piss-pipes. It seems to me, all things weighed, I have earned a more dignified exit.

Good grief, it ages me all the more to know you weren't born until 1983. Are you even old enough to buy yourself a beer?

I didn't know all that business about Moses Picea and the chiefs conference, and I sure appreciate being able to see that photograph. It's proof to me once again that you're the right man for the job. I doubt most would have been attentive enough in their reading to come across the name, or knowledgeable enough to recognize it for what it was. It is no easy chore, reading those diaries that closely. The Colonel's handwriting was neat enough, but so small and crowded onto the page that I always had to use a magnifying glass. And some of it has suffered from water damage and the like. I admire your diligence.

I enjoyed telling one of the nurses about your museum up there. All those strangers coming and going from my room in the hospital, and she was the only one who would give me the time of day. Most of those gals were too busy gossiping to even notice there was an old coot in the bed they were changing. But this one girl was a sweetheart. Actually looked me in the eye and talked to me, rather than around me. Seems she's planning a trip up to Alaska this summer with her boyfriend, going to see the sights. I envy her, and told her so. I also told her she should swing by Alpine and say hello to your museum. Sounds like she won't be much near your neck of the woods, though. I forget just how big that state is.

I've been meaning to ask you — you've mentioned a fellow by the name of Isaac in a number of your letters. Does he have something to do with the museum? It's no matter except my own curiosity.

I've hired a neighbor kid to help me clean out the crawl space. Along with a lot of useless junk, he brought up a rusty cookie tin filled with coins, stick pins and the like. That's where I found this brass button. It belonged to the Colonel, although I can't be sure it made the trip to Alaska.

I'm still thinking on how to get all these artifacts up to you. It's going to take some doing. For now, I thought you might enjoy this little token.

Sincerely,
Walt

Lieut. Col. Allen Forrester
June 4, 1885

Ceeth Hwya has bestowed upon me his moose-hide tunic. It is an impressive garment, beaded with dyed porcupine quills & dentalium shells. When I went to pull it on over my head, however, we found that it was too small for my larger frame. I wrestled absurdly to remove it, which provoked laughter from all, myself included.

One of his wives is altering it with panels of hide along the sides, an opening down the front in the manner of a white man's jacket, so it will better fit me. It is a fine gift. I hope I managed to communicate my gratitude, both for the gift's craftsmanship & intention. He says if I wear it, it will earn us safe passage. He indicates its power is of a magical sort. While I do not hold to such notions, it is plausible that the jacket will mark us as under his protection as we encounter other villages.

Ceeth Hwya will not be swayed to accompany us farther north. At long last, however, he has advised us on a route. We are to take the west fork of the Wolverine River, follow it to a lake called Kulgadzi. There we will find a village on its shores.

With hopes of obtaining a map, I showed Ceeth Hwya how to use paper & pencil. He was quite taken with the implements, spent some time drawing different shapes before I induced him to draw the map.

Based on his crude drawing, Kulgadzi appears to be a narrow lake, running east to west. We will be able to obtain canoes from the Indians. I suggested that we would paddle directly across the lake. The tyone says this is ill-advised & that we should instead travel west, taking the long way near the shore of the lake. I cannot discern his reasoning, though we will soon enough see for ourselves.

On the north side of the lake, we will begin our last ascent to the summit.

— He says the only living souls in this land belong to the Wolverine People, Samuelson translated.

I asked if this is the tribe's name.

— Not that simple, Colonel. They mean what they say. These are wolverines that take human form. No nastier blend of character, man & wolverine. Ruthless enough to steal your last meal out from under your nose & smart enough to do it.

Fables do not concern me. We will make our way.

Once we get into the high mountain pass, the tyone says we should not stop for the night. Samuelson says it will be best to camp while we are still down in the trees, then get an early morning start so we can make it through the pass in a long day. If we get caught out at night, he says we should keep moving. Don't stop to set camp.

Because of the threat of being caught out by a mountain storm?

— Maybe that, too. But Ceeth Hwya says you'll enter a kind of spirit world up there. He says it's a good place, but not for the living.

It seems these people believe the dead spend their days hunting strange beasts like none seen elsewhere, creatures with giant horns coming out of their mouths & legs the size of cottonwood trees. Once we pass over the mountains, according to the tyone, we will travel down to a river. Along the way, he claims, we are likely to stumble upon the bones of these mythical creatures.

From then on, as we come down out the mountains & return to the land of the living, the tyone says we should not trust the people we meet.

Samuelson expected him to say as much, as the groups have battled for bygones, stolen slaves from each other.

The tyone claims to be one of the few Midnooskies who has traveled over the mountains of his own free will. He managed to survive, even make a few trading deals.

— But only by the skin of his teeth, Samuelson said.

When we have traveled that far, the tyone says we should stow away the jacket he has given to me.

Would his enemies recognize it?

— More than that, Samuelson said. — It's got to do with how things work on either side of the mountains.

I asked him to explain further, but it is only nonsense. Because Christian missionaries have traveled far into the country of the Yukon River, & many of the natives have been converted, Ceeth Hwya does not believe the supernatural protection of his jacket will hold sway.

I asked if he could at least tell me this — how long will it take us from here to cross the mountains? His answer was not particularly helpful: maybe 14 days, maybe two months, it all depends.

June 5

Ceeth Hwya has left us to travel back downriver. He goes in the baidarra. We no longer have use for it as the river becomes increasingly rocky & shallow. Several Indians from a nearby camp joined the tyone. I asked if we might trade them for their long-handled fishing nets so that we might feed ourselves on our journey north, but they said we won't find salmon on the west fork. It seems the fish do not travel there but instead spawn on different tributaries. Uncured in this heat, any fish we harvest now will last but a few days in our packs. Once again, we will have to make do with what we can scavenge until we reach the village.

I repaid the tyone's assistance with a generous amount of powder. On a more personal note, I gave him one of my pencils as well as a dozen or so pages torn from my diary. This especially pleased him. I suspect that if given the chance this young man would much benefit from learning to read & write.

After our farewells, Ceeth Hwya boarded the baidarra along with other Indians. I could hear his shouts of 'A-to! A-to!' (Paddle! Paddle!) as they floated down the Wolverine River.

June 6

Today we bade farewell to Samuelson & Boyd. They head to the west, into a valley the Indians say holds copper & gold. It is, too, in the direction Boyd believes he saw his wife traveling.

— You see that fog up that way, Colonel? That's a good sign, don't you think, that I might find her yet?

Tillman asked the two men how long they intend to stay in the valley, to which Samuelson said it would depend on what they find.

— You prefer this territory, then? Pruitt asked.

— It's truly the last of the wild country, Samuelson said. — But it won't stay this way for long.

— The wildness, then, is what you seek?

— Gold & furs are what we're after.

Pruitt asked if there wasn't an easier way for a man to earn a living, which brought a laugh from Samuelson.

— No doubt, no doubt, he said. — I suppose the wilderness does have its draw. She always keeps a part of herself a mystery.

Samuelson said that even after five seasons he cannot claim to know this territory.

— Give it time, though, he said. — Soon enough the proselytizers & the politicians will come & sort it all out. Next thing you know, the Indians will be dressed in cotton getups, going to church, & living in neat little houses that can't hold the heat. We'll go back to thinking we know it all. That's when it'll be time for me to move on.

As we parted ways, Tillman asked if either man might have a drop or two to spare. Boyd said they were all out of spirits, but that they could spare some tobacco.

I paid them both their wages, wished them

the best of luck. It seems unlikely that we will ever meet again. I am sorry for that. Samuelson was a particularly good guide.

He correctly predicted this: Nat'aaggi stays on with me & my men. I did not ask her to join us, nor did she make her plans known except to continue in our company, along with the dog, Boyo.

The Indian woman is capable assistance. She is always at some work or another, hunting food, gathering birch bark for fire starter. I remain, however, somewhat mystified by her desire to travel with us beyond her people's territory.

Does she understand we are to go over the mountains? We will travel quick & light, I said, so it will be no easy journey.

— I'll hazard she knows better than us what we're getting into, Tillman said.

June 7

We camp at the mouth of the west fork. Large bear tracks mark up the nearby sand bars, though we have not seen any animals. Brown bear meat is said to be rank, but in our current condition, we would not turn up our noses. For that reason, as well as our own protection, we will keep a man at guard through the night. I take the first shift.

I think on it more often than is good for me, especially when I'm alone at the campfire like this. Sophie a mother. Me a father. A family together. At the last Indian camp, I obtained a gift for her — an infant strap made by the Midnooskies. The women use the decorated leather slings to secure their babies to their backs as they work. This one is ornately decorated with flattened & dyed porcupine quills. I do not expect Sophie to use it, as I'm sure she will prefer a baby carriage, but I believe she will enjoy this souvenir of my voyage.

I still carry with me the Old Man's silver comb, though I do not know what to do with it. I consider throwing it into the river, or offering it to the Midnooskies. Yet I cannot seem to part with it. More than once I have taken it from my pocket, tried to polish it with my shirt sleeve to see if I can determine any sign of its path to Alaska. The Old Man could have picked it up on Perkins Island, where soldiers & white men come with some frequency. Surely it can be explained.

We learned at one camp that the Old Man remains in our proximity. The Indians were lamenting his theft of fish from their drying racks. They said he was later spied on the riverbank, sleeping with his hands on his fat belly.

Sophie Forrester
Vancouver Barracks
June 6, 1885

"Why didn't you have hired help when you were a little girl — was your family poor? You don't talk like you were raised poor. What do you mean Friends? What's a Quaker? I don't like church a bit. Mam makes us go but I think it's just because she likes that we all have to sit quiet. What about your da, was he Quaker too? We don't have marble or sculptures around here, just trees and hills and more trees. And you can see the mountains on sunny days. No, I've never seen a sculpture before."

In such a way, as we walked today in search of nests, Charlotte drew to my attention the false-fronted and thin nature of civilized discourse. She speaks forthrightly, without guile or manipulation; she means no affront and only asks what any rational person would. Yet how do I answer her honesty? I simplify, even outright lie, all to keep the conversation light and moving forward. Each time she spies a gap, however, the child does not skip over it as expected, but instead pauses at the edge and peers down fearlessly.

"How did your father die, was he old or something? Who lit the barn on fire? Why didn't anyone put it out?"

If only I possessed Evelyn's ease with banter. I have watched how, when it suits her, she deflects and distracts and only talks of that which amuses her, never with sign that there is anything concealed.

I told Charlotte that my father died in a barn fire when I was about her age, and it was not a lie.

I did not say that the quarry boss had long ago sent him away because he fought with the other workers and behaved strangely, nor did I describe how he took to stealing his marble in the night and slept like an animal in the barn and often did not seem to know the faces of his own wife and daughter. I did not share my most fearful memory: the night I looked out my bedroom window to see him standing bare-chested in the rain, how he roared at some invisible entity, his long beard and hair matted like the fur of an unwell animal.

I ran out with a blanket that night, to wrap around his bare shoulders, but he only cast it off so that it lay wet in the yard.

I was there, too, the day he took the sledge-hammer to the bear, and when I tried to stop him, he struck me with a blow that knocked me to the ground, but who would dare to speak of it? When he hid away in the barn, I continued to bring him food each day, but I was too frightened to get near, so would push the tray through the barn door with a broom, and it filled me with shame.

The day after Father went into a neighbor's home and was nearly shot as a thief, a doctor came to our house to say that he should be committed to an asylum, as he was becoming dangerous and his demented brain was beyond healing.

I wanted to shout at the doctor that Father wasn't mad. Anyone could see if they only looked — he was turning into his bear. I begged Mother not to send him away. I would feed him and nurse him, as if I had found him wild and injured in the woods; all this I promised without knowing how agonizing my failure would be.

Yet here again words are lacking, for this is nothing like the story of my childhood. What about the rich hues and variations in the texture of experience? There were the evenings before, when Mother would be preparing her lessons and Father would open his sketchbook and the three of us would talk of everything imaginable, of God and Spirit and free will, of poetry, enslavement, Transcendentalism, good works and the destiny of humankind, such vivid conversations that I believed that Mr Darwin, Mr Emerson, Mr Whittier, and Miss Susan Anthony were our intimate friends. The intensity to those hours of debate! Mother turning to her Bible verse: "That ye should show forth the praises of him who hath called you out of darkness into his marvellous light," countered by Father quoting his own prophet: "Beauty is the mark God sets upon virtue. Every natural action is graceful." I was encouraged, even at a very young age, to enter into the fray and voice my own thoughts, but only if they were well considered and interesting.

Most precious of all, in those hours I witnessed how these two desperately disparate individuals, my Quaker Mother and irreverent Father, had fallen in love.

And what of the morning Father appeared at the kitchen table for breakfast, after weeks of living in the woods? We thought he was beyond our reach, yet here he was before us. He had shaved his wooly beard, and the skin was pale and nicked with small cuts. His shirt was misbuttoned, his voice broken. He had never looked so small to me. His hand trembled when he held up his cup to be filled with water from the pitcher. Mother would not meet the gaze of his blood-shot eyes, and she did not speak a word to him. I have often wondered what guided her — fear, anger, or grief?

That was the last time he entered the house. Several nights later, I saw his lantern light near the barn. I ran into the yard in my nightgown and bare feet, thinking to call him inside. Maybe once more he would sit at the table with me. We could talk again, of the instinct toward art and the capacity of stone, of flying mice and demi-gods. He could tell me of his next sculpture. He could remember who he once was.

Yet I did not call out to him, for as I watched, I saw that Father carried the large kerosene can and that he splashed oil against the barn. When he reached the end of the wall, he knelt beside the barn and poured the oil onto himself, down his back, over his head and wetting his bare face. He knelt there for some time in the lantern light, head bowed and shoulders bent toward the ground, so that I was beginning to think that he had entered some sort of trance. But then he abruptly stood and dashed the lantern at his feet.

He caught fire the same instant as the flames unfurled along the barn wall. I watched as the scene unfolded before me, as Father walked, burning, into the barn, and the flames crawled toward the roof. I watched until the billowing fire consumed the night sky, and Mother came running from her bedroom, then fled toward the quarry to see if there were men who could help put out the fire.

All this time, I did nothing. Still I can remember the cold, rough ground beneath my bare feet, and the terrible heat from the fire, the smell of the heat, and the sound of fire like wind ripping through wood. All this I remember with clarity, but what did I feel? What kept me silent and unmoving? At some moment did my child's mind think of mercy, of allowing one kind of suffering to end another, or was I merely suspended by cowardice? As a grown woman, I often imagine running up to this younger self, grabbing the girl by the shoulders and begging her, Please, please, why don't you do something?

So here lie the darkest, most tender places in my heart, the ones I keep hidden from even a sweet girl like Charlotte, and I would have sworn that never in my life would I share them with another.

Yet, I did, didn't I? I told just one person. I told you, my dear Allen. We were walking in your Mother's garden, and it was like the day at Nantasket Beach — you did not spurn me or counsel me or beg me to leave these memories behind, but instead, when I finished telling you everything, you took up my hands and cupped them in yours, blowing on them and gently rubbing them, as if to keep them safe from some deep cold.

June 9

I have wasted so many precious plates. Each morning these past two days, I have carried all my equipment to the alder near the shed where birds so often come and go, and I have focused my lens on a single branch, for that is all one can do. That and wait. Warblers and sparrows of variety, a robin, several dark-eyed juncos, all made their rounds, and darted about the branches, but rarely did one land within the range of my camera.

The hours of stillness do not test me, nor do I much mind the biting flies that are chased away only by the tiring heat of the sun. I have my broad-brimmed hat and long sleeves, and the task reminds me something of fishing in the pond with Father; much time passes in a quiet meditation, and then in a breath, one is confronted with a quick choice — do I take off the lens cap now . . . or now? And oh, the bird is gone again.

There is a most significant difference, however, for when you jerk at a fishing pole, you lose nothing but the fish, yet with the camera, each time I make the decision to remove the lens cover, I not only startle the bird, but also expose the plate, almost always for naught. For as I reach toward the lens, the bird inevitably darts away, and I am left with yet another useless picture of an empty branch.

It is a nest I must find, I know, for there a bird will come and settle regularly, and I have always pictured it so in my head. If only the robin's nest behind the Bailey house would suit, but in that shady corner, there is never sufficient light for a photograph. I had hoped the large marsh upriver would provide some opportunity, but so far Charlotte and I have only found a few abandoned nests that I suspect belonged to red-winged blackbirds. I have yet to see another humming bird, much less be so fortunate as to discover an active nest.

A profound sense of despair and loneliness settles on me. I allow that I may be so lucky as to someday catch a bird clearly in the frame of my camera, yet my attempts so far lead me to believe that the poor creature will be reduced to nothing more than coarse shadows, with no subtlety or detail.

June 11

I am not given to hysterics, but this morning when the young soldier appeared at my door with a letter in hand, my knees buckled from beneath me and I saved myself from falling only by grabbing hold of the doorframe. The soldier reached toward me. "I am sorry to have alarmed you, Mrs Forrester. It's just a letter from your Colonel."

He spoke as if this were the most common of occurrences, a letter from my Allen, who I have seen or heard nothing of since the 30th of January, four terribly long months ago. It was as if I watched from afar as I took the battered, water-stained envelope. Only much later did I come to my senses and recall that I had turned from the soldier without ever thanking him or bidding him farewell or even closing the front door.

For a time, I could not bring myself to open it. And then, once I tore open the envelope, it was with much difficulty that I slowed myself to read the words, for I wanted to know everything at once.

Now these hours later, I have taken the letter to bed with me and know its contents nearly by rote. "So often I have wished that you could see this land for yourself. We walk past glaciers that would bring tears to your eyes for their majesty, & the Wolverine River is grand." Oh foolish romantic that I am, I even kiss it and hold it to my cheek and kiss it again. It is you, my love, every last word. The paper smells of wood smoke and damp, moldy canvas. Your well-ordered handwriting, the thumb smudge at the bottom of one page, all cause me to think of the smallest details of your presence, so that I can imagine you in this room with me even now. It is all the more painful, then, when I remember the great distance that separates us.

It is dated April 18. And without meaning to, he has abandoned me in a most perilous place. The letter was composed from the cusp of the most dangerous portion of his journey, as he prepared to enter the Wolverine canyon he so feared. And how fondly he wrote of our unborn baby, as if it secured all future happiness. "You carry our child, Sophie, & you become all the more extraordinary to me. Each passing day as I think on it, I love you more."

Dear Allen, what is to become of us?

The letter has made an astonishing journey, by Indian boat and traders' hands, across ocean and uncharted land, to find its way to me, yet for all that it secures me no solace. I am no closer to knowing his fate, or the contents of his heart upon learning my news.

He intended only to comfort me, even in his postscript. "Know that my love is steadfast. I march back home to you."

And now that I have folded up the pages and think of the days ahead of me, I am sapped of all livelihood and impulse. Why have I chased about the forest, as if anything important were at stake? It occurs to me that even if one is able to achieve something of beauty, art is entirely impotent. What can a photograph do? Not a whit. It holds no power to reclaim the life of our child or make me whole. It cannot carry Allen safely home, nor can it preserve his love.

May 3, 1884

Dearest Mother,

Our plans are final. We arrive in Boston the morning of May 19. At last you & father will meet my lovely Sophie, and I think I will ask her to marry me.

You will be surprised to see how happy we are together. She brings out the very best in me. You know how you said when I visited at Christmas that I have become too serious, even severe? Sophie has changed all that. She is so full of joy & wonder, & I am hopeful that these virtues somewhat rub off on me. If only you could see us together when we stroll arm in arm, laughing & talking of all things. You would never guess that I could be so carefree.

Even before we arrive, I want you to have some sense of her. The photograph is a poor representation, as she is not best shown in a stodgy atmosphere. Hers is an uncontrived nature, a beauty in her eyes & laugh, a kind of light that shines out of her very being.

In ways she reminds me of Olivia Stephen. Do you remember her? Maid Becky's niece. She came to stay one summer when I was a boy. Sophie has her same kind of quiet humor, as if she is secretly enjoying everything about the world, but is too humble & shy to tell you all she knows. Also there is something of Aunt Jane's eccentricity, the way Aunt Jane will pick up a book even as someone is having a conversation with her & begin to read it, falling silent. At times Sophie is so intent on her own thoughts or observations that she does not notice anything else around her, & she can be forgetful. She is always misplacing her field glasses, notebooks, or gloves.

I suspect the only reason Sophie is not married yet is because her head is elsewhere — occupied with kestrels & ruby-crowned kinglets (she will have me learn the names of these birds yet). There have been other suitors, I am sure, but they probably mistook her distraction for aloofness. She would not have paid me any mind either, if I hadn't kept returning to her schoolhouse & pestering her. In truth, I won her over not by good looks or distinction, but rather dogged determination.

You are right of course about our age difference; it is significant. Yet I think you will see what I mean when you meet her in person. She is no silly girl. She is witty & kind & settled in some way that I have not yet achieved myself.

I have been thinking that we could have the wedding in Boston & maybe honeymoon at the Nantasket cottage, if you would not mind. Of course I want you & Father to meet her first. I am sure you will love her as I do.

Please don't tell Father of my plans. He will get it in his mind that she does not come from good enough family or that she does not suit me in some way, even before he has had the chance to meet her. I want him to be taken by surprise by her beauty & intelligence. Without even trying, she will win him over.

Do you think she might have the blue guest room? I think it will suit her well, as it is just down the hall from the library & is cooler than the other rooms in this hot weather.

Your affectionate son,
Allen

■ ■ ■ ■

Part Four

U.S. ARMY TIN CUP.
MODEL 1874 ARMY TIN CUP.
ALLEN FORRESTER COLLECTION.

■ ■ ■ ■

Indian War–era Army tin cup of regulation issue, measuring 4 inches in diameter and 4 1/8 inches high. Block tin with soldered seams. Handle stamped with letters "US" and fastened to cup with iron rivets. Some scattered rust and pitting, but otherwise little sign of aging.

Dear Walt,

I am so sorry to hear that you were in the hospital. I hope you're continuing to feel better.

I also wanted to write to you about the second check you sent — it is incredibly generous. Before I accept it, though, I want to make sure you're not sending too much. It really is a lot of money. Are you sure you're keeping enough to live comfortably? Do you have any family to leave it to? Don't get the wrong idea — I can definitely put it to use here at the museum, and I'm not trying to second-guess your financial decisions. But there is no reason to rush. Our budget is set for this fiscal year, and I'm going ahead with the transcribing. Just think about it, and let me know if you are sure. I'll wait to hear from you before I deposit the check into the museum account.

Thank you so much for the brass button. It fascinates me how an object so small and everyday can be transporting, the way it brings you into direct contact with the past. I put it here on my desk beside my computer screen, and I like seeing it there as I go through the Colonel's diaries.

Sometimes it still surprises me that I ended up as a museum curator because I always thought history was boring. It was just this litany of meaningless dates and places I had never seen. I knew I should probably care about Civil War battles, and I'd try to focus on the textbook, but it put me to sleep. And then one summer when I was in high school, I was hiking down by the river with my brother and we came across the old railroad bed. I think landslides in recent years have made it impassable now and property owners have put up "no trespassing" signs in other places, but back then you could follow it for miles along the Wolverine. Sometimes we would find the actual tracks, rusted and half-buried, or sections of railroad ties poking up through the ground, other times we were just able to see the grade of the land and know we were still on it. We were making our way through a particularly brushy area when we looked off the bank. Down by the river were several old train cars on their sides, as if they had been shoved off the tracks.

It wasn't any great discovery, but I think because we had stumbled on them by ourselves, it was like we'd found King Tut's tomb. There were trees growing up through the train cars, and inside there were old tin cans and whiskey bottles. I also found a railroad spike. When I picked it up it occurred to me that it was really old, probably older than anything I had ever held before. I brought it home with me, and I asked Mom when the railroad was built. 1905. It was almost a century old, and by Alaskan standards, that's ancient. That was when I started asking more questions, and reading books about the mine and the river and how my mother's ancestors lived here before. What surprised me the most, though, is how little I could find to read. We hadn't written down much of our own history, and a lot of the old stories had been lost. I think that is what motivates me in my work here at the museum. I don't want to just find and preserve history — I want to keep it alive for Alaskans.

On a separate note, you asked about Isaac. He has as little to do with the museum as he can manage. He's a graphic designer and illustrator (but I still haven't been able to talk him into doing the museum's website pro bono). And he's my life partner. I met him while I was going to graduate school in Seattle, and then I talked him into moving back to Alaska with me. Even though he never stops complaining about the dark and cold every winter, I think we're here for a while.

Warm regards and
best wishes for your health,
Josh

Lieut. Col. Allen Forrester
June 8, 1885

Our steady pace of travel towards the mountains is wearying. 15 or so miles each day, with little time or strength to gather food. As the Indians warned, we have seen no salmon since we began our travels up the west fork of the Wolverine.

Nat'aaggi spotted a moose on a far hillside. Tillman wanted to hunt it, but it would require a day, possibly more, with no guarantee of success. As hungry as we are, I am keen to arrive at the lake. I believe we are within a few days march.

The valley has opened onto a wide plain, the mountains steadily moving away from us east & west. The Wolverine River increasingly becomes rocky & fast moving. In the distance, the land is dotted with bogs & small ponds. Everywhere wild flowers are in bloom. I wish instead for berries, fruit of any sort. We take our doses of acetic acid in hopes that it will stave off scurvy.

It is midnight, yet nearly daylight. We stopped walking an hour ago to set camp, cook supper. We now rest beside the fire, look towards the mountains & a glacier to the northeast.

It seems that her long talks with Tillman have continued to sharpen Nat'aaggi's English. I believe she will be increasingly helpful with translation.

This night she recounted a story she heard told about a nearby mountain — long ago a woman was looking for her people. She had somehow become separated from them. She walked & walked. She carried her baby on her back. She walked many miles up the river. The summer sun was hot & she was thirsty, but she kept walking. When she reached a glacier, it was cool. She drank from a stream. She laid down on the tundra beside the glacier, her child cradled in her arms. There the two fell asleep. They never woke up. She & her infant had turned to stone.

— I see it. Don't you, Colonel? Tillman said. — See, that valley is the curve of her arm, that lower cliff her child. Her face, her long legs.

It took me some time. I could not see what they described. Finally, though, they appeared in the shape of the mountain. A sleeping mother, with child in her arms.

June 9

Boyo found a dead goose this morning. Nat'aaggi skinned it, roasted it over a fire.

Pruitt said he was not as hungry, & he did not touch the goose meat.

The rest of us ate, but I admit my stomach turned when I thought of the feathers at the slave's wrist. If you believe a woman can take such form, how can you ever again eat goose flesh without some distress?

This afternoon we met a man who Ceeth Hwya described as the greatest chief of the Wolverine Valley. They say as a young man he led one of the massacres of the Russians. Now he is old & blind, lives alone except for a woman who cares for him. He wept often during our visit. Nat'aaggi says he was ashamed not to have more to offer in hospitality.

He is one of the oldest men I have ever seen. I suspect he does not have much longer on this earth. Tillman shared with him a small bit of Boyd's tobacco.

June 10

The mosquitoes are incessant. Our first encounters this spring were not so troublesome — the insects large, slow & easy to swat. The Indians, however, warned us of what was to come. With summer, new varieties appear. Small, aggressive, & numerous enough to be a menace. Pruitt claims to have counted 65 mosquitoes on Tillman's back at one time. This annoyed the sergeant.

— You ought to do less counting & more killing, he said.

We stay to the riverbed, where the sand & wind drive back the insects. When we must cross into wooded areas, however, we are besieged. I chose a poor route today so that we found ourselves in the middle of wet land. A dark cloud of mosquitoes surrounded us, attacked any exposed skin & swarmed our eyes, mouths & ears. All the while a sandpiper of some type swept down on us & screeched without stop. It was a maddening, unpleasant scene, one that I thought would break Pruitt entirely.

At night we sleep with our heads pulled all the way into our sleeping bags. Nat'aaggi burns a smudge fire of green leaves. Boyo snaps at the air.

June 11

Mid-day. Sunny, much warmer than one would ever expect this far north. We rest against driftwood logs on a sandy stretch of riverbed. No mosquitoes in this heat, so we will sleep for a few hours in blessed peace. We need not worry about wasting daylight. This far north & into summer, we travel through the night if we choose, as true darkness never comes.

It is remarkable, the transformation of this land. We arrived to snow & ice & gray. When I call this to mind, the landscape before us seems impossible. It has become a verdant, lush place, nearly jungle-like. Swaths of alder roll down off the mountains. The lowlands are thick with cottonwood, birch, & willow, all in foliage. When we enter the forest, we walk through stinging nettles, wild raspberry bushes. There are, too, giant leaves with stalks as tall as a man & barbed with spines that cause welts to the skin. The trapper calls them devil's club. The name is well earned.

We observed a small group of caribou at sky-line this evening, some half mile away. The animals behaved unpredictably, prancing, running in all directions as if they bolted from invisible enemies.

— Mosquitoes, Tillman explained. — Nattie says the poor beasts are trying to outrun them.

June 12
No rabbits in Nat'aaggi's snares today. Ate the last of the salmon two days ago, though it was well turned to mush in our packs. Flour paste for breakfast. Anxious to find the village on the lake.

X. Scurvy (Scorbutus)

Definition. — A constitutional disease characterized by great debility, with anaemia, a spongy condition of the gums, and a tendency to haemorrhages.

Symptoms. — The disease is insidious in its onset. Early symptoms are loss in weight, progressively developing weakness, and pallor. Very soon the gums are noticed to be swollen and spongy, to bleed easily, and in extreme cases to present a fungous appearance. The teeth may become loose and even fall out. The tongue is swollen, but may be red and not much furred. The skin becomes dry and rough, and ecchymoses soon appear, first on the legs and then on the arms and trunk.

Palpitation of the heart and feebleness and irregularity of the impulse are prominent symptoms. The appetite is impaired, and owing to the soreness of the gums the patient is unable to chew the food.

There are mental depression, indifference, in some cases headache, and in the latter stages delirium.

Prognosis. — The outlook is good, unless the disease is far advanced and the conditions persist which lead to its development.

— From *Principles and Practice of Medicine,*
William Osler, M.D., New York, 1893

Lieut. Col. Allen Forrester
June 13, 1885
Kulgadzi Lake

A formidable body of water indeed.

Just as Ceeth Hwya described, it stretches broadside east to west, but is much larger than I anticipated. Nothing like the serene clear ponds we have seen so far. It is at least five miles across to the northern shore. Pruitt estimates 15 miles to the glacier that borders it to the east, most likely just as far to its western end. The waters are cloudy, dark gray, with sizeable white caps. Knee-high, choppy waves wash ashore. The rocky beaches are littered with driftwood.

During the heat of the day, as we neared the lake, Pruitt & I talked of taking a dip. Upon arriving, we are dissuaded.

— That there water would freeze a man's valuable parts right off, Tillman said.

It is indeed frigid. I only cupped water in my hands to splash my face & was chilled.

Tomorrow we search the shore for the village.

I do not sleep well. The wind off the lake stirs the trees, cuts through my sleeping bag. I hear Tillman & Nat'aaggi still awake talking to one another. I long for home.

June 14

We have located the Indians only a mile or so to the west. They speak yet another dialect of Midnoosky so that we have much difficulty in communicating, even with Tillman & Nat'aaggi working together. My Trail River jacket, however, needed no translation.

— Ceeth Hwya! they said.

From then on, we have been treated as royalty. We are offered sleeping quarters in their huts, provided with a feast of caribou meat, trout of some kind from the lake. Without salmon, these are their primary foods.

We have managed to secure two canoes as well as supplies, although it cost us a great deal in gun powder. In retrospect, I believe the Indians' reluctance was not one of bargaining but instead of disbelief. When we told them they would have to retrieve their canoes, as we would be leaving them on the far side, they would not accept the terms. Surely we would be returning, they said. We explained that we would continue on to the north, to cross the mountains.

They wanted to know if I was a shaman. Nat'aaggi said that might explain my behavior. Why else would I come all this way only to lead my men into the land of the dead?

We tried in several ways to explain that we know our direction, that we will travel through the mountains & continue on to the Tanana & Yukon Rivers.

There is little to eat in the mountains, they said. There is no firewood, no good place to camp. Even if we were to find a place out of the weather, they said it is not safe to fall asleep in the pass. They said we could wake to find ourselves lost to a snowstorm or surrounded by dangerous spirits.

The wind from the glacier has ceased this evening. The lake is calm.

Pruitt paddled one of the canoes a few hundred yards out from shore to measure the depth using Indian fishing twine with a rock tied at the end. He had marked the length in five-foot increments. At 100 feet, he ran out of twine but still had not struck bottom.

I suspect it is the fear of the open water that keeps these Indians close to shore — the canoes are not designed to navigate white caps. However, with mild weather such as this, we could paddle hard, be to the far side within hours.

I put forth the plan this evening as we ate. Nat'aaggi, who listened nearby, protested.

— It would cut our journey to the far side well in half, I said. — Why not go straight across?

She endeavored to tell several of the Indian men of our plans. They understood enough to disapprove. An elder in the group came to sit beside me. He spoke earnestly, that much I could see, but we had difficulty comprehending his words. He tried gestures. He pointed towards the lake, then slid one arm smoothly from one side to another, indicating its surface. With the other hand he formed a mouth, brought it chomping up from the depths.

We came to understand that some creature lived in the lake.

— Slook? (Is it a fish?) Animal? What is it?

He pointed to the distance from where we sat to a nearby hut. He indicated that length again & again. He nodded towards the lake.

— Is he saying the thing is that long? Nigh on 20 feet? Tillman asked.

— Yes, Nat'aaggi said. — Udjee.

— Caribou? I don't understand, he says it is a caribou?

— No, sir, Tillman said. — They're saying it eats caribou. Grabs them when they try to swim the lake.

June 15

Pruitt requested we stay in the village for several days. He says he is ill & needs to rest. I inquired as to his specific ailments, to which he replied only that he is generally weary & not himself. He complains of aching bones & shortness of breath even when walking on flat ground. I suggested that he might gain strength in eating more when we have food available, to which he shrugged with indifference.

I asked Tillman how he fared.

— I'm well enough. But Colonel, we've been going hard. A day or two wouldn't put us too behind, would it?

I suspect Pruitt of apathy, Tillman of wanting to consort with the Indians. Both of them are wary of the lake. It all frustrates me to no end. Perhaps I have been too inflexible, however.

I have agreed to an additional day in camp, so as to rest & feed our appetites. The men must find their nerve again. I have no interest in dawdling our way over the mountains. I am disappointed with their softness.

Pruitt reports that the psychrometer has been stolen. I suspected he had misplaced it, but then Tillman caught sight of one of the young Indians showing the instrument to the others. Tillman was ready to start a brawl, but I swayed him otherwise. We are better off to seem as if we approve of the "trade" than to arouse hostility.

This evening, Nat'aaggi brought an old man to speak with us. She helped him raise his hide tunic to his chest. Along the Indian's side were savage, roughly healed scars. Several of his ribs had evidently been broken as well, healed unevenly so that they protrude at odd angles. It is improbable that a man could survive such injuries, certainly not an Indian without medicine or doctor.

I asked what had caused this. Was he in a battle? An attack of some sort?

Nat'aaggi shook her head, then pointed to the lake. It seems the old man was fishing out too far. The creature overturned his canoe. He says he escaped only because he was a strong fighter.

I observed that the scars are well healed, asked how long ago it had happened.

The discussion attracted Tillman's attention.

— Christ Almighty! The thing in the lake did this?

I repeated my question about the timing of the event.

— It happened many summers ago, when he was a young man, Tillman said.

I suggested that if the creature had ever existed, perhaps it was dead now.

Tillman was not put at ease, however. As

he climbed into his sleeping bag tonight, he made his plea.

— Let's just walk around the lake, Colonel. Why risk it? Even putting aside this 50-foot monster, those waves are serious enough. Seems to me they could sink these shallow canoes.

When I would not budge, he tried to convince me that it would improve our mapping if we were to walk the edge of the lake.

— The lieutenant could get better measurements.

I have no desire to overwinter in this territory. I told Tillman as much. I'm ready for home. The lake offers us no danger beyond fear & superstition. With calm weather, smooth waters, we'll paddle straight across without any excitement.

June 16

It is but the early hours of the morning, yet I can no longer sleep. It is quiet. The waves have subsided. The lake is smooth. A mist lays across the water. I am anxious to be on our way. I will wake the men soon.

In September I visited the Chkituk village, where I sang a funeral service for a Kenaitze who had become ill and soon died from a fright. He had seen some scary animal-like monster that was coming from the water. Soon this native lost his speech, his mind became cloudy, and within three days he died.

— From Hegumen Nikolai,
Travel Journal, 1860,
Through Orthodox Eyes

Dear Mrs. Forrester —

I have enclosed your pneumatic shutter. I am quite anxious to learn how it works for you. Although my landscapes are not as prone to jumping about as your birds, I may yet be tempted to try the apparatus. My wife for some time has wanted me to take a portrait photograph of our three young and energetic grandchildren. A quick-acting shutter might be of use in such a situation.

I have also put on order the rapid rectilinear lens — I think the Dallmeyer's will serve you best. I will send it to you as soon as it arrives.

And yes, I know all too well your frustration. It is a rare combination of events that must occur: the illumination at the moment, the length of exposure, the composition of the scene, the development, and then the printing. I am sorry to say that only one or two of my photographs of Mount Hood come close to touching upon the vision that I so often witness. Yet I believe that the more you experiment, the nearer you will draw to your aspiration.

I hope I do not stray too far into my own philosophical thoughts, but let me venture this much: one must learn the mechanics and chemistry, and then allow all that to slip into the background. It seems counter to science and rational thought, but I do not believe one can ultimately calculate perfection. It is an impression, an instinct in the moment, on which one must depend.

All that being said, I see great skill in the two prints you kindly sent me. They may not be your birds, but it is clear that you have an aptitude for both composition and light. It seems to me that already you observe and translate the world with a photographer's eye.

I would be most pleased to see more of your future work.

Sincerely,
Mr. Henry Redington

Sophie Forrester
Vancouver Barracks
June 12, 1885

I would not have gone out today if it weren't for the letter from Mr Redington that arrived just before noon. He is so composed that at times it makes me smile, for his idea of "inordinate pleasure" is a brief discussion on citrate of soda solution and exposure times. Yet his kind words bolster me more than he can know. Can it be that he really finds some promise in my work so far? I write to him pages and pages of all my anxieties and frustrations, and he sends me concise common sense and encouragement. And a pneumatic bulb!

Charlotte was glad as well, for I'm sure she must tire of being cooped up in the house with small chores and my ill mood. Today was a perfectly fine day to go afield, albeit quite hot. She and I settle into a routine — I wear tripod and camera strapped to a knapsack on my back, while she carries the wooden box with glass plates, focusing cloth, etc. (And her sling-shot is always at her side. I must remember to tell Allen when he returns how devoted she was to her promise to protect me.)

In the large meadow on the hill we caught sight of two king birds that behaved like a breeding pair, of which I made notes in my field book, and although we were unable to locate their nest this day, I am hopeful. Then, in a hollow in a dead alder tree, we discovered an occupied sapsucker nest. The darkness of the cavity will not allow for a photograph, I am afraid, but it was a lovely find all the same, and Charlotte was quite taken with the nearly grown chicks.

As we returned to the barracks, we met up with Evelyn, who was strolling with two officers and several young women, and Charlotte and I were obliged to stop and converse with them.

When asked, I explained that we were in search of birds, to which one of the young women said she was fascinated by photography but suggested that it was a rather rough and manly hobby, to go about the forest with a camera. The two young men nodded their agreement.

"What a stupid thing to say!" Evelyn replied. "What on earth makes it more suitable for a man than a woman? Do not for a single moment doubt Mrs Forrester. More than anyone I know, she is capable!"

They all seemed taken aback by the passion of Evelyn's speech, and it occurred to me that they do not know her so well. Nor were they inclined to engage in her debate, but instead began to wander away from us and down the trail toward the barracks, all the while one of the women complaining that they would be late to the band concert at the parade grounds this afternoon.

"Imbeciles!" Evelyn said, once they were out of hearing distance. "But they are the closest I can find to amusement in this place, so I am stuck with them after all."

She left us then to catch up with her party, but before she had gone far, she did in fact say something that surprised me. "I hope you find your humming bird, Sophie!"

I did not think she was listening that day in Portland when I told her of my impracticable desire. How could anyone hope to photograph the ceaseless motion that is a humming bird?

June 13

At long last, after all these days of searching and waiting, I have a bird! A chickadee on the branch of the alder, with more contrast than I would like and faced the wrong direction, but there it is, all the same!

I was so elated, I ran about the house and

469

shouted for Charlotte to come see the developed plate. She agreed it was wonderfully exciting, but remarked that it was unfortunate that all I had caught was the "tail-end" of the bird. I could not argue her point.

Yet I begin to regain some small optimism. More and more I grasp the way in which shadow, light, and shape transfers to the glass, and how I might manipulate the elements both in the field and in the dark room to achieve more subtlety of detail. And if I can catch the tail-end of a chickadee in a hundred hours, then I must only invest hundreds more.

As for a nest, I fear the season grows late. It may be next spring before I am able to attempt such a photograph. Yet I am pleased to know that while I lack the hand to paint or sketch, it seems I possess some of the necessary traits for this endeavor — fortitude and great patience.

June 15

I am grateful that we were not harmed, but now that it is over, I confess I found today's encounter positively exhilarating! We returned safely to the cabin from the forest hours ago, yet even still I can feel my heart trembling.

With the weather fair today, Charlotte and I ventured farther than ever we have before. Where the wagon trail weaves north, we came across a small meadow. It was a picturesque scene, the way the sunlight caught the buzzing insects and tawny grass. Several small birds fluttered up from the grass, landed, flew up again, but I could not identify them with the naked eye. We walked to a small rise, and from there we could see that the meadow turned to marshland at the far side. We set down packs and camera, I brought out the field glasses, and we sat there for some time in silence, watching the tree swallows and dragonflies.

The black bear seemed completely ignorant of our presence. It wandered out from the trees not a hundred yards away, its head down in the grass as if looking for some morsel of food. Now and then it brought its snout up to sniff the air, but never indicated it saw us.

Charlotte was equally unaware as she looked to the distance through the field glasses. I touched her elbow, and when she saw where I pointed, she squeaked, and then reached for her sling-shot. I shook my head and urgently mouthed the words "no, no."

Thank heavens the child obeyed me! At best, she would have startled the bear so that it would have fled, ruining our chances to observe it. A more terrifying likelihood is that the creature would have been provoked to come after us, and I do not think we would have fared well, no matter how straight her aim or fast our legs.

So Charlotte and I remained still and silent, yet it required much willpower on my part, for such nervous energy coursed through my veins. All of my senses and attention were fixed upon the bear, so that the animal became fully formed, magnified even: dusty black fur, small ears that twitched at the insects, the gentle slope of its forehead, the immense weight and bulk of its presence. It was nothing like the cool, white marble bear of my childhood.

And then the bear looked at us. Its eyes were quite small and dark, like wet pebbles in its enormous black head. It watched us for what was surely only a few seconds, but time had become mutable, slowed, so that I had long enough to consider what the bear may or may not do, and it was a disquieting consideration. At last, it turned from us and began to lumber away across the meadow, and time sped alongside it, so that when the bear disappeared into the far trees, it was as if all had happened within the clap of hands.

When we returned to the barracks, Charlotte sprinted to Mr MacGillivray where he was working in the General's garden.

"A bear! We saw a bear!"

"What is all this?"

I confirmed that it was true, indeed we had spied a black bear just a few miles away. Mr MacGillivray seemed skeptical but concerned, and he expressed relief that we had survived the ordeal.

And just now as I write, I have realized that in all the excitement, I left my field glasses at the marsh!

June 16

I am yet unsettled by it, the gaze of the black bear.

For some time after Father's death, I imagined, with both fear and hope, that I would someday meet a wild bear in the forest near the quarry, and that when I looked into its eyes, I would know that it was Father.

Of course, I found no such sign in this bear. In its small, dark eyes, I saw nothing recognizable or connected to my brain, no common affinity or acknowledgment. Only an alien wildness that was grand and terrible.

I am glad of Mr MacGillivray's news. He set out on horseback yesterday and found the bear's tracks in the mud of a nearby creek, yet he saw nothing of the animal itself. (And, kind man, he retrieved my precious field glasses. I am only fortunate it did not rain on them during the night.)

I begged Mr MacGillivray that we might keep the knowledge of the bear to ourselves, for if the men of the barracks, many of them bored and anxious to prove their bravery, learn of its presence, there will be a hunt on.

"I agree with you there, Mrs Forrester. Much rather let the fellow find his way back into the mountains. As long as he doesn't overstay his welcome."

Both Charlotte and I promised we would not wander so far, an agreement to which I was amenable. While I am glad to have seen the bear, for surely it is one of the most extraordinary occurrences of my life, I have no desire to repeat it.

June 17

I have been issued a summons; I am to present myself at General Haywood's house tomorrow afternoon.

Mrs Connor! I have no doubt. It seems she has taken it upon herself to directly or indirectly inform the General of the modifications I have made to the pantry. Insufferable busybody!

Bless the soldier who delivered the message, for he began immediately with, "This isn't regarding your husband. We have no news about the Colonel's whereabouts. The General wants to see you on another matter. It's about your room here, where you do your picture-making."

This evening I cannot stop stewing over it. Is this such a matter of urgency that a soldier must be sent to my door? Again and again, I rehearse in my mind what I will say to the General and his wife tomorrow, and the words I will dish up to Mrs Connor next I see her. For heaven's sake, the cabin is to be destroyed next summer! What does it matter what I do to it? If necessary, I will pay for any damages, and reinstall the door and shelves myself if need be, even if it is just in time for them to knock it down. Beyond that, what I do with my time is my business and mine alone.

Evelyn informed me with great amusement just the other day that I am the talk of the ladies' teas, that Mrs Connor has made it clear that she finds my activities unwholesome, even wicked, and she didn't think the General would approve of the "injury" I had done to the house. Mrs Whithers apparently defends me as much as she is able and says she would like to see my photographs, but she wonders how interesting they could be considering I point my lens only at trees and shrubs.

It is all an incredible annoyance! Why do any of them care how I spend my hours? I certainly have absolutely no interest in their daily comings and goings.

I say this, however: I will not be bullied, General or no General.

Vancouver Barracks, Washington, circa 1880

Lieut. Col. Allen Forrester
June 16, 1885
Kulgadzi Lake

I am only glad to have survived this day.

We left shore around 6 this morning in a cool mist. The lake was dead calm. For some distance out, the water remained shallow so that our paddles scraped the bottom. At about 100 yards from shore, the depth abruptly fell out from beneath us so that even when Tillman thrust the paddle & his arm directly down, he could not strike bottom.

In the stillness of the morning, we heard only the dripping of water from our paddles, one of us occasionally clearing our throats. As we hit our rhythm, the canoes gained speed. Our vessels were well matched in weight & strength — Pruitt rode with me, while Tillman & Nat'aaggi carried the dog in their canoe. It seemed feasible that we would make it across the lake within an hour or two.

Tillman noticed the dog's sudden alertness.

At first it only lifted its head, pricked up its ears. Then came its low growl.

—Will you look at that? Tillman said.

The fur along Boyo's back stood on end. The dog growled again, then began to bark sharply towards some distant place in the middle of the lake.

Pruitt whispered a curse.

That's when I saw it — a large V sliced through the waves, as if an invisible canoe was propelled towards us.

I suggested it was perhaps a beaver or muskrat.

—That's one hell of a rodent, Tillman said without humor. He took out his rifle, began to load it.

The form seemed to quicken its advance, but as it neared within a few hundred yards of our canoes, it abruptly changed direction, began to circle us at that distance.

In the gray depths, I could not determine anything of its shape. When it surfaced, we could see that its length was greater than our two canoes end to end. Nat'aaggi shouted with alarm. She & Tillman began to paddle quickly back towards shore.

— Don't, I said. — It may only rouse its interest. Let's just sit.

I did not yet realize how near the beast was. Just then, it struck our canoe with such force as to nearly capsize us.

It must have dove, for it disappeared, then

resurfaced on the far side of the other canoe. Again its long back was barely visible, but we could see that its skin was smooth, mottled green and black. No apparent ridges, fins, or limbs.

— Paddle! I commanded.

Nat'aaggi & Tillman were making quick progress towards shore. Our own canoe, however, faced the wrong direction. For a few strokes, Pruitt & I worked at odds to each other, until we were at last able to turn about.

We were still several boat lengths behind the others when the creature struck our vessel again. We were overturned, both of us thrown into the cold water.

I descended several feet below the surface. My ears filled with the rush of water. I could see nothing beyond dull gray on all sides. The glacial coldness seized my muscles, so that I could not even let the air from my lungs.

Though muffled by the water, I heard what I took for a cry from Pruitt. I gained my senses, swam upward, surfaced with a gasp. That was when I first felt contact. Cold skin, smooth as if without scales. Large enough to shove me aside with its weight.

Pruitt tried to hold to the canoe as it filled with water. When the creature rose to attack him, for a brief moment I saw its head. A prehistoric beast, with a wide, flat skull & a bill-like mouth.

We gained a brief advantage when the

creature instead went for the canoe. For what seemed like several minutes, it thrashed with the canoe in its mouth as it tried to drag it under.

Tillman & Nat'aaggi paddled their canoe to our aid. The two reached Pruitt first, just as the creature again came near the surface. Nat'aaggi beat at it with her paddle. Pruitt grabbed on to the side of their canoe but lacked the strength to pull himself aboard. His weight upon the side threatened to overturn it.

Tillman tried to help him into the canoe, but it tipped too far, Tillman lost his balance so ended up in the water as well. Nat'aaggi just managed to keep it from capsizing entirely. I swam for the other side so that I could steady it when they tried to climb in.

Tillman held to the canoe, used his shoulder to boost Pruitt aboard. Before he could save himself, Tillman was abruptly pulled down. The creature had hold of him. From my position, I could do nothing except shout an order for Pruitt to shoot.

Pruitt stood with the rifle, took aim. The canoe teetered beneath him. He hesitated. I think he feared shooting Tillman, who was now fiercely engaged with the creature. Nat'aaggi continued to beat down into the water with her paddle. Pruitt finally shot, aiming for the backside of the creature, well away from Tillman. It was enough to at least startle if not wound it.

Tillman climbed aboard as I counter-weighted the canoe. It occurred to me then that it would never hold us all. Already it was sunk to within inches of being swamped. I ordered them to head into shore.

Tillman reached down to offer me a hand out of the lake.

— You could hold to the stern while we paddle, Tillman offered.

They could make no headway with the added drag. Again I ordered them to paddle on.

I swam after them with all the strength I could muster, but by now I was worn out from the struggle & cold. I made little progress. As I thrashed in the water, I again felt the thing pass near me. It was most unnerving. Its bulk & power moved through the water so that I could feel its current beneath me before my feet struck its back.

It would have had me, I am certain, if it weren't for the Indians. I was half frozen & fading. When I saw their canoes approach, I gave one last effort to swim towards them.

I cannot describe the relief of being pulled from that lake. Two Indians helped me aboard their vessel, as those in the other canoe were at the ready with bows & arrows. I was weak & my body felt impossibly heavy, so I lay on the bottom of the boat. In the short time it took to reach shore, I commenced to shivering & teeth-chattering with such violence that my muscles ached. It would be some time before I fully regained my warmth.

The Indians were able to retrieve our water-filled canoe, tow it back to shore. Remarkably our packs were still strapped inside, though one rifle was lost.

As we were helped ashore, it became clear that Tillman had no sense of his injury, only wanted to boast of fighting the creature. — I got in quite a few good clobbers, he said, demonstrating with his fists. Then he began to laugh. — Guess I can swim after all, if I'm riding a 50-foot water snake.

Pruitt insisted that the creature was neither a snake nor anywhere near 50 feet. The two began to argue. Tillman quieted, however, when I drew his attention to his leg where the cloth of his pants had been torn away. He said he was surprised to know he had even been bitten, then he looked down.

— Good God! he said in a weak voice, so that I expected him to faint.

His wounds were clean & cool due to the lake water. Unlike most injuries I have encountered in the field, there was of course no ball or shrapnel to concern us. All that said, it is not pleasant to behold. In their arrangement the wounds reveal the size & shape of the creature's jaws. Punctures to the skin of his upper thigh, as well as that of his lower leg beneath the knee, show the jaw to be nearly three feet wide. The teeth seem to have been comparatively small, concentrated at the back of the jaw, & notably sharp.

Most of the puncture wounds are neat. However, several gashes did require suturing.

When Pruitt brought out needles & silk thread, Tillman protested.

— Not without a drop of whiskey, he said.

I pointed out that there were no such spirits for 500 miles in any direction.

While Nat'aaggi held his head in her lap, Pruitt & I set to work. I credit Tillman — while he did shout & curse, he managed to keep still enough. We went as quickly as we could. I am grateful, too, for Pruitt's skills as impromptu field surgeon.

Nat'aaggi tends to Tillman. She sits by his side tonight in one of the huts, offering him drinks of water.

June 17

My diaries & Sophie's letter are nearly dry. I have laid them along the ground in the afternoon sun, holding them in place with small rocks. It is fortunate that I carry them wrapped in squares of oilcloth within my jacket. They are damp in places, but all considering, they are in decent shape & I am much relieved.

■ ■ ■ ■

A medicine man visited Tillman this afternoon. His ceremony was long & bizarre. For an hour or more, he remained concealed beneath a skin blanket inside our hut. He eventually began to writhe, dance, sing, all the while still hidden. After some time, he had worked himself into such a state of excitement that the skin blanket fell from him, his face dripped with sweat, his voice was gravelly. He next placed the blanket over Tillman's injured leg, spoke incantations, then appeared to catch some unseen entity, which he wrestled with on the ground for some time before dragging it out of the hut.

If it were me, I would not hold to such nonsense. Tillman, however, says it can do no harm.

Dear Josh,

First off, I see now that I might have used language in previous letters that would likely offend your kind. Please excuse that. I've never bothered myself with being politically correct, but truth be told, I don't care much one way or the other about people's sexual leanings. I tend to get lazy and resort to the easy insults. I apologize for that.

It's a limitation in writing back and forth like this. You don't see a whole person in their words. I am surprised, though, that you two landed some place like Alpine, at least how you describe it. It seems the city might be a more accepting place.

I am curious, too, why you mention it at all. Life would be a whole lot easier if you just kept that under your hat. Down the road from me a couple of old spinsters have lived together for as long as I can recall. They don't make a show of it or march to get married at town hall. They keep their business to themselves, and that suits us all just fine.

As for the money, take it. I don't have family to speak of. I was married once years ago, but we never had children. It was probably for the best. I don't think we ever much liked each other. Looking back I think I was only truly in love once, when I was about 18 or 19. She was a sweet girl, and if I'd known how rare that commodity was, maybe I would have done things different. Maybe, maybe not. Sometimes when I think back on my younger self, it's like trying to read the mind of a stranger. And a damned idiot at that.

On to more important matters, it's true what you said about the way a person comes to history. There's nothing like a textbook to bleed all the life out of the past. And for you, a boy all the way up in Alaska, the Civil War might as well have happened on another planet.

Interestingly enough, though, it was at one of those battlefields that I first got interested. It was much like your finding those train cars. My father took me out to Gettysburg when I was a boy, and even at that young age, I was moved. I was still young enough to hold onto his hand, and while we walked, he told me that his uncle, the Colonel, had fought there. He made me to understand that my feet were touching holy ground where men had killed and bled and died. All these years later, I can still recall the day. The clouds were moving fast across a blue sky, and the green grass and trees were so peaceful. Nearly 50,000 men dead, wounded, or missing. I always did have an overactive imagination as a child, and I could hear the cannons firing, and I could see the ghosts of the soldiers walking those gentle hills. It troubled me for some time.

I'll tell you one thing about history — we leave a lot of carnage in our wake. The only way we know, it seems, no matter how many times we see it done.

Sincerely,
Walt

It became very quiet in the house. All sat with downcast eyes. The shaman also remained silent with his head down, thinking for a minute or longer, then, without a word he left the house. In a few minutes, he returned with a dirty, greasy sack and shook from it the objects of his profession, namely wooden rattles used in dancing, colored sticks, strips of wood, feathers, a doll with hair and queue, and other trinkets which were so dirty that one could not handle them without repulsion. Then one or two similar dolls were brought in by some women: All these things were burned in their presence on the street. It was amusing to see the indignation of one old woman when she saw my churchman spitting on a doll brought by her.

— From Hieromonk Nikita,
Travel Journal, Kenai, 1881–1882,
Documents Relative to the
History of Alaska, volume 1
(translated from Russian)

Sophie Forrester
Vancouver Barracks
June 18, 1885

An unexpected turn of events at the General's house this afternoon, although my embarrassment could have been much worse. Mercifully, Mrs Haywood interrupted my outburst before I could say all that I had prepared, about the right of a woman to run her household as she sees fit and the impertinence of anyone to suggest otherwise.

"And do not suppose that my husband will not defend me in this case," I was saying. "I will certainly do everything I can to make amends, but if I cannot, I suggest we take it up with him upon his return . . ."

"Mrs Forrester, Mrs Forrester. Calm yourself," said Mrs Haywood, who was directing her servant to pour the tea. "You have not been called here to be reprimanded."

"What? Of course not!" the General said. (In truth, every word the General spoke was at the auditory level of a shout, but his demeanor and that of his wife indicated that this was his customary voice.)

"What is she talking about?" the General shouted at his wife.

Mrs Haywood placed a hand on her husband's knee and directed her attention back to me.

"I have not seen you at the ladies' tea in some time. And it's so unfortunate that you missed the concert at the parade ground. It was rousing, though of course quite loud."

"Yes," I said, "I was able to hear the drums and horns even as I worked."

"Working on your photographs?" she asked. "We understand you have modified the pantry in your house where you do such things."

I nodded but dared not speak, so instead sipped at my tea.

"We have seen you about the grounds often with your camera," Mrs Haywood continued. "It is the landscape that interests you, rather than portraits?"

"Enough!" said the General. "I don't have all afternoon to natter away. Do you see those over there?"

He pointed to a wooden box near the door of the parlor.

"Plates. From the expedition. They came down the river with the papers. They need to be handled."

I did not understand. Were these photographs from Allen's journey? And did he ask me to develop them?

"Yes! Yes!" shouted the General.

Of course I would do anything to assist, but I suggested that Mr Redington in Portland would be better suited to develop such important photographs.

"We've been in contact. He recommended you. Frankly, I'd prefer he do it. But he can't get to them for some time, and he says you're more than capable. I'll have them sent up to your house."

General Haywood stood then, eager to be free of the parlor, but I could not let him go without asking if he had heard anything from my husband or his men.

"Not a word since Haigh Canyon."

As for the glass plates, it seems no one has opened the box since its delivery, as it was marked "Photographs" and the General prudently wanted them handled only in a dark room. I am anxious to discover their contents.

June 19

Such a disappointment! More than two dozen photographs from the expedition are lost. Not only are the plates cracked and broken, but it looks as if someone stripped them out of their protective slides and exposed them. At first I thought all were destroyed, but I have discovered just nine that were spared.

I sent word to the General, and he replied that he feared as much, as there were rumors that the Wolverine Indians had tampered with the shipment before it was delivered to Alaska's coast.

As I waited for his reply, I found myself hoping that the General would say that he had reconsidered, and request that I send the plates on to Mr Redington after all. I have yet to put any of them into solution.

Some part of my hesitation is irrational. If the men were injured or in danger at the time these were taken, surely such reports would have been sent along with the plates. Yet against my will, photographs from our Civil War come to my mind. What if, alone in my dark room, I am confronted with some scene of Allen or his men in distress? The thought nearly incapacitates me with dread.

A more rational concern, however, is that I may very well ruin these precious plates. I grow more confident with my skills, yet I cannot rule out the possibility that I will wrongly measure my chemicals, or misjudge how long to leave a plate in solution, and it is not as if these photographs can ever be retaken. I hope Mr Redington has not been too generous and reckless in his recommendation.

I know the General is anxious to have this done, but perhaps I will wait until tomorrow, with hopes that I will be calmer of nerves.

June 20

I regained my courage after all. Five plates developed to varying degrees of success late last night, and today I made prints in the sunshine. Mr Pruitt had neatly annotated each with a slate pencil, so I am able to identify them as such.

The first was marked "Wolverine River, April 1885," and showed a wide river made of slabs of ice closely piled up on one another so as to reveal only small patches of dark water. Though the weather is foggy and overcast, one can see in the far distance a stand of evergreen trees along a steep hillside. The terrain makes me think that there must be tall mountains beyond that are obscured by the low clouds. It is an icy and forlorn scene, so that I can hardly imagine anyone living comfortably in such a landscape.

The next plate was irretrievably damaged by fogging, a problem I know all too well. I suspect Mr Pruitt was challenged to handle the plates without a dark room, probably working beneath the focusing cloth in daylight. I am sorry to not be able to see the image, for it was titled "Midnoosky dance" and sounded fascinating indeed.

There then was an image marked as "Kings Glacier," a mountain of broken and towering ice. This was the scene Allen so wished me to see.

"Nat'aaggi." This is a photograph of a young Indian woman, not much more than a teen-ager I would suppose, crouching beside a large, wolf-like dog.

It is petty and vain of me, but I felt a sickening kind of jealousy to see the woman. She is wild looking, with a fur pelt over her shoulders, clothing of animal skins, and her dark hair long and unbound, but she is not unattractive. There is a certain hardness in her face that causes me to think she is of a strong disposition. I am not sure romance, real or imagined, is even the root of my envy. Rather it is the thought that she should be on such an adventure with my husband, while I wait for any scrap of news and go with none. Does she travel shoulder-to-shoulder with the men as they ford rivers and sleep beneath the stars? Does she laugh and joke with them? If so, how is it that she has the good fortune to walk alongside my husband, to know his fate from moment to moment, while I am left behind? What I wouldn't give to be there in her place.

The last photograph I developed today is unmarked. It is of Allen. He sits on a makeshift campstool with his Army tin cup in his hand, and in front of him is a sled piled high with backpacks, crates, and rifles. At first, I did not recognize him, for where he once had

Boyo

a well-trimmed moustache, he now wears a full beard, his cavalry hat is stained and misshapen, more like that of a trail-worn cowboy than a gentleman officer, and all of his attire appears shabby. At his waist is a pistol in holster. He does not look up at the camera, so I cannot see his eyes.

I was overcome with emotion at the sight of him. I am sure it never entered his thoughts that I might be the first person to see this photograph. I wish he had known, for maybe he would have looked into the camera and I might have seen some tenderness there.

Sophie Forrester
Vancouver Barracks
June 21

I wonder if peaceful sleep will ever find me again. Late last night, I developed the last of the plates with hopes that I could then go to bed to rest comfortably. However, the images proved to be greatly distressing.

The first photograph was of a group of Indians standing and sitting outside of a bark hut. There are several small children and women. One Indian man wears an Army cap, which I suppose was gotten in trade. They all appear quite hungry and poor.

Two other photographs are rather unremarkable. One is of a dog, and it is marked "Boyo." The other shows a cliff face, of which I see nothing particular except a black spot in the trees that I cannot make out even with magnifying glass.

The last, however, became more and more disturbing to me as I came to understand its contents. It is a picture of an Indian man standing on one foot, perhaps in a kind of dance, as he leans on a wooden staff or crutch, his arms spread wide. He wears a top hat, a black vest, and a great assortment of decorations about his neck. All this I could see easily enough on the plate, yet it is an oddity of a negative that all that is black appears white, so that there was something nearly angelic about the image when it first revealed itself in the solution. I rinsed the glass plate and fixed it and set it out to dry so that I could make prints in daylight.

Of course, all that appears white in negative is truly black, and now that I have a print, I can see that he is in shadows and wears dark clothing, while behind him the background is quite bright. He is very near to the camera, his head is cocked at a strange angle, and he peers directly into the lens. I have never met this Indian or seen his countenance before, yet I sensed a familiarity in his appearance that took me some time to pinpoint, and then it occurred to me. His shadowy form, with lame leg and odd tilt of the head, recall the raven that plagued me in the spring.

All this was unnerving enough, but then I recalled that I had not found any notation on the plate itself, and I went in search of the sleeve from which it came. There I found it: "Man Who Flies on Black Wings, Wolverine River."

I have since studied the print with magnifying lens for perhaps longer than was good for me. It is the eyes that chill me the most.

Lieut. Col. Allen Forrester
June 18, 1885

A visitor this afternoon — welcomed by some, though not all of us.

Nat'aaggi spotted the canoe coming across the lake directly as if from the north side. Several of the Indians gathered at the shore to watch its approach. A lone figure, only a dark outline at that distance. As it neared, though, Pruitt took out field glasses.

— It's your friend, Colonel.

He handed me the glasses. Through them I made out the black hat & bronze face.

The Old Man paddled with quick efficiency, though the lake was choppy. At times it looked as if his vessel floated just above the waves.

Several of the Indians waded out when it was near enough, helped pull it to shore. I was surprised to note, then, that the canoe was in fact heavily loaded with fish nearly to overflowing. They were freshly caught, gleaming wet & clear-eyed. A few even flapped about in the pile. Mostly whitefish, as well as large lake trout, grayling. Cheers went up from the Indians as it became clear that the Old Man intended the fish as a gift to the village.

I wondered aloud how he could have gathered so many fish without being attacked by the same creature that nearly killed us.

The Old Man turned to us then, removed his black hat, bowed his head in my direction, then laughed. He spoke, but I could not make out any of the words.

I asked for Nat'aaggi to translate, but she refused. When I asked why, she answered that she knows I don't like 'kay-yuni' stories — spirit stories.

I admitted that was true.

The Old Man then pointed from me to the mountains on the north side of the lake.

I said yes, we would travel that way once Sgt. Tillman has healed.

— He goes there, too, Nat'aaggi said. — You will see him, but you will not know him.

I asked what he meant by that.

She shook her head & said no more, then returned to Tillman's hut.

June 20

Tillman is healed enough to resume travel. The sutures are holding. He is able to walk with little pain. I have insisted that we go by canoe, both to speed our progress as well as give Tillman more rest. We will, however, remain near to shore.

June 21
We have made good progress. Even paddling near shore, all of us were on high alert. Boyo's ears were always perked forward. When a splash went up behind Tillman's canoe, the dog woofed & we all startled, then laughed, for it had only been a small trout. We never did see sign of the creature. We camped last night on the northern side, rose early this morning. I believe we were all glad to leave behind Kulgadzi Lake.

During these first hours of the day, we have already climbed several thousand feet in elevation. What appeared from the distance as grassy hillsides, upon closer inspection have proven to be thick with alder & devil's club. We made our way on game trails through the brush, but often they disappeared out from beneath us or ended abruptly so that we were left in a tangle. At one point, we startled a small black bear but were unable to shoot it before it was lost to the dense brush. It is unfortunate for we could have used the additional meat.

Now at last we are above tree line. The heat fatigues us, so we have stopped to rest beside a mountain spring where we can drink, soak our feet. The dog laps water, pants endlessly.

The view below, as we look down upon Kulgadzi Lake & across into the Wolverine River Valley from where we have come, is most stunning. The mountains to the east are lofty & shine white with snow in the sun, their glacial fingers reach down to the river. To the west, the Wolverine River basin spreads flat & wide, a vast green dotted with small lakes & ponds that reflect the blue sky.

Dear Walt,

I wanted to give you an update on my progress — I just finished transcribing the portion of the diaries from Kulgadzi Lake. It's interesting because I remember my mom telling me that when she was a little girl, all the kids believed a monster lived in its deepest water.

I have to admit, I wish there were a giant, mysterious creature in that lake. It would make a better story than the ones we tell about it now. The public access is littered with junk cars, broken glass, syringes, and old trash fires. Every year there is at least one drowning there, usually with alcohol involved. Last summer, two teenagers who were partying overturned their canoe. They weren't wearing life jackets. One managed to get to shore, by some miracle — it's a glacial lake so the water is unbelievably cold. The other boy died. And then last winter, state troopers found out that a man from Anchorage had been killing young Native women, driving them out and dumping their bodies into the lake through holes in the ice. He had a fishing tent, so everyone just thought he was ice fishing. Needless to say, you won't catch me going for a swim in there.

You're right what you said in your last letter, that it might be easier for me and

Isaac to live somewhere else. The people here aren't always the most tolerant, and Alpine copes with some difficult social problems. Isaac says I'm too much like Pollyanna sometimes, that I only want to see the good. When it's 20 below zero, I say, "Yeah, but the sun is shining." When the wind picks up on the river and the air is hazy with glacial silt, I say, "Sure, but at least it's warmed up some." And when a kid on a four-wheeler shouts a nasty comment at us while we're out for our evening walk, I say "That's Wesley. His mother is so sweet." I don't mention that his father died in a motorcycle accident five years ago, or that Wesley has been in and out of rehab for meth and heroin since he was 14, or that a lot of people think he's the one who has been burglarizing the summer cabins.

It is tough here, in a lot of ways — the weather, the people, the history, but somehow that's why I love it so much. It's like when I go for a walk by the Wolverine River. The riverbed here is wide and the channels are lined with gray sand and boulders, and there is a cold wind that comes down from the glaciers. Out there among the boulders and silt, there is a plant called dryas that blooms a small white flower with translucent petals. It seems so fragile and beautiful and unexpected, all the more because it survives in such a harsh place.

I do sometimes wonder what would have happened if the Colonel had never traveled up the Wolverine River, had never broken the trail for the miners and all that came with them. I'm sure someone else would have come along eventually. It doesn't matter what draws explorers — wealth or fame or military power, or even genuine curiosity — they alter a place just by traveling through it and recording what they see. Within 20 years of the Colonel's expedition, largely because of his reports, the mining companies and fur traders had moved into the Wolverine Valley, and by the 1920s, the Wolverine tribe was hit hard by tuberculosis, influenza, and alcoholism. For example, I am fairly certain that the man the Colonel calls "Ceeth Hwya" died in the 1918 flu epidemic. And those who survived were in a fast-changing world where they had little say over their own fate. Where their fish camps had been, trading posts were built. Families were drawn into a cash economy that did not serve them well, and their children were sent off to government schools. But until 1924, the only way Alaska Natives could earn citizenship and the right to vote was to "sever all tribal relationships" and "adopt the habits of civilized life." According to family stories, when my great-grandmother was a little girl, she used to secretly speak Indian words with her sisters, but if they were caught, their dad would punish them.

It is a paradox, though. Where can we go to learn about Alaska's people, how they lived and worshiped and dressed and spoke before living memory? The explorers are witnesses to the before. The Colonel's diaries, like the writings of Meriwether Lewis and Captain Cook, are a kind of cursed treasure. I have to say, when I read the Colonel's description of the men's copper earrings and the red dye on the faces of the women, it was an incredibly moving experience. It's ironic that such details would be preserved by the very man who would set off so much change.

On a separate note, you seem surprised that I mention Isaac in my letters, but I wouldn't have it any other way. I've come to think of you as a friend, Walt, and that means learning more about each other. You shared with me some of your own life, so it seemed natural to tell you something about myself. And of everything, I think the people we love are the most important.

Warm regards,
Josh

Dear Josh,

The rules keep changing around me so damned fast that I can't keep up with it anymore. More times than not, it seems like a bunch of hooey, people worrying about labels and winning arguments instead of just going about their business. I guess I've always liked what the Colonel wrote: "All that matters is how a man lives in this world."

But every now and then, I come out a fool, and I know it. Of course you're right. Friends talk about their loved ones. I wouldn't have it any other way either. I hope that's enough said on the matter.

I've thought a lot about those diaries. As I told you, I liked to read them when I was a boy for the sheer excitement of it. Years later, after the wife and I went our separate ways and I found myself fumbling around in life, I took them up again. I don't know exactly what I was looking for, except maybe I liked the idea that we don't have it all figured out and buttoned up just yet, that maybe there's something out there that can still rattle us. I always wished I'd been around when there was still new country to be seen, or that I'd had the gumption to seek out an adventure of one kind or another when I was young enough to do it.

Your last letter got me to thinking,

though, about what these documents mean to you — they must be bittersweet. You're living the long repercussions of the Colonel and his men. I suppose you've got to feel some loss and mourning over that, and now you're left trying to preserve your culture.

Nothing is as simple as we'd like to make it out.

I do like the idea of that dryas flower, though, blooming along the river.

Your friend,
Walt

Lieut. Col. Allen
Forrester June 22, 1885

An unexpected respite: the dog found a narrow break in the mountainside today, with tall rock faces on either side. In this shaded ravine were hard drifts of snow & ice. Boyo took to rolling in it to cool himself. The rest of us broke off chunks to put to our sunburned foreheads & cracked lips. Tillman tied a piece of it to the top of his head with his neckerchief to keep himself cool, though I cannot think it will last long in this heat.

Pruitt has made an interesting discovery.

As we near the pass through the Wolverine Mountains, a distant saddle between two slopes, we travel in high country along alpine heather with tiny blooms, lichen-covered rocks. No trees or bushes impede us, so the walking is easy.

This afternoon we came to a group of huge boulders. It appears the rocks, some larger than a horse carriage, had many years ago toppled from the nearby cliffs.

Upon reaching them, Tillman & Nat'aaggi climbed atop one for a better view. Pruitt walked between the boulders, inspecting their surface. It was then that he noticed the petroglyphs.

The images are crudely etched into the stone & weathered, but as we identified more of them along the rocks, I had a growing sense of familiarity. Many are simple, geometrical designs. Spirals, patterns of dots. But then, an indication of a mountain. A tebay. A star. A bird.

It occurred to me — these are the same pictures the Midnoosky children made with their strings on the Trail River. To see them again here, miles into the mountains, I cannot explain it, but it strikes me as an uncanny echo.

If these people consider the mountains ahead of us a place where the dead roam, then what do these symbols mean? Are they a caution of some sort, or simply a signpost?

June 23

Whatever the source, human or beast or the rumored Wolverine People, it seems we have suffered at their tricks.

They made their presence known while we dozed in the shade of the boulders. We had removed our packs, used them as rests. I was soundly asleep when Tillman woke me.

— You hear that, Colonel? Some kind of whistle pig or something.

Though my ears are not as keen, I caught the sounds then. From above us on the rocky mountainside — chirps, whistles, then came low chuffs & growls.

Tillman suggested we could eat the animals, though we did not even know its type yet.

At the urging of our empty bellies, we grabbed rifles, Nat'aaggi her bow & arrows. None gave thought to the packs we left behind. We scattered across the hillside in pursuit of the sounds. Boyo leapt from rock to rock, barking excitedly.

The chase went on for too long, our judgment impaired by the promise of fresh meat.

Pruitt at last called out, asking if there were any sign.

— Not hide nor tail, Tillman answered.

I did not trust my ears at first. The chirps & huffs along the mountainside had taken on the cadence of human speech. There were words then, unintelligible but words all the same &, more unnerving, laughter & shouts.

Nat'aaggi began to run back towards the boulders. We followed.

Pruitt noticed my pack was gone. Because of his weakness & Tillman's injuries, I had carried the most provisions, including a good supply of dried fish & tallow from the Kulgadzi Lake Indians.

With Pruitt & Nat'aaggi at guard with the

remaining supplies, Tillman & I followed what appeared to be drag marks across moss & heather. After a half mile or so, we came to my pack.

Its contents were strewn about on the tundra. All the food was gone, as was my tin cup. The loss of provisions is a serious concern, but I feel the loss of the cup, too. It has been with me through many battles, countless marches.

June 24

It has become an all too common woe on this journey, but we once again face near starvation. The wild berries on these slopes are hard & green, though we try to eat them. Nat'aaggi snared several chipmunk-like animals. Pruitt says he is unable to stomach the meat. His lack of appetite is concerning.

Nat'aaggi found my tin cup in a mound of dirt & rock that had been recently scraped. She then pointed out the animal tracks in the mud.

— Nothchis, she said. Wolverine.

62°56'N
143°22'W
Clouds early in the morning.
Does He smile to see His work?

  With His shoulder, & His art, He twisted
the sinews of my heart.

  In this forest, in this night
  I am the tyger, burning bright.

Sophie Forrester
Vancouver Barracks
June 23, 1885

I must endeavor to put these dark fears out of my brain. Since developing the plates from the expedition, I find it impossible to eat or sleep. My worry becomes agonizing. I have made myself a pest to the General's secretary, visiting the department headquarters twice in as many days to ask if there isn't some word of Allen. Is he safe? Does the General know whether the men made it through the canyon, and will they be home before winter comes? Are there any reports as to the character of the Wolverine tribes? Is there a plan to send someone up the Yukon River in search of the party if a report does not arrive soon?

Of course, there is no answer, except to say that we must wait.

Charlotte is impatient with being kept indoors, and so I will allow her enthusiasm to propel us. The fresh air and light may do me some good. We have packed a picnic lunch, along with our photography supplies, and I have promised to see if we can find any pied-billed grebes, for Charlotte has never heard their calls.

And I vow that tomorrow, I will attend the women's tea. Perhaps I will bring cake, or the lemon meringues that Charlotte makes so well, to make amends for my inattention.

It all seems a shallow distraction, yet I do not know how else to continue on.

June 24

Today ended up being a small and unexpected gift. Afternoon tea started out very predictably, but pleasantly enough. I brought Charlotte's lemon meringues, which everyone enjoyed. Mrs Bailey told us all about the elegant dinner a la Russe she attended in Portland last week, and I asked after Sarah Whithers' attempt to learn the flute. (She said she enjoys it very much, has learned to play "Greensleeves," but that her husband finds it vulgar and wishes she would study piano instead. I was sorry Evelyn was not in attendance, for I am sure she would have had something amusing to contribute on the matter.)

Mrs Connor was true to form. She inquired about Charlotte's work at my house, wondering that the girl has enough to occupy her time since I have no family to tend. I replied that Charlotte is of great help to me in my photography, that I have come to think of her more as an assistant than a housemaid.

"Perhaps if the girl isn't needed for common household chores, she might return to me. I find I am short staffed."

I was politely but firmly insisting that the girl remain with me, when I realized a separate conversation was occurring around us.

"We are all interested to know if you have any pictures yet?" Sarah Whithers asked over the din.

"Yes, but they aren't exactly . . ."

"Oh how we would love to see them! Wouldn't we?"

"Well maybe some time . . ."

The women, however, were already on their feet.

Do you know where I've placed my cane? I wish I had more suitable shoes — it's a bit of a stroll down to her house. Will you hand me my coat, Mrs Connor? Should we send for a carriage? No, no you're right. It would take much longer to wait. Oh this is all rather exciting, like a church outing!

On the walk to our house, I tried to remember if I had put away the ironing, and if there were very many dirty dishes in the kitchen. As we approached the yard, I saw Charlotte peer out a window and then dart away. Please let her be straightening the mess, I thought. I tried to detain the women for a moment by the honeysuckle, to ask them about what other flowering shrubs thrive here, but they were impatient to get indoors.

I was much relieved to see the house was not in too appalling a state, and then Charlotte whispered to me, "I saw you all coming down the lane. Did my best to tidy." "Bless you," I whispered in return.

It was overwhelming, having so many eyes suddenly upon my photographs, yet I must say the women were kind and enthusiastic. The picture of the apple tree in bloom, with the parade ground in the distance, was a favorite. They also liked the one of Charlotte on our front porch, and Mrs Bailey asked if I might take such a photograph of herself and her family. I answered that portraiture was not my particular interest, but maybe later in the fall when I will not be so occupied with seasonal birds.

It surprised me that Sarah Whithers should be so smitten with the blurred photograph of the pine siskins in flight. "What is it?" she asked in wonder, and when I explained, she said that it was a most beautiful picture. I told her to take the print as a gift, if she truly enjoyed it. "Are you sure? It is much too precious!" but I could tell she was pleased and so I insisted. She studied it for a time, and then looked up from the photograph, as if taking in the house and myself for the first time. "But what of your husband? What on earth will he think of all of this?"

It seemed to me a very intimate question, but for once, I knew exactly what to say: "I think he will like it very much."

The talk in the room quieted, and the women eyed each other as if unconvinced, but as I think back on my declaration, I am all the more confident. I cannot predict all of Allen's sentiments, yet I am certain of this: he would be pleased to know of my photography, he would say he never doubted me, and he would disdain the notion that my time would have been better spent keeping the house neat in his absence.

June 25

I cannot take it as a good sign. Quite early this morning, a servant from the Haywood house came to our door, asking if Miss Evelyn was in our company. I replied that we had not seen her yet today.

"Or last night?" the woman asked, to which I said no. The line of inquiry concerned me, and I asked if Miss Evelyn was well. The servant only said that we should send word directly to Mrs Haywood if we hear anything of her whereabouts.

I did not encourage it, but neither did I dissuade her when Charlotte suggested she should seek out her mother, who does the laundry for the General and his wife, to find out any more information.

By this afternoon, we learned that Evelyn had in fact been missing since yesterday morning and was discovered to have spent the night at the Quimby House in Portland. She reportedly pleads all innocence and says that she decided to go shopping with a friend in the city and was too tired to return the same day, yet I cannot help but have my suspicions that Lieutenant Harvey is in part to blame. They are too much alike, pursuing happiness in dangerous quarters.

And now I wish I had written none of this. Even within one's own diary, there is thin difference between expressing genuine concern and gossiping, and I do not wish to fall off into that more mean temptation. It is only that Evelyn is the most difficult of any friend I have ever had, for she has so much potential for good and intelligence, yet so infrequently chooses such paths.

June 26
This morning a large raven landed near the privy while I was throwing out some dirty water, and with its appearance, all my will toward composure and rationality dissipated. I must have seemed a lunatic when I ran toward it and cried for it to go away and leave me alone. It shook its wings, and I thought then of Allen in the Alaska wilderness, and how a bird might fly and carry its curses with it. I threw my empty pail with hopes of strik-

ing it. The pail rolled harmlessly across the yard, the bird hopped back several feet, and I saw then that it was just a common raven, with no crippled leg or distorted eyes.

It has occurred to me more than once that I might seek out the raven in order to photograph it. What would I find if I peered into those eyes a second time?

I have not seen that particular bird again since I lost the baby, yet even if it were to return, I do not think I would attempt to focus my lens upon it.

Father always said an artist must be at least half in love with his subject. I do not doubt a beauty of some sort can be found in the capriciousness and hunger of a wild scavenger, but it does not hold my desire. I am in love with the promise of something else.

THE UNDISCOVERED COUNTRY
— Edmund Stedman, 1878

COULD we but know
The land that ends our dark, uncertain
    travel,
Where lie those happier hills and meadows
    low, —
Ah, if beyond the spirit's inmost cavil,
Aught of that country could we surely
    know,   *5*
    Who would not go?

    Might we but hear
The hovering angels' high imagined chorus,
Or catch, betimes, with wakeful eyes and
    clear,
One radiant vista of the realm before
    us, —   *10*
With one rapt moment given to see and
    hear,
    Ah, who would fear?

    Were we quite sure
To find the peerless friend who left us
    lonely,
Or there, by some celestial stream as
    pure,   *15*
To gaze in eyes that here were lovelit
    only, —

This weary mortal coil, were we quite sure,
   Who would endure?

(Typewritten paper, folded, & inserted into Lieut. Col. Allen Forrester's diary of 1885. With handwritten note along bottom: *Dear Walt — save this one for me. It made me think of the Colonel's trip into the mountains. I'm planning a May visit. With love from your sister, Ruth*)

Lieut. Col. Allen Forrester
June 25, 1885

We have stopped to rest from the afternoon sun. If we set out again once evening comes, we will make it through the pass by morning.

Tillman protested the plan. I pointed out that it will be cooler come evening, but with the clear skies, it will remain light enough to see. This arctic sun skirts below the northern horizon for only a few hours each night, so a kind of twilight remains even after sunset.

Tillman was unconvinced.

— Don't you understand, Colonel? Those wolverines, they live off the flesh of the dead. We're getting close to that other world the Indians talk about. We shouldn't be wandering up here at night. If there are ghosts nearby, they'll be haunting the hills.

I have no use for the occult. I said as much. To which Tillman said that while I might not have much use for spirits, they might have some unpleasant use for me.

This caused an unexpected chuckle from Pruitt. Soon he & I were both laughing outright. Nat'aaggi was perplexed at our humor.

Tillman said with some indignation that it was nothing to joke about, that the only way we'd be safe is if we could throw salt over our shoulders to chase off the spirits.

— Not that I'm a superstitious fellow, Tillman gravely added.

This only provoked a new round of laughter from us.

Pruitt said that if anyone had salt to throw over a shoulder, he would follow along on hands & knees to lick up every grain.

— Yeah, boy, Tillman agreed. — What I wouldn't do for a lick of salt & a splash of whiskey to wash it down.

Just as the Indians warned, we find no firewood, no food or shelter. Only sleet & a beating wind. We hoped to outrun the storm before setting camp. None of us want to remain here, yet we have no choice. We hunker down with sleeping bags pulled up over our heads. Nat'aaggi wraps herself in a skin tunic. Tillman offered his coat, which she refused. We are wedged best we can against the rocks. Hard to see to write in this sleeping bag. There is nothing else to do. We wait.

Pruitt keeps shouting above the storm —

Do you feel that? Can't you feel that?

What he says makes no sense. He says there are hands on him. Something pulls at him. He says he has to run. I have warned him to stay put.

(undated entry)
My dearest Sophie. I pray you will read this. You are first & last to me.

I do not know if we will survive this night. They are all around us. They scream & cry so that it is hard to think to put these words on the page.

You must know that I love you.

I am not afraid of death but instead of the passage from here to oblivion, of being aware of its coming. I would rather have been run through with a spear than to face this long dread.

373. After retreat (or the hour appointed by the commanding officer), until broad daylight, a sentinel challenges every person who approaches him, taking, at the same time, the position of *charge bayonet.* He will suffer no person to come nearer than within reach of his bayonet, until the person has given the countersign, or is passed by an officer or non-commissioned officer of the guard.

— *From The Soldier's Hand-Book, for the Use of the Enlisted Men of the Army,* 1881

Lieut. Col. Allen Forrester
June 26

We have woken on a floating mountain. Overhead is sunlit blue sky. The storm that surrounded us last night has settled as white clouds below us in the Wolverine Valley. We see nothing of river or forest below. The view is groundless, only vapor & rock & sky. The mountains on either side are white with new snow. The sun brightly glints off rocks & heather leaves still wet from the melting snow.

Nat'aaggi found a clump of bushes with twigs to start a fire. It's just enough to give us small warmth until the sun heats up the land.

— I'm aching like we spent the night three sheets to the wind, Tillman said.

All of us are the same. We blink against the brightness of the day, our heads & muscles beaten. I attribute our symptoms to the long, sleepless night & near hypothermia.

As we sit beside the fire, which produces

more smoke than heat, we have tried to set straight our recollections of last night's occurrences.

So much is unexplained. What is it that we witnessed? The terror, absurd as it seems, has not entirely left us.

The storm came upon us swiftly. The dark clouds streamed across the mountaintop & moved amongst us, the air turned icy & wet, so our clothes were soaked through, our faces damp. The midnight sun was blotted out.

They walked out of the fog. Yet how can I say they walked? They were only shadows in the windblown mist. Arms, hands, howling mouths. Bitter cold, their touch. Some were of human form, while others were great lumbering beasts.

Confusion swept through us. We were all out of our sleeping bags. Boyo barked madly in all directions as if birds threatened him from above. Nat'aaggi drew her bow, then knelt & wept. Tillman called for his mother. I heard Pruitt scream from far away.

I do not know how I was so fortunate as to find Pruitt without being lost myself. I stumbled through the dark & gray landscape, followed the sound of his cries. The voices moved, circled me & turned me around, until I could not recall which way I had come. I could not find Pruitt or our camp or anyone else. I thought I heard Boyo whining nearby, then came a muffled yelp, as if the dog had been kicked hard in the side.

I walked on blindly. I called for Pruitt. Without warning I was at the edge of a sheer precipice. I could see nothing beyond my feet but blackness. Far below there was the sound of water flowing over rocks.

At this moment there was a hand at the back of my neck. There was no movement or breath behind me. Only a heavy, cold weight that seemed to reach through my skin & flesh & bone, until long cold fingers tightened like a cinch around my windpipe.

What disturbs me most is my impulse. I stepped forward. Rock crumbled from beneath me, fell silently into the black. I would follow it.

Never before had I considered such an act. Yet it was a thirst; I longed for death as one might long for water. To be swallowed by dark & cold & ice & rock. I strained against it, as one pulls against heavy sleep. I reached for my holster.

I was rescued by a sound. It was not Pruitt's voice, that much I am certain. Nor was it the shriek of those banshees.

It was the cry of an infant. It came out of the fog: the bleating, pleading, cadenced wail of a newborn. Conjured by my own brain, I was sure, to remind me of Sophie & our child & all that draws me home.

The cold fingers at my throat withdrew. I turned to face my enemy, but there were only clouds coursing by.

It was as if I had nearly drowned in icy water, my body ached so, my head numb. I walked as if half-dead back towards camp. Not far from the gorge, I came to Pruitt where he scrambled up the rocks. I shouted to him, but he did not see or hear me.

It was a terrifying & sorrowful madness that clutched him. At the highest point that he could reach upon the rocks, he stood with his arms outspread, his face turned up to the dark sky.

— Take me now! You coward. What is this? My God the Father will not have me, you who have made me all that I am.

He clapped his palms hard against the sides of his head, against his chest. — Here & here & here, he shouted — You have made this! You are the devil, if you would make such a man as this.

He folded to the ground like a man who has taken ill. When at last I made my way across the rocks to where he huddled & moaned, I touched his shoulder. He faced me, then, with such wildness in his eyes.

— Did you hear it? he asked. — The baby crying in the fog? It's my doing. A suffering ghost.

He reached for my pistol, but I overpowered him.

— Shoot me. I am begging you, Colonel. He has forsaken me. You must do it for me.

It took all my might to subdue him & bring him back to the others. All the way, his speech was muddled & incoherent.

Upon our return, Tillman shouted for us to identify ourselves or he would shoot. He could see our faces, hear our voices, yet I was hard pressed to convince him. At long last, he pointed his rifle away from us, began firing in all directions. The end of his barrel flared brightly in the dark fog, the shots echoed along the rock faces. I ordered for him to stop.

— You're right, you're right, he said. — No bullet is going to stop what's out there.

We spent the rest of the storm huddled together, our backs to the rocks. Throughout the night, the torment continued, so that we heard screams & cries & arrows flying past, all seemingly within a stone's throw of us. More than once the ground shook beneath us as if giants thundered past. Pruitt sobbed. Nat'aaggi sat with her knees pulled up in front of her, her knife in hand. Boyo crouched in front of her, a low growl in his throat, ears twitching in all directions. I kept my rifle at the ready, though I knew it could do no good.

At some dark hour, snow began to fall.

How can I describe the eerie silence that greeted us when morning at last came? The storm faded, the visions fled, just as daylight broke through the dissipating clouds. We stood, shook the snow from our clothing. As far as we could see in any direction, the landscape was covered in a thin layer of white. Not a single track or footprint in the snow. Not a whisper of sound. Where just moments before we could hear a riot of suffering & struggle, now there was nothing.

We gathered what we could find of our possessions, sought a more sheltered camp to rest, for we are all of us too fatigued to travel far. As we walked, we passed by the gorge where I had nearly fallen during the night. Tillman whistled in appreciation.

— Jesus, Colonel. That would have been a long tumble.

Straight down, perhaps half a mile, a small creek trickled through the jagged rocks.

June 27

The good weather holds so we continue to make our way through the mountain pass. We rested little today, only during the hottest hours of the afternoon. We are all of us anxious to be out of the mountains before another storm develops.

We did stop for a time where an engorged creek had eroded a bank of mud. Protruding from the half-frozen mud were a pair of tusks like those of an elephant, each near to three feet long & of a tawny color. While the rest of us were admiring the strange sight, Tillman cursed.

— That's it, Colonel. That's the horns I saw coming out of the clouds, on these giant furry animals, except they were just fog.

Tillman climbed down into the creek bed, inspected the walls.

— Look here, he called out.

He had found the animal's spine bone embedded in the mud, with each separate vertebra larger than a man's hand. He tried to pull one of the bones loose but it would not budge.

Pruitt would likely know something of these remains, if only his mind were coherent. He does not speak or acknowledge our presence, but only stumbles along beside us. Then, with no apparent provocation, he bursts out with yells or sobs. It startles & disturbs us all. Several times I have ordered the lieutenant to pull himself together, but it is of no use.

June 28

We have done it! We are through the pass, now look out over the Tanana River Valley.

It is as if we prepare to drop into another world. The rocks & glaciers of the Wolverine Valley here give way to a wide vista with a great number of lakes, braided streams. We emerged from the pass at 3 in the morning, just as the sun rose, not in the east, but almost directly north. It was a grand sight — the sun breaching the distant horizon, the valley spread before us in golden dawn. All of us are euphoric. When Tillman let out a whoop, the dog ran in excited circles around him & barked. Even reserved Nat'aaggi is revived.

It is a tremendous relief. We are not home yet, but the worst hardships are over.

Even with Pruitt's pathetic state, I am proud of these men. There were many who thought this expedition impossible, to travel up the Wolverine River, to cross this divide into the heart of Alaska. Yet here we stand. We made the long, steady march up from the coast 500 miles. Ahead of us is yet 1,000 miles to the sea, but we will travel through land charted by white men. We will float at ease down rivers, rather than drag sledges & skin boats up them. There will be trading posts to restock our provisions.

We could reach the coast before summer is out.

Between rising sun & Nat'aaggi's fire, we are well on our way to being drier, warmer & closer to content. Boyo sleeps hard beside the fire, though he kicks & whines in his sleep.

Tillman just took from his coat pocket a small square, wrapped in wax paper & tied with twine with unusual neatness. He set it on his knee.

He asked if anyone cared to guess its content.

None of us answered. Tillman unwrapped it to reveal two bits of chocolate. He broke them into smaller pieces, gave each of us a share.

To taste such sweet flavor after months of unsalted half-raw game, flour paste, wormy rice, & rancid salmon.

— Wooo-eeee, Tillman howled. — I don't know that I've ever tasted anything as good as that. Well, go on Nattie. Aren't you going to try it?

Eyeing us closely, she at last put the chocolate to her tongue. It brought a look of surprised wonder to her face.

— This is more like it, Tillman said.

The others are drowsing in the sun. All is quiet along the hillside. The only living creature spotted so far this side of the mountains is a raven that passed overhead & flew down towards the Tanana Valley.

■ ■ ■ ■

Part Five

ALASKA INDIAN MAN'S TUNIC.
WOLVERINE RIVER INDIANS, 1885.
ALLEN FORRESTER COLLECTION.

■ ■ ■ ■

Moose hide, sinew threading, decorated with flattened porcupine quills, dentalium shells, river otter fur trim, dye of silverberry seeds and ochre. Adornment suggest the garment was owned by a man of high status. Atypically opened down the front as in the style of a European jacket.
Damage: bullet hole left upper torso, staining front and back.

OREGON POST
A TRIP INTO ALASKA
LIEUT.-COL. FORRESTER EXPLORES
WILD NORTHERN RIVER

WASHINGTON, D.C., July 15 — Gen. James Keirn has received the first report from Lieut.-Col. Allen Forrester who this spring left Vancouver Barracks in the Washington Territory to attempt an exploration into the regions of the Far North.

"This excels all explorations on the American continent since the time of Lewis and Clark and the world's record since Livingston," said the General.

According to the report, carried south by wild Indians and then a mail steamer, Col. Forrester reached the mouth of the Wolverine River more than three months ago, and now follows the river deep into the heart of Alaska. Gen. Keirn says the Colonel and his party plan to cross to the head of a river called the Tanana and then on to the great northern Yukon River. After the nearly 1,000-mile journey to the coast, the party hopes to arrive at St. Michael's on the Behrings and return via steamer to the United States.

An expedition up the Wolverine River has long been an ambition of brave explorers, even since before Alaska came into the possession of the United States, but the Russians failed each time it was attempted due to hostile Indians and unforgiving terrain. Since then, several explorations by American officers have ended in failure as well, until among Army officials the feat has come to be considered well-nigh impossible.

Col. Forrester is accompanied on his great journey by Lieut. Andrew Pruitt, of Madison, Wisc., and Sgt. Bradley Tillman, of Carbondale, Penn., but the party also relies on Alaska Indian scouts to assist in the expedition.

Lieut. Col. Allen Forrester
June 29, 1885

We were met this day by a scouting party of Tetling River Indians, as we near their village. They were not so surprised to see us as we might expect but instead greeted us warmly. We came to understand that they received advanced reports that we were traveling in their direction.

Happiest news of all, I learned they hold a letter for me that was delivered up the Yukon River by steamboat earlier this summer. I can only hope it is from Sophie. I am anxious to learn of her health and that of the baby.

June 30

Her letter leaves me to wonder, for whom do I write these pages?

July 1

We remain at the Tetling River, tributary of the Tanana. There are four Indian birch-bark houses here, with 35 men, assorted women, children, & dogs.

Many of the Indians are afflicted with severe coughs, other signs of illness, yet they endeavor towards hospitality. We stay at the chief's house where we are given caribou meat. We eat, then sleep. Pruitt takes some food, has begun to come to his senses, though in the night he often cries out.

Tillman is the strongest of us, in body & spirit. I write here now only because Tillman woke me, helped me to a sitting position, put journal & pencil in my hands.

The day I received it, I crumpled her letter, threw it to the flames of the campfire. I regret it now. Have I misunderstood her words? If I could read it again, would I find something to soothe my anger?

July 2
Our plans to raft down to the Yukon are thwarted. The Indians say it is not possible because of rapids & deadfall, also that there is no salmon to be found in the upper Tanana River. We will need to construct skin boats.

July 3
Tillman & I traveled to a nearby village to secure caribou hides for use in making our boats.

The natives here are well-supplied with guns & ammunition from Fort Reliance. They wear dresses & shirts made of cotton. It seems that most if not all have been converted. Russian Catholic crosses decorate their graves.

When Tillman saw the graves, he made the sign of the cross, said he hopes it keeps the mountain spirits at bay. I had not known he was a religious man. It seems he was raised in the church, though he had fallen away from it.

— All that we've seen, Colonel, I figure it's best to play it safe.

Try as I might, I can find nothing to comfort me.

July 4

Construction of the caribou baidarra is nearly finished.

Food is scarce even among Indians. In exchange for their dried arctic pickerel, sucker fish, grayling, whitefish, we have traded all our remaining money as well as any items we could spare — pocketknives, garments. Tillman even gave up his trousers in the trade, so is left only to his long underwear.

We have been told that once we reach the Yukon, we will be able to obtain provisions from either the trading post near the confluence with the Tanana or at the home of a missionary who lives in the area with his family.

The Indians warn us, however, to pass as silently as possible through the next stretch of river. It seems the nearby tyone is of a warlike disposition. They say it is likely that we will be killed if we are spotted by his people.

It is Independence Day. When it came to my notice this evening, I informed the men. Tillman insisted on building a bonfire. He then stood solemnly in his long underwear, shot several rounds into the air. We attempted to sing a verse or two of 'My Country Tis of Thee.' It was not a rousing performance. The Indians were unimpressed.

July 5

At 6 this morning we launched the boat with myself, Sgt. Tillman, Lieut. Pruitt, Nat'aaggi, & the dog. We paddled 3 hours until we reached the confluence with the Tanana River. Pruitt is still weak but at last coherent. I believe sleep & warm food have served him well, though he still seems uneasy of mind.

We are in a markedly different land from that of the Wolverine Valley. The air is hot. There are no glaciers or rocky cliffs. Instead it is a flat country with rolling hills, mountains only in the farthest distance. Widespread forest fires burn to the north, so the air is filled with smoke. The water in the lakes is stagnant

& undrinkable.

The Tanana River is several hundred yards to a mile wide, with muddy water, loamy banks. We travel 3 to 3 1/2 miles per hour.

The lack of salmon does not bode well for our journey, as it may well indicate falls downriver.

July 6

Pruitt shows signs of advanced scurvy. It was brought to my attention when he spat out one of his teeth during our evening meal. Upon further inquiry, I discovered that his legs & torso are covered with large blackish lesions.

I have no doubt as to the cause. In addition to scarce & poor-quality food, we have worn the same clothes since March 20 & suffered extreme exposure. Our doses of acetic acid have been ineffective. His corresponding lack of appetite only worsen his condition. All this accounts a great deal for his past weeks of malaise, perhaps even his unsound mental state.

July 7

I aimed to shoot the raven.

It would not leave us be, but circled & squawked overhead. I fired a half dozen bullets from my carbine, but none met its target. The men do not understand, but I know who the raven is.

I would have liked to watch the bird plummet to the earth.

I want only sleep. It is a forgiving oblivion.

As written by Lieutenant Colonel Allen
  Forrester
July 6, 1885

I here put down this record of confession. On the 28th of June 1885, I threatened Lieutenant Andrew Pruitt with pistol.

We descended from Tebay Peak on our way to the Tetling when the lieutenant lay down upon the ground and refused to rise. With no food left in our possession and no means to obtain any in the immediate area, we were in no position to set camp. I advised the lieutenant that we should continue the day's march to the river with hopes of finding natives from whom to obtain food.

Still the lieutenant refused to rise. I ordered Sergeant Bradley Tillman to assist me in lifting the lieutenant to his feet. I hoped the two of us together retained enough strength to enable us to travel in such a way to the river.

At this time, the lieutenant forcefully withdrew from our aid and again lay upon the ground. I advised him that if he had strength enough to resist us, he had strength enough to walk. At this time I drew my pistol and aimed it at his head. I told him I would shoot him as a deserter if he did not rise. The lieutenant did not come to his feet, at which point I cocked the gun. I then proceeded to fire a bullet into the ground near the lieutenant's head. Sergeant Tillman at this point interceded, pulled Lieutenant Pruitt to his feet and began to forcefully march him down the hillside. The sergeant then suggested that I return my pistol to my holster.

It is my firm belief that as commander of this expedition, I failed to maintain proper composure. I allowed anger to impinge my judgment. I did not observe the lieutenant's failing health or deteriorating mental state. I am at fault and hereby take responsibility.

Lieutenant-Colonel Allen Forrester

Lieut. Col. Allen Forrester
July 8, 1885

A pair of Canada geese with goslings on shore. The five young are downy gray but begin to grow their pin feathers. They forage in the grass even as we float by in our skin boat.

It is the mother, I presume, who follows after the young. Her head held high on her long, slender neck. White paint down her cheeks. Round eyes. They shine black.

The male watches us. On guard.

Though we are near starving, I will not allow the men to kill them.

I thought I heard a woman call from her black beak.

I am unwell.

Lieut. Col. Allen Forrester
July 9, 1885

This isnt the Colonel but its Sgt Bradley Tillman that wrights here.

Colonel is sick as a dog. Hes burnin with fever an I dont know much what to do about it cept Nattie washes him in the river an the lutenant gives him some asprin pills.

I havnt read watever the Colonel wrights in his little books ever day. Thats his own. I mearley wright here so that thers counting for watever comes next. I dont like it much atall that the Colonel might die as hes a good man best kind there is. Hes the one who spurs us on, keeps us livin even when thers no food to speak of. He might loose his temper now an then but all good men do so.

We know hed like us to move on down the river so we keep at it tho the bugs are bad bitin an when we rapp the Colonel in his sleepin bag hes awful hot. We try an not make much noise threw here as this is the land of the bad tyone. We hope not to meet up with him.

So thats all for today. I pray its the Colonel that wrights here next. Its cleer an hot an the river is slow.

Durned glad the lutenant is on the mend as I dont care to be the lone able body & mind. I never was any good at wrightin. I am sorry for the speling mis-takes. I askd Pruitt to help me but hes sick of spellin words out lowd an he doesnt want to wright in the Colonels book cept I think we awt to.

July 11

Its Sgt Tillman here agin. The Colonel isnt better yet so I wright agin.

We tried not to but we got found by the Indians while we were floatin by in the dark of night. Lucky we had Nattie hide in the bushes when we heard their gun shots so I hope shes safe with the boat. The Indians marched us way from the river. They didnt talk much an carried their guns at ready wich made me & the lutenant nervis. We had to help the Colonel walk an he was too feverd to know what happend. We awt to have taken the Indian jacket off the Colonel but we forgot. The Indians took us 10 miles or so into the woods away from the river then brot us into the chiefs house.

We ate an slept an ate more. All the time more an more Indians come to see us white people. They kept pointin at the Colonel's jacket.

The Indians look sickly. Theres lots of couffin. The lutenant says they have consumptin.

Dear Mrs. Forrester —

First, to address your question, the frilling you describe may be in part due to the exceptionally warm weather we have enjoyed of late. I recommend hardening the negative with a good long soak in alum and water.

Now let me say that your most recent photographs are truly remarkable, though you disparage them. The three young chickadees all in a row on the branch is most affecting, and while the pine siskin is not entirely in focus, it is a wonderful depiction of Nature all the same.

I hope you do not find this too forward, but would you mind terribly if I sent these prints on to a Mr. William Powell? He is an editor in Philadelphia and has long been a friend to me. I do not know if he will have any use for the photographs, as the sciences are not his normal subject matter, but I cannot help but to feel that these deserve a wider audience.

Sincerely,
Mr. Henry Redington

Sophie Forrester
Vancouver Barracks
June 27, 1885

Does he really see such value in my photographs? I am astonished, and not a little intimidated, by the prospect of Mr Redington sharing them with an editor.

I know Mother would not approve of my vanity, but all the same, I did a little skip of joy when Mr Redington's letter arrived. And then I wrote back to say that I would be truly honored, but I also begged him to wait just a while longer with hopes that I might contribute some better photographs.

June 28

Miss Evelyn, as always, you are as much blessing as aggravation!

The sight of her running down the lane toward my house concerned me at first, but then it occurred to me that she is no Mrs Connor; when there is misery to be endured,

Evelyn can be sure to flee in the opposite direction. I therefore could not fathom what brought her in such haste.

She was out of breath and disheveled when she arrived at the porch.

"I've found it, Sophie! I've found it!"

It seems she was out for a walk with Lieutenant Harvey, down through the orchard and near the river's edge, when she first saw it.

"They buzz like giant bumblebees, don't they? One of them flew straight past us, and I ran after it, for I thought it might be your bird. For a while, I could not see it, but then I heard its loud buzzing again and saw it fly into a thicket, and there I found it, sitting in a little gray pouch on a branch."

Before she could say any more, I had laced my boots and retrieved my straw hat and field glasses.

"What about your camera?"

I told her I would fetch it later. In truth, I was not quite ready to believe this stroke of good fortune.

Several times I have walked down to the Columbia River as far as the orchard, but never considered the area for nests. Surely all the activity and noise from the wharves, the ferries coming and going, men unloading crates into wagons and then driving them past with shouts, with all that commotion, who would think that a humming bird would choose to build its nest amid all that? And so late in the year?

Yet there it is, dressed in frilly lichen and lined with downy seeds and no bigger than a child's teacup. The nest is built on a most precarious thimbleberry cane, about four feet off the ground, and with each gust of wind, the stalk waves and trembles. The mother bird was not at home, so I crept closer and closer, scarcely breathing for worry of stirring the branches, until I could peer into the nest, and there I beheld two perfectly small white eggs.

"Was I right? Oh Sophie, is this your nest?"

Indeed it is!

June 29

It does no good to have Evelyn sighing and complaining behind me as I work.

"My God, how can you stand this tedium? Aren't you done yet? When will you have a picture? It's been hours!"

In fact, we had been at the nest for not three-quarters of an hour, and I was only beginning my vigil.

"Honestly, I think I'd rather listen to Mrs Connor lecture me about the ills of whiskey and dancing, than sit here with nothing but the flies and this insufferable heat and you not talking at all."

Perhaps she should seek out some other company, I suggested as kindly as I could manage.

"Yes, I will do just that!" she exclaimed, as if released from some odious duty. "Just tell me as soon as you have a picture I can see."

Now that I am able to sit on my field stool and contemplate the scene in some peace, there is much that gladdens me. The mother bird tends to her nest. As afternoon wears on, with the sun over the river, the light is quite lovely, and I can see already how this pneumatic shutter is essential. With only the subtlest of movement, I can press the bulb and rapidly expose the plate.

Yet I need to be much closer if there is to be any hope of the nest looking like something more than a black dot in the far distance, only I fear that if I press the female, she will abandon it altogether.

Beyond photographs, it gives me joy just to observe the Rufous humming bird through field glasses, as she sits with her long, elegant beak and speckled throat. She shifts now and then, flares her tail feathers, and adjusts herself to her eggs. When the wind gusts along the river, and the cane shakes violently, she settles herself down into her nest, like a fisherman in a boat. I begin to wonder if she is unskilled at choosing her nesting sites, and if maybe earlier in the season she lost one to wind or storm. That would explain this late nest. All in all, I have much to add to my field book.

■ ■ ■ ■

I have taken one photograph, though I know I am still much too far from the nest. It occurs to me that if I could somehow conceal myself and the camera, with only the lens unobstructed, I might be able to place myself much closer without causing a disruption.

June 30
"A hunting blind is what you're after."

My inclination to seek out Mr MacGillivray was entirely correct. I explained my desire to construct a kind of camouflage for myself so that I might position my camera within feet of the nest.

We will need it to be tall enough to accommodate the tripod and camera, so that I might aim precisely into the nest, but should otherwise be as small and unobtrusive as possible. I will send Charlotte to Vancouver tomorrow to purchase canvas from the mercantile, and Mr MacGillivray has promised to help me build a crude frame.

A delightful sense of anticipation flutters within me.

July 1
As I brought my camera to the nest this morning, I found that even as I walked, I studied the angle and nature of the light and

considered how I might compose a picture of this arrangement of trees or the pleasing way the lane runs past the General's house. I noticed that the mountains were flattened of all detail, but remembered how, in the evenings, their ridges and peaks are often brought out in relief by the setting sun.

And then I suddenly arrived at a wonderful consideration: somehow, through these many weeks of study and effort, I have come to see the world through the eyes of a photographer! Mr Redington said it was so, he believed in me even as I doubted myself, and now I find that perhaps he was correct after all.

July 2

I wish I could only be happy on her behalf — I have learned that Evelyn soon goes to San Francisco with Lieutenant Harvey, who has resigned his commission and will become a partner in a shipping business. I am disappointed that she did not tell me herself; I heard it instead through Charlotte and her mother. When I asked Evelyn about her plans, she was too eager to defend herself, saying that while she will travel with Mr Harvey, she will stay with a cousin in San Francisco until the wedding. I care little for propriety, only about her well-being and happiness.

She says she longs for the cosmopolitan, for surprise and newness, for anything but the treacherous hold of the commonplace, and as she spoke, there was a fever in her eyes that appeared less wholesome than that of a joyful bride-to-be; I do not like to echo Mrs Connor, but I suspect Evelyn's many late nights do her health ill.

General and Mrs Haywood cannot be pleased, for she has brought some embarrassment upon her family, and while Lieutenant Harvey has promised to marry her and he has means, he is also known to be impulsive and fiery-tempered. Yet I suspect it is his very unpredictability that maintains Evelyn's attraction.

I might have shared my thoughts with her, that she is too intelligent to marry into trouble just to escape boredom, but who am I to assume wisdom over her heart? Certainly my Mother saw only misfortune in my choice of an Army colonel a dozen years my elder. She begged me to consider her own mistaken path, how she had forsaken her community of faith by marrying outside of the Society of Friends. She was convinced my security lay with a younger and less worldly man than Allen, one who possessed a gentle religiosity. Yet I am convinced such a marriage would have stifled me.

It seems to me that it is most difficult to comprehend love from a removed distance; I can only hope my friend finds more joy than not.

July 4

Charlotte and I have set up the canvas tent some twenty feet from the nest. At first, I intended to decorate the outside of it with branches and leaves, but I no longer think that will be necessary. It is movement that seems to startle the bird more than anything. My hope is to gradually inch closer during the next day or so.

Charlotte is beside herself with excitement about the nest, though she said she wished she had been the one to find it for me. When the mother bird was away, I had Charlotte hold a piece of paper at the nest so that I might focus upon it, and when she saw the two humming bird eggs she exclaimed, "Why, they're no bigger than buttons!"

It is cramped quarters inside the tent, but there is room enough for camera, tripod, and campstool. I have cut several small holes in the canvas so that I might point the lens out one and sit on the stool and watch with my field glasses out another.

Charlotte is vastly more patient than Evelyn, but even her I was forced to send away, as she fidgets and talks incessantly. She was far from displeased, however, for when she asked if she might try making a few prints from the pine siskin plates, I gave her permission, and she ran home to the dark room with much enthusiasm.

July 6

I arrived at not half past five o'clock this morning with my camera. The tent is now well within the thicket and only a few feet from the nest. With the entrance on the opposite side, I am able to tiptoe in without stirring the mother bird.

The location, I find, is too shaded for a decent photograph this time of day, but I am not sorry to have risen so early. It is both peaceful and thrilling to be hidden away in here while all the world goes on around me. The sun rises, the bugler sounds his call, and with it, all the post comes to life. The insects begin to buzz about the tent, the mother bird stretches her neck, and I hear the first ferry come into the wharf along with the distant sound of men and mules and wagons.

Yet amid all this activity, I go entirely unnoticed, nearly to the point of awkwardness. Just an hour or two after reveille, two young soldiers walked by on their way to the parade ground — What's that tent doing there? She's taking pictures. The Colonel's wife? Not much interesting what I can see, just branches and trees. Who is she then? Mrs Forrester. Don't think I know her. Seen her with the General's niece now and then. Now there's a spitfire. Mrs Haywood? Naw, the niece. Evelyn.

I wondered if I shouldn't speak up and reveal myself before they said anything to embarrass themselves, but I hesitated, and the sound of their conversation diminished so that I could tell they had moved on.

It is after noon, and the sun comes in from across the river. The light is strong. I have begun now to photograph in earnest.

One of the eggs is hatching! I was granted only the briefest view, when the mother bird stood at the edge of the nest as if to fly, but then she returned to her brooding.

Three plates today. I restrain myself, for I am still uncertain which hours and weather conditions will serve best.

July 7

Peculiar how near to death a newborn bird appears, its skin thin and wrinkled, its head like a moldy, squashed blackberry. The chick shows no sign of movement, and I would be unsure of its life except for the movement of its small ribs with breath. The sight of it causes me a shudder, much like when I look upon an unsightly wound, yet within days, this wretched creature will sprout feathers and open its beak to the world.

Lieut. Col. Allen Forrester
July 12, 1885

Srgt Tillman agin. This mornin we came to know why they brot us here. They herd we were medcine men with ways to cure the sick. All we have are 3 kinds of Army pill one for malarie, tho we seen no sign of it here, an the pills that eather empty you out or keep you stopped up. The lutenant gave them out willy-nilly but the Indians were glad of it. The chief who is sickist of all got some of each, while others just got 1 or 2 kinds. The lutenant says he feels bad givin them pills that wont do them good but might make them feel worse, but I say he probly saved our lives if nothin else cause the Indians are well plesed an wont shoot our heads off.

Pruitt doesnt look good himself. Hes turnin black all over with the scurvy an he lost a nother tooth.

July 14

Were on the river agin. The Indians didnt want us to take our leave. They kept tryin to look in our boat to see whats in there so they almost found Nattie under the sleepin bags but they didnt. I spect she could fend for herself fine but I didnt want to trust that.

Were probly gettin nere some rapids an I dont like it much. The lutenant uses a stick floatin in the water an his watch an says the water runs about 7 miles an hour.

Rainin. Least the smoke from the wild fires is gone.

Sick an tired of eatin nothing but tallow that goes down hard. The Indians dont have much food to speak of an we have nothin to trade anyways.

July 15

Its me agin. The Colonels fever broke at last so hes gettin better but still just rides in the boat with not much talkin or helpin.

Im scared out of hell with these rapids. Nattie an me do most of the paddlin with poles to keep us out of the sweepers. The water is fast an theres big rocks an trees to run smack into. Seems all the rain is swellin the river more so that trees are topplin in. River like a notted braid so we got to pick wich way to go rite about the time its too late cause the waters fast an were alredy going some way. I

dont like it much atall but I try an not lose
my head.

July 16

Mitey glad the river is slowin. Just one big
channl. Wether cleard up to.

Past by some Indians camped on shore. I
shot a round into the air to greet them. Scairt
the hell out of them. They all took to runnin
into the woods. All but one old woman staid
an we got some dried fish from her to cook
in our tallow wich is a nice change for our
bellies. Cant wait to find the tradin post to
get some real vittles.

July 17

Nothin to report cept a long day on the river.
Lutenant says we made 60 miles. Got some
more meat an fish from some Indians. They
talk a pidgin of English an Indian that we
can kind of figure. They say were almost to
the Yukon. There we mite come across the
steamboat.

Dear Walt,

I'm getting close to the end of the transcribing, and I've been thinking a lot about something you mentioned in your last letter. Do I feel a sense of loss when I read these pages? It's a difficult question for me to answer, because the question itself makes certain assumptions. But the short answer is no.

I also want to give you a long answer, and I hope you don't mind, Walt, because I find the topic really challenging and interesting.

So let me begin by pointing out that I'm not one, or the other. I'm both, or more accurately, many — Wolverine tribe, Russian, Irish, Swedish. And that just pertains to some of my ancestry, which I think is only one aspect of a person. There are so many other labels people like to assign. Where am I an insider, and where am I an outsider? It all depends on where I'm standing and who is trying to put me into which box.

But what makes the question of cultural loss the most uncomfortable, and difficult for me to address, are the inherent definitions built into it. If a group of people is described as existing in a state of loss, it is necessarily therefore lesser, and those that took greater. It's such a limiting and two-dimensional idea. Who defines wealth and success? How can we say this person is valued less or more, is better or worse, because they are a part of one culture or another, and why would we want to?

When I was 9 years old, my mom was making my favorite breakfast — sourdough pancakes with blueberries and black bear sausage. It was a clear September morning, and we were hoping my dad might be home soon from hunting camp, so I'd helped my mom clean up the house and my brother had started a fire in the woodstove. Outside the wind was picking up, and with every gust, yellow birch leaves would get blown off the trees, and I remember thinking they looked like spinning gold coins.

I was just getting the syrup out of the cupboard when there was a strong knock on the door. It startled me, because it was so pounding and unexpected — nobody ever knocked when they came to our house, they just walked in. My mom looked worried, too, and then she opened the door to find a tall Alaska State Trooper standing there in his blue uniform, Mountie-style hat, and holster. He'd come to tell us that my dad had died in an airplane crash in the mountains. He was flying out of his hunting camp when the weather turned bad.

My father was an Irish-Swede — his

great-grandparents were immigrants who had come to America to escape poverty in their own countries. When he was 19, he moved up to Alaska from Minnesota because he wanted to be a big game guide. He fell in love with my mom, and he never left Alaska again.

I remember my mother crying for two days straight, and then she stopped crying and started organizing the potlatch. My dad's friends held a wake at the bar, where they drank too much Jim Beam and shot rifles in the air in honor of my dad. And then my mom's relatives from all around Alaska started showing up at our house. There was this endless amount of cooking and eating — moose meat, salmon, wild blueberry pie — and everyone was telling stories. My great-uncle played fiddle, and the old people danced and sang. They all slept on our living room floor and in tents in the yard, and it seemed like they were here for weeks.

Somehow these memories are both the happiest and saddest of my entire childhood.

So I guess I wonder, where is the line separating me into this culture or that culture, saying I have less or more? I'm just me, and like most people, I've had my heart broken a few times, but for the most part I have been happy.

I don't want you to misunderstand me, though. There are some important and hard questions to be asked of history in Alaska. Native children were abused for many years by missionaries and teachers at territorial government schools. How do those effects trickle down through generations? How do we help families get out of patterns of alcoholism and addiction and domestic violence? These are real problems. But when we use terms like subjugation and loss and the desire to "preserve culture," it devalues and limits people in a way that I don't think is accurate.

You shouldn't assume my opinions represent how everyone feels, though. Even within my own circle of friends and family, you'll find twenty different opinions on one subject. Whenever anyone writes down one of the old stories, several people come forward to say "No, that's not the way it goes. This is how it happened." I think there's this tendency to lump people together, to think that all people who look like this or come from this background must think the same.

Here's an example: a few years ago an environmental group approached the tribe to ask us to support some stance, assuming we'd all agree. But we had to say no, actually, some of our members earn a living working for the exploration companies, even as their relatives are protesting against the mines. Another example: I have a group of friends who formed a band and they use traditional Wolverine River language, music, and dance but interweave them with modern sounds and influences. They performed at the birthday party of one of our elders, who was turning 100, but even though they meant it to honor her, she was upset by it. She is devoted to her church and was raised to believe the old ways are backward and evil.

All of these opinions are packed into one small town, even one family. You can see how complicated it is, even if you just scratch the surface. It's humanity. We're complicated and messy and beautiful.

When I'm reading these diaries and letters, more than anything, I'm thrilled, both as a historian and as a member of the tribe. We know so little about the precolonial Wolverine River, and the Colonel's diaries are rich in information. Every detail, about how people dressed and spoke and prepared their meals, is an exciting discovery. I love the idea that women could turn into geese at the edge of a marsh, that a young girl could marry an otter and then slay him for his hide when he was found to be unfaithful. The dead could go to the mountains to hunt woolly mammoths, and instead of drunken teenagers and a psychopathic serial killer, Kulgadzi Lake could be inhabited by a giant toothy monster. There's this sense in these stories that we were wrestling with a vibrant and fully spirited land.

I wish I could find the tree where Moses Picea was born. It's probably not far from my uncle's old hunting camp, but the journal entries are too vague to be sure. For the Colonel, it was a repulsive and bizarre encounter. He didn't know that spruce tree or that river valley; he never knew Moses Picea or all that he did for Alaska. And certainly he couldn't have imagined that the baby might somehow be connected to him and the "Man Who Flies on Black Wings."

I find it very interesting that once the Colonel and his party cross the Wolverine Mountains and arrive at the Yukon, which by 1885 was already the territory of the Army and missionaries, they never come across another goose woman or lake monster. And during the next few years, when the miners and trappers started pouring up the Wolverine River, not one of them described such occurrences. I'm not saying that other world is gone, because I'm not convinced it is. Maybe we just don't have the eyes for it anymore.

I know I've never been so fortunate as to witness it, beyond stories and imagination. As my professors were so fond of saying in college, the paradigm has shifted.

And then my Pollyanna side, the one that tends to annoy Isaac, kicks in and I think, but thanks to you, we have these journals. And we have all our stories. We have the people who live here now, and our history and fate, even our families, are intertwined.

I've been thinking more and more about the exhibit and what I want to do with the artifacts. It is incredible that your family kept the Colonel's leather tunic. There are very few Wolverine River artifacts from that early in history. And of course when an item is so damaged, especially in such a violent way, people don't tend to hold on to them. The jacket, the artificial horizon (I've always thought that was such a poignant name for that instrument), and his tin cup could make one display. I'm thinking we could also show the journals, open to certain pages, in a glass case. And then there are Sophie's letters, the silver comb, and the baby sling.

There are so many talented artists here in Alaska, working in both traditional and modern media, and I'm wondering if there isn't some way we could do a related art show. In other words, I'm coming up with lots of ideas.

I'm sending you another photograph because it looks entirely different this time of year. This was taken upriver from Alpine, near the pass where the Colonel and his party went over the mountains. Winter is full on now. It snowed last week, and then it cleared up and the temperature dropped to 20 below zero. The water pipes in my mom's house froze the night before last, and poor Isaac spent half the day in her crawl space thawing them with a blow torch. I'm glad he's willing to do it because I'm always afraid I'll burn the place down.

All best wishes,
Josh

Dear Josh,

Your latest photo is in its place on my refrigerator, right next to the other, although I've got to say, this one makes me want to go put on my sweater. It gets cold enough here in Montana, but that looks like something else altogether. And those mountains. It's a magnificent scene.

You've given me something new to ponder, too. I can't say I've ever considered the whole idea of culture and loss just the way you described it, and it's not the first time you've turned something upside down for me. I suspect you do my dusty brain good, even more than the crossword puzzles.

I was sorry to read that story about your father. My own dad died when I was in my twenties, and it left me reeling for some time. I can't imagine how hard it would be if you were just a young boy. My dad was one of those larger-than-life men who I just assumed would always be around. He's the one who first showed me the boxes with the Colonel's papers in the attic, and told me I was free to read as much as I wanted, as long as I was careful with the pages. When he could tell how taken I was with the expedition, he got a map of Alaska and pinned it up in the attic for me, and I marked the Colonel's route. From then on, I always imagined I'd see it in person one day.

I kick myself now that I didn't do it when I had the chance. When I was still working for the highway department, I had a travel agent look up the information for me. I told her I didn't want to go on one of those fancy cruises through the passage. I wanted to see the country the Colonel described. She did her best to put together an itinerary for me, but her papers and brochures just sat on the coffee table for a few months and then I must have thrown them away. I had the money to pay for it and could have taken the time off from work, but it always seemed like too much hassle. And I think some part of me was a little afraid of making the trip. That must sound silly to you. Does to me now, too.

At least I had the good sense to send the Colonel's papers up there. How is your transcribing coming? Are you ready for me to send the artifacts yet? I stopped by a shipping business last week, and it sounds like they can handle delivering them to you whenever you're ready.

Sincerely,
Walt

Lieut. Col. Allen Forrester
July 20, 1885

Tillman has done his best to keep up with my entries. I am grateful for his attention. Though there is nothing slanderous, only personal & revealing, it makes me uneasy to know he has opened these pages. He was quick to say he could not have made out my handwriting even if he had tried.

These past days are confused in my memory. I have not been that ill since I was a child. I am still weak in the legs, quick to tire. I am very much thankful for the work of the men & Nat'aaggi in keeping us on the path to the coast. They say our encounter with the upper Tanana River tyone was eventful, at times worrying. I recall very little of it.

We are disappointed to learn from Indians camped on shore that the trading post downriver is without supplies.

At noon we arrived at the Yukon, a considerable mark of progress.

July 21

We have reached the trading post, overseen by a young Russian-Indian creole & his wife, yet as reported they are out of provisions & wait for the steamboat to return upriver. However, they treated us kindly. The woman gave us breakfast of fresh coffee & hardtack. After these starving weeks, it was a delicacy indeed. Also, the storekeeper provided Tillman with a pair of much-needed trousers.

I suppose it should come as no surprise. I've seen men fall in love with laundry women, Indian girls, other men's wives, whores. Almost always the spell is broken when the men return to regular society. When Tillman today professed his love for Nat'aaggi, I suggested it might only be a passing fancy, based on circumstance.

— I know all about camp affairs, sir. Lock two animals together in a cage, they'll either f—— or fight, sure as the devil. I tell you, though, this is something different. I haven't even asked her to have a go with me & it's been a while, so I could use a poke.

I suggested that it was her skill with a knife that perhaps stayed him. He insists that it is his high regard for her.

—You've seen the way she can hunt & trap. Did you know she can make her own snowshoes?

She is a capable young woman, I agreed. At

times I have wondered if she is under our protection, or we under hers.

He went on to list her many other attributes. He said he had never before met a woman who aimed to out-do him with shooting & games.

— She has a way, too, of joking about things most women are too shy to discuss. But she's not crude like some of the whores I've known, he added.

I observed that they do seem to enjoy each other's company, but wondered how they could remain together.

— You remember when you said your Mrs. Forrester wasn't like any woman you had ever come across, that there was something different about her that set her apart? Well, that's how I feel about Nattie.

I asked if she shared the affection, to which he admitted being perplexed.

— I'm a tomcat, sir. On the rare occasion I get turned down, I don't waste a minute blubbering about it, he said.

With Nat'aaggi, however, he said he is unsure. They will be conversing, as her English has steadily improved, when Tillman will reach over to take her hand or attempt to sit closer to her.

— She just moves right off, & I follow like a mooncalf.

I suggested that perhaps her unfortunate marriage had made her wary of courtship.

Tillman slapped his knee.

— Well, of course! Why didn't I see that? She's gun-shy. I've just got to approach her slow, then maybe I stand a chance.

I said no more. It seems to me a doomed affair. Surely he has no intention of remaining with her in the Alaska wilds. I have seen few Indian women adapt to modern civilization; Nat'aaggi does not strike me as such a woman. Would she be prepared to travel to San Francisco, then on to whatever post he is next stationed? It seems improbable.

Later in the day, Tillman spoke up again.

— Just think, Colonel. Soon enough you'll be seeing your sweet wife & your little one, too.

I could not answer him.

July 22

We have arrived at the missionary's house, though the man himself is not about. It seemed a mirage to our eyes: a kitchen garden with turnips, cabbages, & flowers, a straight little house & several outbuildings of milled lumber. All set down on the bank of this wild river.

— Look at that, even the floor doesn't have a speck of dirt, Tillman whispered as the wife welcomed us into the house & made us coffee. — Sure glad I'm wearing britches now at least.

It caused us all some embarrassment to

581

notice our own condition in contrast to her neat appearance & orderly home. We are in poor shape & filthy beyond acceptable.

The missionary's wife fed us our first real meal in four months, including fried eggs, bread, potatoes, & turnips, all sprinkled with generous amounts of salt. She has welcomed us all, although she serves Nat'aaggi & Boyo their meals outdoors.

The woman also took note of Pruitt's poor health. She offered to prepare some treatments for him to take. She said it probably would not please him much, but that it would greatly improve his condition.

She later showed us to the bathhouse, with woodstove & a large tub we could fill with water to bathe. We were also given leave to raise one of her husband's canvas wall-tents for our sleeping quarters. Nat'aaggi prefers to make her own tent of spruce boughs.

July 23

We are new men, clean, well-fed, & rested. Tillman has even shaved his beard, which gave Nat'aaggi a shock.

Mrs. Lowe, as she is called, has her hands full with seven children, the oldest a 10-year-old boy, the youngest still an infant, but she manages to assist us a great deal.

Already today she has encouraged Pruitt to drink several cups of spruce-needle tea, which he says has a strong, sharp flavor but is not entirely disagreeable. She has also served him the Indian cure of rabbit intestines, just warmed but uncooked.

Pruitt was pale as he prepared to sip all this down, but he did as told.

I mentioned to Mrs. Lowe that he had lost much of his appetite these past weeks, which has only worsened his condition. She is confident, however, that within a week or two of such remedies, Pruitt will improve.

I remarked to Mrs. Lowe on the hardship of mothering so many children in a remote place such as this, with supplies so unreliable. She admitted that it has often been lonely & difficult. Last winter she lost her second youngest child to fever. It seems that her husband was away again on his mission work, so she faced the tragedy alone.

July 25
We helped Mrs. Lowe with some repairs to the roof of her woodshed, which had been damaged in high winds during the winter. She then cooked us an extravagant dinner of caribou roast, potatoes, carrots. She also served a dessert of biscuits with blueberry jam.

She would not let Pruitt have his, however, until he had drank his usual bowl of rabbit innards. Though he is still gaunt & weakened, he is recovering something of his natural character. He has taken up his journal again

& notes the various plants along the river.

I learn more about the Lowes. They are of the Moravian Church, of which I know very little. The husband was assigned this mission in '80 but they did not arrive until '82.

Mrs. Lowe has adapted remarkably to the extreme conditions here. She butchers the game birds her oldest son hunts, hauls firewood by sled. In her husband's absence, she has even shot several caribou when the herd has traveled close enough to their home.

In '83 the Lowes met Lieut. Frederick Schwatka as he completed his renowned journey down the Yukon River.

She says he was a very different kind of Army man than I seem to be. I asked how so.

— He was not so reserved, & he had little humility.

I remarked that any man who has spent time in Alaska should be nothing if not humble.

Lieutenant Frederick Schwatka, 3rd Cavalry,
Military Reconnaissance in Alaska made in 1883 as reported to Commanding Department of the Columbia, Vancouver Barracks, Washington Territory

Yukon River

We camped at 8:30 p.m. near several Indian graves, about a mile or two above the mouth of the Whymper River, which comes in from the left, and just on the upper boundary of the conspicuous valley of that stream. There were quite a number of graves at this point, forming the first and only burying place we saw on the river that might be called a family graveyard, i.e., a spot where a number, say six or seven, were buried in a row within a single enclosure. From its posts at the corners and sides were the usual totems and old rags flying, two of the carvings representing, I think, a duck and a bear, respectively, while the others could not be made out.

. . . Dr. Wilson tried to get a skull out of the many we assumed were at hand, to send to the Army Museum's large craniological collection, but although several very old-looking sites were opened, the skulls were

too fresh to be properly prepared in the brief time at our disposal.

Lieut. Col. Allen Forrester
July 26, 1885

Mrs. Lowe confided in me that her husband has fathered a child with a young Innuit woman, is gone more than he is home. She believes he has taken the native woman as a kind of second wife.

Why does she remain? Does she not have family to assist her? & wouldn't the church dismiss him if they knew of his misconduct?

— I must leave it to the Lord, she said.

She asked if I have such faith. I admitted that I do not.

— Sometimes I fear that our prayers are not strong enough for this wild place, she said.

This evening I sit outside the wall-tent. I notice for the first time a true darkening in the sky with sunset. The air is cool. Autumn comes early to this country.

Tillman & Nat'aaggi play their hoop game

down at the river. They race each other & laugh. When once they both threw rocks into the hoop at the same time, he grabbed her at the waist & lifted her into the air.

It is selfish, but the sight of them causes me some loneliness.

July 27

It is good that Tillman came for me tonight.

I stayed too late in Mrs. Lowe's home. She & I talked of our families in the East, our childhoods. She had visited Boston often when she was a young girl. When it grew late, she helped the older children into their beds in the attic, lit a lamp at the table. I stood to go, but she asked if I might stay to visit a while longer. The children were soon asleep, all but the infant that suckled at her breast.

When the babe had fallen asleep, she gently pulled its mouth from her breast. I could not look away. The wet milk upon the child's lips. The soft curve of her full breast. She did not hurry to cover herself, but sat there for a moment, then she brought her eyes up to mine.

The world narrowed to such a small point so that I forgot all but that warm flame of the lamp.

Then came the sergeant's knock. — Sir, it is late. You wanted to rise early.

I cannot sleep. I sit outside the wall-tent where Pruitt & Tillman are in bed. I hold in my hand Sophie's letter & the silver hair comb.

July 28
We left the Lowes' home this late morning. The children ran about shouting, helping to dismantle the wall-tent & load the skin boat. The baby cried in her arms. Once we were on the river, it took much effort on my part to not look back for her.

Just before Nulato we came upon Mr. Lowe at an Indian camp. He waved to our boat when he saw that we were white men. I would have preferred to float past, but it would have seemed markedly unfriendly, so we stopped.

The man is cheerful, quick to shake our hands & bless us. He said he was glad to know we had found rest & food at his home. He asked briefly how his family fared. I fought the urge to pummel him. When he began to introduce us to the natives in his company, Tillman interrupted, said that we must be going if we hope to meet up with the steamboat.

Mr. Lowe seemed surprised by our abrupt departure, but not in the least put out. He waved happily from shore as we rounded the next bend in the river.

We sleep tonight in an abandoned trapper's cabin well below Nulato. No sign of the steamboat, though it is expected any day now.

We landed only briefly at the village, but found the Indians in a state of unrest. They have heard that the Alaska Commercial Co. will close down its Nulato station. Anvik has already been abandoned. Several Russian-Indian creoles have stirred the hostility by explaining to the natives what poor terms they have been receiving on their trade. They get less than half the San Francisco value for their furs, but are charged 25 per cent more for goods.

The Indians wait for the steamboat with rifles in arms. All in all, this cabin down-stream seemed a better place to spend the night. It holds no food or supplies. It does, however, provide comfortable enough quarters. It is a quiet & picturesque spot, with a creek running nearby.

Pruitt was the first to notice the large tusk lying in the creek bed, just a foot or so beneath the clear running water. Wooly mammoth, he says, from thousands of years ago. It is the same as the ones we saw in the mountain pass.

July 29
Pruitt today asked me if he might find some peace along this creek. It struck me as odd. All that we have seen & endured in this territory, peace was not among them. I said as much.

— There is a certain stillness at the center of it, he said. — You must feel it, too?

I looked where he did, down where the clear water washed over the mammoth tusk. He said that it was perhaps the creek. I could not follow all he said, as his speech had a rambling quality to it, but he talked about the immensity of it, drop by drop down the mountain valleys, then this rush out to sea.

— That is a comfort, isn't it? he said. — Each day, we rise. Wash in cold water. Gather wood for the fire. Eat to stay alive. The next day, do the same again. Maybe it can be simple enough when so reduced.

There's also rain & mosquitoes & rotten salmon & walking for days on end while your boots rot off your feet, I offered, but he was too focused on his own philosophy to see my humor.

Elemental. That is the word he used again & again. Hunger, sun, cold. Pure unto themselves. No false veil between a man & the world around him, he said. No pretenses. Nothing to hide behind.

I supposed that is what a man like Samuelson finds in this country.

Pruitt then told me he would like to spend his last days here.

It took me aback. Did he mean to kill himself?

— I think I would like to live here alone for a time, he said.

Just then a group of ducks floated down the stream. We watched as they bobbed in the current near the far bank.

— At Elk Creek, sir, I was no bystander or deserter.

We were both of us quiet for some time.

— That might have been tolerable, he went on. — To have watched & done nothing & live with that shame alone. To have fled & been shot. That would have been a relief. I might have wished for it even.

Men who are afraid often make poor choices, I said.

— That cannot explain the capability, he said. — Don't you think evil itself must exist already inside of a man for him to commit such acts?

I could not give him an answer except to say that for all creation men have done such things, the strong misusing the weak. Every civilization has its own versions of cruelty.

— I've spent the past three years telling myself that, but it does me no good, Colonel. It's as if that day I entered hell itself, &, God help me, I cannot find my way back out again.

He began, then, to weep openly.

— Forgive me, Colonel. Forgive me, he said.

It is not for me to forgive him. Who on earth can? A boy like him was never suited for war. It saddens me, to think of the young Andrew Pruitt, intelligent yet so feeble-hearted. Had he been a school teacher or a lecturer, he never would have been tested so, never would have faced his own moral deficiency.

— Do you read the Bible, Colonel? he asked.

I admitted that I did not. Religion has never held much interest for me.

— There is a poetry to it, he said. — That's what always draws me back to it. Even with all the ways it fails, I can still find that to admire. The poetry of it. At my best, I imagine it the highest of arts. An expression of what we wish we could be. There is hope in our wanting to be something better, even if we never manage it. Maybe that is what I can hold to. The wanting. Do you know what I mean, sir?

I am not sure I do. All that matters is how a man lives in this world.

Pruitt has given me his journals. I expected detailed notes of flora, fauna, geology, & the like. Not this. I have asked him to copy out all the pages of meteorological readings & mapping data. As for his rambling entries, they serve no purpose in our reports to headquarters, but would rather be an embarrassment. They are nearly incomprehensible. Yet he says he would like me to have them.

He officially resigns his commission. I will arrange for his salary to be paid through the trading post at St. Michael's. When we meet up with the steamboat, we can likely obtain enough supplies to sustain him until then.

I take him at his word, that he seeks a life here & not a death. I hope I do right in agreeing to his resignation.

Indians passed through our camp this morning with news — the steamboat nears Nulato.

64°42' N
158°08' W
Rain.
Prevailing winds from the west.
I am set down in this valley. A cold wind washes over me like water over unearthed bones.

The land is open and wide and blown clear. The mountains are far.

Can something half-dead and rotted to pale be resurrected? Can the clean breath of this land enter me?

From whom shall I beg forgiveness?

And I will lay sinews upon you, and will spring up flesh upon you and cover you with skin, and put breath in you, and ye shall live.

Thou knowest.

My dear Sophie,

These words do not come easily to me. Since I received your letter at Tetling, I have been seized with such emotion as I cannot express.

I am not like you. I am ill-equipped to know, much less speak of, my heart. Yet as I waited to board the steamboat, I recalled an incident from my childhood that has allowed me some small understanding of myself.

My cousin Robert & I planned to sail to Africa to search for the source of the Nile. We drew maps, made our supply list, & for months wrote letters to one another about our impending expedition. I was 10, Robert two years older. I looked up to him a great deal.

It was my poor mother who had to inform me on a summer day that Robert had drowned trying to swim across the family pond. She must have expected me to collapse into her & weep, for I was still a child, but I did not. Instead I ran to my upstairs bedroom & retrieved the box where I kept our maps & plans. I opened my bedroom window & threw it all out, so that the papers scattered through the trees & the wooden box shattered in the yard. I did not cry. Anger was all I could comprehend.

Your letter cut me deeply, Sophie. How could you so belittle me as to think that I would abandon you or lose my love for you because you suffer some ailment beyond your influence? In so few words, you lessened every act of love between us.

I cannot explain all that we have encountered on this journey, though I will share my diaries so that you might know as much as I. Yet even as we marched, half-starving, & faced something of our nightmares, all the while I thought of you & our child & knew I could endure any hardship in order to return home.

Can you then know how much your letter robbed of me, not just to learn that we will not have a child, but to know that you could doubt my love? Did you believe that I loved you only for a mother you might be, rather than the woman you are? When I looked up to see you in a treetop with the schoolchildren, I fell in love with your courage & intellect & sweet voice. I thought, 'I should like to climb trees & mountains with this woman.' All those afternoons at the boarding house when I courted you, we did not talk of children — we talked about what I had seen of the wild country & all that you hoped to see.

I was to show you Yosemite; you were to teach me the names & songs of all the birds. As we grew braver in our affection, what did we whisper of but how we would spend nights together in a tent? Was all this forgotten?

Sophie, it is our loss together, this child & all others that might have been born in our future, but it surely is not all that binds us together? You left the schoolhouse, I would leave the Army, so that we might have the life each of us has always desired.

Yet I see now, recalling Robert's death, that I am quick to anger in the face of grief. I read of your anguish & loneliness, yet I was stranded thousands of miles away. I could do nothing in your aid.

I have calmed & can now comprehend that you did not set out to injure me with your words, but instead to share with me your truest pain.

I have not been so brave. I have kept things from you & you are right to question me. It was not from any lack of respect for you, for you possess more insight than many officers I have known. Nor is it shame on my part — I have endeavored to be good & decent even in the throes of warfare.

There have been grim days, though, I will say that now. At times it has been at my orders, even my own hand. Even within the bounds of order, morality can be hard found.

You asked me about the day with the telegraph machine. I will tell you now. I had accepted the surrender of a renegade band of Indians, with my promise that I would send them back to their reservation to be with their families if they agreed to our terms. Once the Indians were within my custody, however, I received orders from Washington, D.C., to march them to Florida, where they would be incarcerated in the dungeons of Fort Marion.

I did everything in my power, but my superiors were not to be persuaded. In the end, I was made to break my word. It sickens me all the more to know that many of the Indians, acclimated to the deserts of the Southwest, perished in their dank cells.

Can you understand my reticence now? Not only to be forced to recall the incident but then to speak of it? I would not cast such a shadow over you.

Yet I did a discredit to your fortitude. I should have remembered that you, too, have known grief. You are by no means naïve or unwitting, yet somehow you still find beauty in each day. It is a gladdening thought, & one that saves me just now.

I am able to count on my hands the number of men I have left in the field, & now I come home without Lieut. Pruitt. He is well provisioned, improves in physical health. Yet I cannot be sure I do well by him. He is unsteady & irritable of heart. I leave him along the Yukon River, a land more tame than the Wolverine River, but this wild territory is still beyond our explanation.

I can find no means to account for all that we have witnessed, except to say that I am no longer certain of the boundaries between man & beast, of the living & the dead. All that I have taken for granted, what I have known as real & true, has been called into question.

I am certain only of this — I come home to you in love.

Allen

Lieut. Col. Allen Forrester
August 2, 1885
St. Michael's

We left Pruitt at the cabin near Nulato. I asked again if he would fare well alone, to which he replied that it was his last hope, as he could no longer find such hope in humanity. A gloomy answer indeed. Yet I see little choice but to honor his resignation. There were firm handshakes all around. I left him a spare pencil I still had in my possession. He thanked me. He also asked me to give his good wishes to Sophie.

Despite the unrest at Nulato, Tillman, Nat'aaggi, & I then boarded the steamboat with little incident. We did, however, encounter some difficulty in enticing Boyo to come aboard.

Tillman, true to nature, was engaged in a fistfight with a white trader before the night was out. I suspect it had something to do with Nat'aaggi, though none of the parties involved would give explanation. Considering we are so near the end of our journey, I chose not to pursue the matter further.

We arrived this afternoon at St. Michael's on Norton Sound, where we will wait for the revenue cutter. I hoped that I would find a letter from Sophie waiting for me, but there is none. I try hard not to think on it.

The young Mr. Troyer, the trading agent for the Yukon area, has welcomed us with much hospitality. Tillman & I have been given quarters in his home. Today was devoted to arranging back pay for Pruitt & additional supplies to be sent to him.

We now have little to do but wait for the revenue cutter. No one can provide an estimate on its arrival — it could be within days or as long as a month. Never have I been so anxious to return home. More than once I have pictured myself jumping into the cold gray waves to swim south.

St. Michael's is a sparse settlement. There is but the Alaska Commercial Co. post, some small & weather-beaten houses, the old Russian church. Only a few outbuildings remain of the Russian fort. The way these structures are set out on this small point into Norton Sound, with long views in all directions over seascape & vast, treeless land, the ocean wind whipping at it, it is as if we have reached the edge of the world.

August 3

I read most of the day, catching up on a stack of newspapers in Mr. Troyer's office. He must be an avid reader, Mr. Troyer, for every shelf & desktop is piled with newspapers & books.

Tillman & Nat'aaggi have wandered off together. The dog has chosen to sit at my feet while I read & I do not mind.

August 5

After traveling for months on end, it is unnatural to be still for so long. I am impatient beyond measure to return to Sophie.

Mr. Troyer tries to engage me in frequent conversation. He is a philosophizer with little opportunity in this territory, but I make a poor partner in such discussions. He asks much about our journey. I have relayed some of the more bizarre details.

— Amazing! Simply amazing! But what do you make of it all? he has asked enough times to become a bother.

Make of it? Is it not enough that we survived? The more Mr. Troyer burdens me with such talk, the more I avoid his company.

Tillman is restless, too, though I do not think he is keen to leave. Nat'aaggi does not make her plans known. Could she intend to travel south with us on the ship? It seems unlikely. Yet it is equally implausible that Tillman will want to part from her. She keeps her feelings concealed, from what I can tell, but he is clearly lovesick.

The three of us often walk along the gray beach together. Tillman throws sticks for the dog, though Boyo is wary of the water. Nat'aaggi has found a few sea-shells.

This afternoon Tillman & I came across some houses for the dead near the shore. They are cone-shaped constructions of drift wood, with the body laid inside & wrapped in cloth & animal skins.

August 6
All these days at the beach & rocky points, I find nothing suitable.

Nat'aaggi asked me today what I seek. I told her I look for some small gift to bring to my wife — a feather, a pretty sea-shell, perhaps even the egg-shells of some shore-bird.

August 7
We were invited to an Innuit meal. Their favorite food is seal oil, which they eat voraciously, dipping with fingers from bowl to mouth. Tillman & I politely declined. We did, however, venture a go with their dessert — a whipped concoction of seal oil, berries, & tallow. It looked appetizing, almost like a sweet cream, but we could each only manage a few bites.

August 9
More than a week with no sign of the revenue cutter. I cannot tolerate this waiting.

August 11
Today Nat'aaggi brought two Innuit boys to me. Their English is quite good. She told them I wanted to find an egg for my wife.

— To eat? one of the boys asked.

— No, I said. — She thinks they are pretty. Just the shells would be fine.

At this they became quite animated, beckoned for me to follow them. They led me away from the sea, out through the grass & hummocks. We walked for so long, I thought perhaps they led me on a wild chase. Now & then they would poke around in the low bushes, but then continue their walking.

At last one of them shouted with excitement.

They had indeed found a small nest. It had long since been abandoned but inside the bed of grass & feathers were two broken shells.

The boys indicated that often these nests hold as many as a dozen eggs. The villagers gather them to eat in the spring.

I thanked them, gave them each a coin, carefully collected the bits of shell.

When I showed them to Nat'aaggi, thanked her for her assistance, she indicated I needed something to put them in. A tin can will be fine, I said.

Tillman has spiffed himself up for the evening. There is a gathering at the trading company. Several villages will bring in their furs. They will celebrate with a feast & dance.

Tillman borrows my Indian moose-hide jacket. He thinks it will impress Nat'aaggi. He spent a long time in front of the mirror, readying himself. He still looks a frightful mountain man, I joked, & the jacket is too small for him. He was all seriousness. He said he would dance with her tonight, find out once & for all if she loves him.

He asked if I wouldn't come, too.

— I hear these Eskimo men are something at wrestling, he said. — Wonder if we could best them?

I declined, told him I have never been much for socializing, but I wished him a good time.

Sophie Forrester
Vancouver Barracks
July 8, 1885

The second humming bird chick has broken from its shell. The mother bird leaves her nest only briefly, but spends most hours brooding over her newborns.

I now know the limit of my days, for within three weeks they will fledge, and the mother bird will have no need to return. The only chance I have to catch her image is when she is perched, in stillness, in a place where I have already focused my camera. The nest is my only hope.

Last night I developed what plates I have. Even in the negative, I can see the mother bird in focus, the lines sharp and the textures varied. It is exhilarating indeed, yet I do not lose sight of my original desire. It is the light that I must come to understand.

July 12

Evelyn is most disappointed with me, and I do feel as if I have behaved poorly as a friend. I did not attend the Fourth of July festivities in Portland, though she begged, for I had no desire to brave the pressing crowds, roman candles, and cannons. And then I again declined an invitation from her, this time to resort to the coast for several days to take in the sea air. I would not leave the nest.

As it turns out, I might as well have gone. It has been especially windy along the river, so that the nest bobs on its thimbleberry cane and I can take no pictures. In the end, I am left alone in the house. Charlotte is away with her own family. I spent a few hours in the dark room, experimenting with the new printing solutions Mr Redington supplied me, yet it could not hold my interest.

During these past few weeks, an anxious loneliness has grown within me that not even the distraction of my camera can ease. Against my will, I watch the wharf as men disembark the ferry, and I think, can that be him? It changes nothing, this desperate watching, yet I am provoked by the knowledge that he might well appear one afternoon, without warning, for he will have no way of sending word from Alaska that he is on his way.

I have done my best to resist, but yesterday I visited the department headquarters yet again and asked after Allen, a futile endeavor though I know it is.

Tonight I straightened the dining room and put on my best dress, thinking that it might cheer me, but instead it only served to sharpen my heartache.

July 14

Dear Allen, do you know why I persist in keeping this diary? My field journals, my photography notes, those I keep for myself. They are the mode with which I am most at ease. This diary, however, is something different; I would not place all these emotions on the page for my own sake.

Despite the gloomy letter I sent to you, despite my hours of anguish and worry, each time I take up this diary and put pen to paper, it is with the hope, no the faith, that you will someday come home to me and want to know how I have spent my hours.

Each entry, every word contained here, is devoted to you.

July 18

Today the mother bird perched at the side of the nest, the two tiny beaks opened up at her. The exposure is fine enough; one can distinguish birds and nest from foliage. Yet when the shutter clacked, the mother bird startled, and so her image is blurred.

And still I am not entirely pleased with the angle of light.

July 20

It was a risk, yet it had to be done. With Charlotte's assistance, I moved the camera tent so as to better position myself to the arc of the sun.

We made a comical pair, the two of us. We stood inside the small structure, each lifting a side, and shuffled awkwardly, slowly, foot by foot, like two actors doing a pantomime of a horse. Because we were trying to be as quiet as possible, we were all the more pressed toward laughter. By some blessing, however, we were able to make the change with only the two wide-eyed chicks observing us, as the mother bird was out gathering food. By the time she returned to the nest, we were quietly in our place as if we had never been elsewhere.

This evening I officially promoted Charlotte from housemaid to photographer's assistant, although I can only afford a small raise in her salary. She positively beamed when I presented her with a handwritten business card:

Charlotte MacCarthy
Photography Assistant
For at home photographs, landscapes,
and ornithological portraiture
Vancouver Barracks,
Washington Territory

July 23

I confess that my most recent print of the humming bird at the nest is lovely, with the sunlight fast upon her, her two chicks beneath her, beaks open, the background in shadows, the nest and birds in lit clarity. It is perhaps my best photograph yet. I mounted a print of it with parlor paste to cardboard and placed it in a simple gold-leaf frame I had purchased in Portland.

When I presented it to Evelyn, wrapped in a set of white linen pillowcases that Charlotte had embroidered with Evelyn's initials, I was not sure how she would respond.

"Is this my wedding gift? It is, isn't it! Even so, I won't wait to open it."

She then fell silent as she held the photograph, and I could not read her expression. I asked her finally if she did not like it.

"Sophie, it is beautiful . . ." Her voice was quiet and I saw that she might cry, all of which took me entirely by surprise.

"I will deny it!" she said as she wiped her cheeks with a handkerchief. What would she deny? "That your little picture made me teary. Word must not get out that I am tenderhearted after all."

She says we must see each other again soon, that I will have to come to San Francisco once she and Mr Harvey are settled into their domesticity. Yet I am already nostalgic for these days I have shared with her at Vancouver

Barracks, for I do not think they will likely return.

I will miss you, Evelyn. Let tomorrow be kind to both of us.

July 27

I am filled with a terrifying hope. Can it be that at last I have a worthy photograph?

The nest is empty; both young birds fledged this morning and the mother is gone. They have become unobtainable vibrations of color and feather among the branches.

And I am left with two exposed plates. What will they hold? Can it be that I have caught something at last? Yet I will not risk any drop of sunlight that might ruin them in developing. I must wait for dark.

Lieut. Col. Allen Forrester
August 14, 1885
St. Michael's

Bradley Tillman is dead. It does not seem possible, yet it is so.

At 5 this morning, I woke to shouts, then gunshots. Tillman's voice. — Come on, there. We're all having a good time here, aren't we?

I could tell from his speech that he was drunk, as were they all.

I hurried to pull on my clothes when I heard Tillman's voice again. I have come to know Tillman well enough to guess that events might get out of hand.

Yet he was not the one looking for a fight this time. He was drunk & happy. As I approached the trading post, in the gray morning light I saw a man pointing a rifle at the crowd that had gathered outside. Before I could speak, Tillman stepped towards him with a friendly hand out. The man shot him just then. Tillman slumped to the ground.

He was not to be revived. The crowd broke into confusion. The shooter dropped the rifle & ran.

I have only come to understand the details as this day progresses. It was Mr. Jacob Wheeler, the one who had scuffled with Tillman aboard the steamship. It seems Mr. Wheeler spent this past evening drinking more than he should, fuming over the incident. At some point, he perceived that he had been slighted by Tillman, who had jostled into him during the dancing. Mr. Wheeler retrieved his rifle from his tent, began to shout & fire rounds outside the trading company.

The noise brought many of the revelers out of doors, who thought the shooting was part of the night-long festivities. Tillman seems to have been the first to notice that the man was in a bad temper. Tillman approached, hand out in reconciliation. Like a child who steps thoughtlessly into the street to retrieve his toy even as a carriage bears down upon him. The man shot him once in the chest.

Mr. Wheeler was later found hiding beneath one of the Innuits' skin boats on the beach. He will be taken by the revenue cutter to stand trial in San Francisco. For now he is locked in a closet in the trading post under guard. It is as much for his own protection, I suspect. I would have delivered upon him considerably more than a bloodied face if Mr.

Troyer had not interceded.

There is no counting the deaths of my comrades, yet it does not lessen my grief. Tillman was never measured in his ways, but he possessed a kind & self-less nature. That is a rarity amongst men. The General was right to appoint him to my party. I am sorry beyond words that I do not bring him home to his family.

I have written dozens of such letters. This one will be no easier, though they have most likely expected such news for some time. Bradley Tillman was never one to stick to safer trails.

August 16
Nat'aaggi left this morning at dawn. I watched as she & Boyo disappeared into the willows. She carried her bow & quiver of arrows; she & the dog both wore their packs.

I do not know what to make of her journey. It is impossible, of course, but if one allows that it might be, then it is a noble & terrible thing. For myself, I would not willingly enter those mountain storms again.

Despite my reservations, if I had known she would leave today, I would have arranged transport for her up the Yukon. I would have provided her with supplies.

She will need boat passage along the way, but she knows where she can find safe help

— Pruitt, Mrs. Lowe, the friendly camps we encountered. Perhaps she can travel quietly & unnoticed through the more dangerous territory until she gets to the mountains.

When I saw her go, I wanted to call out to her. I wanted to tell her it's no use, but what do I know?

She sang a song over his body yesterday in the Russian church, before we had built a coffin, so Tillman was wrapped only in fabric. She knelt by his body & sang. Her words were both English & Midnoosky, but still I could not make out all she said. I had a senseless & fleeting thought — Where was Tillman to translate for me?

I understood only this much:

We walk by the river.
Not the same words.
Not the same { — }
We walk beside the river.
My friend, my { — }
My friend
I cry to you.
{ — } in the mountains where kay'egay
    spirits walk & sing
I go to look for you.
Will you walk out of the clouds?
My friend, my { — }
I cry to you.
{ — } in the mountains.
That kay'egay place.

I come to look for you.
I cry to you.
I come to you.

At times like this, I wish I were a praying man.

I wonder that Nat'aaggi didn't give it to me herself, but maybe she feared I would try to stop her leaving.

— She says she made it for your wife. Something about putting some egg-shells into it, Mr. Troyer said.

It is a basket made of birch bark & spruce root, much like the one I have seen Indian women use to hold food. This one, though, is small enough to fit into the palm of my hand.

August 17
We sat up late into the night, Mr. Troyer & I. By dinner, we were forced to light the lamps, as summer's midnight sun has left this land. A strong rainstorm had moved in from the Bering Sea, so that the wind beat against the side of the house in the darkness. There are no trees or hills to slow storms on this barren island. For once I was willing to be confined indoors.

When we finished eating, Mr. Troyer opened a fine bottle of Glenlivet. Perhaps it was the whiskey at work, but I was willing to sit through his talk. Mr. Troyer offered up his thoughts on death & mourning, how we suffer more because we have done away with the rituals that might otherwise comfort us. He is interested in the burial habits of the Innuits, the shaman practices of the Indians. He wanted to know more of what I had seen amongst the Wolverine tribes, so I told him best I could. I even described the infant I had cut from the bloody roots of a spruce tree.

— My God! To witness such epiphanies! he said.

He begged for as much detail as I would give, only to spend far too much time speculating aloud about the birth, what it might signify, who the child might be. A pointless endeavor. I said as much.

— Yet you must desire to make some sense of it? he said. — An event of that magnitude must mean something.

His zeal brushed me wrong.

— Tell me this, Mr. Troyer, what meaning do you find in the death of Sgt. Bradley Tillman? An event of some magnitude, I'd say. You were witness to it as much as I. You tell me, what significance shall we take from it? What great knowledge does it bring us to watch him be shot dead by a drunken fool?

I saw then just how young Mr. Troyer is, for I had startled & shamed him.

— You're right, he said. — There is nothing decent to be taken from that.

He was quiet for a time, though not long enough to suit me.

— But don't you think, Colonel, that soldiers are strengthened by such grief? You all have been tested in battle. You've lived by your own wit & hands.

— How old are you, Mr. Troyer?

— 26 come December.

I could not help but laugh. I could be his father.

— So you have not seen war.

— No, sir.

— I would be careful, then. It is all too easy to love a thing you've never had to live with.

Still, he would not leave it be. I was sorry to find he is a maudlin drunk.

—You're a great, great man, Colonel. I wish I could see the things you have seen. Surely you've learned so much from your journey.

— Nothing I didn't already suspect, I said.

—What is that? What did you already know?

—That it's a d——d hard life.

— For the Wolverine Indians?

— For any of us.

August 18

I cannot stop thinking on it. The day Mr. Troyer & I carried Tillman's body into the old Russian church, a raven flew overhead as we walked. As we neared the church doors, the bird landed to perch overhead on the tallest cross. It turned its head down towards us,

opened its black beak. Its sounds were uncanny, a gurgling, human-like croak that rose
& rose to a shrill cry.

I am certain — in that bird's strange call, I
heard the voice of the Old Man. Yet I could
not make out its meaning. Was it the sound
of weeping? Or of laughter? Or was it only a
raven's cry for its next meal?

My dearest Allen,

It is with great and perhaps unreasonable optimism that I send this letter north in hopes that it, and the enclosed photograph, will reach you. I feel I might as well have corked it into a bottle and tossed it into the Columbia River, yet General Haywood has promised to dispatch it to Sitka on the very next mail ship, and from there he says there is a possibility it will find its way to the USS Corwin. I suppose I will not know for weeks, months perhaps, whether you have received it.

I am armed, however, with renewed good cheer. Word came to Vancouver Barracks this week, on a long route among Indians and traders from what I understand, that you had passed safely into the Wolverine Mountains in June. If it is true, the General says there is some chance you will arrive at the coast by the end of August, just a month from now, and be home before winter! Oh please let it be true! I know the General was hesitant to say so much but wanted to give me some peace of mind, for I become more and more anxious about your welfare as the weeks go by.

My dear Allen, I miss you more than I could ever imagine a heart could bear. Nearly half a year you have been gone from me. Again and again, I read the letter you sent from Alaska. I am sorry that all scent of wilderness and camp smoke is gone from it now, for I like to hold it to my face and close my eyes and picture myself beside you.

You will be proud, I think, to know that I have not squandered my days in melancholy, however. In the spring, I purchased a camera and these past months have endeavored to photograph wild birds. I thought often of how you would counsel me, how you would say that I should step bravely, and so that is what I have done. Our ledger book, my housekeeping, and our little cabin at the barracks have all suffered for it, but I hope you will find it has been a worthwhile pursuit.

I have been blessed with some praise for my work, and am astounded to find that an editor in Philadelphia has passed several of my photographs on to an ornithologist who is compiling a new book, and they have asked if I might provide them with at least a dozen more photographs of varying species from Oregon and the Washington Territory. I have not agreed yet. I have ventured no more than a mile from home with my camera, and I admit I am somewhat daunted by the scope of the request. I wonder if you will think it feasible.

This particular photograph that I send you, however, I have not shared with anyone else. I took it just days ago, and I wanted you to see it first. It is, I think, what I have aspired to from the beginning.

Look closely — do you see? Is there not something to it?

This is all that I can manage to write just now, as the messenger is at the door and I am out of time.

Let this token of my love find its way to you, and bring you safely home again.

With all my heart's love,

Sophie

100. U. S. R. C. Corwin. Sitka, Alaska.

Lieut. Col. Allen Forrester
August 20, 1885
Aboard the USS Corwin bound for San Fran-
cisco

Sophie, my dear, I am on my way to you at last. Your letter, dated nearly a month ago, along with your photograph, greeted me aboard the revenue cutter when it arrived at St. Michael's yesterday. It was a most welcomed surprise.

These words that I write in return will not be passed to Indians or mail ships, but instead I will deliver them to you myself, & then I will grab hold of you & never let go again. Now more than ever, we are in need of each other's comfort.

I come home without my men. After all that

we endured, Bradley Tillman was killed in a senseless & drunken misunderstanding just days before our ship was in sight. Never is it easy to lose a soldier & friend, yet a man who dies in battle at least gives his life for some purpose, if only in protection of his comrades. This, this absurdity, is a blow. My task was to bring my two men safely home from Alaska, & I have failed both of them. It troubles me terribly.

The loss of our baby, my fatigue, all that you & I have experienced in our separation — I am unkeeled by it. My emotions rise too quickly.

Yet this alone cannot explain how your photograph has affected me. I have removed it from its wrapping many times to study it, & I cannot get my fill. It is stirring in a way I am hard pressed to describe. There is texture & depth to it that seems born more of brush strokes than camera work.

You have an eye for the extraordinary, Sophie. It makes me wish all the more that you could have seen Alaska, only without our hardships, for I believe you would have spied something beyond what my poor senses could fathom. I found myself inadequate in the face of it. Only now, as I leave these shores behind, do I begin to try to comprehend: gray rivers that roar down from the glaciers, mountains & spruce valleys as far as the eye can see. It is a grand, inscrutable wildness.

Never are the people here allowed to forget that each of us is alive only by a small thread.

Perhaps this is what young Mr. Troyer so longed to hear from me. I could not find the words then. It is you, Sophie — you make me want to express myself more profoundly. You give me hope that we may yet find meaning in our days. Your photograph serves as evidence.

I am reminded of something the trapper Samuelson said of Alaska's wild country.

Here, I have found the passage in my diary: — She always keeps a part of herself a mystery.

You have focused your lens on just such a mystery.

These months I've been gone, I have thought often about the narrowness of your life at the barracks. I know all too well how meddlesome that society can be, & it grieved me to think of you so confined. I should have known you better. Of course you would buy a camera & build your own dark room. School teacher or officer's wife, you are every bit the woman I fell in love with.

This is what we will do, as soon as I am returned to Vancouver: I will leave the service, as we have planned & I have so long desired. We will pack up our camp, your camera too, & we will go to the wilderness, you & I. Yosemite, yes. But for your photographs, the Cascades, the upper reaches of the

Columbia River, the high deserts to the east of the mountains, or we'll go to the Coast, the tide marshes. We'll sleep in a tent beneath the stars & make love & listen to the wind through the trees, & the hours will belong to us alone. We will report to no one. When dawn comes, we will go looking for your birds, & you will teach me their names.

Yes, there is most certainly something in this photograph, Sophie. It is in that blade of light at the edge of the humming bird's wing. Something wild & beautiful. It is something of you, my love.

Sophie Forrester
Vancouver Barracks
July 29, 1885

I cannot categorically name it, any more than I can be sure of my own faith, for it is not the photograph itself as much as the impression it leaves upon me. The moment the fledgling humming bird perched at the edge of the nest and stretched its small wings, and the late sun shone along the river, my breath caught in my throat, and I released the shutter.

It was just as Mr Redington described — all my days spent in experiments and failures and near successes, and in an instant I was presented with this scene, a young bird preparing to take its first flight, and I allowed instinct to lead me.

All along I had imagined that it would be the mother bird that would figure large in any photograph. Yet when I returned to my dark room, I was full of the sense that I had something at last in this picture of the fledgling, even as I was afraid to hope for so much. Could the young bird have held its position long enough to be more than a blur of motion? I was cautious and methodical in my every step. I waited until dark before I bathed the glass in pyrogallic solution. I then fixed it in hypo-sulphite of soda, and at sunrise this morning I prepared to make the prints. When the sun was high, I latched negative plate and nitrite of silver paper into the frame. I made many prints, varying the exposure from less than a minute to more than ten minutes, tempering my developing solutions. I moved back and forth from the bright day to the red glow of my dark room, testing and looking.

Still I was not sure, not until I chose the best print, not until I toned it in chloride of gold, floated it for some time in clean water and let it hang to dry, not until I brought the print out into the day.

There, along the bird's still, outstretched wing: an unexpected sliver of white light.

It is only an effect of a beam of sun glancing off a branch behind the subject and can be explained rationally & scientifically.

Yet this cannot account for the remarkable sensation it evokes in me, a trembling, thrilling exhilaration, as if I have set something right, and long to do it again and again.

My excitement comes, in part, from the

knowledge of how easily it might have slipped past me. It was a singular event, the tentative young bird at the edge of the nest, that allowed me to photograph the unfolded wing. Within seconds of my releasing the shutter, the humming bird took flight, its wings beating so rapidly as to be invisible to the human eye. I doubt it will ever return to this nest again. What if I had not been at the camera at that precise moment? What if I had hesitated with the shutter, or the day had been overcast, or my eye had been drawn away? What if the wing had extended slightly higher, or slightly lower, so as to obscure the gleam along the branch?

The dark foliage and gray nest, the bird's small eye and pale breast, the slender black beak and, then, the wing — like a hand that has drawn back a curtain — and my gaze is seized by that unexpected, graceful arc of light.

When I look upon it, this bend of bone and feather and sunlight, a tender place in my heart is healed even as it is torn, again and again a thousand times over.

I am left to wonder, will anyone else see it?

That day in the forest when I looked upon the marble bear, alive with the setting sun, what did I witness? Was it only sunlight on stone, or Father's spirit, or a reflection of my own?

It seems to me now that such a moment requires a kind of trinity: you and I and the thing itself.

■ ■ ■ ■

Part Six

MIDNOOSKY BIRCH-BARK BASKET.
1885.
ALLEN FORRESTER COLLECTION.

■ ■ ■ ■

Birch-bark basket formed in traditional style with flat, square base, oval mouth, folds in bark at either end. Reinforced with spruce root stitching. Used for gathering and storage of food. Also for cooking by filling it with water and heated rocks.

This example, however, is unusual for its small size: 3 inches in diameter.

SITKA HERALD, MAY 14, 1907
STRANGE REPORT OF INDIAN KILLED BY HARPOON BOMB

BYERS ISLAND, ALASKA — An Indian witch doctor was killed by a harpoon bomb aboard a whaling ship in Alaskan waters earlier this month.

The Indian had been employed as a guide by Grady Whaling Co. of Sitka. According to the company's reports, he accidentally detonated the bomb attached to a whaling harpoon and was killed instantly.

Such news would not have traveled far beyond Byers Island except for the strange reports that followed.

The captain of the ship was informed that the Indian was considered a powerful witch doctor among the nearby tribes. Apparently a colorful character, the Indian was known to have a pronounced limp and to wear a black top hat and an elaborate necklace of teeth and trinkets. The Indians said he could provide healing and hexes in equal measure. Because of his worth, they demanded exorbitant payment for his death.

Grady Whaling Co. was not amenable to the payment, however, and conflict seemed imminent. US Revenue Cutter Bear was dispatched to serve as peacemaker by force if necessary.

However, all negotiations were called off when it became known that the Indians believed the witch doctor had not in fact died but instead had taken up residence in a spruce tree on Byers Island, in the form of a black bird. The Grady Whaling Co. argued that no compensation should be paid in such a case, for while there was a corpse, the bird was very much alive and well.

NOTICE OF LOCATION
~~State of Washington~~ Alaska Territory
~~County of~~ No counties in this territory
Wolverine River Mining District

· Notice is hereby given that the undersigned did, on the *6th* day of *July* 1887, discover and locate a *quartz lead containing valuable minerals,* to which they have given the name the *Gertie Lode,* under the Act of Congress of May 10, 1872; they claim *1,500 feet in length on the line of the lode, starting at the center of the discovery shaft and running west 1,500 feet, and 300 feet in width on each side of the center of the lode for the whole distance in length.* The said lode is located *in the Wolverine River Valley, Alaska Territory, northwest of the Trail River's confluence.*

William Samuelson and Jeremiah Boyd
Locators

Dear Walt,

I'm enclosing a couple of things I think you might find interesting. Earlier this winter, a university student offered to do research for me, so I asked if she could find any references to the "Old Man" from the Colonel's expedition. It was a nearly impossible request, since we have no name or other key information. But she went through online archives of Alaska newspapers, and she found this article on an Alaskan "witch doctor" being killed aboard a whaling ship in 1907. The similarities are amazing, and it certainly makes me wonder.

I'm also sending you a photocopy of the mining claim for the Gertie Lode that began the gold rush here in Alpine. We have it on file here at the museum, but I just thought recently to look it up. I hadn't noticed the names before, but now I recognize them — Samuelson and Boyd! I haven't been able to find any other records for them.

I'm finished going through all the journals and letters, and have most of them translated into digital documents, and I have to say that I was surprised in the end — I didn't realize that the Colonel and Sophie eventually came up here together.

On another note, the Anderson Museum in Portland doesn't seem to be open anymore, but do you know where Sophie's photographs and plates went to? Depending on where they are kept, I thought we could offer digital copies of her diaries to add to their collection, if you think that would be appropriate.

But the main reason I'm writing is I have an idea, and I'll apologize now because I'm afraid I might bombard you with my enthusiasm. Here's my thought — Why don't you come up here and visit us in Alaska?

I can already guess your arguments about why it wouldn't work, but before you say no, give me a chance. We've got it all figured out.

You could fly up this summer for just a week or two. My cousin owns a rafting business, and he has already said that he would be happy to take us on a float trip down the Wolverine River. He has an opening in mid-July. It only takes about 5 days if we put in near Alpine and float to the coast. We could also take it at a more leisurely pace if you wanted.

Although it is a big, fast river, the only serious white water is at Haigh Rapids, and even there we can skirt around the rougher water. Clients well into their 70s have rafted down the river before. It sounds like you've recovered well from your recent illness and have spent a lot of time in the woods throughout your life, so I don't think this will be outside your comfort zone. My cousin is used to having some pretty hoity-toity clients, so he serves great meals, and you'll have a warm sleeping bag and a cot in a roomy tent.

Isaac has already checked into it, and we can get you a cabin at the Wolverine River Lodge so you could spend a few days here in Alpine too. It's nothing fancy. The main lodge has a restaurant and bar, and there are a half dozen cabins nearby. Each one has its own bath, telephone, and television. It's only about a 10-minute drive from the museum, and it's right on the bank of the river. Just imagine — It's very likely that the Colonel camped in this same area.

We are all so excited about this idea. You could see the museum and meet everyone here. Mom is already planning to have you over for dinner, and Isaac wants to take you up the old mining road so you can see the ruins there.

I know this must seem overwhelming. But please just give it some thought. On a practical level, it would also solve the problem of the artifacts — you could bring them with you on the plane. It would be safer than sending them via the mail. And we've got the money you donated to the museum, so we can easily cover all the expenses of your trip.

OK, I hope this hasn't been too much of a "hard sell." I really want you to consider this, Walt. I know it has long been a dream of yours to come to Alaska, and we would love to have you. Please say yes.

With warmest wishes,

Josh

P.S. You'll see that I've also sent you a brochure about the rafting trip, just in case it might help persuade you.

Raft Alaska's Magnificent Wolverine River

Calving glaciers, soaring mountains — float from the mountains to the sea and experience Alaska on its grandest scale.

Our river trip begins in the historic mining town of Alpine, Alaska. For the next five to six days, you will float through one of the most scenic landscapes in the world: dramatic Forrester Canyon, cascading waterfalls, coastal mountains with their ever-white peaks, the misty stretches of Boyd Flats, and the beautiful Tillman River. You'll also see the crumbling signs of a bygone era — the abandoned railroad line that was built in 1905 through some of the most rugged terrain on earth. You'll see tunnels through the mountainsides and timber railroad trestles. Wildlife too abounds along the way: bears, seals, salmon, and bald eagles are common sights. Near the end of the trip, we will float past Kings and Stone Glaciers, which regularly calve giant slabs of ice into the river.

You can look forward to:

- Friendly, informed guides.
  - Freshly prepared meals.
    - Comfortable sleeping quarters.
      - The adventure of a lifetime.

Dear Josh,

You knocked me right off my feet with your last letter. Alaska!

Right off the bat, I can think of a lot of reasons why the trip would be against my better judgment. I'm too old for such adventures, and I hate flying more than having teeth pulled. Consequently, I haven't been in one of those death traps since 1980, before you were even born now that I think of it.

It also seems to me that your little museum could put that money to better use than bringing my useless bones up there.

All that said, yours is the kindest invitation I've received in a long time. As you well know, ever since I was a young boy and learned about the Colonel's journey and studied that map up in the attic, I've dreamed of seeing Alaska. It's hard to even imagine what it would be like to step foot in that country. And now, it seems like I've got some friends up there to boot.

I won't deny it. I'm nervous about making that long trip. I'll check in with my doctor, and we'll just see how this pans out.

As for Sophie's photographs, the Anderson Museum burned in 1965. The family had donated her photographs, plates, and camera equipment to the museum, and all of it was destroyed. What you have there is all that's left.

Thank you for your kindness, Josh. I'll be in touch. I sure would like to see Alaska.

Walt

Willow Ptarmigan Nest, Near Nome, Alaska, 1915. **Photograph by Sophie Forrester**

Oregon Post, April 19, 1929
Bird Photographer Sophie Forrester Recalls Life of Adventure:
Anderson Museum Will Open Show of Her Photographs Next Week

One would guess upon first meeting Mrs. Sophie Forrester that she has led a common, quiet life. She is a slight and elderly woman with white hair pinned up neatly, long dark skirt, old-fashioned high-necked blouse and a soft-spoken, Victorian manner.

Yet visit her home on a quiet little pond outside of Portland, and one will find evidence that contradicts this ostensibly ordinary life.

There is a wooly mammoth tusk above the fireplace, a framed letter from the National Audubon Society in gratitude of Mrs. Forrester's work, and on her bookcase an Indian birch bark basket that holds what Mrs. Forrester says are the eggshells of an Alaska ptarmigan.

Follow her upstairs to her studio, and one finds a lifetime of photography equipment, including the original American Optical field camera that began her career.

For nearly four decades, Mrs. Forrester photographed the birds of Washington, Oregon, and the Alaska Territory. Among many others, the renowned American ornithologist William Norland highly praises her work.

"She is a true birdwoman, and don't let her tell you otherwise," Mr. Norland is quoted as saying. "But there is a rare genius to her photographs. The birds aren't the subject of her lens, as much as light itself."

And surely her avocation has exposed her to much adventure. She and her husband, the late Col. Allen Forrester, made six journeys to the wilderness of Alaska where she photographed ptarmigan and terns among many other birds.

When asked if she was ever afraid she would drown in a river or be eaten by a bear, she laughs and waves off the question.

"I have only ever been truly frightened of boredom and loneliness," she says.

It takes much effort on this interviewer's part to get her to talk about her notable career. When asked about her photographs appearing in the celebrated "Wild Birds of North America," she says, "Why yes, Mr. Zimmerman did use a few in his book." In fact, more than 30 of her photographs appear in the pages of that much-acclaimed publication. Over the years, both her photographs and her meticulously noted field observations have been printed in many scientific journals and magazines. Her particular interest has been nests and fledglings.

Her life work as photographer and naturalist went hand in hand with her husband, who passed away in 1918. It seems that the Colonel was known in his own right, as he led an important expedition into the Alaska Territory in 1885, according to Mrs. Forrester.

"He liked to tease that he was my field assistant, but he was the one who actually made it all possible," Mrs. Forrester reminisces. "I would look up at a nest on a cliff and wonder how on earth I could ever get that photograph. He would lead me up and around and farther on until we were on top of the cliff, then he would tie me off with ropes and lower me down until I was face to face with the nest. And then I'd get my picture."

Surely then she must have been frightened?

"My stomach did give a flutter now and then," she admits, "but I knew he could tie a good knot."

Mrs. Forrester insisted on naming several other people for this article. She credits much of her success to the early encouragement and guidance of a Portland pharmacist by the name of Henry Redington. In 1885, he sent her photographs to a book editor and so launched her career. And those many years ago when she was first starting out at Vancouver Barracks, Army Sgt. Joe MacGillivray helped design what she says is her most valuable invention — a photography blind. She describes it as a small canvas tent where she could sit inconspicuously with her camera lens aimed out a hole in the canvas.

Many of her photographs required days on end of sitting in such a tent. But what of her dread of boredom? Mrs. Forrester insists she was never bored when there was the promise of catching a bird in a picture.

Her patient efforts resulted in the creation of more than 500 negative glass plates, and she does have her favorite. It is of a flock of wild geese in the delta of the Wolverine River in Alaska.

"Allen never forgot his expedition to Alaska. He had an extraordinary encounter that led him to believe that the wild geese there had a certain enchanted quality. More than anything he wanted to take me there to photograph them. That was our first trip together to the north," she says.

She recalls that it was early on a May morning in 1892, and she was still sleeping inside their tent when she heard the calls of geese flying along the river. She rushed out of the tent, still wearing her night clothes and with her camera equipment in hand. Her husband, the Colonel, was making coffee on the campfire.

"He said, 'There they are, love. Get your picture quick!' Of course, there was nothing quick about it. It wasn't until the next day that I was able to get that particular photograph, when the flock had gathered in a marsh near a group of Indian women. It was one of the most beautiful scenes I have ever witnessed, and I am afraid I did not do them justice, but it is still my favorite."

This interviewer also asked about the only photograph in the house that shows Mrs. Forrester herself. In it, she is wearing high boots, sporting trousers, and a broad-brimmed hat. Her husband, the Colonel, stands beside her, and behind the two stretches a treeless plain.

"That was Nome in 1915," she says. "We were there to photograph the nesting willow ptarmigan. I'm afraid it was our last journey to Alaska, as my husband's health began to fail."

With wistful expression she adds, "I see that and I think, oh my Allen, if only I could be with you now."

Through June 1, more than 100 of Mrs. Forrester's photographs will be on display at the Anderson Museum of Art.

Last Frontier Airlines

A friend has sent you the below itinerary:

Traveler Information
Walt Forrester
E-ticket

July 10 Departure

Flight 2743, Seat 15C
Departs: Missoula MSO 1:15 pm
Arrives: Seattle–Tacoma SEA 1:47
pm *388 miles*

Flight 101, Seat 27A
Departs: Seattle–Tacoma SEA 3:15
pm
Arrives: Anchorage ANC 5:41 pm
1445 miles

July 21 Return

Flight 96, Seat 20C
Departs: Anchorage, ANC 9:20 am
Arrives: Seattle–Tacoma SEA 1:40
pm *1445 miles*

Flight 2396, Seat 17C
Departs Seattle–Tacoma SEA 5:30
pm
Arrives: Missoula MSO 7:52 pm *388
miles*

ACKNOWLEDGMENTS

This novel was very much inspired by the real-life 1885 journey into Alaska led by Lieutenant Henry T. Allen. His *Report of an Expedition to the Copper, Tanana, and Koyukuk Rivers in the Territory of Alaska* was both a starting ground and a constant source of information. In addition, I am grateful to the University of Alaska Anchorage/Alaska Pacific University Consortium Library, which holds the Fred Fickett papers. Fickett served as private in Allen's Copper River expedition, and his diaries and letters are a treasure trove.

Further invaluable research was made available by Alaska's Digital Archives (vilda.alaska.edu), the Alaska Historical Archives, and the Anchorage Museum, in particular the 2013 exhibit *Dena'inaq' Huch'ulyeshi* and accompanying book. Thanks also to Gregory Shine and Doug Wilson of the Fort Vancouver National Historical Site.

The Rasmuson Foundation not only provided me with grant funding to raft a remote section of the Copper River for research, but also, perhaps more important, gave me a boost of confidence just when I was having doubts very early on in the writing. Alaskan artists are incredibly fortunate to have this source of support and encouragement.

In addition to Lt. Allen's report, I relied on many research books, but I would like to note Richard Nelson's *Make Prayers to the Raven* and *The Athabaskans;* Frederica de Laguna's *Tales from the Dena,* with beautiful illustrations by Dale DeArmond; *Chickaloon Spirit* by Katherine Wickersham Wade; *Shem Pete's Alaska* with James Kari and James Fall; and *K'tl'eghi Sukdu: The Collected Writings of Peter Kalifornsky.* Thanks also to the University of Alaska Press and Amy Simpson for their generosity in allowing me to use excerpts from *Through Orthodox Eyes.* And even as I worked from my home in Alaska, I had a vast library of nineteenth-century texts about everything from dry-plate photography and military history to ornithology and obstetrics at my fingertips thanks to the digitalized Google Books.

Andrew Pruitt's entries owe much to the poetry of William Blake and the Bible. The geese women were inspired by a reference in Richard Nelson's *The Athabaskans,* the spruce root baby by "Xay Tnaey" by John Billum in *Our Voices: Native Stories of Alaska and the Yukon.* The passage "When I First Saw White Men at Trail River" was influenced by "When Lieutenant Allen Came into the Country" as told to Katie John by her mother, included in *Tatl'ahwt'aenn Nenn': The Headwaters People's Country,* transcribed and edited by James Kari. And while most of my Native language references come directly from Allen's and Fickett's writings, I also relied on the work of linguists James Kari and John Smelcer, though of course any errors are my own.

Many people generously lent me expertise and inspiration, and books, along the way. In particular I would like to thank Melissa Behnke and David Cheezem as well as all the staff at Fireside Books; Mary Ann Cockle, who has the eyes of a hawk; Dr. Susan Lemagie; artist Annie Aube; David and Wendy Carter; pastors Tim and Leisa Carrick; and Jenny and Craig Baer.

I would also like to thank Argent Kvasnikoff, who not only shared with me his personal experiences and insight, but also showed me yet again the power of the artist to help us see the world in new ways.

From the beginning, I envisioned this story with maps, sketches, photographs, and vintage artwork — thanks to artist Ruth Hulbert and photographer Stephen Nowers for their work to make this possible.

I am tremendously grateful to my editors,

Reagan Arthur of Little, Brown and Company and Mary-Anne Harrington of Tinder Press — this book and *The Snow Child* before it would not have been possible without their perceptive edits, enthusiasm, and patience. Heartfelt thanks also to the wonderful teams on both sides of the Atlantic, including Carrie Neill, Keith Hayes, Lisa Erickson, Peggy Freudenthal, Tracy Williams, Olivia Aylmer, and Matt Carlini at Little, Brown and Company, and at Tinder Press, Vicky Palmer, Katie Brown, Patrick Insole, Amy Perkins, and Sarah Badhan. And I am forever thankful to my agent Jeff Kleinman of Folio Literary Management, who has expertly guided me from the beginning of this adventure and has an army of kind and discerning readers.

Most of all, thank you to my family near and far, but especially my mom, Julie LeMay, who helps me to see when a swan is more than just a swan; my dad, John LeMay, who liked Sophie from the start and hated to lose Tillman; my husband, Sam, who makes everything possible; and my daughters, Grace and Aurora, who inspire me every day — your love sustains me.

PHOTOGRAPHY CREDITS

The author and publisher are grateful for permission to reproduce the following images:

Thibodeau Photograph Collection, ca 1897. ASL-PCA-538

page 625, U.S.R.C. CORWIN. Sitka, Alaska. Alaska State Library, Wickersham State Historic Site. Photographs, 1882-1930s. ASL-PCA-277

page 645, from iStock.com, Jeff D. Samuels

ABOUT THE AUTHOR

Eowyn Ivey's debut novel, *The Snow Child,* was a finalist for the Pulitzer Prize and an international bestseller published in twenty-six languages. A former bookseller and newspaper reporter, Eowyn was raised in Alaska and continues to live there with her husband and two daughters.